THE BLIND DETECTIVE

THE BLIND DETECTIVE

CHRISTINA KONING

Allison & Busby Limited
11 Wardour Mews
London W1F 8AN
allisonandbusby.com

First published as *Line of Sight* in 2014 under the name A. C. Koning
This edition published by Allison & Busby in 2023.

10 9 8 7 6 5 4 3 2 1

ISBN 978-0-7490-2953-1
Typeset in 11.5 Sabon LT Pro by Allison & Busby Ltd.

FSC
www.fsc.org
MIX
Paper | Supporting
responsible forestry
FSC® C171272

The paper used for this Allison & Busby publication
has been produced from trees that have been legally sourced
from well-managed and credibly certified forests.

Printed and bound by
CPI Group (UK) Ltd, Croydon, CR0 4YY

In memory of my grandfather and First World War veteran, Charles Frederick Thompson (1890–1964)

'I am the enemy you killed, my friend.

I knew you in this dark.'

WILFRED OWEN, *Strange Meeting*

Chapter One

The fog had made all the trains late. He'd need to get a move on. As always, he was on his feet and had his hand on the catch, ready to lower the window, as the train slowed down. He'd timed it so that he was pushing down the handle as the engine halted; its loud, final expulsion of steam was the signal for the door to be opened. Although this had to be done with caution; it wouldn't do to knock some poor bloke for six. The juddering lurch as the carriage stopped gave momentum to his first step onto the platform. He'd found that a swift – or at least, confident – progress through the crowd was best. Not that this prevented occasional collisions – '*Oops, sorry!*' '*Don't mention it, old man.*' – but, on the whole, people tended to get out of one's way, if one seemed to be moving with sufficient purpose. Crossing London Bridge, the smell of the fog was intense, and left an acrid taste in the back of the throat. He resisted the temptation to spit, although others around him were not so restrained. Disgusting habit. Still, the fog was beastly. The way it filled one's mouth and nose with its sulphurous odour – like a mixture of coaldust, rotten eggs, and bad drains – awakened memories he'd as soon have forgotten: *bluish lips fringed with blood and froth.* He was still hemmed in by the surging crowd. The inexorable slowness with which it moved was like that of a column of men wading through mud: he remembered the suck and heaviness of it, the way it clogged one's legs. But it was starting to thin out a little; soon he'd be able to stride more freely. From the traffic lights it was six hundred and seventy paces. After seven years, he knew the route so thoroughly he could have walked it blindfold. St Paul's was to his left, Tower Bridge to his right, although both of course would now be invisible in the fog. He heard the ghostly booming of a ship's siren in the distance. From closer at hand, behind and ahead of him, came the steady trudge of footsteps: his fellow toilers in the City's stony vineyards. Disembodied voices floated towards him.

'. . . filthy weather.'

'. . . nil–nil draw.'

And, from the pavement, 'Spare us a copper, guv'nor. Wife an' kiddies to support.'

'What was your regiment?' he asked, bending towards the seated man.

'Manchesters, sir.' The whining note was absent, now.

He fumbled in his pocket, found the shilling he had intended for his lunch. 'There you are.'

A hand reached up to take it.

'Thank you, sir.'

'I was with the RFA Wipers. A bad show.'

'It was that, sir. Good luck, sir.'

'The same to you.'

Another ten steps brought him level with the Monument. Close as it was – no more than a hundred yards away – it wouldn't be visible in this. He'd climbed it once, when he was a lad. He remembered the view from the top, the river's brown ripples sparkling in the sun, its forest of ships' masts, clouds scudding past, and the face of the girl he had been with that day. Maud O'Sullivan. Yellow hair she'd had, coiled in a bun, and beautiful, light green eyes, with pale lashes, that turned to gold in the sun.

'Look out!'

The impact of a shoulder colliding with his nearly knocked him off his feet.

'Sorry!' He put out a hand to steady himself, and encountered the iron spears at the top of the steps leading down to Monument Underground station. 'This fog . . .'

'I know. Dreadful, isn't it? One can't see a blessed thing.'

A dray lumbered past, with a steady clip-clopping of hooves, leaving a whiff of horseflesh and leather in its wake. It was followed by the rumble of a motorbus, going more slowly than usual, he guessed.

'I say, do you mind telling me the time? My watch seems to have stopped.'

'Not at all. Let's cross, though, while the lights are in our favour.' At the far side, his new acquaintance tapped his sleeve. 'It's five and twenty past eight.'

'Thanks awfully.'

'Don't mention it, old man.'

Another three steps brought him to the heavy oak doors, whose bronze handles were shaped like a bundle of sticks, with an axe-head protruding. Fasces. Carried by the lictors in front of Roman magistrates, he recalled. Denoting that the said officials had the power of life and death. As a firm specialising in criminal cases, Saville's dealt with all of it: insurance fraud and embezzlement, but also murder, suicide, and what the newspapers liked to call 'sex crimes'. One never knew exactly what each day would bring. He entered the echoing vault of the foyer just as the lift arrived. Its doors clashed open, and someone got out, bringing with him a pungent stench of tobacco.

'Morning!' Jackson. A pipe smoker. His teeth clenched around the said article. He returned the greeting, stepping past his colleague into the open lift. The concertinaed cage doors were slammed shut, their oily wheeze setting his teeth on edge as always. 'Well, toodle-oo,' said Jackson, having performed this operation. 'I'm off. The Houndsditch case. Back lunchtime, if anybody wants me.'

'The Houndsditch case,' he repeated automatically, feeling behind him for the concave brass disc of the lift button. 'Right you are, Mr Jackson.' He pressed the button and, with a convulsive jerk that threw him momentarily off-kilter, the lift started to ascend. At the third floor it stopped again, to allow two more people to get on. Miss Poole and Miss Johnson. The Ladies' Cloakroom was on the third floor, he recalled – a fact which gave rise to frequent complaints from the female staff as to the inconvenience of this arrangement.

'Morning, Mr Rowlands,' said Miss Poole, with the note of false cheerfulness he'd come to expect from her sort. Miss Johnson's greeting was more restrained – either from natural reticence, or as befitted her dignity as secretary to the junior partner.

'Shocking weather, isn't it?' continued the irrepressible Miss Poole.

He agreed that it was. Then there was no more conversation until they reached the fifth floor, where a little squabble ensued as to which of them should go first. 'After you,' he said, but Miss Poole wouldn't hear of it of course.

'Oh no! After *you*,' she simpered, so that he had no choice but to give in or risk making more of a fuss than the occasion warranted. With a grudging murmur of thanks, he moved past her, out of the lift, catching a whiff of her sickly-sweet perfume. *Californian Poppy*. Loathsome stuff. He was glad Edith didn't use it.

The big clock that hung out over the street above the window was just striking half past as he entered the office: its chimes reverberated through the room.

'There you are, Mr Rowlands, sir. I was wondering where you could've got to.'

A powerful smell of hair oil assailed his nostrils. 'Morning, Bert,' he said.

'I was just saying to Mr Cheeseman here,' the post-boy went on in his nasal sing-song, '"Mr Cheeseman," I says, "what do you suppose could've happened to make Mr Rowlands so late? Seeing as how he's always in by a quarter past at the latest."'

'Trains, Bert,' he said, suppressing the irritation he felt at this inquisition. Of course he wasn't late – not even by a minute – but his nerves felt jangled, just the same. Perhaps it had been Edith's sharpness that morning, their row of the previous night still unresolved. Her furious scraping of the blackened toast (how *did* she manage to burn it quite so often?) and the irritable way she had of banging down her teacup conveying her feelings more eloquently than words. Poor Edie, he thought, with a guilty flush – for *this* to happen, when she'd worked so hard to make ends meet, and they'd almost saved enough for her to take the girls to Bournemouth for a week in the summer. It was just their luck. Still, it was hardly the end of the world – a point he'd tried to make to her the night before. 'It's all right for *you*,' had been her reply. With a sigh, he hung his coat on the rack inside the door, and after switching on the lamp over his desk, for it wouldn't do to sit in darkness, sat down at the switchboard.

'I said it must be them blessed trains. Didn't I say it must be them blessed trains, Mr Cheeseman?'

'You did that,' agreed the janitor, with a bronchial wheeze that lent a portentousness to even his lightest remarks. 'Well, best be getting on.'

'Yes, thank you, Mr Cheeseman,' he said automatically. 'Anybody in, yet, Bert?'

'Mr Jackson's been and gone.'

'Yes, I spoke to Mr Jackson. Nobody else? That's all right, then.'

'It's just that . . .' Still the boy hovered. *There was a definite whiff of halitosis. If he'd only stand further off.*

'Just *what*, Bert?' He tried to keep the impatience out of his voice.

'If the tellyphone was to ring, like . . . an' you wasn't here.'

'Then one of the secretaries can answer it. Or you can let it ring. We've been through all this before, haven't we?'

'Yes, Mr Rowlands.'

'Well, then . . .'

Still muttering under his breath, the boy shuffled off. From anyone else it would have seemed like cheek but

Bert wasn't that sort. *Not quite the round shilling, poor lad, the mother a widow, out Dalston Junction way. A cramped little flat over a butcher's shop.* Unhooking the earpiece from its cradle, he slipped the wire frame to which it was attached over his head, checking that the mouthpiece was at just the right distance – no sense in deafening them – and made a minor adjustment to the swivel chair. Then, as he did every morning, he ran his hands lightly over the board, feeling the beautiful intricacies of its switches and sockets under his fingers, and making sure that everything was as it should be: the dolls' eyes open, each cord ready to be connected to its particular jack a each switch in the correct position. It was, he thought, like a great brain: a network of ganglia, across which electrical pulses darted and flickered. Sound waves, communicating information, in a flash, from one mind to another. All done through the magical electromagnetic technology of which he was the conductor. When he'd started this job, the switchboard had been newly installed – a Stromberg-Carlson model, with an oak frame and a bakelite front-panel. Its shape resembled an upright piano, with a high back panel consisting of rows of female jacks ('jills' might have been a better word, he thought) and a bank of switches and cords where a row of ivory keys would have been in the musical instrument. There were fifteen lines for incoming calls and the same number of internal lines. A buzzer sounded when the call came in, and you took your cord and plugged it into the right jack, before pushing back the front key in line with the jack. 'Number, please,' you said. Then you took the cord which was directly in front of the back cord and plugged it into the jack for the called number, simultaneously pulling the back key towards you to ring the called party's telephone. When the called party answered, and the call was connected, you closed the talk key. A convex disc called a doll's eye dropped down when the circuit was in use, retracting when it was idle. At busy times, he'd have five or six calls on the go, whisking the cords in and out as if engaged in a complicated bit of weaving. It had taken him all of a week to get the hang of the system; now, of course, it was second nature. It didn't bother him in the least that his was generally regarded as a job for women.

His arrival was followed by that of Mr Jardine, *smelling strongly of wintergreen*, who'd been with the firm eight years, and Mr Mullins, who had joined them six months ago, straight from Oxford. He greeted them both and handed them their letters, already sorted into piles. Miss Foy, one of the younger secretaries *tip-tapping on high-heels*, appeared next, complaining of the trains. Then came Mr Fairclough, another of the lawyers, who asked that his nine o'clock client should be shown straight in. At five to, a very flustered and out of breath Miss Taylor arrived. She'd walked all the way from Ludgate Circus, she said, the bus having broken down. At five past, the doors swung open to admit the senior partner. 'Morning, Rowlands.'

'Morning, Mr Saville.'

'Any messages?'

'None so far, sir.'

'Mr Willoughby in?'

'Not yet, sir. The fog—'

'Yes, yes.' *His lumbago must be playing up again.* 'Well, send him along as soon as he gets here, will you?' By a quarter past, the dolls' eyes were dropping down, with that peculiar ticking sound they made, as his colleagues started making the first calls of the day. The buzzers signalling an incoming call were going every couple of minutes now, sometimes two at a time, but he was used to that. Most of these were routine enquiries, some of which he dealt with directly – one woman wanted to know if they handled breach of promise cases; from the faint tremor in her voice he guessed it must be her own case she was referring to, and put her through to Mr Jardine, whose manner towards the ladies was more sympathetic than that of most of his colleagues. At half past nine he put through a trunk call for Mr Saville: the Scottish fire insurance case proving a bit sticky, he surmised. It took him all of fifteen minutes, but in the end he got his man. Well, he and the five other operators between here and Inverness-shire. Being in the telephone service, like being in the army, was all about teamwork.

For the next hour, he barely took his hands away from the board: it was all switch, flick, switch – deftly putting the cords in and pulling them out of their sockets as the calls came in. He didn't mind it, being busy, the rhythm of it, the constant click and shift and after seven years he'd grown pretty quick at the game. The trick was not to let your concentration slacken, even for a moment. Knowing just where to find everything was another must. He prided himself on running a neat switchboard: no tangled cords, or switches left carelessly open for *him*, thanks very much! It was pretty much like operating a battery, he'd sometimes thought. There was the same need for absolute precision, the same series of meticulous actions to be gone through – whether what you were doing was focusing a sight on a target, or managing a row of 'supervisories'. Discipline. Order. Taking pains. These were his watchwords. It was all about having a system and sticking to it, no matter whether it was a network of telephones one was minding, or an 18-pounder gun. A vivid image of the weapon he'd spent three years of his life getting to know filled his mind for a second: the shine of its brass fittings and its great barrel, painted dark green for better concealment (mud colour would've been better), the oily gleam of its firing mechanism, the delicate calibrations of its adjustable sight. He saw in his mind's eye the great wheels – nearly as tall as a man – on either side of the gun, and the little saddle-shaped brass seat where you sat. But what he remembered most was the way the whole thing recoiled, when the shell was fired. That, and the smell of the cordite after.

At ten o'clock, he was relieved by Mrs Gilbert, who

did the mid-morning shift. Carrie Gilbert's husband (*who'd escaped with his life but with his nerves in pieces from the tunnels at La Boisselle*) couldn't be left until there was a neighbour on call to see to him. Sometimes, when the nights had been very bad, Mrs Gilbert didn't get in till nearly eleven; then it was up to him, as the senior telephonist, to cover for her, although the partners had turned a blind eye so far.

'Morning, Mr Rowlands.' She brushed past him with an apologetic murmur, bringing with her a smell of cold. 'Sorry if I'm a bit late. The fog . . .'

'Dreadful isn't it? Don't worry. It's been a slow start.'

These courtesies having been exchanged, he went outside for a smoke. If anything, the fog was worse than it had been before. Choking, filthy stuff, that clung to one's face with a palpable clamminess like the touch of dead fingers. Sounds, in this dense atmosphere, had a curious quality, seeming at once to come from very far off and, disconcertingly, to be close at hand. A laugh jumped out at him, as if from a hole punched through glass. A snatch of talk: '—find the necessary, never you fear . . .' Out on the bridge, a klaxon hooted softly. The traffic must be at a standstill, he guessed. What it would be like by this evening, he hated to think. He hoped it didn't make him too late home. Edith was in a rotten enough mood as it was. Not that she didn't have cause to be, poor old girl. Ever since she'd found out there was another on the way – and how were they to feed the two they had already, on the pittance he earned, and the small return she got from those shares her father left her? – she'd been out of sorts. He hadn't made matters any better by saying he'd look for another job. 'What kind of job?' she'd replied scornfully. 'There *are* no other jobs, or none that – Oh, never mind!' She'd meant jobs that he was fit to do. She was right of course, there weren't many. Still he'd persisted (he never did know when to shut up), 'I could get an evening job. They're looking for staff at the Brockley Jack.'

'What! And have the girls know that their father works in a public house? I don't think we've quite come to *that.*'

It was at times like these that the gulf between their respective backgrounds, which had seemed of no account when they'd first been married, seemed all too apparent. Because of course they were from different worlds, he and Edith. That she, who'd grown up in a big house with servants, whose brother had gone to Oxford, and who might have married a doctor, or a solicitor, should have ended up with him – a mere telephonist, although, admittedly, one that worked in the City – was a come down, to put it mildly. To have given up her world of ease and privilege for the one they now inhabited – a world of narrow streets, and mean little houses, and front gardens scarcely big enough to house the dustbins – was surely more than most women would have endured without complaint. 'Do you think I *like* living here?' she had wept, towards the end of last night's quarrel. 'Being surrounded by these *people* . . .' She meant their neighbours: the Wilkses on one side, the Dooleys on the other. Mrs Dooley was impossible for several reasons. She was fond of drink; and she dyed her hair. As for Mrs Wilks . . . 'No one, I hope, could accuse me of being a snob,' said Edith, 'but *really*, when that woman insists on discussing her husband's difficulties with his "waterworks", I draw the line, I really do.'

For his own part, he thought Mrs Dooley a pleasant enough soul, even if she did like a drop now and then. Mrs Wilks wasn't a bad sort, either: she'd been very kind that time Margaret had been taken bad with croup. But he saw Edith's point. 'I don't mind for myself,' his wife had said. 'But the *girls*, Fred, it's so hard on them.' Privately, he doubted that their neighbours' carryings-on could mean much to children of seven and five. It was Edith he was sorry for. She'd been brought up to expect a different sort of life, that was all. 'Stuck-up,' Dorothy called her. His sister had never been one to mince her words.

The rest of the morning passed quickly enough. *Flick. Switch. Flick.* Two more trunk calls, Bristol and the Coningsby case; and Stratford. At lunchtime, he eschewed, as he often did, the society of the office canteen for the anonymity of the city streets which, after seven years, he'd come to know with a thoroughness that would have made the Major proud.

'Think of it as reconnaissance,' the Major used

to say. 'Like making a mental sketch map of enemy territory.'

On fine days he'd walk down Gracechurch Street and Cornhill Row and along Cheapside towards St Paul's, and Hatton Garden. There was a bench in Bleeding Heart Yard where he liked to sit and eat his sandwiches. Or he'd go the other way, along King William Street, past the Bank of England, to Finsbury Circus or when he was in the mood for a good walk, to Bunhill Fields, *it was Bone Hill really – a hill full of bones*, and the company of its illustrious dead. Blake. He'd always liked Blake. Although all that stuff about Albion was a bit beyond him. There was the one about London. How did it go, again? *I wandered through each something street, near where the something Thames does flow . . .* Today the filthy taste of the fog in his throat made him disinclined for a long walk, so he settled for a cold pork pie, washed down with a cup of tea in the Kardomah Café in Clement's Lane, with a cigarette for afters.

Walking back towards the office, he could hear the strains of the organ of St Mary Woolnoth, as he neared the intersection with Lombard Street. He checked his watch: there was still fifteen minutes before he'd be expected back. Too good a chance to miss. He slipped into a pew near the door. It wasn't a piece he was familiar with. Bach, or Handel, he guessed. He wished he could say for certain. Although there was a gramophone at home – a parting gift from Ashenhurst and the rest of his Pals at the Lodge – there hadn't of late been the money for new recordings. The few discs he had – Melba singing arias from *La Traviata*, John McCormack's 'She Moved Through the Fair', Elgar's *Enigma Variations*, Chopin's *Nocturnes*, and Beethoven's *Eroica* – had been played almost to death. Of course there was always the wireless. But by the time he'd got home, and had his supper, and the children had been put to bed, they'd usually missed half the classical concert. In the early days of their marriage, he and Edith had been in the habit of going along to the weekly concerts at Wigmore Hall. Of late, there'd been no time for such civilised amusements. Now, their social life revolved around the monthly game of Bridge which took place at the house of one or other of their group of friends – couples, for the most part, in the same situation as themselves. He focused his attention once more on the music. How grand to be able to make a sound like that! To fill a great space like this with such cascades of notes, such peals . . . Like bells, like the skirling of pipes and the beating of drums, all rolled into one . . . How it made one's heart beat! Such intricacies of sound . . . Lifting one's spirits up, far above the misery, the *pettiness* of life . . . ''Scuse me, is this seat taken?'

It was a woman – a girl, really – who'd spoken. He realised that he'd had his eyes closed all this time. He opened them, and got to his feet, to allow her to get past, catching as he did so a whiff of her violet scent. 'Thanks. It's ever so nice, isn't it, the music?'

There was a slightly over-eager note to her voice, a tone Edith would have called 'gushing'.

'Yes.'

'I often come here, in my lunch break.'

'Do you?' He'd really rather not have got into conversation.

'Oh yes. D'you know, I've seen you here before? Last week, it was. Or maybe the week before that. I watched you for ever such a long time, but you never once caught my eye. Lost in the music, you were.'

A sort of horror came over him. He got to his feet. 'Awfully sorry.' He made as if to glance at his watch. 'Is that the time? I really ought to be getting back.' Before she could say anything more, he turned on his heel, striking his elbow sharply on the end of the pew as he did so.

Back in the office, he settled to his work again. Hours passed, without his being aware of their passing, so caught up was he in the intricate patterns of what he was doing. *Flick*, *switch*, *flick*. His hands moving over the rows of switches with the deftness of a concert pianist – if the piece he played had been an arrangement of human voices. He put through calls from Cherrywood, seeing in his mind's eye drifts of pink and white blossom; the South Wimbledon exchange; and Coppermill, which was Walthamstow, a fiery-red gleam of hammered metal; from Dreadnought – Earls Court – an iron hulk painted battleship grey and Hogarth – Shepherd's Bush, a vision of Gin Lane.

When he'd first started this job, it had taken him quite a while to learn the names of the exchanges, to remember that 'Trafalgar' was Whitehall, 'Laburnam' Winchmore Hill; that 'Museum' was Bloomsbury, and 'Primrose' St John's Wood. Now he had them all by heart – the poetic and the mundane.

It was the same when he'd first arrived in Flanders: the way everything had its particular name. Each trench and dugout christened with whatever the incumbent regiment thought fit – so that for the Jocks it was all Balmoral and Stirling Castle; for the Taffs, the Rhondda Valley and Swansea Town. At the Salient, he'd been with a crowd of London boys, and so a city had grown up in those first months, that seemed a shadowy version of the one they'd all left behind. In Ploegsteert Wood – 'Plug Street', as it soon became – you'd follow the line of a trench called 'The Haymarket' to get to 'Piccadilly Circus', off which branched not only 'Regent Street', but, by some topographical incongruity, 'Fleet Street' as well. One dugout he'd been allocated during the autumn of 1914 – an image of its thick clay walls, lined with sheets of tin, came at once to mind – had rejoiced under the name of 'Claridges'; 'The Ritz' was across the way. Funny, the things you remembered.

Mrs Gilbert left at three-thirty, to be home in time to cook her husband's tea. After that, Rowlands was on his own again – not that he minded a bit. He put through a call to Holborn (Chancery) for Mr Fairclough, another for Mr

26

Saville to Grosvenor Square. He connected a trunk call to Harrogate for Mr Jackson in under ten minutes. Asked a client to wait (Mr Jardine being occupied with another). Sent Mr Mullins' four thirty straight through. Then, just after five, one of the buzzers went. He inserted the rear cord into the jack and flicked the front key forward.

'Saville and Willoughby. Good afternoon. How may I help?'

'Oh, hello.' There was a slight, but perceptible, pause, as the speaker, a woman, appeared to consider the wisdom or otherwise of proceeding. Evidently she decided she would risk it, for she went on: 'This may seem an odd question, if it turns out not to be the case but . . .' Again, she seemed to hesitate. 'I'm looking for Gerald Willoughby,' she said at last. 'Is that by any chance his office?'

'It is.' Suddenly it was as if everything else fell away – Edith's cross mood that morning, and the fog, and the trains, and that girl in St Mary's – annihilated in an instant, by the sound of a voice. Creamy, he'd have described it as. Satiny. Low. *An excellent thing in a woman* . . .

'Oh, good. I was hoping it might be. Is he there, do you know?'

He was suddenly at a loss for words. He cleared his throat. 'I'll just see. Who should I say is calling?'

'It's Celia West. Although he'll remember me as Celia Verney. Just tell him it's Celia. He'll know.'

Celia West. The name rang a bell, but he couldn't at

once say why. With a conscious effort, Rowlands pulled himself together. 'One moment, please.' He plugged the front cord into the jack, and pulled the front key backwards. Willoughby answered on the second ring. 'Hello?' It was well disguised, but there was still the trace of a boyhood stammer. *H-hello*.

'A Mrs Celia West for you, sir.' Old habits died hard. Even though it was ten years since he was obliged by the difference in their respective ranks to call the younger man by that honorific, he'd never dropped it. 'She said you'd known her as Verney.'

'Celia Verney. Good Lord!' It was hard to tell from Willoughby's voice whether he was dismayed or pleased. 'It's ages since . . . Well, well. Do put her through, Rowlands. And, by the way, it's Lady Celia. Not that you were to know.'

Now he knew why the name had seemed familiar. Celia West belonged to that select set whose comings and goings between Mayfair and Monte Carlo, Westminster and Biarritz, were regularly chronicled in the Society pages of *The Times*. Not that he bothered with all that sort of thing, but Edith took an interest. He transferred the call, waiting just long enough to make sure that the two were safely connected, and to hear his employer's voice – now registering unqualified pleasure – say: 'Celia? How v-very nice. It's been a long time.' And the reply: 'Yes, I suppose it has. Five years or more. Isn't it too absurd?'

* * *

He arrived home at half past six, to a smell of charring lamb chops and a clashing of saucepans, and Edith's black mood still filling the house like smoke from an ill-extinguished fire. Setting down his briefcase in the hall, Rowlands hung up his coat – he never wore a hat – and ran a hand over his hair to smooth it. No excuse for looking as if you'd been dragged through a hedge backwards.

'Daddy!'

There was the soft thud of feet descending the stairs, and then Anne hurled herself at his middle.

'Steady on!' He dropped a kiss on the hot tangle of her hair. 'You almost knocked the stuffing out of me. And I wouldn't be of much use then, would I? A daddy with no stuffing to hold him up.' He sagged at the knees, like a puppet whose strings had been cut, and she gurgled delightedly. 'Silly Daddy.'

Margaret, with the gravity of her two years' seniority to her sister, waited until he and Anne had finished larking about, before resting her small hand upon his sleeve. He bent to kiss her. 'How was school today, Meg?'

'All right. We did Long Division. I know how to carry.'

'Good show.' He knew not to tease Margaret. 'I'll test you after supper, shall I?'

'Girls!' came Edith's voice from the kitchen. 'Go and wash your hands.'

As his daughters scrambled back upstairs to obey their mother's injunction, she came out into the hall. He leant to kiss her, but she moved swiftly past him, towards the dining room. 'You smell of the fog,' she said. 'I suppose it's still bad out there.'

'Pretty bad.' He followed her into the room, as she started laying the table for their evening meal. There was an energy to the way she did this – as there was to the way she did everything – that struck him, in his present mood, as excessive. *Flap* went the cloth. *Crash* went the plates. *Clash* went the knives and forks as she set them down. 'Edith,' he said quietly, so that the girls wouldn't hear. 'Just stop that a moment, would you?'

'Supper's ready.' But there was a pause in the crashing of plates and the jangling of cutlery, as she waited for what he had to say.

'Look, I'm sorry about last night.' *If you could hear yourself*, he'd said.

She sniffed. 'Nothing to be sorry about.'

'Yes, there is. Edith . . .' He held out his arms. There was a moment's hesitation, before she came into them. 'Dearest girl . . .' He stroked her hair, lovely soft hair. Why she'd had it shingled, he couldn't imagine. Women and their ridiculous fashions. 'We'll manage. I promise.'

'Will we?' Her face was against his chest, so that the words sounded muffled. But she let him hold her; he felt her soft weight, her solidity. Did he imagine it, or was she already heavier, more substantial, than the last time he had her in his arms, her newly gravid state declaring itself in the increased heat of her skin, and in the faint exhausted sigh with which she disentangled herself at last? 'Come on, girls,' she said, suddenly brisk, as the two of them came clattering in. 'Don't stand there dawdling. Margaret, you can fetch the potatoes. Anne, you can put out the napkins. Left-hand side, remember?'

He returned from washing his hands to find his wife and daughters already seated, Anne kicking the table leg as usual, until reproved by her mother. 'For these and all Thy gifts,' he murmured, his fingers automatically straightening the knife and fork on either side of his place mat, and positioning his glass, side plate, and the napkin in its bone ring, so that they were just so. There was an answering sound from his wife signifying 'Amen', and they began eating. And, after all, the chops were not too badly burnt, and the mashed potatoes only slightly lumpy. The cabbage was undeniably overcooked, but he'd had worse. When she married him, Edith had never set foot inside a kitchen, except to pass on her mother's orders to the cook. Her efforts in that department, though better than they had been in the beginning, were often a bit hit and miss. Not that he would ever have dreamt of saying so. 'Awfully good rice pudding,' he said.

'Hmff,' said Edith, as if she did not quite believe him.

'Rice pudden's my fav'rit.'

'Don't talk with your mouth full, Anne. Margaret, if you've finished, you can help me clear the table.'

Crash. Bang. Crash. It was a wonder they'd got any crockery left that wasn't chipped. At once he reproached himself for the disloyal thought. Poor Edie. She couldn't have had the least idea what she was letting herself in for, when she'd thrown in her lot with him. Not only having to be her own cook general, but her own scullery maid as well. From the kitchen came another series of crashes and bangs, as his wife, assisted by their elder daughter, got started on the washing-up. 'Leave the saucepans,' he called, knowing she'd probably do them anyway. 'You never get them quite clean,' she'd say, if pressed. For all her practical inexperience in household matters, Edith had firm views as to what constituted men's and women's work. Putting out the rubbish, mowing the lawn, sweeping up leaves and, under supervision, cleaning the windows all counted as men's jobs. The rest was her department, like it or not.

'Daddy . . .' Anne scrambled up onto his knee. He smelt her sweet baby smell. 'Tell me a story,' she said.

'Later. When you're tucked up in bed.'

'Do you want to hear my two times table?'

'Rather.'

Anne was just coming to the end of her sing-song recitation, when his wife returned with the tea tray. 'Bath time, girls.' There was the usual cry of protest. He intervened, as he usually did.

'Let them have another five minutes.' Then there was just time for Margaret to demonstrate her prowess at long division – *she'd a good grasp of mathematics, that one, unusual in a girl* – and for Anne to sing him the song the infants were learning for assembly:

Jesus bids us shine with a pure, clear, light
Like a little candle, burning in the night.

After this, the girls went upstairs for their bath, which they had to share, because, as Edith was never slow to point out, hot water cost money. He poked up the fire and threw on a shovelful of coal, to get it burning brightly. Coals cost money too, but it was a miserable night and if they couldn't have a decent blaze every now and again, then what had things come to? He wondered, as he sat there, crouched over the fire – any closer, and he'd be *in* the fire, his wife was fond of saying – whether other men felt like this. So . . . so *unequal* to what was expected of them. Or was it just those like himself? He thought of Ashenhurst – 'Hello-ello, old man' – was it like that for him too? Or Pearson, always so cheery, poor chap; though God knows he had little enough reason to be. No, on reflection, *he* had no right to be blue.

As if she divined his thoughts, Edith leaned across and put her hand on his. 'You look all in,' she said, in a gentler tone than before. 'Want me to read to you?'

'That'd be nice.'

'Just let me get the girls settled.' She got up and went to the door. 'Margaret! Anne! Don't forget to clean your teeth. I'll be up in five minutes to switch the light out.' She returned to her seat. 'What's it to be?' she asked. 'Another chapter of *Bleak House*, or just the paper?' This was their nightly ritual, instigated by Edith when they'd first started walking out together. It was better than the wireless, in his opinion, although when he'd said this to Edith once she'd laughed. 'At least,' she replied, knowing his fondness for all things musical, 'you don't expect me to *sing*.'

On most nights, he'd have gone for the Dickens. There was nothing like a bit of fiction for lifting one's mood. But tonight his concentration wasn't up to it. 'Oh, just the paper, I think,' he accordingly replied. 'It's in my briefcase.'

'I'll get it.' Before he could stop her, she jumped up again. He heard the click of her heels on the hall's tiled floor.

'You oughtn't be running around like this. You'll tire yourself out,' he told her, as she settled back down again, with a creaking of springs, in the armchair facing his.

'You know me, I was never one for sitting still,' she replied, disregarding this allusion to her condition as if it were of no account. She'd been just the same when she was expecting the other two: always on the go. Apparently, it slowed some women down, being in the family way, not his Edith, though. She unfolded the newspaper with a brisk little shake. 'Now. Where would you like to start? Births, Deaths, and Marriages?'

'It's as good a place as any.'

She began reading, and he closed his eyes. Already he felt calmer, the strains of the day conjured away by a soothing litany of names, dates and places. Although it wasn't so much what she read as the sound of Edith's voice that soothed him. It was the first thing he'd noticed about her: her voice and its distinctive timbre. She'd laughed at him when he'd called her beautiful. 'How on earth can you tell?' she'd said. But he'd insisted that it was how she sounded to him. 'Then it's lucky you can't see me,' she'd said, but she'd been smiling as she said it. That woman who'd rung this afternoon to speak to Mr Willoughby, she'd had a lovely way of speaking, too. Honeyed. *Was that the word?* He'd never understood what it meant till now. A voice like that hinted at a world of possibilities.

'*On January 14th, at 19, Queen's Gardens, Ealing, a son, to Muriel, wife of Roderick Brooke,*' read Edith. 'Now it's just the Deaths. *At Hyde Park Gate, on January 16th, after a brief illness, Sir Percival Harrington, Bart., aged 84.*'

He checked her with a wave of his hand. He didn't want to hear about those who'd died in bed, after long, comfortable lives. 'Read the On Active Service column.'

'I was just about to.'

'How many are there?'

'Not many today. Three. No, four.'

'Of course the main push didn't start until April.'

Edith cleared her throat. '*In loving memory of my husband, A. B. Burgess-Smith . . .*'

'Doesn't ring a bell.'

'*. . . died January 17th 1922, of an illness contracted in the Great War . . .*'

'Probably a lung case. Like poor Perkins, you

remember.' *That terrible, gargling cough he'd had. Poor devil, he hadn't lasted long.*

'Yes.' A brief pause in acknowledgement of poor Perkins. '*In loving memory of Ralph, only son of Mr and Mrs P. L. Cotton, Second Lieutenant, Manchester Regiment, died of wounds, aged 18, January 17th 1915 . . .*'

'Does it say where?'

'No. Just "in France" . . . *In ever-beloved memory of Brian (Frederick Brian Arthur) Fargus, Lieutenant commanding Machine Gun Section, Queen Victoria's Rifles, 9th London Battalion, killed in action at Le Petite Douve, Wulverghem . . .*' She stumbled over the word, he corrected her:

'Say it as if you've got a frog in your throat.'

'*Wulverghem, Flanders, January 17th 1917 . . .*'

'That was a beastly show.' Bodies all flung down together and frozen in mud.

'*In loving memory of Henry, 2nd Baron Gorrell, Major RFA . . .*'

'Did you say Gorrell? I think I knew a Gorrell.'

'*. . . killed in action in Flanders, January 16th, 1917.*'

'It has to be the same one. Major Gorrell. Well, well. D'you know, I think it was Major Gorrell who took us for our first training session when we got to France. Quiet sort of chap. Looked as if he wouldn't say boo to a goose. Damn good officer, though.'

'I don't think you've mentioned him before.'

'No. Well, one lost sight of people. Except those in one's own detachment, of course.'

'Yes.' Edith sounded as if she was swallowing a yawn. 'Shall I read on?'

'Not unless there's anything particularly interesting in the news.'

She skimmed through the next few pages. 'There's not much. Another big demonstration in Trafalgar Square . . .'

'Oh dear.'

'"Oh dear" is right. We're getting just like Berlin, or Rome. Fascists shouting abuse from the tops of buses. Communists spouting a lot of hot air about goodness knows what.'

'I heard a couple of chaps talking about it on the train. "Minimum wage." I'd give 'em a "minimum wage" all right. String 'em up, I would. Bloody Reds.'

'I suppose your sister was there.'

'I've no idea.' He knew his wife's view of Dorothy's activities well enough by now not to want to prolong this discussion. 'I haven't spoken to her this week.'

'Well, I just wish she wouldn't get involved in all that kind of thing.'

'Edith, we've talked about this before. You know that nothing I can say will make the smallest bit of difference.'

'It's not a woman's place, in my view, to get herself mixed up in politics. I suppose it's Viktor's influence.'

'I expect you're right. Is there any other news, or shall we have the wireless?'

'I mean, I know she *means* well, but I can't help feeling that all this speechifying and campaigning she does is rather beside the point. There'll never be a revolution here – and thank heavens for *that*, I say!'

There were tanks in Piccadilly last year, he thought but did not say. He didn't feel like getting into an argument. And it was true his sister could be a bit much sometimes, with her causes and her crusades. Her heart was in the right place, though – even Edith had been known to admit as much. Edith yawned. 'There's not a lot else. "*A Morris Cowley two-seater, belonging to Mr L.G. Greatrex of Harrow, was stolen from outside the Northwick Park Lawn Tennis Club, Wembley, on Saturday night . . .*"'

'What colour was the car?' Not that it mattered tuppence, but he liked to be able to picture things. 'It doesn't say. "*Four Whitstable boys were bound over at Canterbury for breaking into a store . . .*" Oh! How dreadful!'

'Doesn't sound especially dreadful to me . . .'

'No, I meant the murders. Quite horrible. Listen to this: "*At Riverview Villas, Barnes, on Saturday morning, Mr Alexander Filson (47), his son Robert (19) and daughters Catherine (14) and Mary (7) were found shot dead . . .*"'

'Daddy . . .'

Neither of them had heard the child come in.

'What is it, Margaret?' Edith said sharply. 'You're supposed to be in bed.'

'Daddy said he'd read us a story.'

'Your father's resting. Now run along before I get cross.'

He got to his feet. 'It's all right. I'll go up. You carry on with your paper.'

As they went upstairs, Margaret said thoughtfully, 'Seven. That's the same age as me.'

It took him a moment to realise what it was she meant.

Chapter Two

He was glad he'd only got daughters. He wouldn't have wanted a son. Because who could say when it might not start again, the nightmare? Then all that effort of watching over the boy, his shining face looking up at you, of feeding and clothing him, and teaching him to know right from wrong, would have been for one purpose only: to have him sent away at eighteen – or even younger – to be blown to bits, or shot, or to die in a beastly swamp like Ypres, coughing his lungs out from poison gas . . . No, he'd never wanted a son. Edith felt differently, of course. But then she hadn't seen the things he'd seen. He thought of the man he'd stumbled across that time in the trenches at Zonnebeke, with half his face shot away. A horrible look in his one remaining eye, as he lay there, the blood gurgling out of the ragged hole that was his mouth, as if he cursed those that were trying to help him for being alive, while he was in agony. Or poor young Earnshaw, with a bloody stump instead of a hand, a fragment of exploding shell having blown away his fingers. Staring at the dripping thing, as if he couldn't quite believe what he was seeing. 'Funny kind of thing to have for a hand,' he'd seemed to be saying. Not that he'd said a word. These, and other no less hideous images, came back to Rowlands still, on the edge of sleep or, sometimes, when he was thinking about nothing at all. All of a sudden, that bloody head would rear up, with its one-eyed glare, *such hatred in that look*; or Robin Earnshaw would turn, with that frightened half-smile, holding up what was left of his hand.

Strange that these sights should have been the last that remained to him. Men scrambling up the ladders, and ducking under the wire. Star shells exploding all around – *ah! those bursts of white fire!* – quite beautiful, he remembered thinking, like a particularly deadly kind of firework. Then there was the trench they'd taken over near Bellewaarde Wood, with the dead men lying at the bottom of it: arms and legs sticking out stiffly in their field-grey uniform, like terrible, life-sized dolls. What a mess that had been! Broken rifles and entrenching tools all flung down in the mud, with cartridge clips and machine gun ribbons, empty food tins, water bottles, unexploded shells – all of it turned to rubbish, just as they had been turned to rubbish . . . a ghastly sight, all told.

What he wouldn't have given to see it all again.

At once he pulled himself up. There was nothing to be gained from such thoughts. Better to keep your eye on the road ahead, as the Major would have said. And in truth he'd never been bitter about what happened, knowing, as he did, how much worse it had been for some. Pearson, for example, who had lost his hands as well as his eyes, when a grenade went off in his face – such injuries being all too common. He wondered what had happened to poor Earnshaw. He – Pearson – had made light of it, of course, in the way so many of them did, joking that the only thing he missed was being able to fill his pipe. He'd still managed to feed himself, though, with the aid of that pincer-like contraption they'd rigged up for him in the workshops. Necessity being, as ever, the mother of invention, a man without hands will starve faster than a man without eyes. 'Good as new,' was how Pearson said it had made him feel, the first time he'd used the thing. 'You almost don't miss the old system, once you've got the hang of it.'

Then there was Ashenhurst, who'd lost not only his sight, but the one bit of happiness he might have hoped for, to make up for that loss. It was Ashenhurst who'd taken him under his wing when he'd first arrived at the Lodge. That was the way it worked there, with all of them teamed up with a Pal. Showing them the ropes, was what the Major called it, 'Quite literally, in our case!' he'd laughed. That was one of the ways you learnt: following the guide-rails, or wires, that were strung along the corridors. It wasn't difficult, Ashenhurst said, you just had to make sure you knew which direction you were setting off in. After that it was simply a matter of keeping the wire to your left, or your right, as the case might be. This place was all right angles, he'd find. Or he could try keeping to the strip of linoleum that ran along beside the carpet – all the corridors had it. When he was ready to go out into the garden he'd find the same arrangement, only with gravel paths. A wooden board marked the top of every step. You soon learned to distinguish one kind of surface from another. Gravel or grass. Granite slabs or cobblestones. To tell one season from another by this method, too. Autumn leaves, by their smell and sound, as well as the way they felt underfoot. Snow, of course, its soft crunch when new-fallen; its smooth treachery, as it melted and froze again to ice.

Not that he wouldn't take a tumble or two, while he was finding his feet, Ashenhurst said. 'For the first six weeks after I got here, I gave myself some wonderful black eyes.'

When he'd registered surprise (thinking himself, absurdly, the only one in darkness), Ashenhurst seemed amused. 'Didn't you realise? We're all in the same boat, here. Except for the doctors, and the girls, of course.'

He'd heard women's voices on more than one occasion since his arrival, but had assumed they must be those of visitors. 'Girls?' he'd echoed.

43

'Yes. Our VADs.' Was there the faintest trace of irony in Ashenhurst's voice? 'You'll meet them soon enough – in fact, you'll probably be assigned one of your very own. Like dancing, do you?'

He was taken aback for a moment. 'Well . . .'

'Oh, don't worry – we'll have you tripping the light fantastic in no time. That's where the girls come in, of course. It's one of the things they're good at, getting us back on our feet, so to speak.'

And in fact it was only a week later that he'd had his first dancing lesson, with a VAD named Vera. 'We don't stand on ceremony here.' She was a cheerful sort, he remembered her firm, round body pressed against his, her smell of talcum powder, and had kept up a constant stream of chatter about all sorts of things, as she'd steered him, quite skilfully, around the floor, to the strains of the 'Missouri Waltz'. It had felt all wrong to him, not to be the one leading, even though he'd quite enjoyed her chaff. 'What's your name, Tommy?' had been her first question, and when he'd told her she'd hooted with laughter. 'Frederick! *That's* a bit grand. I think, if it's all the same to you, I'll call you Freddie.'

The sandman is calling when shadows are falling,
While the soft breezes sigh, as in days long gone by . . .

When it was over, he'd found he was trembling, as much from the novelty of having a woman in his arms again, as from the strain of having to concentrate so hard on the music. Although wasn't that what he'd always done? For the life of him, he couldn't recall. So many things were different now. Things one had taken for granted, descending a flight of stairs, say, or where one's feet went in dancing a waltz, had become fraught with difficulty. Other couples were circulating; he could hear their talk and laughter above the music, a foxtrot this time. How they managed it he couldn't imagine. It was worse than firing practice.

In fact, he'd gone back the following week for his lesson but only because Ashenhurst said that if he didn't find dancing to his taste, then he might like to try sitting in with the orchestra: 'You did say you played the piano, didn't you, old man?' The second time wasn't so bad. By the third, he was quite looking forward to his spin around the dance floor with Vera. But when he got there, Vera was not to be found. Another VAD was there in her stead.

'It's Miss Tremlett's afternoon off,' said this new voice. A nice voice it was, pitched agreeably low, with the rounded vowel sounds and crisp consonants that denoted a lady. Some of them were from very good homes. Wanting to do their bit, he supposed, although why they should have chosen to spend their time with a lot of stumbling crocks, he couldn't for the life of him imagine. 'I expect she's gone shopping for her trousseau. She's getting married next month.' His surprise must have registered on his face. 'Oh dear, have I disappointed you? I'm Edith Edwards, by the way. I do hope we'll be friends.'

He supposed that this had been the turning point, for him: the moment when it began to seem as if his life might once more have a purpose. It had taken him a while to realise it, of course, since at the time he was much too preoccupied with not treading on Miss Edwards' toes. No, it wasn't until several weeks had passed, and he and Edith had started walking out together – quite literally, since, with her assistance, he was now venturing as far as the Brompton Road – that he'd come to see the progress he'd made, since the dark days after his return from Flanders. It wasn't just that he was capable of doing more for himself, that came with practice, as Ashenhurst never tired of telling him. It was the way he *felt* . . . as if he'd come alive again, after lying for so long in a black tomb. He'd never known what it meant before, that story about Lazarus coming out of his grave. He was Lazarus. Death had wrapped him in its embrace but he'd broken free, and walked out, into the light . . .

Not that it was light, exactly, where he was now: a sort of twilight, rather. Yellowish, like a dirty pea-souper. He'd one-eighth of his vision in his right eye, the doctor who'd patched him up had told him. That meant he could distinguish light from dark, and shapes of things, if the light was good enough. Everything else was lost to him. People's faces, flowers, the colour of the sky, but if you said the word 'blue', that was what he saw, or thought he saw, like an echo of long-ago heard music in the brain.

Still, his case was a lot better than some. Young Atkinson, for instance, who'd lost both eyes to a sniper's bullet, when he was taking a sighting through binoculars. The damage wouldn't have been so great if one of the cylinders hadn't exploded, driving splinters of metal into his unprotected face. They'd had to extract these with a magnet, Atkinson said proudly, his voice from the next bed sounding painfully young. Or there was Parry, who'd lost his sight to gas, in that beastly show at Langemarck, in '14. *He'd* been one of the lucky ones in his platoon. The rest had died, choking on their own blood and the froth from their corrupted lungs.

Knowing he himself was luckier than some wasn't much consolation, all the same, when he'd woken every morning to nothing but darkness. Even the terrible dreams from which he woke, sweating and terrified, were preferable to this. In those dreams he was always back there and he could always see – only too clearly. That trench with the dead Germans, their legs sticking out so stiffly; the look of hatred in a dying man's eye . . . He'd had a bad spell, soon after he'd been discharged from hospital. He was perfectly fit, they'd told him, as fit as he'd ever be. No sense in taking up a bed that some other man might need. So he'd gone home to Camberwell. His mother had still been alive then. It was then that he'd understood what his life would be. Other men, those who'd lost limbs, or suffered nervous collapse as a result of what they'd been through, might recover; he would not. He found himself envying them: the men with damaged bodies and minds. You could replace a limb with something almost as good; heal, in time, a shattered spirit. What *he* had lost could never be replaced, or healed. He was shut in for ever, in this smothering dark.

Sometimes, waking from sleep, he'd forget, for a split second, what had happened. Opening his eyes in the expectation of seeing, only to find that expectation cruelly thwarted. Those were the worst times. Once his mother had come into his room when she heard him sobbing – harsh, tearless cries that seemed to tear the throat. Because what *use* was he now, what use would he ever be? He couldn't read, he couldn't write, he couldn't walk down the street unaided, he couldn't even feed himself without spilling the food all down his front like a little baby. Worst of all, as far as his pride was concerned, was the fact that he was now dependent on his mother and sister, the household economy being precariously based on the miserable pension his mother received from the lamp factory, combined with what Dorothy could earn from her dress making. It was true that she, his sister, had hopes of getting a better situation soon, in a bigger factory, but that was beside the point, he felt. Why she should work her fingers to the bone to support a useless hulk like him, he couldn't imagine. She made light of it, of course, that was Dottie all over. Still, it wasn't right: a girl of seventeen having to be the head of the family. In his worst moments, he wondered if it wouldn't have been better if he'd died that day – the day he'd got his 'Blighty one' – instead of living on, a burden to everyone.

It must have been around this time, a few weeks after

his return home, that Mother had spoken to Dr Standish about him. She was ill by this time, poor Ma, although she'd said nothing about it. Typically, she'd been more worried about him than she had about her own health, although by then she'd only another five months to live. One of the things he most regretted about that dreadful time was how, wrapped up as he was in his own misery, he'd failed to see the truth of the matter. So it was that he found himself at the Lodge. Dr Standish knew a man, a very good man, in his opinion, who'd agreed to take a look at him. It was on his, Mr Altringham's, recommendation that he was sent to Regent's Park. A place called St Dunstan's Lodge, which specialised in the rehabilitation of the war-blinded. 'They're doing good things there,' said Altringham, whose hands had smelled of the expensive soap he'd washed them with, between patients. 'I think you'll be just the type they'll be able to do something with.'

He remembered his first interview with the Major (he hadn't thought of him as the Major then). His mother had accompanied him, it having been one of her better days. At first it had been she who'd done most of the talking. But then the man who'd introduced himself simply as Ian Fraser had interrupted one of Mother's nervously rambling sentences to say, 'D'you know, Mrs Rowlands, I think I'd like a few words alone with this young chap, if you don't mind.' When the door had closed behind her, Fraser had been silent a moment. Then: 'Tell me a bit about yourself,' he'd said.

'There isn't much to tell.' It had sounded sullen, even to him.

There was a pause. It occurred to him that Fraser might be studying him. He hated that: the feeling of being so very much at a disadvantage.

'You enlisted in '14, didn't you?'

'Yes. Sir,' he thought to add.

'First Battle of Ypres, Loos, and Passchendaele, wasn't it? I was with the BEF in France,' went on that calm, quiet voice. 'It wasn't exactly a picnic. But not, from all accounts, quite as wretched as that Flanders show.'

'I wouldn't like to say, sir.'

'No, of course not. So tell me, what was your job, before the war?'

'I was a proofreader at Methuen.' He was unable to keep the bitterness out of his voice. 'I've always liked reading.'

But if Fraser heard the sour note, he gave no sign of it. 'Good show. We need some men with literary interests here. We've actually quite a decent lending library.'

The obvious reply was on his lips; he bit it back.

'How long is it since you came home?' was Fraser's next question.

'I don't know. Three . . . no, four months. I was in hospital six weeks. I'm afraid I've rather lost track of time.'

'The very first thing we'll do is get you a watch. Here, take a look at mine, if you like . . .' It seemed an absurdity, but then he felt the other man put something into his hand. It was an ordinary watch, without a glass, but with a hunter lid to protect the face. There were little raised dots around the outside edge, and a dot against each numeral, his exploring fingers found, with double dots at the quarters. The hands were slightly raised, he discovered.

'Very important, in our situation, to have a sense of time,' said the Major. 'I'll have it back, thanks. Now, unless you've any questions for me, I suggest we take a look around the place.'

They'd emerged from Fraser's office into the corridor, where a crowd of men milled about, laughing and talking. A smell of cold air and muddy fields clung about them. A chorus of voices greeted Fraser's appearance:

'Morning, Major.'

'We missed you this morning, Major.'

'Not slacking, are you, Major?'

'How was the match? asked Fraser.

'Not so bad,' was the reply: a soft north-eastern accent.

'5–3 to the Durhams, worst luck!' somebody else chipped in.

'Ah, that'll be Sid Ridley's doing,' said the Major. A burst of rueful laughter greeted this remark. 'Sid played inside left for Newcastle before the war,' he explained. 'Didn't you, Sid?'

'Aye,' replied that gentleman. 'I did that.'

'This is Frederick Rowlands, by the way,' Major Fraser went on. 'He'll be joining us, just as soon as he can get his kit together.'

'Any good at kicking?' said another voice – a Mancunian. 'We could use a good striker.'

'I've played a bit . . . before the war.'

'Don't tell him that!' laughed the Major. 'He'll have you signed up for the team before you know what's hit you, won't you, Hancock? Give the man a chance to settle in first.'

They'd visited the workshops where men were making baskets – 'not so difficult, when you get the knack of it,' said the Major – the cobbler's, strongly redolent of leather and blacking, and the joinery shop, with its smells of fresh sawdust and glue, and its agreeable sounds of men whistling and hammering. They'd put their heads into one of the classrooms, where a female instructor was giving a typewriting lesson. With his mother in tow, they'd taken a turn around the garden. All this was to become familiar territory, a place he'd come to know like the back of his hand. But on that first day, it wasn't the cheerful sounds of men working, or the smells of the vegetable garden and the chicken-sheds, or the, to him, more attractive prospects offered by the tap-tapping of the typewriters that'd had affected him the most. No. It was that moment when Hancock had called back over his shoulder, as the laughing group of football players moved off down the corridor, 'See you at next week's practice!', a remark that, when he came to think about it afterwards, he wasn't even sure was meant for him. But he'd known then it was going to be all right.

Although, in point of fact, he'd never taken to football, at least, not in the form in which it was played at the Lodge. Kicking around a ball with a bell inside it, merely for the pleasure of feeling the impact of boot against leather, and then trying to get the thing in the net by directing one's kick towards the sound of the goalkeeper's clapping hands, wasn't enough of a challenge, in his view. Although he could still remember the smell of the air on those winter mornings, in Regent's Park. Freshly churned-up mud and leaf mould and a hint of frost. Rowing was more his cup of tea. That was hard, physical work; he found that he had a flair for it. There was a rhythm to it that he liked: the feel of the oars in his hands, the *resistance* one felt as blade pressed against water so that one had to judge each stroke just right to achieve the desired rate of propulsion; the recovery that followed the stroke, and then the feathering of the blade . . . Firing a gun was demanding enough: with a rate of twenty rounds a minute to maintain, you couldn't afford to slacken for a moment. You caught each shell as your Pal passed it to you, feeling its cold, deadly weight in your cupped hands, loaded it, and held your hands ready for the next one as the first was being fired, in a smooth, unbroken sequence. After a few hours of this, he'd fallen down upon his bedroll like a dead man each night, so that even the bursting of the five nines close at hand had failed to wake him. But if he'd been fit before – and soldiering toughened up even the weakest man – it was nothing compared to the way he was now. As if driving himself to the limit could obliterate the horror of those wasted months when he'd first come out of hospital, thinking himself useless, a cripple. If nothing else, he'd prove he was anything but that.

With Edith acting as coxswain (and by this time, she was definitely *his* VAD), he'd rowed around the lake in Regent's Park; as his confidence increased, he'd taken to the river. His four – Ned Corrigan, Bobby Shelton and Alf Doubler – had taken first prize in their class at the Putney Regatta that summer. He'd also distinguished himself (second prize) in the Single Sculls. He still had his medal somewhere, along with the one he'd received for serving his country. He knew which of the two he cared more about, and it wasn't the one with the King's face on it and the blue and gold ribbon.

It must have been not long after his triumph at Putney that he and Edith had taken a boat out on the river at Richmond. It was a beautiful summer's day: he remembered the feel of the sun on his face, and the wind ruffling his hair, as they'd moved out into mid-stream. The only sound, apart from the wind rustling the leaves, and the rhythmic dipping of the oars, was Edith's voice, keeping time. A mile or so downstream, they'd steered between the leafy fronds of a weeping willow, and tied up against the bank, to eat their lunch. Cheese and ham sandwiches, he recalls, washed down with a bottle of beer. He'd never tasted anything so good. Afterwards, he'd had a smoke, and she'd washed the plates and glasses in the river. A feeling of contentment he hadn't known in years filled him. It was then that he'd asked her to marry him. She was silent for so long that he was afraid she hadn't heard him, and that he'd have to say it all again but then she laughed – a warm and throaty laugh she had; it was one of the things he loved about her. 'If you could see your face,' she'd said. 'It's a real picture. Yes, of course I'll marry you, Fred. I thought you'd never ask.'

When Celia West had rung up again, a couple of days later, he'd wondered if perhaps he'd mistaken the tone of that first exchange, and this might be no more than a professional call. But if it were just that Her Ladyship were consulting his employer in his capacity as legal adviser, then the warmth of Gerald Willoughby's response then and now had suggested otherwise. Instead of his usual cool, polite manner when dealing with clients, this was effusive, even boyish. It was 'perfectly ripping' to hear from her, he'd said, and no, she wasn't disturbing him in the slightest. Work was 'frightfully dull' at present; he was only too happy to be interrupted. All this and a great deal more in the same vein suggested an easy intimacy, an intimacy, moreover, which intensified as the weeks went by, as Lady Celia's calls became a regular occurrence.

The calls always came at around the same time, just after office hours had ended, and Willoughby was always in his office to receive them. It got so that he,

Rowlands, could predict when it was her from the very sound of the ring, although that was absurd, he told himself, because all telephone bells sounded the same. How to explain, then, that on the – admittedly rare – occasions when a late call from someone else came in, he knew it even before he heard the caller's voice? There was a *flatness* to the sound, he somehow felt, which couldn't be confused with the – to him – very different *timbre* of those calls from the Mayfair number. Call it intuition, or a sixth sense, it amounted to the same thing: a shiver of excitement in the pit of the stomach; a prickling of the hairs on the back of the neck as, a split second before he heard her voice, he switched the line to open: 'Put me through, would you?' she'd say. She didn't need to announce herself. He'd do as she asked, lingering just long enough to hear Willoughby say, 'Celia! I've been dying to talk to you all day.'

Except that, as the weeks went by, he found himself keeping the line open for just that little bit longer each time. It wasn't something he set out to do; it happened, that's all. And it wasn't that he cared what these two had to say to one another, as that he wanted to hear anything *she* had to say, however inconsequential. She could have read out a shopping list, and he'd have listened, entranced. He was under no illusions as to what this signified. Hadn't he fallen in love with a voice once before? It wasn't as if he could stop himself this time, either. To suppose himself less susceptible than other men, merely because his head would never again be turned by a pretty face, was to suppose that desire can only be kindled through looking. Whereas if a decade spent in darkness had taught him anything, it was that in love, *all* the senses were implicated. The feel of a woman's skin, her smell, her taste – above all, the sound of her voice, apprehended as it was through the intimate whorls of the ear – could fire the imagination in a way the eye's banal appraisals could not.

He told himself that it didn't matter, what he felt for Celia West, for who, apart from himself, would ever know? If he permitted himself this small indulgence, this brief immersion in another's being, what harm could it do? Although, as his hand hesitated for a few seconds longer each time before closing the channel between them, her murmuring voice and his listening ear, he couldn't help but feel a flicker of guilt. A small betrayal had been committed. And, whether the one betrayed was aware of it or not, his . . . infidelity seemed too strong a word . . . his *transgression* had altered, if only by a hair's breadth, the nature of his marriage.

It had been Willoughby who'd saved his life. Not, as it happened, in any literal sense, although he *had* been the officer in charge of getting them all to the field hospital that day, his nervous stammer more in evidence than ever, on being confronted with the battered remnants of his platoon.

'Can you m-make it, do you think?'

'Yes, sir.'

'Good man.'

A quick clap on the shoulder and he was gone, to put the same urgent question to the rest of the walking wounded: Naylor, who couldn't get over his luck at having been hit in the shoulder, *I'm going home, boys!*; and Duncan, whose jaw was fractured, poor fellow, so that he groaned aloud when anybody touched him; and Partridge, who'd seemed the best of the lot of them, with only a shallow scalp wound – a scratch, he'd called it – but who'd later taken bad and died from blood poisoning, it was said. There must have been others, whose names he can't remember or never knew, but these were the ones nearest to him, as he crouched there in the dugout, the graveyard smell of earth all around him, holding the handkerchief that someone had given him against his face to staunch the bleeding, and wondering how long the darkness was going to last. It hadn't crossed his mind that it might be for ever. Even on the way to the clearing station, with Naylor walking alongside to guide him over the slippery duckboards – although it hadn't stopped him putting his foot in a hole, so that he'd been drenched up to the knee in ice-cold, filthy water – it hadn't really hit home. He'd been more intent on trying not to bring them both down into the stinking mud that lay on either side, to have time for such thoughts.

It was only when he was awaiting his turn to be seen in the tent at Mendinghem (as the dressing-station was humorously called, the others in the vicinity being 'Bandagehem' and 'Dosinghem'), that he'd had an inkling of the truth. He'd heard the orderly say, 'Another eye case, sir,' and it had struck him with the force of a blow to the stomach, *I might be left blind*. Until that moment, he'd been too numb with pain and shock to consider anything beyond what he was being asked to do by the doctors. Simple instructions – *come over here, sit down, turn your head towards me* – having acquired an ambiguity they did not have when one could see. Now he confronted the terrible question: *how bad is it?* Another: *how long will it last?* followed on from this. Without being able to read the doctors' expressions, as they probed and stitched, he could gain no sense of the severity, or otherwise, of his case. It wasn't until the next day, when Captain Willoughby stopped by to see him, bringing a gift of cigarettes, and the news that they were sending him home with the next consignment of wounded, that it had hit him. His war was over.

Willoughby, who up until that day had struck him as a nice enough young chap, if a little bit green, the way these young fellows straight out of Sandhurst tended to be, had been in uncharacteristically sombre mood. 'Is there anybody you'd like me to write to?' he'd asked. 'Your m-mother, perhaps?'

He'd supplied the address, thinking, *I'll write to her myself, as soon as these bandages are off*. 'How's Wilson?' he'd thought to ask.

The other was silent a moment. 'I'm afraid Wilson's

dead. The same blast that . . . well. I don't have to tell you. You were there.'

Now it was his turn to be silent.

'Was he a Pal of yours?' said the officer, with awkward sympathy.

'Not particularly. He was a good sort, though . . .'

'Yes.' Willoughby cleared his throat. 'I'll be writing to his people of course.'

'Yes, sir.' What a lot of writing he must have to do, he'd thought. Wives, mothers, sweethearts. *I regret to inform you . . .* They'd had a letter like that when Harry was killed. 'It's a comfort,' his mother had remarked, folding up the letter after he and Dorothy had read it, 'to know how popular he was with all the others.' He hadn't had the heart to point out that the phrase 'well-liked by all his comrades' – supposedly descriptive of his brother – doubtless featured in the majority of letters of this kind.

'Well,' said Willoughby, pushing back his chair, so that it made a scraping sound on the hospital's bare wooden floor. 'If there's anything I can do . . .'

'Thank you, sir.'

'No, I mean it. Anything at all. You'll let me know, I hope?'

'Yes, sir.' Although what was there to be done? The only thing he wanted, which was that his life should be as it had been before, was not in Willoughby's – or anybody's – power to give.

* * *

It wasn't until two years after that conversation that he had cause to remember Willoughby's promise. He'd just qualified as a telephonist and gained his typing diploma. Now he was looking for a job 'because,' the Major said, 'it's time you were out in the wide world, old chap. There's not a lot more we can teach you, here at the Lodge.' Whatever the truth of this, it was certainly the case that he needed to make a living. He had a wife to support, with a child on the way. Opportunities for those like himself, although by no means plentiful, were – theoretically, at least – available, the hiring of war veterans by the larger corporations being promoted by the government of the day as a civic duty. The Major, as ever, was sanguine about his chances. 'With your brains and quickness at picking things up, you shouldn't have too much trouble,' he'd said, before going on to list the numbers of men the Lodge had managed to place in the past two years. Men as 'handicapped' as he was (the golfing analogy was a favourite of the Major's) had found work as carpenters, shoemakers, chicken farmers. Some, who'd trained as masseurs, were now involved in the rehabilitation of the war wounded. Others, with the assistance of compliant bank managers and industrious wives, had started small businesses: a tobacconist's in High Holborn, a tea shop in Amersham.

The reality was a bit different, of course. Because with all the men returning from the war – to say nothing of those who'd been thrown out of work by the closing-down of the munitions factories – there just weren't enough jobs to go round. The shipyards and mines were laying people off, too. No, it wasn't a good time to be looking for a job, especially for someone whose previous experience was no longer of any use to him. So that when Edith came across the advertisement in *The Times* that day, Rowlands had been almost at the end of his tether. They'd been living in furnished rooms in Marylebone at the time; the sofa on which they were sitting doubled as their bed at night. Edith was reading out the requests for *Smart Lads Willing to Use Initiative*, and for *Reliable Ex-Servicemen Seeking Responsible Positions*, as she did most evenings, and he was letting his mind drift, thinking, *I'll write to the Major tomorrow – maybe he can suggest something . . .* when suddenly a phrase caught his attention.

'Read that one again.'

'*Situation Vacant for Respectable Couple as Chauffeur and Cook?*'

'No. The one before that.'

'*Established Firm of City Solicitors Saville & Willoughby Seeks Receptionist . . .*'

'He was training to be a lawyer . . .'

'Who?'

'Captain Willoughby. My O.C. It has to be the same one.'

The very next day he'd presented himself at the firm's offices near London Bridge. He hadn't been kept waiting long. The moment he'd walked into the room and heard the other man's voice, he knew it was going to be all right. 'Good Lord! It *is* you. Gunner Rowlands, as large as life. I m-must say, old chap, you're looking a lot better than when I last saw you.'

He'd felt himself flush with pleasure at the remark which was, admittedly, no more than the truth. The broken man he had been and the man he was now belonged to different worlds. He'd made some reply, remembering to keep his head up, and his gaze looking forward, as he did so. Nothing was more disconcerting, Edith had told him, than a gaze that wandered vacantly around the room. 'Remember: eyes front,' she'd said. 'Just like in the army.'

He'd been glad of his military training a moment later.

'I gather you want to come and work for us?' Willoughby said. He was smiling as he spoke – Rowlands could hear it in his voice. He remembered that smile from before – the way it had lit up the younger man's face. A good-looking chap, was Willoughby. Fair-haired, with blue eyes, and a fine, straight nose. A face saved from girlish prettiness by the reddish moustache its owner had cultivated during those war years, and by the small scar bisecting his left eyebrow – although whether this had been brought about by an encounter with a stray bit of shrapnel, or was merely the result of a particularly energetic game of rugby when he was at school, Rowlands had never had the nerve to ask.

'Yes, sir.' Unconsciously, Rowlands had squared his shoulders. If disappointment were to follow, he would meet it face to face.

'Think you can do the job?'

'Yes, sir.'

'Good.' He pressed a bell. 'Then you'd better report first thing on Monday morning.'

It had taken a moment for the sense of what he'd said to sink in. 'Thank you, sir,' he'd managed to say at last feeling, to his horror, the tears starting to rise. 'You won't regret it.'

'I'm certain of that. Ah, here's Miss Johnson, my secretary. Miss Johnson will show you where you're to sit, and all that. Sometimes,' Willoughby went on, as – understanding that the interview was at an end – his new employee rose to take his leave, 'I think this whole show is run entirely by the w-women. We men are just a sideshow. What do you think, Miss Johnson?'

And the young woman who – tactfully, he thought – had taken his arm to guide him towards the door, had paused for a moment on the threshold. 'Now, wouldn't that be a fine thing?' she'd replied.

He'd never known it so busy at work: the telephones didn't stop ringing, from morning till night. Buzzers sounding. Answering cord plugged in, with a resonant *clunk. Number, please* . . . Ringing cord plugged into called party's jack. *Hello, I have a call for you* . . . Hands moving mechanically over the board. Front key back. Front key forward. *Tick, tick, tick* as the dolls' eyes dropped down. *Thunk* as the weighted cord sprang back, at the call's end. *Buzz, buzz, buzz* as another call came in, in never-ending sequence. He was dead tired by the time he got home. It got so that he was connecting calls in his sleep. He wasn't one to make a fuss about a bit of hard work, but he'd started to wonder if they didn't need another person working full-time on the switchboard, besides himself. Needless to say, he hadn't said this to anyone else, not wanting it thought that he couldn't cope. Nor did he wish to undermine Carrie Gilbert's position although he was doing twice the work she was, for not a great deal more money.

'It's time you had a pay rise,' Edith said. 'It's been over a year since the last one.'

He shook his head at that. 'I'm sure Mr Saville will think of it in due course. He's got a lot on his mind, what with the Cheltenham case.'

Her only reply was a sigh then, after a silence: 'You know the girls need new coats, don't you? I saw some in the sale at Barker's the other day.'

'All right,' he said. 'I'll see what I can do.'

'It's just that I can hardly bear to send them off to school in what they're wearing now. Margaret's growing so fast that I've had to sew an extra piece onto the hem of last year's coat, and as for Anne's, it's a disgrace.'

'I've said I'll speak to him, all right?'

Her offended silence told him he'd gone too far. At

once he felt contrite. 'I'm sorry, Edie. It's just that I've been so busy.'

Although in truth he'd had plenty of opportunity. It was just that the thought of going cap in hand to the senior partner made his stomach turn. As for raising the matter with Mr Willoughby, that, for reasons he couldn't bring himself to examine, had become impossible. It was as if, since the arrival on the scene of Celia West, their relationship – his and Willoughby's – were no longer strictly one of business, but had changed into something else. He knew it would be presumptuous to call it friendship. But, he couldn't help feeling, he and Willoughby now had something in common: call it a shared obsession. More than this, he was all too aware that at least a part of his squeamishness about asking his employer for more money was because it cheapened the way he'd started to feel about *her*. Which was all wrong, he knew: he was a married man, wasn't he? He had no business having feelings for other women. As for listening in to private conversations: that was wrong, too. Somehow its very wrongness only added to the pleasure.

Chapter Three

People appeared with a suddenness out of the perpetual fog in which they existed, or rather, in which they existed for him. He'd trained himself not to find such apparitions untoward. Because things were the way they were – it was no use fretting about it. In the years since he'd had to get used to this, he'd learned to pay attention to all the signs by which animate creatures announce themselves. The sounds they made: sighs, groans, sniffs, coughs; the creaking of a mackintosh, or of a new pair of boots. Also their various smells, some pleasant, most not. The way they disturbed the air around them. Because if people were noisy enough when stationary, you could run out of words to describe the sounds they made when in motion. The footsteps of those in a hurry – the young and fit – thudded, pattered, or skipped, although some people glided, like dancers. Those of the slower moving – the old, the wounded, and the drunk – shuffled, limped, or staggered. But all of them made their presence felt, in one way or another, even if it was merely by the simple expedient of stepping between him and the light. People spoke of the sixth sense of blind men; for himself, he didn't believe in any such thing. It was just that he used what senses were left to him more fully than most, perhaps.

The darkness in which he lived was full of accidents waiting to happen. A chair moved a few inches out of its usual position was one such, as was a knife with its blade pointed the wrong way. A glass placed too near the edge of a table. A piece of soap, left carelessly on the rim of the bath. He thought of the occasion, only last week, when he'd almost broken his neck tripping over one of the children's dolls that had been dropped on the stairs. Edith had blown up at them about it: 'Do you realise you could have *killed* your father, leaving that there?', reducing Anne, the culprit in this instance, to howls of anguish. He sometimes wished Edith were less severe with Anne, but of course, young as she was, she'd got to learn. Because if you couldn't *see* something was there, then you were almost bound to fall over it. In the dark, the smallest thing could pull the ground from under your feet. Doors left ajar were another hazard. The edge of a door could deal a blow hard enough to knock a man to the floor. Yes, he knew it was hard on the girls, but being sure that there was nothing out of place was the only way he could find his way through the maze the world had become.

It was why, he supposed, he'd become such a creature of habit. He wasn't always like this; it was something that had come with age . . . or rather, with the premature ageing of the spirit that had afflicted him after Passchendaele. Overnight, it seemed, he'd assumed the cautious habits of a man much older than he was, along with the grey hair of middle age. That, too, had been a legacy of the war, although Edith, who'd never seen him with the dark hair he was born with, had told him it became him rather well.

It had been an averagely busy morning. There'd been a fair number of calls to put through, and calls to make, with the usual number of enquiries to fill the spaces in between, some time-wasting, some not. He was dealing with one such – a particularly obstreperous customer who wanted to know whether Rowlands could recommend a 'good man' who'd 'take on' a litigant in a traffic accident, of which it transpired he himself was the perpetrator – when something alerted him to the fact he wasn't alone. Not to put too fine a point on it, the *smell* of the newcomer alerted him. What was disconcerting was that he hadn't heard the man approach. So that if it hadn't been for the smell – acrid, like that of a spent match – he wouldn't have known the other was there until he spoke.

'Willoughby in?'

Rowlands allowed a pause to elapse before replying. 'Perhaps you'd like to start by telling me your name,' he said. 'And what exactly your business might be with Mr Willoughby.'

'"What h'exectly my business might be . . ."' A guffaw of incredulous laughter followed this inexpert mimicry. 'Ho, very grand an' I *don't* think . . .' The hoarse voice grew suddenly confiding. 'What if I was to tell you, *my man*, that I've a piece of "business" your Mister Willoughby'd give the eyes in his head to know.'

'If you'd tell me your name . . .' Rowlands persisted.

'What's it to you?' was the gruff retort. Then: 'Say it's *Mister* Jarvis. Come with some very interesting business indeed.'

Now would have been the time to have sent him on his way – he saw that, with hindsight. 'Put it in writing,' he should have said. 'Mr Willoughby can't see you now. He's a very busy man.' But, as he hesitated – and there *was* something horribly convincing about Jarvis' manner – the man leaned closer, so that Rowlands could feel his smoke-smelling breath against his cheek. 'Tell him,' he muttered, 'That it's about the Count. *That'll* fetch him.'

* * *

70

It was a case they'd been working on for some months. Later, it would become known as the 'Fire Conspiracy Case', notorious, not only because of the scale of the operation, but for the sensational events which brought it to a conclusion. At that moment, however, it was just another case. A suspected insurance fraud, centring on a string of arson attacks on shops and warehouses, scattered across London and the Midlands. One recurrent factor was the connection with the garment trade; another was the name of Giovanni Caparelli – known to interested parties as 'The Count', for his dandyish style and exquisite manners. London had become something of a haven for men like him since the war. Men who seemed to have sprung from nowhere, and who made their living from who knows what. Caparelli was a case in point. On the face of it, his activities seemed no more and no less dubious than those of any other businessman; he had never, in fact, been in trouble with the police. And yet there was something not quite right about him. Ventures in which he was known to have been involved – a private members' club in Shepherd's Market, a furrier's in Knightsbridge – had ended badly, like some of the people, it was whispered, he had got in to run them.

Although nothing bad seemed yet to have adhered to Caparelli himself. He moved in circles which, if not precisely those of the top drawer, were at least respectable. It wasn't unknown for him to turn up at Ascot, or the Derby, when the two-year-old in which he had a share was running. Nor would it have been unusual to find him in some of the West End's smarter drinking dens. But how did he make his money? That was the question.

At least part of the answer was to be found in the complexities of the case on which they were now engaged. Because it was Caparelli who owned the warehouse in the Goswell Road, full of bales of silk and velvet, which had gone up in flames six months before, and for which he had received compensation to the tune of £20,000. How fortunate that he had thought to insure such valuable contents only the week before! The books recording the transaction had all been in order, and the claim had been duly passed by the Sun Fire Insurance Company's representative, Mr Alexander. Since then, there had been other fires and other – no less lucrative – claims, put through by the obliging Alexander: a shop selling fancy goods in Poland Street (prop. G. Caparelli), insured with Sun Fire for £10,000; a warehouse full of fur coats in Ealing (£30,000). The result was that London, these past few weeks, had smelt increasingly of burning. The smell was everywhere, it seemed to Rowlands. It was borne on the wind that came by way of Blackfriars, and Mansion House, and Temple Bar, and all the other dark warrens of the City of London. It came from the river, with its timber yards and warehouses full of cotton, jute and art silk (all of it beautifully suited to burning); from the narrow little streets of Soho and Clerkenwell, with their dress shops and furriers, and fancy goods emporia, to the grand squares of St James'. It lodged, this smell, in the nostrils, driving out all others, so that for Rowlands, perhaps more sensitive to such things than most, it was as if the very air tasted of ashes.

Quite what the Count's involvement was in the whole affair remained uncertain, however. 'He's much too downy a bird to get his hands dirty,' was Jarvis' grudging admission. But that the Italian was in it up to his neck was not in doubt. Wasn't it, after all, his property that, set on fire by unscrupulous hands, gave London such a stench of the inferno?

After his initial truculence, there was a certain degree of professional pride in the fire-raiser's unfolding of the secrets of his trade: 'This is how we goes about it, see? We starts with the place itself – shop or warehouse, or what-have-you. Getting it ready, like. We throws the stuff about . . .'

'By "stuff" I suppose you mean the silks and other materials?'

'Stuff. Yes. We throws it all about, making sure there's plenty of flimsy bits where they needs to be . . .'

'Close to the source of the conflagration . . .'

'Come again?'

'The fire. Go on.'

'Then . . .' Jarvis emitted a hoarse chuckle, as if delighted by the ingenuity of his methods, 'we places a tray inside another tray—'

'I'm afraid I don't quite follow,' interrupted Willoughby. 'What are these "trays" you're referring to?'

'Photographers' trays,' was the reply, delivered in the mildly exasperated tone of one stating the perfectly obvious.

'Ah! For developing photographs, you mean?'

'Yes. Trays, like I said,' said Jarvis. 'We places a tray *inside* another tray, and then tucks a wax taper in between. Then we lights the taper and leaves it to burn.'

'I suppose these trays you mention must be highly flammable?'

'If you mean do they burn easily, they *do* burn easily. Like billy-oh,' said Jarvis happily.

'And how long after the, ah, taper, is lit, does the conflagr . . . the fire . . . start?'

'Depends on how much stuff there is to burn,' was the considered response. 'About half an hour, mostly. Not less than twenty minutes, anyhow.'

'Leaving you . . . that is, the perpetrator . . . plenty of time to get clean away before the alarm is raised,' said Willoughby, perhaps for Rowlands' benefit, since Rowlands had been present throughout this conversation. A necessary precaution, when dealing with a man like Jarvis, of course. 'Very ingenious. Thank you, Mr Jarvis, you've been most helpful.'

It wasn't only unpleasant surprises that the darkness delivered. He was just finishing up at the end of the day, when the door to the office opened. Light footsteps crossed the floor towards him. Even before she spoke, he knew it must be her. It was something to do with her scent. Expensive, he supposed, yet it didn't have the vulgar chemical tang he associated with such stuff. This was delicate, like roses after rain, but with an underlying aroma suggestive of something more exotic. He thought of Turkish cigarettes, and that peculiar green drink he'd had a few times in France, which turned cloudy when you mixed it with water. *Absinthe. Was that it?* He couldn't remember now. All he knew was that her perfume put him in mind of it. A nightclub smell. Not that he'd ever set foot inside a nightclub.

'Oh, hello. I wonder if you can help me?' Close to, her voice was even more alluring than when he'd heard it at the end of the telephone line: its slight huskiness more apparent, its note of mocking amusement more pronounced.

'Of course, Lady Celia.'

There was a moment's startled silence. Then she laughed. 'I must say,' she said, 'you're awfully good. At recognising voices, I mean.'

'One gets into the habit, in this job.'

'I suppose one must,' she murmured. 'It's Mr Rowlands, isn't it?'

'Yes.' He hoped his expression wasn't as foolishly delighted as he felt.

'I was hoping Gerald might be in. Would you mind awfully trying his number for me?'

'Not at all.'

While he was ringing the extension, she must have

moved across to the window, because her voice now came from behind him. 'Why, you can see straight across London Bridge from here,' she said. 'This building must be absolutely dead-centre.'

'I believe it is . . . Oh, good evening, sir. I have Lady Celia for you in reception.'

'Tell her I'll be out in just a moment,' said Willoughby.

'Yes, sir.'

He relayed the message, but if she heard him she made no acknowledgement that he was aware of, her attention seemingly occupied with what was in front of her. 'Quite a lot of traffic on the bridge,' she said. 'Isn't London becoming *clogged* with motor cars these days? And there are boats on the river – barges, I suppose one should say. Quite pretty at this time of day, with all their lights reflected in the water . . .'

'Can you see the Monument?'

'Is that the tall thing with the golden flames? Yes, you can just see it, above the roofs of those office buildings . . . although it's almost dark, you know.'

'Yes, of course.' Six o'clock. It would be dark by now. From her silence, he guessed that she was still standing there, looking out at the view she had so casually sketched for him. Then she sighed. Although what could a woman like her have to sigh about, he wondered.

The door to the internal office opened, and Willoughby came out. 'Hello, Celia. Sorry if I've kept you waiting, I had a letter to finish. Old Saville wanted it on his desk first thing tomorrow.'

76

'Oh, I know how busy you are, you working people. Not that it matters a bit. I've been having such a nice talk with Mr Rowlands.'

'Oh, Rowlands knows everything there is to know about the running of this place, don't you, Rowlands?'

'Well . . .'

'Anyway, if you're finished for the day you can go,' said Willoughby, still addressing his employee. 'I'll lock up.'

'Very well, sir.'

He started to gather his things, conscious, as he did so, of something in the atmosphere. It was a crackle, like electricity. *Chemistry*, it was called, meaning that peculiar frisson of attraction between two people. He supposed they must be smiling at one another. He could picture Willoughby's smile: a flash of strong white teeth, under the neat sandy coloured moustache. *Hers* he could only imagine. If it was as lovely as her voice it must be worth looking at.

'Well, goodnight, Mr Rowlands,' said Celia West. 'So glad to have met you.'

'Goodnight, Lady Celia.'

There was a faint swish of a silk dress against silk-clad legs as she moved past him towards Willoughby's office, followed, he supposed, by Willoughby himself, because a moment later there came the sound of the office door closing, then silence.

* * *

All the way home, making his way through streets still crowded with early evening traffic, and then in the packed train compartment, he couldn't get her out of his thoughts. *The way she'd smiled, because she* had *been smiling, surely, when she'd made that remark*. 'You're awfully good at recognising voices'. As if she'd half-guessed how enraptured he was with hers. Sitting over his tea, after supper, with the fire for once throwing out a delicious heat, so that he felt a pleasant glow all over, he revisited their conversation. The fact she'd remembered his name. The sound of her laughter. If he hadn't known better, he'd have supposed she was flirting with him.

'What are you looking so pleased about?' Edith said, breaking into these thoughts. From the next room could be heard the halting notes of 'Au Clair de la Lune', as Anne, supervised by her sister, stumbled through her piano practice.

'Am I looking pleased?' He felt himself flush, as if he'd been caught out in a lie. And yet, surely, there could be no harm in *thinking* about another woman?

'You've been grinning like a Cheshire cat ever since you got in.'

'Have I?' He made a mental note to keep better control of his facial expressions in future. 'Maybe that's because I've some good news,' he improvised, feeling like a cad. But really, it *had* only been a passing thought. A brief moment of felicity, in an otherwise dull day. It wasn't as if he'd ever have the chance to act upon his feelings.

At once she was out of her chair. 'Oh, Fred. You don't mean to say . . .'

'As of the beginning of next month, my pay is to go up by two pounds a week. Mr Willoughby called me in to tell me this afternoon.'

'Oh, Fred!'

'I was going to wait until the children were in bed to tell you, but you've wormed it out of me.' He reached for her. 'Aren't you pleased?'

She leaned against him for a moment, so that their faces were almost touching. He could smell the faint musky tang of her skin – stronger now she was with child – and the soft green soap she used to wash her hair. 'Of course I'm pleased.' She straightened up from the embrace, giving him a little pat on the shoulder to indicate that their moment of closeness was at an end. 'Only . . . I'd hoped it might have been more. Did you tell Mr Willoughby that you'll soon have another mouth to feed?'

'Not exactly.' In fact, he hadn't mentioned it at all. It had been Willoughby who'd brought up the subject of the pay rise, saying that he hoped that he, Rowlands, would accept it as a small mark of the firm's gratitude for his quick thinking in the matter of the Caparelli case, for, as he put it, 'having the good sense to see that Harry Jarvis might prove an important witness, which he has, I don't mind telling you.' Now the pleasure occasioned by Willoughby's words was extinguished, to be replaced by the old, familiar, dread: money, and the lack of it. 'Edith, I'm doing my best.'

'I know.' A sigh. Then she brightened. One thing about Edith, she never remained out of sorts for very long. 'You haven't forgotten that we're going to the Faradays' tomorrow, have you?' she said. It was their regular Bridge evening. He'd developed a taste for the game during his days at the Lodge. Afterwards, he and a few of the others had kept the thing going. It helped to have a sighted partner, of course. Fortunately for him, Edith had turned out to be a better player than most.

'I haven't forgotten,' he said.

That night he had the old dream. He was back in Flanders again. It was the same as it always was, with that grey light over everything – the scarred and pitted fields, the stumps of trees, the shell holes gleaming like mirrors, reflecting a leaden sky. Nothing moved in that landscape, and yet movement was what he looked for. A twitch at the periphery of vision, which might turn out to be nothing but a scrap of rotting cloth, clinging to the wire, but which might equally prove to be a concealed enemy. He got it in his line of sight. Now it was a matter of watching and waiting, to see if the thing – friend or foe, he couldn't tell – would betray itself.

He woke with a start, his mouth dry. The grey fields, with their tangled wire, gave way to familiar darkness. Beside him, Edith breathed effortfully through her mouth, as she did when sleeping on her back – now the only position she found comfortable. He reached to turn her onto her side, feeling the astonishing heat of her, her solid weight in his arms, then thought better of it. Poor old girl. It wasn't easy for her. No, it wasn't easy for her at all. Having the children to look after, and the house to run, and then the constant worry about how it was all to be paid for. Nor, if he were honest, was their precarious financial situation the only thing she had to complain of. Not that she was aware of this, of course, but still . . . It felt all wrong. To be thinking all the time about another woman was disloyal. Shabby. He resolved to have no more to do with such thoughts. For a long time, he lay there, his eyes wide open, until the clockwork cheeping of sparrows in the cherry tree outside the window told him it must be getting light.

His resolution to have as little as possible to do with Celia West lasted no longer than the evening of the very next day. He'd lingered, as he usually did, to set things to rights before he went: untangling the weighted cords and letting them slip back into their places, sweeping his hands over the board to check that all the switches were exactly aligned. It was what he'd done every night except Sundays for the past seven years, and yet now what had been mere routine was infused with a shameful excitement. As his fingers moved amongst the rows of keys, he knew the real reason he was waiting was for her. Because whether he liked it or not, he'd become part of their little ritual, hers and Willoughby's. If one were being fanciful, one might say he was playing Cupid, although he knew there was a grosser name for what he did. Not that he cared about that. All he *did* care about was hearing her voice. *And what choice did he have, after all*, he thought angrily, as, precisely on time – you could have set your watch by her – the buzzer sounded. *It was his job, wasn't it?*

'Mr Rowlands.' Fortunately, she didn't seem disposed to chat.

'Lady Celia.' He was equally terse. 'I'll see if Mr Willoughby's in.'

He connected the call, pausing this time no longer than it took for her to announce herself 'Darling, it's me.', then resumed what he'd been doing before. Untwisting the cords. If it was a long call, he'd leave before it was finished, which meant leaving the outside line open . . . As it happened, though, this call was shorter than most. The buzzer sounded on the internal line. 'Rowlands, we seem to have been cut off,' said Willoughby, sounding faintly aggrieved. 'Have the goodness to get Lady Celia back on the line for me, will you?'

He did so, wondering what had caused the hitch – most unusual, in a local call. Perhaps some unlooked-for 'works' on the line. He'd check up later. The telephone rang only once before being answered. 'Hello?' It was a man's voice. Crisply authoritative, with just the hint of a South London accent. The butler's, Rowlands supposed.

'Who is this?' said this voice, with some impatience.

'Is that Lady Celia's residence?'

'It is. And who might *you* be?'

An instinct told him not to announce himself. 'I have a call for Lady Celia.'

'Do you indeed? Well, for your information, my wife is not at home. You may transfer the call to me.'

Rowlands didn't hesitate. He pulled the cord from its jack. Cutting off the call, and ending his brief but unwelcome conversation with Lady Celia's husband. Even he had heard of Lionel West. It was men like him who were putting the country back on its feet, the newspapers said. Providing jobs and offering hope for the future to the working man. His was a fine example of the spirit which would make Britain great again. 'The New Entrepreneur', one enthusiast in the press had called him. A man who embodied the notion of 'get-up-and-go'. Rowlands' heart was hammering like an overwound clock. The buzzer on his desk went again. 'Rowlands, I'm still waiting for that call.'

'I'm sorry, sir,' he said. 'But there seems to be a bit of disruption on the line.'

'How tiresome. Well, look, there's no sense in your hanging about. I can try later, from home. Perhaps it'll be fixed by then.'

'I hope so, sir.'

The buzzer sounded for an incoming call. It was the Mayfair exchange. 'We've had a complaint,' said the operator, in that affected voice so many of them used. He hoped his didn't sound like that. *We've hed a complaint.* 'Caller says he was cut off. Would you like me to reconnect the call?'

'Yes, please.' He took a breath, to steady his nerves, already half-prepared for what would follow.

'Hello?' It was Lady Celia who answered, sounding strained, on edge, almost, he sensed, with that peculiar intuition which had served him on other occasions, *frightened.* 'Who is this?'

'It's Frederick Rowlands, of Saville and Willoughby's, Lady Celia.'

'Oh yes. Of course . . . The . . . the draper's. I suppose it's about that order of sheets . . .'

Afterwards, he congratulated himself at the speed with which he'd picked up his cue. 'Yes, m'lady. Will you send someone to collect them, or would you like them sent?'

He was pleased with the improvisation, although in no doubt as to what it signified. This was the moment of no return. From now on, they were in it together, whatever that entailed.

'Oh, send them, by all means.' The brittle tone had given way to one of bored disdain. To hear her, no one would have guessed that she was anything other than what she seemed: the mistress of the house, dealing with some trivial matter of household economy.

'Of course, Lady Celia. Will there be anything else?'

'No. That will be all.' There was a faint click, as of a receiver – perhaps elsewhere in the house – being replaced. Then another, more definite, click, as Lady Celia hung up. He wondered if she was feeling the way he felt now: as breathlessly exhilarated as if he'd just run a race, and won.

A light rain was falling as he left the office; the feel of it speckling on his face was a sensation he loved. The fresh smell of it, after a long, dry spell, never failed to delight him. He didn't know why people complained, living in the city, it wasn't as if you ever got really wet. He recalled the black, unremitting deluge which had made their lives such a misery in Flanders. Men joked they were as likely to die from drowning as from shellfire, as of course many of them did, slipping into unconsciousness in a flooded crater. It had happened a lot that last summer. He remembered seeing a stretcher party, returning with its grisly burden – the corpse so caked in mud you'd have taken it for some relic of the Neolithic past, instead of a man who'd been alive not twelve hours before. Banishing the dreadful image with a shake of his head, he allowed a bus to pass, then crossed Fenchurch Street and turned in the direction of Leadenhall Market. The home-going crowds had thinned out by this time, and so he got along quite briskly, using his furled umbrella as a rudimentary cane, to determine his distance from the kerb. Being inconspicuous was what he strove for – one of the reasons why he preferred not to carry a stick, white-painted or otherwise. He'd always loathed being an object of pity.

Although he'd given sixpence that morning to the blind beggar at the entrance to Bank station, who'd been playing 'Tipperary' on the mouth organ. Not everybody who'd ended up like him had had the luck to land a decent job.

The wind dropped abruptly as he passed under the iron and glass canopy of the market – now deserted – and, bracing himself for the assault on the senses that would follow, pushed open the door of the Lamb's saloon bar. A confused roar of voices all talking at once was the first thing; that, and the sudden warmth, after the chill of the streets. Pungent smells of tobacco and beer mingled with the odour of damp woollen overcoats, and the sour reek of a coal fire. 'Over here, Fred, old chap!' After seven years in England, his brother-in-law's accent had diminished to no more than the slightly over-precise enunciation characteristic of the foreign-born. Yet Rowlands couldn't help but wish he would pitch his voice a little lower. Even though nine years had passed since the Armistice, having a German accent could still get you into trouble. 'Good to see you, Friedrich,' Viktor went on, in the same hearty tones. 'Now then, what will you have?'

'Usual, thanks.' It was a quiet pub, but even so, Rowlands wondered if he was imagining the faint chill that descended upon the place: the scraping of a chair, as the man next to them along the bar moved further away. Evidently one of those who disliked Germans on principle, although Viktor had never taken part in any fighting. He'd been in prison for the whole of the war, for trying to organise resistance to it. He'd had no quarrel with the English, he explained to Rowlands – just with the German government.

'Of course. A pint of bitter,' Viktor said. 'And a pint of mild.'

'Right you are, love,' carolled the barmaid.

The drinks arrived. Both took a long draught.

'So,' said Viktor. 'How is life with you?'

'Not so bad.'

'Which means "good" in your English way of speaking, does it not?'

'If you like. How's Dottie?'

'Oh, Dottie she is fine. Very busy, you know.' Viktor took another sip of beer, and smacked his lips appreciatively. 'Organising the strike,' he added, into what seemed to his companion to be an unfortunate moment of silence. This was a pub for working-men, but even so . . .

'What's it about?' he asked, not entirely sure he wanted to know.

'Didn't I say? We're getting the women out – the seamstresses. It was Dorothy's idea, of course.'

It would be, thought Rowlands. Ever since she'd started her first job, at the age of seventeen, Dorothy had been in the thick of it, with regard to union politics. All other politics, if it came to that. It drove her wild that, at twenty-seven, she still didn't have the vote, 'although it won't be long, if things go the way they ought to,' she said. Of course, he could see that for a woman with her brains, working in a factory didn't offer much scope. Even though it was working in clean conditions, at what might have been regarded by some as a not-unpleasant activity – cutting out and sewing evening gowns and trousseaux for Society ladies – it was hardly very fulfilling. But when he'd suggested that she should train as a typist – *because that was how he'd got started, wasn't it?* – she'd only laughed. 'I can't quite see myself in an office, can you, Fred? Making cups of tea for the boss, and all that rot. I think I prefer working in a sweat-shop.' Which was Dorothy all over. Her own worst enemy, Edith said.

Viktor was still talking about the proposed strike: 'It will be a fine show, I think. Not, perhaps, as good as last year's.' – Rowlands supposed it was the General Strike he meant – 'but still a useful protest. You may not be aware of it, but some of these women earn less than twelve shillings for a forty-nine hour week. Which is less than some of these types – these so-called "entrepreneurs" – would spend on a fine dinner for themselves and their wives. As for the conditions . . .'

Something in what Viktor had just said arrested Rowlands' attention. 'Speaking of entrepreneurs, what do you know about a man named Lionel West?'

Viktor said nothing for a moment. 'Why do you ask?'

'Just curiosity. He telephoned the office today, that's all.'

'I hardly thought that type would be a friend of yours,

old chap! Not a very pleasant man, I think.' Viktor gave a dry little laugh. 'A very rich man, is Lionel West. He owns very many factories in our part of the world, you know. Factories for making dresses and the like. I believe he made his money from making guns, however. Guns to blow German boys to bits, the swine.' He laughed again, the same dry sound, with no mirth in it. 'You have spoken to him, you say?'

'Briefly.'

'I should keep it that way. The less you and I have to do with men like that, the better, I would say.'

Their talk turned to other things. Football; Viktor was a keen follower of West Ham. Music; he'd recently lent Rowlands a new recording of Brahms' *Requiem*. But all the while they were talking, Rowlands was thinking about Lionel West. Despite his brother-in-law's words of caution, he couldn't help feeling curious about the man who had succeeded, amongst all other men, in capturing Celia West – Celia Verney, as she was then. From Edith's occasional readings aloud from the Society columns, he'd learned that the beautiful Lady Celia was Lady Verney's only surviving child, that she moved in a fast set, but had remained so far untouched by the breath of scandal, and that her marriage was generally held to be of the 'modern' variety, which meant that she and her husband – 'some wealthy businessman,' said Edith – spent as little time in one another's company as possible. Which accounted for a lot, Rowlands thought, but did not say. Who could blame a spirited young woman, neglected by her spouse, for seeking consolation elsewhere? Not he.

Lionel West himself proved more elusive – businessmen, wealthy or not, being of little interest to the readers of the Society columns. Since he owned no racehorses, and had never been linked to any well-born beauty, other than his wife, he remained, for the time being, an enigma.

By half past nine on Sunday morning, the girls had their hats and coats on, even though the train that would take them from Honor Oak Park to New Cross Gate in time for the Whitechapel train didn't leave for over an hour. But that was Edith all over. Even though she'd made no secret of the fact that she found these visits trying, when it came to getting ready to go, she was efficiency itself. He'd only just finished shaving – taking care, as always, to fold the razor up safely, in case one of his daughters should take it into her head to suppose it a plaything – when his wife called from the bottom of the stairs, 'Aren't you ready, yet?'

Carefully, he wiped the last flecks of foam from his cheeks. 'Coming.' He buttoned up his shirt, a clean one, crackling with starch, and reached for his collar. 'Could you just help me with this?' It was the collar stud at the back he meant; the others he could manage perfectly well.

Wheezing a little with the effort of climbing the stairs, Edith complied with this request. 'Would you like me to do your tie for you?'

'If you wouldn't mind,' he replied meekly.

She took it out of his hand and slipped it around his neck, under his collar. A few deft flicks completed the operation. 'There! You look very smart,' she said.

'Thank you, dear.' She was standing close enough for him to be able to smell the chalky scent of her face powder, the only cosmetic she allowed herself. In Edith's opinion, only fast women wore lipstick. It was a view he'd shared, until recently. Now he found himself wondering whether Celia West wore lipstick, seeing in his mind's eye the image of a pair of perfect, Cupid's-bow lips, painted in vivid scarlet . . . He brushed the thought away. Very lightly, he ran his fingers down the curve of Edith's cheek – a habit from their courting days. It helped him to 'see' her. Her well defined cheekbones, thin, straight nose, and delicate lips. Her brow, still smooth, but given to wrinkling in anxiety or vexation . . . 'I say! You've got your hat on.'

'Of course I've got my hat on. *Some* of us have been ready for hours,' she said, in the tone of humorous exasperation she habitually used towards her husband. She made as if to move away.

He wasn't quite ready to let her go, however. He slid his arms around her, drawing her closer, until he could feel the small bump of her belly against him. 'Is it a new hat?' he asked, to prolong the moment, the slightly resistant weight of her, not quite yielding to his embrace.

Edith laughed. 'Now, when did I last have a new hat?'

'You should get yourself a hat. For spring,' he improvised. He had only the vaguest idea what hats looked like, these days. The last he remembered, they were enormous, and shaped like cartwheels; now, it seemed, they were bell-shaped, made of felt, and pulled down over the face.

The suggestion seemed to please her, for he felt, to his surprise, the swift moth's-wing brush of her kiss upon his cheek. 'Silly old boy,' she said. 'Perhaps I will, at that.'

He'd always looked out for Dorothy – and she for him, if it came to that. A plucky little thing, was his sister; he'd never known her to be afraid of anything. Even as a child, she'd been a tomboy, forever getting into scrapes. Smart as a whip, too; she'd been top of her class in every subject. Mother'd encouraged her. She'd wanted Dottie to go to the teacher training college at Avery Hill. Then of course the war had come. Having to be the breadwinner all those months had been the end of any aspirations she might have had towards a better kind of life. Not that she cared two straws, or so she said, she could earn good money at the dress factory. And her income had certainly been a godsend during all those months when he was getting back on his feet; he didn't know what they'd have done without it. Dottie had never complained although he knew by now how much she'd hated it. Not just the work itself, which, though exhausting, was at least relatively clean, but having to 'toady', as she put it, to their wealthy clients. The fittings were the worst, she said. Crawling around on the floor with a mouthful of pins, while some idle socialite whined about how dreadful the weather had been last time they'd been in 'Monte', or how frightfully tiresome it was keeping up with all the invitations she'd had to parties that Season. It was hardly surprising, Rowlands thought, that his sister had turned out such a Red.

When Mother had died, not two years after Harry, they'd had no family left but each other, he and Dorothy. Even then, she'd been a brick, not expecting, as many unmarried sisters would have, that he'd provide a home for her although he'd had a job by then. He was already engaged to be married to Edith, of course. Still, it had been decent of Dottie not to prevail upon family obligation. 'You know me,' she'd said, on the one occasion the subject had come up – he'd taken her out to tea, he remembered, to break the news that he and Edith were getting hitched. 'I like my own way in everything. Always have. I can't see me sharing a house with another woman, can you?' Especially, she hadn't needed to add, when the other woman in question was her sister-in-law.

It was a pity, he thought – if hardly surprising – that his wife and sister didn't get on. They were both so very decided in their views. Of the two, he supposed Dottie was the more uncompromising; 'strident', Edith said. It was true that she could be opinionated, but her ideas were so heartfelt, he for one couldn't blame her for holding them. It was different for Edith – she hadn't had the upbringing they'd had. With a father grown old before his time, on account of a lifetime spent slogging his guts out in a succession of punishing jobs; the lamp factory had been the last and best of them, but even that had done for him in the end; their mother struggling to make ends meet, with three children to feed and clothe (two others had died in infancy, which had been a blessing of sorts, he supposed). All in all, it hadn't been the easiest of childhoods, not a patch on Edith's, he was sure. Although she was making up for it now, poor old girl.

Yes, it was wasn't all that surprising, when you came to think of it, the way Dottie had turned out. Getting herself mixed up in union politics at the dress factory where she was working, and from which she'd subsequently been sacked, and then announcing she was going to marry a German. That had turned out all right, as it happened, Viktor being such a steady sort of chap, but it had been typical of his sister's way of doing things. With the child arriving so very soon after, which at least explained the unseemly haste, said Edith, he'd hoped she might have settled down. Most women did when they had children, didn't they? Dorothy had proved to be the exception.

There were ten years between them; she was the baby of the family. Spoilt rotten, of course, being the youngest, and the only girl. And even though she was a grown woman, with a husband and child, he couldn't help picturing her as she was the very last time he saw her, on that last leave home: a skinny kid of seventeen, all big eyes, tumbling dark hair, and forthright opinions about the way the war was going. Billy had her looks, apparently. 'A handsome little chap,' Edith had admitted. Knowing how much she'd have liked a son, Rowlands suspected it was something of a sore point, that her sister-in-law had managed to produce one with so little apparent effort.

Just now, as she welcomed them into her house, Dottie seemed on her best behaviour, giving Edith a hug, and exclaiming at how much the girls had grown in the six weeks since she'd last seen them. 'Will you look at Anne? She's taller than Billy although she's six months younger. Vic, don't you think Anne's taller than Billy now?' Laughing and talking, she drew them into the narrow little house, which had become as familiar to him as his own. The bumpy feel of the Anaglypta paper that covered the wall to the height of the dado rail in the hall was linked in his mind to the smell of the place – floor polish, and cooking, just now, an appetising smell of roasting mutton – and to the comforting weight in his hands, as they sat down to dinner, of the bone-handled cutlery that had come from his mother's house. That was the thing about objects, he thought, they acquired a freight of significance far beyond their everyday use, which had to do with the memories associated with them: all the times they'd passed from hand to hand . . .

'More meat, Edith?' said Dorothy, breaking into

these reflections. 'Viktor, do carve another slice of meat for Edith.'

'Oh, no more for me,' said her sister-in-law. 'I couldn't manage another mouthful. Although it was delicious,' she added. Edith was making an effort, Rowlands thought.

A pity Dorothy couldn't leave it at that. 'You're eating for two, remember?' she said. An observation, he knew, which would only embarrass Edith, who disliked references to the body and its functions. These, in her view, belonged to the realm of topics – politics and religion being the others – which ought never to be mentioned in company. Dorothy, of course, thought just the opposite. 'I remember how ravenous I was when I was expecting Billy,' she was saying. 'Viktor was convinced it was twins, I got so big. Out to *here* I was, wasn't I, Vic?'

Edith's only response to this was a dry cough – a signal, to anyone willing to hear it, that there were children present. But Dorothy seemed oblivious to this hint. 'Oddly enough, not a lot of it was the baby. Quite a little scrap *he* turned out to be, didn't you, my pet?'

Perhaps it was out of sympathy for his guests, or merely that he'd heard this remark too many times before, that prompted Viktor to change the subject: 'You know, it's a funny thing, your asking me about Lionel West, the other day. Because Dottie knows him, don't you, *schatz*?'

There was a brief silence. Then Dorothy laughed. 'You could hardly call it "knowing".'

'But you've met him, you told me so yourself.'

'Oh, yes. I met him several times. We were as thick as thieves, Mr Lionel and myself.' There was an edge of irony to her voice. 'As a matter of fact, he owned the factory where I was working in those days. So naturally he did pop in from time to time. Billy, you'll have that glass over if you don't take care.'

'Tell them about the dress!' Viktor seemed barely able to contain his glee. 'It's priceless, really . . .'

'Who's this we're talking about?' enquired Edith sotto voce.

'Just someone I've come across through work,' he told her. Really, it was too bad of Viktor, bringing it up like this.

'We made his wife's wedding dress,' said Dorothy. Was it his imagination, or was there a steeliness in her voice that had not been there before? 'Valenciennes lace over satin, sewn with seed pearls. It took us three weeks. *Very* particular he was, Mr Lionel. Everything had to be just so. I was the one doing all the buttons – a great long row of them, all down the back; they had to be covered with satin to match, of course, and I can tell you, he kept me at it, sometimes half the night. It had to be perfect, he said. And I must say,' she added, 'she did look lovely in it, the young lady. Like a princess, Mr Lionel said.'

'But surely that was bad luck?' said Edith. 'I mean, for

the bridegroom to see the dress before the wedding.'

'Not when the bridegroom owns the factory and a great deal more besides,' laughed Viktor. 'I'd call that very good luck indeed. More potatoes, anybody?'

When they'd eaten as much of the roast lamb and potatoes and greens as they wanted, and had followed it with a piece of plum pie and custard, there was still plenty of room, as Dorothy put it, for a cup of tea, and a slice of Madeira cake. 'Because Vic's got something he wants to say,' she said, setting down the tray on the Benares brass occasional table, another relic of their mother's house, which had pride of place in the sitting room. 'Haven't you, dear?'

'Yes.' As if suddenly overtaken by embarrassment, Viktor cleared his throat. 'The fact is' he said. 'Dorothy and I are thinking of clearing out of London.'

'What he means is,' Dorothy went on, 'is that we're moving to Kent.'

'I say! This is all very sudden.'

'Oh, Viktor's been on the lookout for just such an opportunity for weeks, haven't you, dear? It turns out there's a chap in Staplehurst who's selling his share in a chicken farm . . .'

'It sounds like a good idea.' Although, to Rowlands' knowledge, Viktor had never had the smallest experience of farming. Still, you could always learn.

'And what I was wondering . . .' the note of embarrassment in Viktor's voice grew more acute. 'Is . . . the fact is . . .'

'He's in need of a loan from the bank, aren't you, dear? And we thought that, as your brother's a bank manager,' Dorothy said, addressing Edith, 'he might be in a position to help.'

'Oh. I see.' Money was another topic Edith thought unsuitable for general conversation. 'I'm afraid I can't imagine how. I mean, he doesn't *know* you . . .'

'Well, we thought that's where you might be able to help,' was the reply.

'Dottie thought . . .' put in Viktor, 'that is, we both thought . . .'

'We wondered if you'd write to your brother, on our behalf,' said Dorothy. 'Explaining the circumstances. We do have some money put by,' she added. 'So it wouldn't have to be a very large loan.'

'That's right,' said Viktor, with an awkward laugh. 'I'm hardly a Lionel West.'

'Thank God for that,' said his wife. 'More tea, anybody?'

The plutocrat's name came up in a different context, a few days after this. A summons came from the inner office. 'J-just wanted a quick word. S-something rather important's come up.' There was the sound of a match being struck. The smell of the Special Mixture cigarettes that Willoughby had made up for him at a tobacconist's in St James' filled the air. 'Oh, sorry, Would you like one?' he asked, pushing the packet across the desk towards Rowlands.

'Thank you, sir. I wouldn't mind.'

'Here. Let me light it for you. Yes, as I was saying, there's been a development.'

He nodded, to show that he was listening. Funny taste these gaspers had. Sweetish, you might say. Aromatic. On the whole, he preferred his Churchman's.

'It's about our f-fire case.' His stammer was much worse today, Rowlands thought. 'Thought you should know. It appears that our friend "Count" Caparelli isn't working alone. That is, he has a b-business partner.' He paused a moment, as if to consider the wisdom or otherwise of saying what he was about to say. 'We d-don't yet know the extent of this individual's involvement, you understand.'

Rowlands made a sound indicative of comprehension.

'As it happens, it's Lionel West. The City magnate. I don't know if you've come across him?'

'Yes.'

'The fact is . . .' Willoughby was silent a moment. 'It's all terribly awkward, but I happen to know his wife.'

'Lady Celia.'

'P-precisely.' There was another pause. 'I don't have to tell you,' Willoughby went on, 'how important it is that *her* name should be kept out of things.'

'I understand.'

'Yes, I believe you do.' When Willoughby spoke again, it was as if he'd momentarily forgotten that their relationship was merely a professional one. As if, in that moment, they might have been friends. 'I've known her

100

almost all my life,' he said. 'Since we were both kids, in fact. She—' He broke off. 'That is, I . . . The fact is, we were awfully fond of one another, at one time. I simply can't allow anything to happen to her – no matter what the man she's married to has done . . . or not done. Do you see?'

'Yes, sir.'

'Good man. Because if these investigations go the way I think they're going to go, then things could get rather unpleasant. I don't want her dragged into it. If I had my way,' said Gerald Willoughby, as if to himself, 'she'd have been out of that unfortunate business long ago.'

Chapter Four

There'd been a change in the weather. Stepping outside one morning, he felt the warmth of sunshine on his face. There was a smell of moist earth and flowers, rising from somewhere beneath his feet. On an impulse, he reached down, and was rewarded by the light brush of a daffodil's trumpet against his fingers. At once his mind's eye was flooded with a colour. *Yellow*. It was as if some high, pure note had been struck. Even though he'd be thirty-seven next birthday – an old married man – the coming of spring never failed to fill him with thoughts of a different nature. Joyous thoughts. Thoughts of new life, of the stirring of hope, of awakening desire . . . It had been weather like this that spring before the war. With the blossom just fallen from the boughs of the apple trees, the day he and Maudie had bicycled down to Kent. He'd borrowed the tandem from Alf Richards two doors down, and they'd made a day of it, cycling past orchards, and oasthouses, and through hop gardens, already showing a touch of green. They'd stopped for an hour in a quaint old village of brick and shingle houses, with a pub where you could get bread and cheese to eat with your half pint of cider, and a church with a Norman font, and funny old-fashioned inscriptions on the leaning gravestones. He remembers singing 'Daisy Bell' at the top of his voice as they'd freewheeled down the hills, and Maudie shrieking with laughter, saying he'd have them both in a ditch if he carried on like that.

Daisy, Daisy, give me your answer, do!
I'm half crazy, all for the love of you . . .

He wondered what happened to Maudie. The last he heard she was married, and living out Sidcup way. She'd written to him after he was first posted to Belgium; it had been one of the things that had kept him going, her letters. He remembered the way she'd clung to him when they parted. 'You will come back, won't you, Fred?' she'd whispered, her green eyes swimming with tears as she saw him off at Charing Cross on the boat train to Folkestone. Girls, wearing their prettiest hats, had turned out to see them go and the band played 'British Grenadiers'. It had seemed a great adventure: the first time he'd ever been abroad. It hadn't taken him long to discover his mistake. His first leave, in the spring of '15, had been a shock for both of them, he supposed. For Maudie, because her newly returned 'hero' was so very unlike what she must have imagined a hero to be. Instead of some swaggering fellow, covered with medals, and full of talk about all the Huns he'd killed, there'd been only poor old Fred, who'd looked, Maudie said, in one of her bursts of frankness, as if he were scared of his own shadow. As for himself, he'd spent the whole week wondering what on earth he was doing there, in a city grown strange, during the months he'd been away, full of the loud-voiced and overfed, and with those whose lack of experience of the war hadn't prevented their having opinions about it.

After he went back, she'd carried on writing for a bit, then the letters had stopped. He didn't entirely blame her for that; he wasn't what you'd call a good correspondent. But he was glad it had happened then, and not after he was wounded, the way it had with poor Ashenhurst. What made it worse was that Ashenhurst had been engaged to be married to *his* girl. She'd been to see him once in hospital, and found the shock of it was more than she could bear. 'She decided she'd prefer to marry a man with eyes,' was Ashenhurst's laconic summing-up of the disaster. He thought, I must write to the old boy again soon . . . A shame they couldn't see more of one another but Cornwall was such a long way away. Ashenhurst seemed to have made a go of it, though, running a small hotel with his widowed sister. 'It's a quiet life here,' he had written, 'but none the worse for that. I think we've all had quite enough noise to last us a lifetime . . .' Ashenhurst had been at Ypres, too, stationed with the Suffolk Regiment at The Bluff, in '16. When the bombardment was at its height, he'd said, you couldn't hear a blessed thing, even when the chap who was standing right next to you shouted in your ear at the top of his lungs. 'I suppose you could say I was lucky,' Ashenhurst remarked, with his dry laugh, 'not to end up deaf as well as blind.'

Edith had found a piece in the paper the other day about the memorial they'd put up at the Menin Gate to all the fallen, or at least, to those that died in that particular 'show'. The Battle of Ypres, or rather battles, because there were at least three, weren't there, in those four years? Although some you'd hardly dignify with the name of battle. Dirty little skirmishes, at best. Which made it all the more ridiculous, to Rowlands' mind, that they'd felt the need to put up a blinking great wall, engraved with the names of those who'd perished in that string of squalid encounters. Some of the names would be of those he'd known. Cartwright, and Maugham, and Norris, and O'Casey; Wilson, too . . . Wilson, who'd been beside him when he got hit, and whose face had been the last face he'd ever seen: a white mask, freckled with blood.

'There's a ceremony of dedication at the end of July,' Edith said, when she'd finished reading out the article. 'You should go.'

He'd shaken his head at that. 'Whatever for?'

'Why, to pay your respects,' she'd replied.

But he'd no stomach for that kind of thing: parades, and medals, and fine speeches. 'A Day to Honour Our Fallen Heroes' had been the headline his wife read out. Most of the men he knew had died without any kind of honour.

If he'd had a touch of spring fever lately, he wasn't the only one. Far from slowing down, as she entered the seventh month of her pregnancy, Edith seemed to have been overtaken by an attack of the fidgets. In bed, she tossed and turned, complaining that she couldn't get comfortable. The baby's kicking nearly drove her to distraction, she said. She was plagued by backache, swollen ankles, and heartburn. When he tried to persuade her to rest, she grew agitated. Resting wouldn't get the housework done, she said, or the dinner on the table, either. One day, she took it into her head to spring-clean the whole house; he came home to find the furniture all awry, and barked his shins on a pail of dirty water she'd carelessly left in the way. When remonstrated with, she'd insisted that the house had got to be clean. You couldn't bring a baby into a dirty house. His offers of help were rejected, almost with scorn. You can't *see* the dirt, she objected, so how on earth will you know where to clean? He was at his wit's end, knowing what to do with her.

Then, one morning, he came downstairs to an altered mood. Instead of the smell of burnt toast and the irritable crashing of china, he was met by a pleasing silence, broken only by the gentle sounds of Anne slurping her milk, and the rustle of turning pages. 'I've had a letter from Ralph,' Edith said happily, in the tone of voice she reserved for talking about her brother. It was a girlish, slightly breathless tone, as if she'd shed the years that separated her from her childhood, when they'd lived in a big house in one of the nicer parts of Poole, and life had seemed full of promise. 'We're invited there on Saturday. They're having a garden party.'

'That's nice.' He was conscious of choosing his words carefully. 'It's a while since we last saw them.'

'Yes, well, Ralph's very busy,' she said.

Ralph, he thought, seemed always to have been busy, even during the war, when running his bank had been deemed too important to abandon for mere soldiering. Now he lived, in considerable comfort, in Surrey. Three years before, at the age of forty, he'd acquired a young wife and, more recently still, a son, whose name he had already put down at Uppingham.

Edith turned a page. 'Oh!' she said, having read what was written there. 'Well, I must say, I call that very generous of Ralph, I really do . . . He's invited

107

your sister and her husband along on Saturday, too. So they can discuss "that little business matter", as he puts it.'

'That's decent of him.'

'Isn't it, though?' she said. 'I suppose it would make sense for us all to travel together,' she added, sounding rather less than enthusiastic at the prospect.

Since that abortive call to the Mayfair house, which had resulted in his brief but all too memorable encounter with Lionel West, Rowlands' dealings with the latter's wife had been of the most perfunctory. Now, instead of being inclined to chat for a moment or two, she'd ask to be put straight through to Willoughby, her tones as clipped and cool as if there were nothing at all between them, which, he reminded himself severely, was no more than the truth. To what had happened that day, she made no allusion. He supposed it must have given her a fright, to be so nearly discovered. It had shaken him up, too, he had to admit, although he couldn't help feeling he'd acquitted himself quite well. It wasn't every man who'd have picked up his cue, the way he had. Which was why he found it hard to suppress a slight feeling of . . . call it disappointment. It wasn't that he expected her to thank him for saving her neck; it was just that some acknowledgement that her neck had needed saving seemed called for. So that when she rang at last, he was doubly unprepared. Both because it was at an unaccustomed time of day for her (first thing in the morning) and because he didn't recognise her voice at first. Instead of the low, musical tones he'd come to relish, there was an ugly stridency: 'Is Gerald there?'

'Who should I say . . .' he started to reply, before he realised.

'It's Celia West.' It sounded as if she were trying not to cry.

'Of course, Lady Celia. I'll see if he's in.'

Willoughby's manner, when he answered, was breezy. 'Ah, Rowlands! I was just about to buzz—'

'A call for you, sir. Lady Celia.'

'Really?' He sounded faintly perturbed. 'F-fine. Put her through.'

He did so. But before he could throw the switch that would consign their conversation to secrecy, he heard her say, 'My God, Gerald. You don't know what he's done.'

To hear more was a temptation he was unable to resist, although he despised himself for it.

'Darling, what is it? Tell me.'

'I can't. I'm too ashamed . . . He . . .'

'Celia, darling. Please don't cry.'

'He *forced* me. It was after I got back last night. He'd been drinking and . . . Oh, Gerald, I feel so . . . so filthy. So humiliated. I wish I was dead.'

'Don't say such things.'

'But it's how I feel. You've no idea what my life has become.'

'The man's a brute. He doesn't deserve you . . .'

'You might say I brought it on myself.'

'That's utter nonsense, and you know it.'

There was a silence, broken only by the sound of her sobs.

Then Willoughby said: 'He's gone too far this time, Celia. He ought to be stopped.'

At Cobham station, they were met by Ralph's chauffeur, Dodds, despatched to fetch them in the Vauxhall. Fortunately, the vehicle was large enough to take them all but it was a squeeze, nonetheless. Edith and Dorothy sat in the back with the girls and Billy between them, Viktor on the fold-up seat opposite them, and Rowlands in front with Dodds. It was only the second time the girls had been in a motor car, and the novelty hadn't yet worn off. Even the prospect of seeing cousin Peter – 'A very little boy. Younger than me,' said Anne at every opportunity – couldn't compete with the charm of this superb vehicle, with its interior smelling of new leather, and its mysterious engine noises. Best of all was the klaxon, which Dodds let the children sound for a treat. Dodds, it emerged, was a veteran of Vimy Ridge. 'Gassed,' he said, when asked what had brought him home. 'My lungs still play me up a bit. Doesn't stop me smoking these, though.'

'Which brand do you prefer?' asked Rowlands.

'Chesterfield's, if I can get 'em. Though they're dear at one-and-three for ten.'

'I'm a Churchman's man, myself.'

'Look, girls!' Edith said brightly, interrupting this masculine colloquy. 'There's Uncle Ralph's house. Do you see, through the trees?'

'Is it the one with the chimbleys?' Anne wanted to know.

Edith laughed; it sounded forced to Rowlands. Perhaps she was feeling some trepidation at the thought of what lay ahead. 'No, not that one, silly! The one with the yew tree in front – remember?'

'*I* remember,' said Margaret stoutly.

Even though his own recollections were necessarily partial, he'd seen enough of such establishments before the war to have a pretty fair idea of what it looked like: a great big barn of a place, with a deep, sloping pantiled roof and twisted brick chimneys like a fairytale cottage, Tudor beams and an oak door studded with iron nails, to make it look three hundred years old, instead of a mere thirty. 'A very fine house,' remarked Viktor diplomatically. 'It reminds me of some I have seen in the Wannsee district of Berlin. A prosperous area,' he added, perhaps unnecessarily.

There was the crunch of gravel under the wheels as the car turned into the drive, and they slowed to a halt. Then Dodds got out and went round to open the door for Edith and Dorothy. As he did so, a frantic barking heralded the appearance of Diana's Sealyham.

'I remember the *dog*,' said Anne, in a rapturous whisper.

'Down, Raffles!' came the shouted command. Ralph, with his best Lord of the Manor air. 'You got here, then?' he said, addressing his remarks, initially, to his sister. 'Trains all right, I suppose?' When he had been reassured on this point, he turned his attention to Rowlands: 'What do you think of the new motor? Runs a treat, doesn't she?'

'Yes,' his brother-in-law agreed. 'Ralph, this is my sister, Mrs Lehmann,' he added, gesturing in her general direction. Since she had spoken not a word since they had arrived, beyond a whispered injunction to Billy to pipe down when (doubtless under the influence of his cousins) he seemed to be exhibiting signs of over-excitement, he had only the vaguest idea where she was standing.

'How do you do?' said Dorothy, with icy politeness.

'And this is her husband, Viktor.'

'Delighted,' said Viktor. Then, perhaps feeling that this did not go far enough. 'We are most grateful to you, my wife and I, for agreeing to see us today.'

'Oh, don't mention it,' replied Ralph grandly. 'Glad to be of help, I'm sure. If I *can* be of help but we'll have to see, won't we? Time for a little chat before the fun begins . . .' Still talking, he drew them after him, into the house. 'Diana'll be down in a jiffy. Just getting Peter up from his nap. He's teething, poor little brute. I say, girls, are you looking forward to your tea? I know *I* am . . .'

Tea, he explained, would be served on the terrace

that afternoon. 'If the rain holds off, that is. Diana thinks it'll stay dry. If it doesn't, we'll have to make a run for it, what?' Laughing loudly at his own joke, Ralph shepherded them through the house and into the garden. It wouldn't be a large gathering, he assured them. Just a few people: forty or fifty, all told. 'Our local JP has said he'll drop by.' There'd be several fellow members of the Rotary Club and their wives. 'And some of Diana's friends . . . I couldn't tell you their names, but some awfully nice couples. We see them quite often for cocktails.' The vicar would be there of course. 'Although if you ask me, he's much too high. Personally, I like my religion without frills . . . Ah, here's Diana, now! Darling, you left me all alone, to entertain the guests,' he said reproachfully, although so far they were the only ones.

'Well, I must say you haven't made a very good job of it,' came the reply, in Diana's relentlessly cheery tones. From her handshake – firm – and the heartiness of her manner, he'd always envisaged a suburban Amazon. Since Diana and Ralph had met on the golf links, this was not unduly far-fetched. 'Poor Edith left standing with not so much as a cup of tea . . . Lovely to see you, by the way, Edith dear.' She kissed Edith, then himself. The kiss didn't touch his cheek, but was bestowed some distance from it. He was aware his presence made Diana uncomfortable. He wasn't entirely sure why. As far as he knew, his face wasn't scarred or disfigured. He was careful, in company, to keep his eyes lowered, not closed. He prided himself, in fact, on not being conspicuous. And yet Diana shrank from him, as if he were a staring madman, or one of those unfortunates – all too common just after the war – forced to wear a painted tin mask, to cover the horrors beneath.

Having dealt with those she already knew, Diana turned to her other guests. 'Hello,' she said, in a voice whose tone was nicely balanced between cordiality and condescension. 'I suppose you must be Fred's relatives.'

'I suppose we must be,' said Dorothy sweetly.

There was a slight, but perceptible, pause. Then Diana rose to the occasion. 'Girls!' she cried, sounding as astonished as if she'd just laid eyes on them for the first time. 'How smart you both look! Can those be new frocks, I wonder? And who's this dear little fellow?' addressing Billy. 'Why, I do believe I can see a family likeness! But look here—' Diana's voice assumed a note of perplexity. 'You do know it's fancy dress for all the kiddies? Oh dear! Don't say you've come without your costumes?'

Edith started to say something about not having realised, but before she could get to the end of her sentence, Diana was off again: 'Oh, don't worry, we'll manage somehow. Nurse'll organise everything. Nurse!' A young woman duly arrived in answer to this summons. 'Ah, there you are, Nurse. And how's my little sweetums, then?' This last presumably addressed to her infant son. 'Nurse, I want you to find some costumes for Miss Margaret and Miss Anne. This is their little cousin, Master William. I'm sure you can find him a nice picture book to look at, while the grown-ups are talking . . . That'll be all, Nurse. You can take Master Peter away with you (*sweetums*!) and bring him back when you're ready. We don't want him dirtying his frock before the visitors get here, do we? Precious babykins! Isn't he a perfect pet?'

'Let's leave the women to it, shall we?' said Ralph, taking hold of Rowlands' arm, a sensation the latter could not help but find disagreeable. Even though he knew it to be a perfectly reasonable act on the part of his wife's brother, still he felt himself grow hot with annoyance. He wasn't a blasted invalid. 'We should be undisturbed in here.' Still holding onto his brother-in-law's arm, Ralph opened a door, releasing a smell of pipe tobacco and leather. 'My inner sanctum,' he said, with a self-satisfied laugh. 'Do come in, Mr . . . er . . .'

'Lehmann,' said Viktor. 'Thank you.'

'Cigarette?' said Ralph, letting go, to his relief, of Rowlands' arm. 'I'll stick to my pipe, if you don't mind.'

'Not at all.'

'Sit down, sit down,' went on the bank manager, rubbing his hands briskly together. 'Fred, there's a chair just to your right.'

'Thanks,' said Rowlands, with as much civility as he could muster. 'But I really don't think I should stay. It's

Viktor who wants your advice, not I . . .'

'Stay if you like,' interjected Viktor. 'There's nothing I have to say that you needn't hear.'

'Thanks, but if it's all the same to you, I'll let you both get on with it.'

'Suit yourself,' said Ralph carelessly. Then, to Viktor: 'Well, what have you got for me?', the rustle of papers indicating that Viktor had not come unprepared.

'I have some figures I worked out . . .' Viktor was saying, as Rowlands opened the door, only to collide with Diana, coming in.

'Oh!' They'd only touched for an instant, but she recoiled as if this fleeting contact had burnt her. 'Darling . . .' This to her husband. 'Frightfully sorry to interrupt your little pow-wow, but the Cavendishes have arrived. And old Mrs Sattersthwaite.'

'I say! A bit on the early side, what?'

'I *know* I said three-thirty, but they must have thought I'd said three,' wailed Diana. 'And there's still so much to *do*. I really have to supervise Gladys. These girls never get anything right if you leave them to themselves, do they?' she added, presumably to Viktor, since he made a small sound indicative neither of agreement nor of dissent. 'So I need you to come and *talk* to them, darling.' Again, this was to Ralph. 'Because it looks so odd if one just leaves people *standing*.'

'It looks as if we'll have to postpone our little chat, Mr . . . er . . .'

'Of course,' said Viktor.

'Duty calls, you know.' As he spoke, Ralph was ushering his guests out. 'Mustn't keep the little woman waiting. And *he's* quite a big pot in the City,' he muttered to Rowlands. 'Cavendish of Cavendish and Peabody, the merchant bank, you know. Wife's a great chum of Diana's. Charming girl . . . ah, Lillian!' he cried, setting eyes on that lady. 'I see you've met my sister.'

'Yes,' drawled Lillian Cavendish, in an affected manner. 'She was just about to tell me all about your misspent youth. Was he a *very* horrid little boy, Mrs Rowlands?'

Edith gave an embarrassed laugh. 'Well . . .' she began, but the strenuously charming Mrs Cavendish didn't wait to hear the answer. 'I don't believe we've met,' she said, evidently addressing Dorothy, for the latter replied coolly, 'No, I don't believe we have.'

'This is Mr and Mrs Lehmann. Relatives of my brother-in-law's,' supplied Diana, her tone conveying how utterly mortifying she found the idea of being forced to entertain such a pair, and not only that, but having to introduce them to her friends. To have called them socially unacceptable wasn't the half of it. Why, the husband (although, admittedly, he spoke very nicely, with no dropping of aitches or anything like that) was some sort of *Bolshevik*, wasn't he? As for the wife . . . Rowlands couldn't suppress a smile at what he guessed must be going around in Diana Edwards' head, as she struggled to accommodate these unprecedented demands on her social skills.

'Name's Cavendish,' boomed another voice. The merchant banker, Rowlands surmised. 'And what's your line?'

This must have been to Viktor, for the latter replied, with some bemusement, 'My "line"? *Ach*, you mean my job.'

'Viktor's about to move into property, aren't you, old man?' Ralph put in smoothly. 'Nice little place down in Kent, what?'

'Oh, land's always a good investment,' said George Cavendish sagely. 'Never loses its value. You can be quite safe with land.'

'Gladys!' cried Diana, perhaps judging that this might prove an unfruitful line of conversation. 'Where *has* that girl got to, I wonder? Ah, Gladys, there you are. You can put the tray down over there. And bring some more hot water. Do sit down, Lillian dear. And Mrs Sattersthwaite, too. Glad to see you looking so *well*, Mrs Sattersthwaite. Are you sure you're quite comfortable there? Gladys! Bring another cushion for Mrs Sattersthwaite's chair.'

'Mummy, Mummy!' came a child's voice from across the lawn. 'Tell him he can't have it, Mummy.'

'Oh Lord,' sighed Lillian Cavendish. 'One's offspring can be so tiresome, can't they? I thought that girl of yours was supposed to be looking after them, Diana. Yes, Bobby, what is it?'

'My lanyard an' whistle,' replied the child. 'Said he could look at it an' now he won't give it back.'

'Now, Bobby, you know what I've told you about sharing.'

'But it's mine,' objected Bobby.

'What's all this about, Billy?' said his mother, joining the conversation for the first time since her snubbing of Mrs Cavendish's polite overtures.

'He said I could have it,' said Billy. 'And now he wants it back. Here!' he added, evidently addressing his rival. 'Have your silly old whistle. I don't want it.'

'Boys will be boys,' said George Cavendish heartily. 'Now run along, old chap. The grown-ups are talking.'

'Bobby's getting so tall now,' put in Diana Edwards tactfully. 'Such a splendid costume, too. Now don't tell me – let me guess . . . Bobby Shafto!'

'Yes, he does look rather a lamb, doesn't he?' said her friend. 'And how old's *your* boy?' This to Dorothy.

'He'll be five in July. What's the matter, Billy?' For apparently he was still of their number.

'I don't like that boy.'

'Well, come for a walk, then,' said Dorothy, getting up from her chair. A moment later, she could be heard pointing out the salient features of the garden to her son.

'Handsome gel,' observed a voice Rowlands could only assume, from its penetrating tones, must belong to the elderly Mrs Sattersthwaite. 'Walks like a thoroughbred.'

* * *

The next couple of hours passed in a babble of – to Rowlands – meaningless talk, as more guests arrived, and mingled on the lawn. Since he had met none of these people before, and was unlikely ever to meet them again, he found it hard to interest himself in Diana's fulsome but curiously unenlightening introductions: 'Now do come and talk to dear Mrs Peachy. She's a perfect lamb though she is about a hundred years old . . .' Nor did Ralph's muttered commentary on his guests fill him with any greater desire to spend the afternoon conversing with the likes of 'Beamish – a sound chap. Very sound on the economy'; or 'Entwhistle – just back from Malaya. Doing very well for himself in rubber . . .' Extricating himself politely from a conversation with Mrs Peachy about wasps, and their annoying tendency to get into the jam, and side-stepping another with Entwhistle, on the deficiencies of the England cricket team, he wandered in the direction of the shrubbery. As he threaded his way between little knots of people, he heard a woman say, 'Of course they're terrible snobs, but they do give amusing parties . . .' and then someone else: 'My dear. Isn't it *too* killing?' Silly women with silly voices. Not that the men were any better. Pontificating about share prices and the German mark, in voices thickened by cigar smoke and too much preprandial sherry.

As the drone of conversation grew fainter, he was guiltily aware that he was neglecting his familial responsibilities. Because at the very least he owed it to Edith to keep an eye on Dottie, given that his sister was the one most likely to 'let the side down', by giving vent to her violently egalitarian political beliefs, in company doubtless ill-disposed towards such notions. Viktor, whose ideas were every bit as extreme, he could trust not to disgrace himself, Rowlands thought. Viktor tended, on the whole, to play his cards close to his chest. To talk to him, you'd never have guessed that this was a man who'd once been jailed for setting fire to a police station, nor that the injuries he'd sustained during his subsequent incarceration were what had kept him out of the fighting – 'a blessing in disguise, you might say,' was his only remark on the subject. Whether Dorothy would show the same restraint as her spouse, her brother had cause to doubt, having been subjected to her diatribes on the appalling complacency of the bourgeoisie on more occasions than he cared to recollect. Although when he'd left her, she'd been chatting amiably enough to the vicar's wife about soup kitchens. Well, he must just hope for the best. Perhaps the thought of the bank loan she and Viktor hoped to solicit from Ralph would stop her behaving too badly.

Yes, all things considered, it was turning into a rather unrestful afternoon, he thought. Not that it had promised to be anything else, given the relations that existed between himself and Ralph, which, frankly, had never been of the warmest. He found Ralph a bore and a braggart, always boasting about his connections. The owner of the bank where he worked, old Lord Rutland, was childless, his son having been killed in the war. 'Always had a soft spot for me, if you know what I mean,' said Ralph. 'Thinks the world of Diana, too. Sends us a crate of champagne *without fail* every year at Christmas. Between you and me . . .' Here his tone became confiding. 'I shouldn't be at all surprised if we were to do rather well out of it when the old boy dies.' Nor was the elderly peer the only such luminary to be assiduously courted by Ralph. 'Because you never know where it might lead.' he was in the habit of saying, after describing some outrageous piece of flattery offered by himself to this titled personage or that. 'And of course I've Peter to think of . . .' He was sure it must have been a disappointment to Ralph when Edith first turned up with *him*. Had there been a family conference, he wondered, before he and Edith got married? *A pity she couldn't have done a bit better for herself, poor darling. Not quite Our Sort, is he?* He could just imagine it.

A branch whipped suddenly, and painfully, across his face. Damn. He must have walked straight into a bush. His fingers clutched at twigs and glossy leaves. A heavy-headed waxen bloom spilled, at his touch, the residue of last night's rain. Camellia, was it? Edith would know. He strolled for a while in the little wilderness, enjoying the mild warmth of the sunshine on his face, and the blessed quiet. Quite a garden, this. 'It's two and a half acres,' Ralph had boasted, when they'd bought the place. It had been dirt cheap, too, he'd gone on to say. 'Fellow selling up and going to Hong Kong. Only too glad to get it off his hands.' Of course, he'd added, it was far too big for just the three of them, and the girl – he meant the live-in maid – but Diana had quite refused to look at another house. 'You know what woman are,' Ralph said complacently. 'Once they get an idea in their heads, nothing on earth will get it out again.'

From the direction of the terrace came an ecstatic cry. Diana's, he supposed. Something was *too delightful* or *too frightful* – he couldn't make it out exactly. At least Edith didn't *shriek*. He wondered if she'd missed him yet. Perhaps, surrounded for once by all the company she could want, she'd let him skulk by himself a while longer. It was a relief, he thought, not having to *talk* to people. All day their voices jabbered in his ears. Sometimes it was as if they were inside his head. Invading his very thoughts, his dreams, with their unending babble. And yet, however hard he tried, he wasn't able to keep *her* words out of his mind for long. *You don't know what he's done* . . . It made him sick to his stomach to think of what had prompted that cry. Its note of shame, of sexual disgust . . . Ever since that call yesterday, he'd been unable to think of anything else. That she, of all women, should have been subjected to such . . . such *vile* treatment filled him with disgust. He found that his hands had clenched into fists. What he wouldn't give to teach that brute a lesson.

'Daddy, Daddy!' Across the lawn, his younger

daughter came running. '*There* you are, Daddy! Daddy, you've got to come and see . . .'

'What am I to see?' he asked, as, out of breath, she collapsed against him.

'It's her costume.' Margaret arrived, at a more sedate pace. 'She's Little Bo-Peep. Peter's nurse made her a bonnet out of cardboard and pink crêpe paper.'

'And my lamb! You haven't said about my lamb!'

'Nurse said she might borrow Peter's toy lamb,' explained his elder child. 'She'll have to give it back, though,' she added, under her breath.

'And what's your costume like?'

Holding his daughters by the hand, he walked back with them towards the house.

'I'm the Queen of Hearts,' said Margaret flatly. 'I've a cloak made from an old velvet curtain, and a crown Nurse made me out of cardboard and silver paper. And a tray of tarts. They're cardboard, too. With red poster paint, for the jam.'

'It all sounds lovely. Has Mummy seen you yet?'

'Yes, she liked my crown. Billy's Little Jack Horner,' she added kindly, since that young man had now joined them. 'He's allowed to wear one of Uncle Ralph's motoring caps.'

'I'm sure he looks splendid.'

They had by now joined the throng of guests on the lawn.

'There you are, Fred! I was wondering where you'd got to,' said his wife.

'I was just . . .' he started to say.

But then came another voice: 'Why, Mr Rowlands! How very nice to see you.'

For what seemed a long moment, he stood there, gaping like a fool. 'Lady Celia,' he managed at last. 'I didn't expect . . .'

'It *is* rather unexpected, my being here,' she replied, as if they were in the habit of meeting every day. 'My husband and I have just dropped in for a moment.'

'Ah.'

'We've a house over the way, you see . . .'

It was an effort to take in what she was saying. All he could think was, *she's here*. Only a moment ago, he'd been thinking about her, and now here she was. Conjured up out of the aether, by the sheer force of his desire. *Don't be absurd*, he told himself severely. People don't just materialise out of nothing. He caught a whiff of her perfume. *Jasmine. Roses.* 'A lovely afternoon,' he managed to say.

'Yes, isn't it too delightful?' There was an artificial brightness to her tone he found disconcerting. As if she were playing a part, in which she was not quite at ease. More unsettling still was the knowledge that Lionel West must be close by. He'd never been more conscious of being in the dark.

'Ah, Lady Celia!' Ralph's officiously cheerful tone conveyed his view that his brother-in-law had detained their guest of honour long enough. 'Lady Celia has very kindly agreed to distribute the prizes this afternoon,' he explained, for Rowlands' benefit. 'Lady Celia, do let me get you some tea.'

'I was just telling Mr Rowlands that my husband and I are neighbours of yours,' she said, ignoring this.

'How very good of you to say so! *Neighbours*. I suppose we are,' murmured Ralph reverently. 'Lady Celia's family seat is Claremont,' he added, again for Rowlands' edification. 'Quite the finest house in these parts, I always say . . .'

'But inconveniently large, and difficult to heat,' came the reply. There it was, Rowlands thought. That silvery note. As if she were laughing up her sleeve.

'Mr Rowlands,' said Lady Celia abruptly. 'Do introduce me to your wife. I assume this must be your wife – with the two little girls? No, please, don't get up,' she said to Edith. 'It's much too hot for standing about. I'm Celia West, by the way.'

It said a great deal for Edith's self-possession that she replied calmly, 'Oh yes, of course. How very nice to meet you.'

A drowsy, late afternoon mood hung over the Edwards' garden, with its heady smells of roses, lilac, cigarette smoke, cucumber sandwiches, and trampled grass; its murmuring bees, its aimlessly circling crowd of party-goers. Their voices, perceived by Rowlands as a tapestry or mosaic of sound, offered tantalising fragments of talk: '. . . she hasn't a penny, you know. All the money comes from his side . . .' '. . . splendid lobelias . . .' '. . . hard to tell if she paints or doesn't. Although she'll never see thirty-five again . . .' 'Yes, we thought of Monte this year. Such fun at the casino . . .' '. . . not a bad return on my steel holdings. Of course, rubber's where you'll make your money. Take it from me . . .' All this was no more than a backdrop to the central drama. Of this, Lady Celia was the undisputed star, surrounded by an admiring cast of supporting players, his relations foremost amongst them. 'Oh, Lady Celia, won't you have some cake?' begged his sister-in-law.

'No, thank you. I never eat cake.'

'Lady Celia, do let me introduce you to some people,' his brother-in-law exhorted, to equally little effect, Lady Celia remarking languidly that she had met some very nice people already, although in point of fact she had talked to nobody but Rowlands and his wife.

When called upon to award the prizes for the best iced cake and the best flower arrangement, she proved no less capricious. She was not a judge of cake, she insisted, only she preferred cakes to *look* homemade – therefore that one, with the slightly burnt edges, was probably the nicest. As for the flowers, she supposed the one with the daisies was the prettiest. She couldn't abide gladioli – such *ostentatious* flowers. On being told that it was the arrangement with the gladioli that had won, she burst out laughing.

'There! I told you I was bad at judging things.'

'What's all the fuss, Celia?' said a voice Rowlands

knew. Hearing it again made the hairs on the back of his neck stand up on end.

'Oh, hello, Lionel.' Lady Celia's voice was coolly polite, *guarded*, Rowlands thought. 'Where've you been?'

'Just taking a look about,' was the reply. 'You have a very pleasant garden,' said the plutocrat, in louder tones, to his hostess.

'But how very kind!' Diana sounded quite overcome. 'I have *help* with it, of course.'

'Well, it's very nice indeed. Who's this?' said West to his wife, turning his attention, in an instant, from the garden to his fellow guests. 'I don't believe I've had the pleasure . . .'

There was a barely perceptible pause, then Lady Celia said, 'Of course. How stupid of me. Do let me introduce Mr and Mrs Rowlands . . .'

'Delighted to meet you, Mrs Rowlands,' murmured West. 'Are these your children?'

'Yes. That is—'

'Charming,' he said, before she could explain further. 'Quite a picture they make. Dear little girls. You're a lucky man, Rowlands.'

He mumbled his acknowledgement of this fact, all the while, conscious that West's eyes were upon him. It was an uncanny feeling, knowing you were being looked at, without being able to look back.

A brief pause ensued.

'Rowlands,' said Lionel West, in a thoughtful tone.

'That name's familiar. Have we met before?'

'I don't believe so.' Rowlands' heart was hammering.

'Strange. I could have sworn . . .'

But at that moment, to Rowlands' enormous relief, a distraction appeared in the form of Billy. 'I say, what a fine little chap!' exclaimed the entrepreneur. 'Yours, I take it?'

'As a matter of fact he's my sister's boy.'

'Indeed. And I suppose this must be your sister . . .' said West, for Dorothy, it seemed, was now approaching. 'A good deal younger than yourself, I'd say. But I can see a resemblance . . . I was just admiring your son,' he went on, now presumably addressing Dorothy. 'Jolly little fellow.'

'Yes.' There was a guardedness in her tone that Rowlands could only attribute to a dislike of the present company. He felt just the same, as it happened. And then it struck him: she knew West, of old. He'd been 'Mr Lionel' to her then. Hardly surprising if she felt awkward, under the circumstances.

Lionel West seemed not at all put out by her manner. Nor did he appear to have recognised her, which was a small mercy, Rowlands thought. 'How old is he?'

Again, there was a slight, but perceptible, pause, as if she were weighing up the advisability of replying. 'He'll be five next month.'

'Five years old, eh?' West seemed delighted by this information. 'That's a fine big chap. He's very like you,' he added, to Dorothy.

'So I've been told,' she replied curtly.

'Yes, I'd say he's the dead spit of you,' went on West, in the same lazily amused tone. 'With that dark hair, and those big brown eyes . . . Although,' he added, as if he had just noticed, 'your eyes aren't really brown. I'd have said they were green.'

'Would you?'

'Oh yes. A very unusual shade. Hasn't anybody ever told you?'

He's flirting with her, Rowlands realised, uncomfortably aware that Lady Celia, who was now saying something to Edith about the rain's having kept off, might well have come to the same conclusion. This, he saw, would be another way that West exerted his power, one he'd doubtless enjoy very much. Humiliating one woman in front of another. Yes, he'd like that, Rowlands thought.

Fortunately, the object of his attentions seemed in no mood to encourage them. 'No,' she replied coolly. 'I can't say that they have. Come on, Billy,' she added, to her son: 'Let's go and find Daddy, shall we?'

'Oh, you mustn't go yet.' It was said in the same silky tones as before, but it was a command, not a request. 'We've only just got acquainted, you and I, and your charming family. As my wife will tell you, I'm very fond of children. Now then,' turning his attention to the little boy, 'Billy, how would you like to earn yourself half a crown?'

Before the child could reply, his mother said: 'He's

not allowed to take money from strangers.'

'Very commendable,' West said drily. 'As to our being strangers, that's easily remedied. Shake hands, Billy. There! Now we're the best of friends. If you cut along to the stables,' he went on, still talking to the boy, 'you'll find my chauffeur – that's the one wearing the peaked cap, and the smart green uniform with the silver buttons. Tell him I want my cigars. They're in the glove compartment of the Rolls. Then dash back here as fast as you can, and I'll make it worth your while. But be quick, mind! Any dawdling, and our little arrangement's off.'

Bracing himself for an indignant outburst from his sister, Rowlands was surprised to hear her laugh. 'I see,' she said. 'That's how you do business, is it?'

'I never take no for an answer, if that's what you mean,' said Lionel West. 'Wouldn't you agree, my dear?'

'Oh, you can be very persistent when you want something enough,' said his wife.

There was an uncomfortable silence.

'Ah, Mr West!' Rowlands could not have been more relieved at the reappearance of his brother-in-law. 'So very good of you to come. *Do* let me get you some refreshment. A cup of tea – or something stronger, perhaps? We have whisky, gin . . .'

'Thanks, but I never drink spirits before sundown. A cup of tea would go down very well.'

'Tea it is.' Having conveyed this request as a matter of urgency to his wife, Ralph turned again to his guest of honour. 'Well,' he said, 'I know there are some people who'd very much like to make your acquaintance, Mr West, if you'd be so kind. Blenkinsop, who's Chairman of the Conservative Association this year, is keen to have a word.'

'Is that so? Ah, here's my little friend (for the child had come running up, out of breath from his exertions). Well done, Billy! You've been no more than three minutes, by my watch. Here's your half-crown. A fair wage for a fair day's work, wouldn't you say?' he added slyly.

If the remark was meant for Dorothy, she paid it no attention. 'Come along, Billy. Your father wants you.' A moment later, she stalked off, with her son in tow.

'Quite charming,' murmured Lionel West, although it seemed to Rowlands that his sister had been anything but that. Which was all to her credit – what a rotter the man was! He was glad, after all, that Dorothy had given him the cold shoulder. 'You were saying?' the entrepreneur said to Ralph, still hovering at his elbow, Rowlands guessed.

'It's just that rumour has it . . .' Here Ralph became positively arch, 'that old Chalfont is thinking of stepping down before the next election.'

'Really?' West's voice was non-committal.

'So they say. And Blenkinsop was wondering – that is, all of us in the Conservative Association were wondering – well, what *your* intentions might be.'

'My intentions?' West emitted a little bark of

laughter. 'Oh, I'm nothing but a simple businessman. I make it a rule never to meddle in politics. Thank you, dear lady.' This to Diana, Rowlands assumed. A pause followed, while West took a sip of tea.

'Do say a word to Blenkinsop, though, won't you?' There was an edge of desperation in Ralph's voice. 'And perhaps one or two of our senior members . . .'

'Delighted to.'

'And then we really ought to be going,' said Lady Celia, a little too quickly. 'You haven't forgotten we've got people arriving later?'

'Just as you like,' was her husband's reply. 'Although it seems to me we've only just got here.'

'But you can't go yet!' Disappointment got the better of their hostess' good manners. 'There's still the prizes for the fancy dress competition to award. I promised the kiddies specially.'

'Well, we certainly mustn't disappoint *them*, must we, my dear?'

Was it Rowlands' imagination, or was there an edge of menace in that silkily insistent voice? He shivered slightly, in spite of the heat of the day.

Diana tapped a teaspoon on the side of a cup and the murmur of voices on the lawn was hushed. 'Come along, children,' she cried. 'Let's form a nice straight line for Lady Celia.'

While this injunction was being fulfilled, with a great deal of excited chatter from the children themselves, Rowlands was privy to another, whispered, conversation.

'It's really too absurd. I had no idea I'd be let in for this.'

And the suavely unconcerned reply: 'You wanted to come, my dear.'

With a – just audible – sigh, Lady Celia moved past him towards the lawn. As she did so, her hand brushed, as if by accident, against Rowlands' sleeve. A warning, perhaps, to say nothing that would betray her.

'We should be going, too,' he said to Edith.

'Hush!' she whispered. 'They're going to announce the winner. It'll be that child with the ringlets. Miss Muffett, I suppose she's meant to be. The lengths some people go to, to make sure their child comes first! There must be five yards of satin in that frock.'

On the lawn, a subdued conversation was taking place, of which only snatches were audible. 'Oh, but surely . . .' came Diana's voice, and then: 'Well, if you really think so . . .'

There was a momentary, and unaccountable, pause.

A restlessness made itself felt amongst the waiting crowd. 'Ladies and gentlemen,' said Diana, sounding as if she was putting a brave face on things. 'Lady Celia is of the opinion . . . that is . . . a difference of opinion has arisen . . .'

'Definitely the child with the ringlets,' muttered Edith.

'So the judges – that is, Lady Celia and myself – have decided to award *two* prizes. The first, to Mary-Ann Fawcett-Smythe, as Miss Muffett.'

'Told you,' said Edith.

'The second, to . . .'

'The Queen of Hearts,' said Lady Celia in a clear, high voice like the striking of a bell.

'The Queen of Hearts,' echoed her hostess uncertainly.

'Well,' said Edith. 'Aren't you going to tell me?'

'Tell you what?' Although he knew perfectly well. They were on the train home by this time, the last stage of their journey, the Lehmanns having left them at Waterloo to catch the Underground back to Whitechapel. And so they were alone together for the first time that day – alone, that is, except for the children. Anne was asleep on his lap, her head lolling heavily against him. Worn out with all the excitement, poor little mite. Margaret might have been asleep, too, for all he could tell. Either that or she'd been rendered speechless by her unlooked-for triumph.

'Aren't you a lucky little girl?' Diana had burst out, the minute the guests had gone. 'Fancy Lady Celia taking such notice of you!'

It wasn't only Margaret's success that was remarked upon. 'I say, old man, you never said you knew the Wests,' Ralph had said, sounding quite aggrieved.

'I don't. She . . . Lady Celia . . . came into the office once, that's all.'

'Fred's office deals with some quite important clients,' Edith had been unable to resist saying.

'Yes, *he's* quite a big noise in the City,' her brother

had replied. 'Rich as Croesus, of course. Although,' he gave a spiteful little laugh, 'you couldn't exactly say he was out of the top drawer. I mean, you'd hardly even call him a gentleman.'

'Oh, darling, what a thing to say!' cried Diana delightedly.

'It's no more than the truth. Father was a brewer, down Bermondsey way, it's said. Mother no better than she should be. They say he'd do anything to get himself a knighthood. I suppose it must be rather awkward for him, seeing as his wife's already got a title. Points up the contrast, don't you know.'

'Darling! *Really*!'

'We should go,' Rowlands said, embarrassed by this outburst on Ralph's part. 'Or we'll miss our train.' A fragment of conversation overheard towards the end of the afternoon, as he was coming downstairs after visiting the lavatory, was doubtless the reason for this venom. The door of Ralph's inner sanctum had been ajar, or so he assumed, since the voices issuing from that direction had been quite distinct.

'You must be mad!' It had been Ralph who was speaking, his blustering tone not obscuring a note of rising panic.

'I can assure you I've never been saner.' The soft voice had a steelier edge, now, but it was still the same voice that had bandied words with Rowlands' sister an hour or so before, and remarked on the good looks of her little son. 'You knew what the arrangement was, from the start.'

'But it'll ruin me, if it comes out . . .' Ralph sounded close to breaking down.

'That's not my affair.'

'But . . . how am I to repay a sum of that amount?'

'Again, that's your concern.' There was a pause, during which Rowlands stood frozen to the spot, afraid that the slightest creak of a floorboard might give away his presence. 'But don't fret, *old boy*. I'm sure you'll think of something. Try one of these Havanas – they're really rather good.'

'Damn your Havanas.'

'No need to take that tone.' It was evident that West was enjoying himself. 'We can still behave like gentlemen, can't we?'

Yes, it was that remark which had stung, Rowlands thought. He wondered what it had all been about. It sounded as if Ralph had got himself into a bit of a spot, financially. Whatever it was, he didn't imagine he'd ever hear about it from Ralph.

Rowlands' observation about the trains gave Viktor his cue. 'We must be going also, must we not, *schatz*? Thank you,' he said to their hostess, 'for a most pleasant afternoon.'

'So glad you enjoyed it,' trilled Diana.

'So glad,' echoed her husband, his thoughts evidently elsewhere. 'A pity about our little chat. Some other time, perhaps.'

With which off hand remark Viktor had had to be content. He had said little during the journey back, perhaps reflecting on the inherent untrustworthiness of the middle classes. After what he'd overheard, Rowlands wasn't the least surprised at Ralph's failure to keep his promise, but to Viktor it must have seemed like mere carelessness or a deliberate snub. He wondered, as the train chuffed slowly from one near-deserted station to the next, what had suggested the idea – not a bad one in itself – of setting up in business. A smallholding. It was what a number of men he'd known during his time at the Lodge had decided upon, by way of making a living. There'd been a chap called Haycock who was doing quite well, the last Rowlands had heard, running a market garden near Ely. Another – *Gotobed, was it?* – had taken on the family's pig farm. But these, for the most part, were men born to such a life. Viktor, to the best of Rowlands' knowledge, was a city boy, born and bred. Quite how he would make out in rural Kent remained to be seen, to say nothing of Dorothy, her brother thought wryly. She was hardly what you'd call the domestic sort.

She, too, had seemed unaccountably subdued, as they sat together in the train. He'd been prepared for indignation, or at the very least, sarcasm, but all she'd said was it was a shame Viktor hadn't had his talk with Mr Edwards after all. People were a mystery, Rowlands thought. Just when you felt you knew how they ticked, they said or did something to surprise you.

'You still haven't said how it was you came to meet her,' said Edith, cutting into these reflections. 'Celia West, I mean.'

'It's really not terribly interesting,' he said, choosing his words carefully. She's a client of Mr Willoughby's. She came in to consult him about something, that's all.'

'I must say, she's awfully attractive,' Edith said.

'Is she? I must say I hadn't noticed.'

'Very,' she went on, ignoring his dry joke. 'And her clothes are simply lovely.' She was silent a moment. 'I don't know that I've ever seen clothes so beautifully made. Dorothy said they had to be Paris models. *Such* lovely materials . . . *crêpe de Chine*. Silk chiffon. And that hat . . .' There was a wistfulness in her voice he hadn't heard before.

'I didn't know you cared about such things.'

'I don't. Not really. But seeing her today . . . and then the way she spoke to you . . . as if you were . . . I don't know . . . old friends.'

'Edith, I hardly know her.'

'I know. But don't you *see*?' Her voice cracked slightly, as if the strain of keeping up appearances these past few hours had been too much for her. 'It *meant* something. That you were the only one she cared to speak to, out of all those people.'

'That's just the way she is,' he said, forgetting for a moment that he had disowned the acquaintance. 'Perverse. She likes going against what's expected.'

'Does she?' She digested this. 'I thought she seemed genuinely interested. I suppose that's just good breeding.'

'I suppose so.'

'I'll tell you one thing, though,' Edith went on, still in the same meditative tone, 'her husband didn't like it one bit, her talking to you. If looks could kill, you'd be stone dead by now.'

He laughed. 'Fortunately, I'm impervious to all such looks.' They talked of other things. But for the rest of the journey, and for what remained of the evening after they got back to Honor Oak Park, he was unable to shake off the feeling of unease engendered by her words.

Chapter Five

When he came to look back on those few weeks, in the summer of 1927, it was with a sense of their having been a period of almost unnatural calm. Like the calm before the storm, he thought afterwards, or the deafening silence that preceded the onslaught of battle. He remembered how eerily quiet it had been, the night before Messines Ridge. As if something held its breath. Just after three in the morning they'd let off the first of the mines; after that, it was as if all hell had broken loose. The earth shooting up in a column fifty feet high, with a noise like that of a giant hand slamming down on a metal table. Even twenty miles away, the shock was palpable. So it was with the events of that summer. All of a sudden the life you'd known was blown apart, and scattered to the winds. Nothing would ever be the same, although of course you'd not the slightest inkling of that then. It was as if it would go on forever – that dull, safe, settled existence. Only when it was over, did you realise how much it had meant.

They'd been sitting in the garden, he and Edith, in order to get the last of the sunshine, the girls having been sent to bed, with instructions not to stay awake talking, although when it was light like this, Edith said, you couldn't expect them to be anything but wakeful. She herself seemed to have succumbed to the prevailing mood of lassitude – the heat, Rowlands surmised, combined with the fact that she was nearing her time. Even Edith couldn't keep going at the same rate, in this, her last month of pregnancy. Now she sat sighing and fanning herself with the paper, from which she had been reading out items of interest, as usual. 'Oh,' she said suddenly. 'Look at this. It's that friend of yours . . .' It was thus she had taken to referring to Celia West. 'She's given a dance for her smart friends. There's a piece about it here. Would you like me to read it to you?'

'I don't mind.' He lit a cigarette. Edith didn't object to his smoking in the garden, although when he lit up indoors she complained it made the house smell like a smoking compartment.

'Quite a grand affair, according to this,' she was saying. She cleared her throat and began to read: '"*At Claremont Court, Esher, last night, a summer ball was given by Mr Lionel West, in honour of Lady Celia's birthday. Amongst the guests at this glittering occasion were the Duke and Duchess of Marchpane, and Lady Cynthia Marchpane; Lord Canovan and the Dowager Duchess of Vauxhall; the Honourable Flora Poore and Mr Guy Fulbourne; Mr and Mrs Flint and Miss Emily Flint; Mrs Hermione Lawless and Mr Ronald Wootton; Miss Angela Carstairs and Mr Douglas Amory; and Mr Gerald Willoughby* . . ."* That's your Mr Willoughby,' put in Edith, in case he might have missed this.

'Mm.'

'"*The theme of the evening was 'Fête Champêtre' and with this in mind, many of the guests had excelled themselves. The Honourable Flora looked charming as an eighteenth-century shepherdess, in a gown of pale pink satin beauté draped with swags of old Brussels lace. Miss Flint wore apple green silk with a flounced skirt, and a matching hat of fine straw, caught up at the side with a green satin bow. Mrs Lawless – with the wit and élan her admirers have come to expect of her – was a shepherd boy, in striped satin breeches and a ruffled shirt – a Corydon to Miss Carstairs' Phyllis (the latter being clad in a gown of palest blue spotted georgette, with a blue silk ribbon tied around her shepherdess' crook). But the* pièce de résistance *of the evening was the exquisite costume worn by Lady Celia herself, who, as Marie Antoinette, has seldom looked lovelier. Her gown of white silk scattered with seed pearls, though simplicity itself, was a perfect foil to the wearer's delicate beauty, her ash-blonde tresses being concealed under a powdered white wig, ornamented with a silver filigree rose. The Verney diamonds completed the* ensemble, *which drew admiring glances from not a few of the guests. The delightful grounds of the Georgian mansion (c 1770, by a pupil of Robert Adam) had been illuminated for the occasion by a thousand fairy lights. Dancing took place in the main ballroom, to the mellifluous strains of a string quartet. A champagne supper was served at midnight, and more dancing followed, for those not already danced off their feet, to the lively sounds of 'Coco' Cavendish and his Red Hot Band."* I must say,' said Edith with a certain wistfulness, 'it does sound lovely.'

'They need something to fill the papers with, I suppose,' he said, yawning, as if the image this account had painted . . . *white silk* . . . were of no more than passing interest. 'Shall I put the kettle on?'

But Edith seemed reluctant to let the subject drop. 'Quite lovely,' she murmured dreamily. 'Do you know, I don't think I've ever been to a proper ball. Although there were dances, when I was a girl, in Alverton Avenue.'

But his sharper ears had detected a step on the path. 'Who's there?' he said.

'Sorry to disturb,' said Viktor. He sounded choked,

tearful. 'Only I saw the garden gate open, and . . . the fact is, I have bad news. About Dorothy. She's been arrested.'

There was a gasp from Edith.

Rowlands had the sensation often described as that of stepping into an empty lift shaft. A sickening, vertiginous feeling – as if one had put out a hand in the dark to steady oneself on a wall and encountered only air. 'Was it because of the strike?' he said, conscious that his wife knew nothing of this.

'They hadn't even got as far as the strike,' said Viktor angrily. 'She was putting up some posters, that is all. Advertising a public meeting.'

'She must have done *something* to get herself arrested,' said Edith, finding her voice at last.

'*Edith* . . .'

'Edith is right. She *must* have done something wrong to be treated so, but she did nothing. All she did was to protest. To the policeman who arrested her – the brute! – she said that what she was doing was not a crime, and that it was a free country.' Viktor's laugh had a bitter undertone. 'Free! That's quite funny, I think.'

'Where is she now?'

'In Holloway prison. Which is why I have come,' said Viktor. 'I have a favour to ask. I need someone to look after the boy.'

'Where is he now?' asked Edith.

'I left him with a neighbour. Mrs Higgins. She said she would have him for a day or two, but . . .'

'You should have brought him with you,' said Edith. 'Now you'll have to make another journey.'

'How can I ever thank you?' cried Viktor, in a voice that trembled with emotion.

'You needn't,' said Edith. 'I'm not doing it for you. I suppose,' she added in a softer tone, 'you'll stay for a cup of tea?'

'Thank you.' His voice was still unsteady. 'But I really shouldn't stay long. The child . . .'

'Sit down,' said Edith. 'You're looking quite done in. Fred, give him a cigarette.'

'I was just about to. Now,' said Rowlands, when he judged that their visitor was master of himself once more, 'why don't you tell us about it from the beginning?'

But in truth there was nothing more to say that had not already been said. It was simply another example of Dorothy's predilection for putting her heart before her head.

When Viktor had had his smoke, and taken his leave, they sat for a while in silence. The sun had gone in by this time, and around them the air had grown cooler. Soon the stars would come out, the Evening Star first of all. If Rowlands had one regret above all others, it was that he would never again behold its beauty. Its white radiance against the darkening blue . . .

'I know it's going to make things difficult . . .' he started to say.

'We'll manage.'

'Yes. But it was good of you to say you'd have him, just the same.'

When Edith spoke again, she sounded close to tears. 'I know you think me heartless.'

'Edith, I never said—'

'. . . but even *I* draw the line,' she gave a choked little laugh, 'at turning a child of five out of doors.'

'I know, I know . . .'

'No matter what his mother might or might not have done.'

'I'm not defending her.'

'Aren't you?' Again came the dangerously brittle tone. 'I rather thought that was what this was all about.'

The smell was what he noticed first, of course – a mixture of floor polish, disinfectant and institutional food overlaying something more unpleasant. Bad drains, he thought, but then wondered if it wasn't just the smell of misery. All the souls cooped up within these walls, with nothing to do but dwell on the painful realities of their situation. The sounds were another horror, magnified as they were by miles of tiled corridors. Sounds of doors being slammed and locked, of voices upraised in anger or despair. 'You would, would you?' The jangling of the wardress's keys as they passed along the corridor, the clang of the gate as it was shut behind them. *God, what a beastly hole!* He wondered, as he sat there, on one side of the splintery deal table which separated him from his sister, whether she could have had the faintest idea of what this place would be like. Surely not, or she would never have risked it, poor silly girl. He blamed himself, although he couldn't help blaming Viktor a little, too. *She was his wife, wasn't she?* He ought to be looking after her, not encouraging her in all this political nonsense. Although, even as he had the thought, he knew the chances of any man's being able to control his sister were slim, to say the least.

'Are you all right?' He kept his voice low, although those seated on either side of him could have had no more interest in what he and his sister had to say to one another than he had in *their* conversations, of which murmured fragments reached him, like scraps of talk on a party line.

'I've been better,' replied Dorothy. 'The food isn't up to much.'

'I meant, are they treating you well?'

'Perfectly well. You worry too much, dear old Fred.'

'Can you wonder at it?' It was an effort to keep his temper with her, sometimes. 'Seeing you in a place like this.'

'I didn't *ask* to be put in here . . .'

'That's a matter of opinion.'

'. . . but there are certain things one can't put up with. Injustice being one of them.'

'Have you thought of the injustice to Billy? Being separated from his mother can't be good for a child of his age.'

148

'Do you think I haven't thought of that?' she cried.

'No need to take on.' He could just imagine the stares they must be attracting. Not that it would bother Dottie. She'd never cared tuppence for what other people thought.

But she wouldn't be quieted. 'There isn't a day – or night – that I don't think what I've done to my child. And do you know what?' she said, working herself up in a way that was all too familiar, 'I'd do it again! For him! Because I couldn't hold my head up, otherwise . . .'

'Pipe down a bit, can't you?' he admonished her but Dorothy, once mounted upon her high horse, wasn't easily subdued.

'It's *because* of Billy that I had to make a stand,' she said, close to weeping now. 'You do see, don't you, Fred?'

'Yes, of course.' Although privately he wondered if she had things the wrong way around, putting others before those whose welfare should have been dearer to her.

But she wasn't to be mollified. 'What sort of a world are we handing on to them, our children?' she demanded, in what Edith would have called her soapbox voice. 'What sort of a world?'

'Two minutes,' said the wardress, in a loud, harsh voice. The murmur of conversation which surrounded them was momentarily subdued, before starting up again with renewed urgency.

'I'll come again next week,' he said. 'Is there anything I can bring?'

'Books. And some decent soap. The stuff you get in here practically takes your skin off. Oh, Fred . . .' His imminent departure seemed to bring home to her all at once the hatefulness of her situation. 'I'm sorry about all this.'

'Shh,' he said, reaching to take her hand. 'Don't upset yourself. Is Viktor coming in later?'

'Tomorrow. They've warned him about taking any more time off work.'

'Time's up!'

'Oh, Fred,' she cried again, still clutching his hand, as he stood up to go.

'Chin up, old thing.' He forced a smile. But it felt as if his heart were breaking. 'Oh, the silly, silly girl,' he muttered to himself, because that was what she would always be to him: a wayward child. His Dorothy, his little pet, who'd made him laugh with her quips and sallies, and had cried her eyes out when he'd returned to the Front. 'How could she have been so stupid? How *could* she?' was his anguished thought, as, released once more into the blessed quiet of Parkhurst Road, he heard the gate clang shut behind him. For someone with her fine nature to be shut up in such a place – it wasn't right . . . It was then that – too late to move out of the way – he heard the purr of a powerful engine, and a car drew up, splashing him with filth from a standing puddle. 'Have a care, can't you?' he shouted, all his anger at the rottenness of things unleashed at once.

'Not my fault, mate,' said the chauffeur, getting out to open the door for the visiting plutocrat – some wealthy philanthropist, perhaps, doing his duty by the less fortunate.

'But you must have seen me standing there.'

'Shouldn't have *bin* standing there, should you?' was the reply. 'Now hop it. My guv'nor's waiting.'

It was on the tip of his tongue to consign the man and his guv'nor to the devil. But he knew he'd only get a dusty answer. So he turned on his heel and walked away. A guffaw of rude laughter from the chauffeur followed him down the street. Cheeky little sod. Thinking himself such a fine fellow in his uniform, although it was ten to one he'd never worn a better one. One of those Dorothy would doubtless have called a 'class traitor'. Maybe she had a point, at that.

'Oi! You! Hang on a minute, can't you?' The lad caught up with him. 'You don't half walk fast, for a blind 'un. My guv'nor said to give you this.'

He stopped, but kept his hands by his sides.

'Go on, take it. A shilling for your trouble, he said.'

'Tell your guv'nor I don't want it. I'm not in need of charity.'

'Suit yourself.' The chauffeur went off, whistling. Yes, maybe Dottie, for all her wrong-headedness, had a point.

There was a moment of silence after he finished dialling, then the faint – but to his ear, perceptible – sounds of the connection being made. A series of dull clicks and

151

muted bleeps. Then the dialling tone proper started up: a soft but insistent purring. Two beats, followed by another pair, and another . . . Perhaps, he thought, there was no one in. But then the receiver was lifted. 'Grosvenor five-nine-four-oh,' came a voice: the maid's, he surmised. He pressed Button A, then made his enquiry.

'I'll see if he's in,' the girl replied.

A minute passed, during which he had time to reflect on what he had to say, as well as on the wisdom of saying it. But what choice did he have? Too much was at stake for faintheartedness now – not least *her* reputation.

The maid returned. 'The master's out.'

'What time do you expect him back?'

'I couldn't say. He's dining at his club. Do you want to leave a message?'

'No, that's all right. No message.' Because, after all, what form of words *was* there that was at once discreet enough for the ears of servants, and urgent enough to convey what needed to be said? He couldn't say. He'd been dumbfounded as it was, that afternoon, when the call had come: 'Saville and Willoughby. Good afternoon. May I help you?'

There'd been a moment of silence then, too. A laugh had followed. Not a pleasant laugh. Self-satisfied, he remembered thinking. 'You see I was right. We *do* know one another. Or rather,' said Lionel West, with the nasal twang that marked him as being not quite a gentleman, 'it's *I* who have the pleasure of knowing *you*. Since I have the advantage not only of having *spoken* to you but of having *seen* you. Not a claim . . .' again, came that odiously knowing laugh, 'I repeat, *not* a claim that you yourself could make, eh, Mr Rowlands?'

To which Rowlands had said nothing, finding himself, at that precise moment, unable to speak. Lionel West seemed not at all put out by this. If anything, his good humour had increased. 'So you see – or rather, you do *not* see, you must let me have my little joke – I'm now entirely, as you might say, "in the picture". Tell me . . .' Here he was momentarily overcome with his laughing fit. 'How *is* the drapery business, these days?'

'I'm sorry, sir, I don't know what you mean.'

'Don't you? Perhaps I should refresh your memory. You telephoned and spoke to my wife last week about an order of bed linen, it was. That, at least, was how the call was represented to me. I confess I was quite taken in,' West chuckled, 'that is, until I had the luck to run into you again . . . A charming party, wasn't it?'

Rowlands was silent.

'Yes, that was a very good trick you played, Mr Rowlands – a very good trick indeed. As a rule, though,' the entrepreneur went on, in a voice from which all laughter had vanished, 'I don't like being made a fool of . . . any more than *you* would, Mr Rowlands . . . or your friend Willoughby. My wife's friend, too . . . Ah, I can tell from your silence that this isn't exactly news to you. Well for your information, I know all about their little affair, too.' Lionel West allowed a pause to elapse.

'For a man in my position, you know, such knowledge is easily come by. Where one's wife spends her afternoons, say, or her evenings, and with whom. Oh, it all comes at a price,' went on the insidious voice in Rowlands' ear. 'But then, knowledge always comes at a price, don't you agree?'

Rowlands made a sound indicative of assent. Trapped as he was, alone in the after-hours office, he could only sit and listen, as the poison poured itself into his ear.

'What *has* surprised me,' West said, 'is how *comprehensively* my wife has managed to betray me. Not only in the usual way, but in my business life, too. Consorting, I'm afraid that is the *only* word, with the man who is doing his best to ruin me. Quite shocking behaviour, don't you think, Mr Rowlands? Would your wife – such a charming lady, I thought her, by the by – behave in such a way to you, do you suppose?'

'I don't wish to continue this conversation, sir.'

'Ha, ha! I don't suppose you do. The truth is always unpleasant, isn't it? But I was sure that a man of your *integrity* would not flinch from hearing it. One more word before I go: as a man of honour myself, I feel it's only right to let you and your friend Willoughby know what kind of man you've got yourselves involved with. I don't mean myself, you understand, but my business partner, Mr Caparelli. A very *irascible* sort, is Giovanni Caparelli. Were the truth about the part you and young Willoughby have played in bringing about his downfall to reach his ears, I'm afraid I couldn't answer for the consequences. Being, as you might say,' West laughed, 'only the *sleeping partner* in the affair. Ha, ha! Very good, don't you think, Mr Rowlands? If you know what's good for you, and him,' here the voice turned suddenly colder, 'you'll lose no time in telling your master what I've said.'

There was a click, as the receiver was replaced, followed by a dull purring. In the silent office, Rowlands found himself trembling all over with the shock of what had passed. *Tell your master*. The cold contempt with which it had been said was with him still, as, replacing the heavy receiver in its cradle, he pushed open the still weightier door, and found himself once more in the street. After the stuffiness of the telephone box, with its olfactory reminders of previous occupants, the air smelled fresh and sweet. The scent of new-mown grass drifted from a neighbouring garden. It struck him that it must be getting close to the longest day. He checked his watch: half past six. It wouldn't get dark for hours. Suddenly, as if a voice had spoken, he turned on his heel, his irresolution at an end. There was a train to Charing Cross at a quarter to. If he hurried, he could just make it.

By a quarter past seven, he found himself on the pavement outside the well-known gentleman's club of which his employer was a member. He remembered a conversation once in which the name of the establishment had been mentioned, Willoughby joking that the place was a refuge for unwanted bachelors like himself, and saying that he envied Rowlands' having a wife to go home to. The truth of the matter was that a man like Willoughby – good-looking, well set-up, and not yet thirty-five – would be a catch for any woman. Quite why he hadn't yet married, with London so full of young women crying out for husbands, was a puzzle, although not one with which Rowlands had ever been inclined to concern himself. And yet, during these past few months, he'd come closer, he felt, to penetrating to the heart of the mystery. For no matter how many pretty and eligible girls there were, the fact remained that none of them were Celia West.

At the top of the short flight of steps that led to the main set of doors, his progress was arrested by a large solid body: the porter's, he surmised. 'May I help you, sir?' boomed this individual. Former Sergeant Major, Rowlands thought. He stated his business. 'Ho. Mr Willoughby, is it?' said the porter. 'Hi, you!', this to some passing Buttons, or Boots, 'Have we seen Mr Willoughby this evening?' The answer being in the negative, he repeated this in substance to Rowlands, still without moving an inch to let him pass.

'But . . .' He was aware that he cut a poor figure, hatless and in his well-worn suit, beside the club's usual clientele; one of whom, at that very moment, alighted from a taxicab, and was greeted with suitable deference: 'Evening, my lord,' before sweeping past him up the steps, leaving a pungent trail of *Romeo y Julieta* in his wake. '. . . I was told he was dining here.'

'Then you was told,' replied the porter, 'incorrect.

If you'd care to leave a note,' went on this superb individual, 'I'll make sure as he gets it . . . sir.'

The thought of struggling to write a note under the eye of this Cerberus was enough to dissuade him from the attempt. 'No, thanks. That won't be necessary.'

'Then what name should I say?' persisted the porter, as Rowlands, taking care to hold onto the brass handrail, started to descend the steps. He'd lost enough face already, he thought, without pitching himself head-first into the street.

'The name's Rowlands. I work for Mr Willoughby, at the Gracechurch Street office.'

'*Do* you, sir?' You should've said straight orf, sir,' said the porter, grown suddenly affable. 'Only you can't be too careful these days. Just this evening there was a pair of gentlemen . . . not that you'd call their sort gentlemen . . . asking for Mr Willoughby.'

'Was there, indeed?' said Rowlands, sharply. 'Can you describe them?'

'Oh yes, sir. One was about my height – that's six foot one – and wearing a blue suit, with a collar and tie. One of them celluloid collars,' the porter added, with some distaste. 'Nasty piece of work he was, I'd say. When I asked him his name, he told me to mind my own business . . . only he wasn't quite as civil as that.'

'When was this exactly?'

'No more than an hour ago. I sent him packing, you can be sure, sir. Didn't like his looks, nor those of the other one. Ugly brute *he* was.'

Rowlands hesitated no more than a second. For if this unsolicited visit meant what he thought it meant, then the threat implicit in Lionel West's words to him that afternoon had not been an idle one . . . He addressed the porter once more: 'As you will no doubt have noticed, writing letters isn't my forte. But if there's a typewriter on the premises I could use, it would be of enormous help to me.'

Fifteen minutes later, he'd left Pall Mall, and was walking up St James' Street, with the letter in his pocket. A copy had been left, in a sealed envelope, with his friend the porter (ex-Devonshire regiment), in the event that Willoughby should look in at the club later that evening. He had thought carefully about the wording of the message, not wanting to appear alarmist, and yet aware that there might indeed be cause for alarm. *I could not answer for the consequences*, West had said, referring to his business partner Caparelli's likely reaction to the news that his fraudulent scheme had been discovered. Now Caparelli's men, it appeared, had come looking for Willoughby . . .

Mr West rang the office this afternoon, at 5 p.m., he accordingly wrote, or rather, typed.

He appears to have learned of Saville & Willoughby's involvement in the proceedings against him. I also received the impression that he intended to mention his discovery to Mr Caparelli . . .

He had hesitated at this point, not knowing how best to phrase what had to be said.

I understood from Mr West that he was angry not only about this, but about a matter concerning yourself and Lady Celia. He made certain remarks of a most unpleasant nature, concluding with threats against your personal safety. I felt it my duty to warn you to be on your guard . . .

Waiting to cross Piccadilly, he was surrounded by a laughing group, emerging from the Ritz hotel. A woman in a cloak made of some soft fabric, velvet or silk brocade, half-collided with him. For a startled instant, he breathed the scent of her hair, her expensively perfumed skin . . . She gave a little scream. 'Oh!' It was as if she had inadvertently brushed up against something foul.

'I say! Look where you're going,' came a man's voice, loudly belligerent. 'Clumsy oaf!'

'Don't shout, Rupert darling,' said another voice, a woman's, not the squealer's. 'People are staring.'

'Let them stare. This fellow might have injured Daisy.'

'But Rupert, can't you *see*? He's—'

'I'm really very sorry,' said Rowlands, restraining his anger with difficulty. 'I hope the young lady isn't hurt. But it *was* an accident.' Then, without waiting for a reply, he stepped out into the roaring torrent of the great thoroughfare, trusting to fate and to the quick-wittedness of taxi drivers, that he would not be run over and killed.

'Serve them right if I *were*,' he muttered furiously. 'Damn them.' The cocktail-drinking set. More money than sense, and no manners at all, it would seem. He wondered if this was what Viktor meant when he talked about the idle rich. He'd always dismissed it as Bolshevik ranting; now he thought there might be something in it. He was still fuming as he walked up Berkeley Street. The way that woman had shrieked! As if he'd been trying to pick her pocket. His anger, he was vaguely aware, was exacerbated by the knowledge that, only a moment before, he'd been thinking of Celia West. When she, that silly flapper, had walked into him, he'd felt a split second of foolish delight. *That perfume she'd been wearing* ... Footsteps were approaching. 'Excuse me, but is this number one, Berkeley Square?'

'No, it's number fifty. The numbers go the other way, do you see?'

'Perfectly, thanks.' Allowing a cab to pass, he crossed the street, and began walking in what he thought must be the right direction. He counted off the gaps in the railings in front of each house as he did so. Big houses, these. Through the open window of one of them he caught a snatch of music. Banjos, he thought. Clarinets. 'Hot' music, wasn't it called? The new American fad. They played it on the radio all the time. Not really his kind of thing, although he'd admit it had a certain swing to it.

Come to me, my melancholy baby
Cuddle up and don't be blue ...

Humming the silly refrain under his breath *Smile for me, my honey dear / As I kiss away each tear . . .* he counted off one, two, three sets of railings before arriving in front of what he hoped was the right house. Well, if it turned out not to be, he'd find out soon enough. His foot was upon the bottom step of what he judged must be a short flight leading up to the front door, when it happened. A violent blow that knocked the breath from his body. He thought for a moment that he must have miscalculated, and walked into a wall, but then a second blow followed, harder than the first. A voice hissed in his ear, '*That'll* learn you . . .' As he staggered, trying to right himself, a vicious kick took his legs from under him. He fell to the ground.

Of what happened next he had only a fragmentary recollection afterwards. His assailants – for there were certainly two of them – did their work swiftly and, after that initial outburst, silently. It was as if the darkness itself had grown fists and steel-tipped boots. All he could do was to protect himself as best he could. Curled up as he was, he couldn't escape a savage kick to the belly, nor another, that caught the edge of his jaw. Through a haze of pain he thought, *I must protect my eyes.* The scrap of vision that was still available to him was too precious to be lost to this assault from blind chance. Then a more profound darkness than the one to which he had become accustomed closed over him.

* * *

He came round to the sound of voices. A woman's, *elderly, indignant*: 'What *is* the world coming to? In Berkeley Square . . .' Then a man's, retired Colonel, Indian Army, at a guess, 'Dead drunk, I'd say. Disgraceful.' Someone started shaking him, none too gently. A voice – not the Colonel's but with a London accent, *Kentish Town*, he thought woozily, addressed him gruffly: 'Now then, what's all this? You can't lie here, you know.'

Rowlands made an effort to sit up, provoking a shrill scream from the elderly lady. 'Look, Reginald, he's covered in blood. How perfectly dreadful!'

'Don't distress yourself, my dear. Constable, can't you see to it that this man is moved on? He's upsetting my wife.'

'You leave it to me, sir. Now then, my lad. Can you stand?'

'I think so,' Rowlands mumbled, through a mouthful of blood.

'Good lad. Here, give us your hand.'

Rowlands did as he was told. A moment later, he was once more upon his feet.

'That's a very nasty shiner you've got there,' said the policeman.

'I suggest you take this man to the nearest police station and charge him with causing a public disturbance,' interjected the Colonel.

'Right you are, sir. Come along, Sunny Jim . . .'

But when Rowlands tried to walk a sharp stab of pain made him gasp aloud.

'Broken rib, too, I shouldn't wonder,' said his amiable custodian, relaxing his grip somewhat on Rowlands' upper arm. 'Take it slowly, and you'll be all right.'

They had by this time gone a few paces further along the street, Rowlands couldn't tell in which direction. 'Constable,' he said, finding it difficult not to slur his words, with a tongue that felt swollen to twice its size, 'I'm not drunk. I . . . I fell down, that's all. The fact is . . .' He explained his predicament.

'Old soldier, are you?' said the policeman. He let go of Rowlands' arm. 'I was too young for the war. Wish I could've been in it, sometimes.'

'You didn't miss much.'

'No. Well, I don't suppose, under the circumstances, you need come down to the station after all.'

'Thank you, Constable.'

'Mind, you ought to get that eye seen to. Want me to call a cab to take you to the hospital?'

'I'm sure it looks worse than it is,' Rowlands said, trying to suppress the violent shivering that now threatened to overtake him. 'If you could just point me in the direction of Hill Street.'

'Why, it's right behind you. On your way home, were you, sir?'

'That's right.'

Because, Rowlands thought, what did he have to lose? If Willoughby was there, he could simply hand him the letter. But when he fumbled in his pocket, the letter

163

was gone. Dropped in the scuffle, he supposed. Well, there was no help for it – he must deliver his message in person. Conscious that the eyes of the young policeman were, in all probability, following his progress down the street, he made an effort to walk without betraying the agony each step cost him. As for which house it was, he hadn't the faintest idea. He chose a door at random. Rang the bell. 'Is this Lady Celia West's residence?'

'That's two doors down,' said the startled maid, before she had fully taken in the condition of the visitor. 'I say, you get off out of it,' she hastened to add. 'Or I'll call the coppers . . .'

But he was already walking away. Steadying himself on the railings, he came at last to what he hoped was the right door. Pulled the bell pull with all his might, letting lose a wild jangling within. But there was no reply. *Come on, come on, come on* . . . The house remained silent as the grave. He pulled the cord again. He was still holding onto it, as he felt himself begin to fall . . .

'Oh good. You're awake,' said a voice. Hers, unmistakably. He felt a dizzy surge of joy. He'd found her at last. Now all he had to do was to tell her what it was he had to tell . . . But when he tried to sit up, nausea rose in his throat. 'I should lie quiet for a bit, if I were you,' said Celia West.

He did as he was told. A silence ensued. Something, perhaps no more than the sound of an exhaled breath, made him think they were not alone. 'Who's there?' he said.

'Just ourselves,' she replied. 'It's the servants' night off. Why? Did you think I had company?'

He took a breath. 'I thought I might find Mr Willoughby here.'

'Whatever made you think that?' She gave a brittle little laugh. 'I'm afraid you're quite mistaken. He isn't here. Nor am I expecting him,' she added, as if it were important to make this clear. She must have come closer, then, for he felt a soft rush of breath upon his cheek. 'Goodness,' she said softly. 'They *have* made a mess of you, haven't they?'

It didn't occur to him until afterwards to wonder how it was she knew that there had been more than one assailant. Nor how, in the absence of anyone to help her, she had managed to carry a man of his size from the doorstep where he had collapsed to the sofa where he now lay. These questions only returned to trouble him later. All he could think of at that moment was that he had to warn Willoughby. 'You don't understand,' he said, making another effort to sit up. 'He may be in danger.'

'I'm sure Gerald can take care of himself,' she said. She laughed again, and he thought he detected a certain uneasiness in the sound.

'But your husband said . . .'

'Let's leave my husband out of this. Now,' she added, suddenly matter-of-fact, 'I've a glass of brandy here. If you raise your head a little . . . carefully, mind! I'll help you to drink it.' He did so, bringing his lips towards the glass. It was then that he caught a whiff of her scent, the same that had captivated him the first time she came to the office. Now it was mingled with another smell, one with which he was also familiar . . . An intimate, salty smell. At the realisation of what it was – what it *meant* – he felt the hot blood wash over him. *Could* it be? But there was no mistaking it. Sweat, and that other, animal smell, which was the smell of love-making. For a moment he froze, unwilling to believe the evidence of his senses. 'Careful!' murmured the woman now bending over him. 'You'll spill it all over you.'

He managed a sip of the stuff – *its* smell, and the burning taste of it, affecting him less powerfully than the shock of realisation that had come before. The smell of her warm bare skin. The smell of sex. He wondered, for a moment, if the beating he'd suffered had made him lightheaded, distorting his perceptions in this gross way, but knew that it had not.

'That should do you good.' She must have moved away from him towards the table, because there was a clinking sound as she set down the glass. 'Sing out if you'd like another, won't you?'

He nodded, not trusting himself to speak. He'd never been more aware of her nearness, of the physical fact of her. In those few seconds her being, which had been, for him, merely ethereal – as of a creature spun out of air, of tones of voice, of the faint rustle of clothing – now assumed solid flesh. With the scent of her in his nostrils – that unmistakably carnal smell – he couldn't stop himself picturing her thus. As a woman, with breasts and belly, and with arms and legs which, though doubtless as slender as fashion dictated, were made, not of air, but of flesh and blood . . . His own flesh could not help but respond to this beguiling image.

'If you can sit up a bit, I'll see what I can do for that eye of yours,' she said, her voice as coolly detached as it had always been. If she was aware of his confusion, she gave no sign of it. 'You look as if you've gone a couple of rounds with Jack Dempsey.'

It hurt him to laugh, but he didn't mind. He was grateful for anything that might distract him from the turmoil in his brain.

Smile for me, my honey dear,
As I kiss away each tear . . .

'That's better,' she said. 'You know, you had me quite worried for a while.' She must have come closer, again, although he wasn't aware that she was beside him until he heard her speak. *Strange, that*, he thought, half-drowsy with the pain in his ribs, and with the brandy he had drunk – because even the most light-footed woman usually made some kind of sound, if only a tapping of heels. Unless the floor was very thickly carpeted. He couldn't work it out. But then, there was a lot he couldn't work out. 'Now,' she was saying, and as she spoke the sour-sweet tang of her was overlaid by a sharper, medicinal smell. 'This is going to hurt quite a lot. Hold still.' She cupped his chin in her hand, and drew his face towards her. Electrified, he forgot to breathe for a moment. Seemingly oblivious to the effect she was having on him, she applied herself to the task of cleaning the wound with a piece of cotton wool soaked in iodine. He barely felt its burning, so on fire was he from her touch. 'Nearly done,' she said at last. 'I think you'll heal up beautifully.'

He mumbled his thanks. All the while, he was conscious of her face close to his; her breath upon his cheek; her gaze upon him. 'Can you really see nothing at all?' she said softly.

He shook his head. His mouth was dry. The words, when they emerged, sounded hoarse. 'I can tell light from dark. Shapes of things, sometimes. Otherwise nothing.'

'Perhaps it's best,' she murmured, 'if we keep it that way.' She shivered slightly.

Again, he was aware of something left unsaid, of an *atmosphere* in the room he couldn't explain. He strained his ears, but there was no sound. Unless . . . was that the sound of someone breathing? No, it was nothing. The sound of his own breath, in all probability. Still he couldn't rid himself of the uncanny sensation that he was being watched. He angled his head, to get the benefit of his 'good' eye. Was that dark shape against the light a human figure? Could it be that there was someone else in the room with them, after all? But she'd said they were alone, hadn't she? What reason did she have to lie? He was on edge, that was all – the result of shock, and the helpless confusion her presence inspired. 'Lady Celia,' he nonetheless persisted, forcing the words through bruised lips. 'Your husband has made certain *threats* against Mr Willoughby. I felt that I should warn him – and you . . .'

She laughed. 'You think I'm in some kind of danger from my husband?'

'I . . .' He knew he couldn't admit to what he knew. That conversation he'd overheard between her and Willoughby. *You don't know what he's done* . . . Her fear and disgust. *He forced me* . . . No, he could never confess to what he'd heard, nor would she have admitted the truth of it, if he had. 'I got the impression he meant what he said.' He was conscious of how lame it sounded.

'There's something you should know about my husband,' she said, evidently taking pity on Rowlands. His blunderings in the dark. 'He enjoys making people afraid of him.' She gave a small, dry laugh. 'But he seldom carries out his threats.'

Except when he knows that the victim won't fight back, thought Rowlands.

'So you see,' Celia West went on, in the languid tone she had used all along, as if she were discussing some completely unimportant matter: a minor change to a dinner menu, perhaps, or an order of sheets she wanted delivered. 'You really shouldn't give it another thought.'

'It's not Mr West I'm worried about,' he said abruptly. 'Although he made certain remarks about yourself and Mr Willoughby . . .'

'Lionel's always been a jealous man.'

'It wasn't your husband who set those thugs on me.'

Now it was her turn to be silent.

'Not that they were meant for me. It was Mr Willoughby they were meant for. And Giovanni Caparelli who set them on. Your husband's business partner.'

'Oh, I know all about Mr Caparelli,' Lady Celia said lightly.

He'd never known Edith angrier. 'How *could* you have gone off and left me like that? For all I knew, you might have been dead.'

'You knew I wasn't dead. I telephoned to say I was all right.'

'Yes, after you'd been gone nearly three hours. I was going frantic, thinking about what might have happened to you . . . and then to have that dreadful man from the pub come knocking on the door with the message . . .'

Like the rest of the street, they'd no telephone, and so this arrangement had to serve.

'It's just his manner,' he said. 'Bert's a good sort, really.'

'Casting aspersions,' she went on, ignoring this. 'He obviously thought you'd gone off on some kind of a spree . . .'

'I'm sorry. It was the only way I had of letting you know.'

'. . . and then when you *did* turn up, to see you looking like that. All covered in blood . . .'

'I wasn't covered in blood.'

'. . . and with your suit all torn. Really, Fred, you try my patience sometimes!'

She burst into tears.

'Edith, don't. It's bad for the baby.'

'A lot you care about that! You didn't give much thought to me – or the baby – when you went off, without a word.' A fresh storm of weeping overtook her. He tried to take her in his arms, to comfort her, but she pushed him away. 'Don't touch me.'

'Look,' he said. 'I've said I'm sorry. I never meant to frighten you.'

'What I don't understand,' she said, blowing her nose fiercely, 'is why you had to go out in the first place.'

'I told you. I had an important message to deliver to Mr Willoughby.'

'So important that it couldn't wait until morning?'

'Yes.'

Edith sniffed, as if she didn't quite believe him. 'And then getting set upon like that. It shows,' she went on, her tears giving way to tartness, 'what the West End is coming to, if one can't even walk the streets there without some . . . some *hooligan* attacking one.' He'd given her a necessarily simplified account of his encounter with Caparelli's men.

'Let's forget about it now, shall we? Given that there's no harm done.'

'If you could see the state of your face, you wouldn't say that.'

Feeling the state of it is quite enough, he thought. There'd be some fine bruises around his ribs, too, he supposed.

'You were lucky it happened in front of her house,' said Edith. 'If you can call it luck.'

He got up, wincing a little with the effort. 'Come on, let's go to bed. We can talk about all this in the morning.'

But she wasn't quite ready to let the subject drop. 'Yes, I must say, I got the shock of my life when that great big car of hers pulled up outside, and you got out,' she said. 'I thought for a moment the police were bringing you home. Next door didn't miss a thing, of course. How we'll ever live it down, I can't imagine.'

Chapter Six

The probable speculations of the neighbourhood regarding his whereabouts the previous evening were of less concern to Rowlands than what people in the office were going to say, when he turned up looking – as Celia West had put it – as if he'd been the wrong end of a prize fighter's left hook. With Edith's help, he'd managed a shave of sorts, although it was hard not to flinch at the touch of the razor against his raw skin. 'Keep still,' Edith told him. 'Unless you want another scar to add to your collection.' His suit would have to go to the cleaner's; he'd have to wear his old one. A good thing it hadn't yet been put out for collection by the British Legion, Edith said. Arriving at the office, he had to put up with more of the same. 'Ooh, Mr Rowlands! Whatever have you done to yourself?' exclaimed Miss Poole. 'Did you walk into a door or somethink?'

'As a matter of fact, I did.' It was easier than telling the truth. And walking into doors was a common enough accident for someone like him.

Mrs Gilbert no less solicitous: 'That's a nasty-looking eye you've got there, Mr Rowlands. However did you do it?'

Repeating the lie for her benefit, Rowlands reflected with a certain grim humour that his appearance had never been more commented upon in all the years he'd worked there. Until now, his colleagues, taking their cue from him, had learned to refrain from such comments. It suited him to be as invisible to them as they were, perforce, to him. Now it was as if the embargo on what his mother would have called 'personal remarks' had been lifted. Everyone, from Bert the office boy upwards, had an observation to make. Nor was his former O.C. any exception. At half past four, the buzzer for Extension 13 sounded: 'Step into my office a minute, would you?'

He realised that he'd been unconsciously dreading this moment all day. What on earth shall I say to him? he wondered. In the end, he said nothing, of course. As soon as he was in the door, he felt his hand grasped and warmly shaken. 'I w-wanted to say, good show,' said his former O.C., speaking rather fast. 'Jolly brave of you, taking on those ruffians like that. I say, they *have* made a mess of you, haven't they?'

To which Rowlands could only smile and shake his head, as if it were of no consequence.

'Took you for me, I shouldn't wonder. S-so Lady Celia said.'

'Yes, sir,' he managed at last.

'I was out late . . . at the th-theatre, as it happens . . . or I'd have copped it for sure!' There was something a little forced about Willoughby's laughter, Rowlands thought. Perhaps it was just embarrassment. 'Thanks to you, I've been spared a nasty black eye.'

'That's all right, sir,' Rowlands muttered, very much wanting this interview to be over.

But Willoughby wasn't yet finished with the subject. 'Lady Celia also said . . . that is, when she rang last night . . . that you'd an idea they were Caparelli's men who did this.'

'Yes.'

'What gave you that impression exactly? Did one of them say something?'

'No, sir. It was what Mr West said.' Briefly, he explained about the telephone call, and the letter he'd tried to deliver.

Willoughby listened to him without interruption. Then he said: 'I shouldn't p-pay too much attention to anything Lionel West says. He rather likes throwing his weight around, I gather.'

Rowlands said nothing.

175

'The important thing is that *she* shouldn't be drawn into any of this.'

'No.'

On that point, at least, they were in agreement, Rowlands thought.

He was just putting his coat on – rather more gingerly than usual on account of his bruises – when he heard the lift doors open at their floor. Rather late for a delivery, he thought, and in any case, all the lawyers had gone home. 'I'm afraid the office is closed,' he was on the point of saying, when his visitor spoke:

'Glad to have caught you, old man . . . I say! What's happened to your face? Been in the wars, what?'

Rowlands didn't bother to smile. 'Hello, Ralph. This *is* an unexpected visit.' Unprecedented, in fact. 'What can I do for you?'

'Oh . . .' After his initial ebullience, his brother-in-law seemed suddenly bashful. 'It's what you might call a delicate matter. Let's talk about it over a drink, shall we?'

'I can't stay long. Edith'll be expecting me.' And she'll be all the more anxious after last night, he thought ruefully.

'You've time for a quick one. Tell you what,' said Ralph. 'If you'll join me for a pint of the foaming, I'll run you home afterwards. Got the motor with me, you know.'

'That's decent of you,' said Rowlands, wondering

what had brought on this sudden burst of affability, 'but the train'll do me.'

'Suit yourself,' was the reply. 'The George, then? There's a nice little room at the back where we can be quiet. You still haven't told me,' he added, as they got into the lift and began to descend, with the faint groaning sound the mechanism always made, 'how you got that beastly black eye.'

'It's a long story,' said Rowlands. Nor was it one he was inclined to tell. Fortunately, Ralph seemed distracted by whatever was on his mind, and so there was no more conversation until they were seated in the Snug at the George, Rowlands with the pint of mild Ralph had insisted on paying for in front of him, the former getting started on the whisky he'd decided after some humming and ha-ing he'd prefer to beer, before broaching the subject that was uppermost in his mind.

'Bit of a what d'you call it . . . *conundrum*. That the right word?' he eventually began. 'I take it you know this West feller?'

'If you mean Lionel West, then yes, I have had some dealings with him,' said Rowlands cautiously. 'But nothing of any significance. Why?' Although, even as he awaited the reply, he knew it had to do with the conversation he'd overheard: with Ralph's fear and anger in the face of his interlocutor's smiling ruthlessness.

Ralph took another gulp of whisky before replying. 'The fact is,' he said, 'he wants to ruin me.' From the public bar next door came a burst of laughter. '*I should jolly well cocoa!' someone shouted. 'Oh yes,' Ralph went on. 'He's an unpleasant type, is Lionel West. I don't mind telling you I bitterly regret ever having gotten involved with him. But that's my nature,' he added with a gusty sigh. 'Too trusting by half. And now I'm paying the price for it.' He lowered his voice, although to the best of Rowlands' knowledge, they were the only ones in the room. 'I suppose I'd better come clean. About six months ago, he – West – asked if he might deposit a sum of money with the bank. Quite a large sum, as it happens. I agreed, as a favour, even though he wasn't one of our regular customers, and—'

'Ought you to be telling me all this?' interrupted Rowlands.

'Oh, you're *family*,' said the other. 'I'm sure you wouldn't say or do anything to show me up. Think how upset Edith would be,' he added casually. 'Anyway, the gist of the matter is that West wants his money back immediately even though the agreement was conditional on his leaving it in place for at least five years. Which has put me in a bit of a tight spot, I don't mind telling you! The fact is, the money isn't *there* at the moment. It's been . . . *invested* in various ways.' Rowlands thought of the grand house Ralph had bought so recently. 'and I couldn't get it back without . . . well, without going to an awful lot of trouble. But when I pointed this out to West, he just laughed in my face. "That's your affair, I'm afraid," was what he said. The man's a fiend,' said Ralph dejectedly.

There was a silence. Both men sipped their drinks. 'I need another one of these,' said Ralph, after a moment. 'Join me?'

'No thanks. I'm not sure,' Rowlands said carefully, 'that I'm really in a position to help, as regards large sums of money.'

On his way to the bar to replenish his glass, Ralph gave vent to a guffaw. 'Money! Oh, I wouldn't dream of asking you for *money*, old boy. You and Edith have little enough as it is. No, it was help of a different sort I was after . . . Another of these, if you'd be so good, landlord,' he said to the latter, who now appeared. He waited until the man had gone, before going on. 'The fact is, I was wondering . . . well, seeing as you've a certain clout with the individual we've been discussing . . . Oh, don't look so surprised! I saw you talking to him at our party, and very chummy you seemed. He was rather smitten with that sister of yours, too,' added Ralph slyly. 'Well, it seemed to me that a word from you . . .'

'I'm afraid you've got the wrong idea about my influence with Mr West. He and I aren't on friendly terms at all.'

'That's not how it seemed.'

'I can assure you, that's how it is.'

'Well then, what about his wife?' said Ralph, after a moment. 'You're great chums, Edith says.'

'Edith's exaggerating. I hardly know the woman. And, even if I did, I don't see what good my talking to *her* would do.'

'I see,' said Ralph bitterly. 'That's the way it is, is it?'

'There's really nothing I can do,' said Rowlands. 'I only wish there were.'

Ralph emitted another loud sigh. 'It's just that I'm at the end of my tether,' he said. 'What Diana will say when she hears . . . We might have to sell the house, you know.'

'I'm sorry,' said Rowlands gently.

The landlord returned with Ralph's whisky. The two men sat in silence until he had taken himself off. Then Ralph returned to his theme: 'A man like *that*,' he said, with a vehemence Rowlands hadn't heard him use before, 'doesn't deserve to *live*, in my opinion. I say, old man, you won't say anything about this to Edie, will you?' he added, putting his hand on Rowlands' sleeve.

Rowlands resisted the urge to shake it off. 'No,' he replied. 'I won't say anything.'

And indeed his brother-in-law's troubles receded into the background almost as soon as the two of them had parted, he to catch his train, and Ralph to drive back to his Surrey mansion, and the contemplation of all it had cost him. Because Rowlands had other things on his mind. Other people, to be precise. Since their encounter the night before – strange and dreamlike as it now seemed to him – he was unable to stop thinking about Celia West. All he could hear was her voice – its soft caressing notes echoing in his mind, over and over: *You know, you had me quite worried for a while* . . . The memory of her touch drove him to distraction. The way she'd run her hand down his face, before cupping his jaw in her hand, while she attended to his wounds, as if she were trying to learn its salient features by heart. He allowed himself to think what *her* face would feel like under his hand, and felt a shiver of desire run through him.

But it wasn't that alone which made him go hot and cold by turns, so that he wondered if he were coming down with a fever. No. It was something else. Something about the way she'd seemed to him that night, that had been different from all the other times they'd been together. What was it? He couldn't say. Only that it was connected with the animal smell of her, which had so disturbed him with its suggestion of carnal pleasures. It wasn't until later that night, as he was lying in bed, sleepless beside his wife's sleeping body, that it had struck him with the force of a blow to the viscera what it was. It *couldn't* be, he thought, and yet he knew it must be so . . . Because as he'd lain there, turning over and over in his mind the events of the night before, it occurred to him that there'd been something missing. Or rather, there'd been something that should have been discernible to his acute senses, that night in Celia West's sitting room, and something that should not have been. The first was suggested by the soft rustle of art silk, as his wife undressed before bed. Women's clothes – especially the clothes worn by women like Celia West – were full of such flutterings and swishings, even in that era of flimsy undergarments and short skirts. The absence of all such sounds from that room where, like Circe, she had held him enthralled, was what he remembered now.

The other thing was the smell – oh, not *that* smell –which had so aroused his senses, but another, almost as unsettling. Cigarette smoke. If it had been Celia West who'd been smoking, he hadn't heard a match being struck. Then it hit him: *she wasn't alone*. There'd been somebody else with her, and that somebody must have been Willoughby. It explained her strange lack of anxiety, on Willoughby's account, and also, perhaps, Willoughby's oddness towards him earlier that day. It explained something else, too: the sensation he'd had, all along, that something untoward was going on. The *atmosphere* in that room, of barely suppressed excitement; it was as if the air had been charged with static, like the seconds before a storm breaks. Because what he'd stumbled into, dazed and bleeding as he was, had been nothing less than an assignation between lovers. He recalled the tremor in her voice. The shocking intimacy of her touch. It had been a performance for her lover, not for him.

Yes, it all made sense to him now. The smell of her skin, and that muskier, animal smell which was the smell of love, he'd caught, as she first drew near. That would explain why there was no rustle of clothing, no brush of a silken sleeve against his face. She'd been naked, or as near as made no difference, as she tended to his wounds. Her lover had watched her as she did so, all the while smoking one of his Special Mixture cigarettes.

Another day went by at work with nothing to distinguish it from all the others, which was the way he preferred it; he'd had enough of the extraordinary. He got his train home at six and got off at his usual station and made his way back along the streets which led to 39, Gabriel Street just as he'd done a thousand, or nearer two thousand, times before. It wasn't until he let himself in at the front door that he knew something was different. 'Hello! Anybody home?' he called, pushing open the door to the sitting room, where a mysterious silence reigned. But they were in there, he could tell from the small, explosive sounds of laughter, and from something else in the atmosphere . . . A feeling of suppressed excitement, yes, but it was more than that. A feeling of . . . *triumph*, one might almost have said. 'Well,' he said loudly, 'since nobody seems to be at home, I suppose I'll have to make the tea myself.'

The giggles grew increasingly irrepressible. Somebody darted towards him across the room. Somebody flung their arms about his neck. 'Oh, Fred . . .'

'Why,' he said. 'Who can this be? Surely it's not my favourite sister?'

'Dear old Fred!' She kissed him soundly.

He winced a little. 'Steady on!'

'Oh, I'm sorry. Your poor face.' She studied him a

183

moment. 'The rotters. Edith told us all about it. I wish I'd been there – *I'd* have given them what for! But aren't you surprised to see me?'

'A little. It's sooner than expected, isn't it?'

'Your tea's poured,' interjected Edith, before her sister-in-law could reply.

He took the cup she had put into his hand. 'So who else is here?' he said. 'I can detect a child or two, I think . . .'

'Daddy, we were hiding!' cried Anne, delighted at this subterfuge, the success of which depended only on those involved keeping absolutely still. He would not have dreamt of spoiling his daughter's pleasure by pointing this out, however.

'And very good at it you were, too.' He ruffled her hair.

'Dottie wanted it to be a surprise,' said another voice.

'Hello, Viktor, old man. Well, it's certainly that. When did they let you out?' he asked, turning his head towards where he judged his sister to be standing.

'Girls, off you go and play,' Edith said sharply. He remembered, too late, that they'd agreed to say nothing to the children of Dorothy's having been in prison. 'They're too young to understand such things,' Edith had said, and for once, he'd agreed with her.

'Oh, let them stay,' he said. 'It's a celebration, after all. You must be glad to see your Billy,' he added to his sister.

'I should say so! I've missed him every single minute.' Dorothy must have caught hold of the child,

184

because there was the sound of a kiss. 'Have you missed your silly old mummy, too?'

'Yes,' replied the child. Then, after a moment's thought, 'Do we have to go home, now?'

'That depends,' said his mother, with a certain calculation in her tone. 'I suppose if you had the choice, you'd like to stay with your cousins, wouldn't you? Especially Anne. You're so very fond of Anne, aren't you?'

The child must have nodded, because Dorothy's next words confirmed her brother's suspicion that she was up to something: 'We'll have to see what we can arrange with Uncle Fred.'

Viktor had lost his job at the printer's, it transpired. 'It was on account of my union activities,' he explained, 'although that is not the reason they gave. My work is satisfactory, they said – they could not in truth say otherwise! – but they would rather give my job to a younger man. An Englishman also.' To make matters worse, he and Dorothy were being evicted from their house in Whitechapel. 'Somebody put the landlady wise to the fact that she'd been harbouring a jailbird,' Dorothy said, in a withering tone. 'Being a respectable sort, she couldn't put up with this a moment longer . . .'

Fortunately the children were out of earshot when she said this, having been shooed out into the garden after supper. Even so, it wasn't the most tactful thing she could have said in front of Edith, of whose attitude to the whole affair she must have been well aware. But that was Dorothy all over, Rowlands thought, never thinking through the consequences of anything she said or did.

'Of course we had been planning to move, as soon as the sale went through,' said Viktor, meaning the chicken farm, his brother-in-law supposed. 'But it appears that might take some weeks.'

If Rowlands hesitated at all before making his offer, it was at the thought of upsetting Edith. She was sitting next to him on the sofa. He felt her stiffen slightly, as if preparing herself for the worst. But damn it all, they couldn't let his sister and her family end up on the streets. Even though they'd little enough room for themselves. 'Well,' he started to say, 'if it's only for a few weeks . . .'

'Of course you must stay here,' said Edith, cutting across him. 'You can have the girls' room. They can go in the back bedroom. I'm sure we'll manage.'

'That's very good of you,' said Dorothy.

'Very good,' echoed Viktor. 'But then, you have been good to us already.'

'Don't mention it,' said Edith. 'You're family, aren't you?'

It was no more than the truth; still he knew what it had cost her to make the offer. Unobserved, he hoped, by the others, he gave her hand a squeeze.

It was five steps to the pavement from the front door, with its stained-glass panels set into a frame like that of a church window, *a poor man's Gothic*, he thought.

He listened for traffic, as he always did. The milk cart went by, with a clip-clop of horses' hooves, and the paperboy whistling on his bicycle. When he judged it was safe to do so, he crossed the street. To his right was the turning into Lessing Street, which would take him to Honor Oak Park. It was not a long road – two hundred yards or so – and he took it at a brisk pace, passing small front gardens smelling of privet, cats, and laburnum, where women emerging to shake out a duster or polish a step, passed the time of day with neighbours similarly inclined. 'Morning, Mrs Gillespie. How're you keeping?' 'Mustn't grumble, Mrs Price . . .' They always said that. As if there were in fact a great deal to grumble about. Turning left up the main road, he passed a row of shops: Briggs' the baker, exuding, at this time of day, the heavenly smells of bread just taken from the oven; Sawyer's the butcher, *smells of blood and sawdust*; Dawson's the newsagent, where he bought a copy of the *Express*; Rollinson's the ironmonger, setting out his stall with a crash of galvanised-metal buckets; Mabb's the greengrocer, *the crisp sweet smell of Kentish apples and the earthier smell of potatoes*. Mabbs, a friendly soul, called out a greeting. 'Fine day, Mr Rowlands . . .' He agreed that it was. Another three hundred yards brought him to the station. He arrived with three minutes to spare before his train.

On the platform, he unfolded his paper. He'd long ago adopted this subterfuge, which served, if nothing else, as

187

a screen against unwelcome approaches. From around him came the rustle of turning pages, and an occasional comment: 'I see Hot Night's 2:1 favourite for the Prince of Wales Stakes. Thought I might have a little flutter . . .' to set the tone of the day. The train arrived. He waited until someone else had opened the door, before getting into the compartment with all the rest. It was all just as it had always been, and would go on being forever.

Since that night when, he'd come to realise, she'd made such a mockery of him – as if, being blind, he were somehow less of a man – he'd been unable to stop thinking about her. Haunted by her, day and night, nights being the more inescapable. Because it was when he lay in bed, beside his wife – whose body, known to him in all its intimate particulars, had hitherto been enough for him – that the shameful way Celia West had treated him became all too apparent. Bluntly put, she'd ruined him for all other women, even, perhaps, the one who shared his bed. Not that he'd put this to the test lately, Edith's body having become, in these last weeks of her pregnancy, by mutual agreement, 'out of bounds', but he dreaded it might prove to be the case. That he'd never be able to take his wife in his arms again without the spectre of another woman rising up between them. It was in these moments, tossing and turning on his unrestful bed, that he'd almost come to hate her – Celia West. Now all he could hear was her voice, cooing softly in his ears; all he could smell was her smell, its heady mixture of sex and expensive scent.

Envisaging, as far as he could, from the memories at his disposal, a face, a beautiful face, he would never see. A body, no less beautiful, he would never touch . . . Oh yes, she'd ruined him, all right.

The more he reflected on that all too brief hour, the more he understood how limited his world had been. Such a solid, predictable world it was, with its narrow streets of mean little houses, its starched collars (clean every other day), its rolled umbrellas, its shillings in the collection plate on Sundays. Such a *respectable* world, and one so lacking in any sense of danger or beauty. It was as if he, and all the others like him, with their collars and umbrellas and shillings, had decide en masse that they'd had enough of danger and beauty, and all such things. Let those who could afford it seek excitement. For *them,* the collar-wearers, there was only hard work, and the satisfaction of 'putting a bit by'. How he despised them! Despised himself, too, of course. This was not a way to live, not when you'd been given your life back again, as he had been. Why hadn't he done something fine with that life, instead of becoming a miserable wage slave? A man who flicked switches for a living, and pushed wires in and out of a board.

Chapter Seven

He'd hung up his coat and had just settled in behind his switchboard when Willoughby came in, whistling that tune they'd been playing on the radio all week. 'Morning, Rowlands. How's the eye?'

'A good deal better, thank you, sir.' He was aware that he sounded stiff, but he couldn't help it. Since that night – still as vivid in memory as ever – his relations with his former O.C. had altered, and not for the better. No longer was he able to feel that sense of perfect respect, tempered with affection, *surely not too strong a word?*, he had once felt. Now their exchanges, kept to a minimum on his side, were polite to the point of awkwardness. 'I don't like being made a fool of,' Lionel West had said. Well, no more did he.

Not that his employer seemed aware of this change of attitude; or if he were, he made no allusion to it. 'Splendid.' He whistled another bar or two of the maddening little tune.

Ain't she sweet?
See her walking down the street . . .

'I thought you should be among the first to know,' he went on, 'that there's been a development. A break-through, you might say.'

'Do you mean with regard to the fire case, sir?'

'I do. The fact is . . .' Here Willoughby lowered his voice, as if afraid they might be overheard although, as far as Rowlands knew, no one else was in yet. 'Lionel West has said he'll make a statement. Outlining all the details. The fires, and Caparelli's part in arranging them. On condition,' he added wryly, 'that we keep him out of it.'

'That's good news, isn't it?'

'Oh, yes. It means our case is as good as won. The best thing is, *she* doesn't have to be involved.'

'I'm very glad to hear it.'

'Thought you might be.' He whistled another snatch of tune. 'Well, must be pushing along . . .'

'Yes, sir.'

'Oh, and Rowlands . . .' There was the faintly

percussive sound of a glass panel a little loose in its surrounding frame, as Willoughby opened the door of the inner office. 'If an Inspector Douglas rings, put him through at once, will you?'

An hour passed. He'd just finished connecting a trunk call to Mr Saville's office – the Margate matricide case, which was proving extremely tricky, with the accused now claiming to be suffering from amnesia, although all the evidence pointed to the fact that he'd been planning the thing for weeks – when there was the clashing sound of the lift doors being opened. A moment later, a man walked into the office, almost colliding with Bert, who'd just brought in the second post. 'Here!' he heard Bert say, with some indignation, 'Watch where you're going, can't you? Nearly knocked me flying, you did.'

But the stranger paid no attention to this, marching straight up to Rowlands' desk. 'Where's Willoughby?' he demanded. Both the cold fury with which the words were spoken and the accent with which they were pronounced told him all he needed to know.

'I haven't seen him today, sir,' he replied, quite truthfully. He offered up a silent prayer that Willoughby would not choose that moment to emerge from his office. 'Perhaps you'd like to leave a message?'

The interloper gave a short, and not very pleasant laugh. 'Tell him,' he said, 'that Giovanni Caparelli wants to see him.'

'Mr . . . Capa . . . relli,' Rowlands repeated

deliberately, writing it down on the pad in front of him. 'Very well, sir. I'll tell him. Will that be all, sir?' Hoping by this display of punctiliousness, to bring their interview to a speedy conclusion.

But for some reason the intruder seemed to want to prolong the conversation. There was a silence, during which Rowlands had the uncomfortable sensation that he was being studied. 'I know you, don't I?' said Caparelli, in a voice whose softness did not detract from its menace.

'I don't think so, sir.'

'Oh yes,' said Caparelli. 'I know you all right.' The Italian laughed. 'How's that eye of yours? A little better, I hope? You know,' he added, no longer laughing, 'you really should take more care. We don't want you to have another *accident*, now do we?'

Then he was gone, letting the doors slam shut behind him.

With fingers that trembled only a little, Rowlands pressed the buzzer. 'Mr Willoughby, we've had a visitor.' Briefly, he explained what had happened. 'I hope I did the right thing in sending him away, sir?'

'Quite right, Rowlands. But there's not a m-moment to lose. Telephone Scotland Yard at once, will you?'

But Caparelli, it seemed, was not so easily caught. He seemed, in fact, to have vanished into thin air. For when the Flying Squad arrived at his offices in Mincing Lane, they found nobody there but a couple of secretaries. A raid on the lock-up in Borough High Street proved more satisfactory. A further raid on the Sun Fire Insurance offices collected the obliging Mr Alexander, whose willingness to pass so many of Caparelli's claims had proved so lucrative for them both. Of the man himself there was no sign. 'Not a trace of him can we find,' said Inspector Douglas, who was in charge of the case. A Scotsman. His manner of speaking put Rowlands in mind of men he'd served with at Loos and Ypres. 'Hell-hags' the Germans had called them, on account of their kilts; also, perhaps, because they had the reputation of giving no quarter. 'Although I've had half the Metropolitan Police Force combing the Square Mile in search of him.'

'I blame myself,' said Rowlands. 'If I'd only managed to keep him talking a little longer . . .'

'Och, it's no' your fault,' replied the Inspector. 'A man like Caparelli has ways and means of making himself scarce. But never fear. We'll catch him yet. And once we've got him . . .' There was the sound of palms being rubbed briskly together. '. . . he won't find it so easy to get away. Oh no! Twenty years in a nice, safe cell is what our Mr Caparelli has to look forward to, I'd say.'

'And I, for one, am grateful that you *d-did* send him away,' interjected Willoughby, in whose office they were sitting. It was five o'clock; nearing the end of the working day. 'Because with a d-desperate character like that, who knows what might not have happened? Why, I might be sitting here with my throat cut . . .'

'Eye-talians are certainly partial to knives, by way of settling their disagreements,' said the Inspector. 'Although I believe Caparelli himself favours a Beretta semi-automatic pistol.'

'Then I am all the more grateful for Gunner Rowlands' quick thinking,' said Willoughby. The buzzer sounded on his desk. 'Do excuse me a moment, Inspector . . . Yes, Miss Johnson, what it is? I thought I said no calls . . . Oh, I see. Well, in that case . . . Yes, I'll tell him. It's for you,' he said to Rowlands, with the ghost of a smile in his voice. 'I believe congratulations are in order.'

By the time he arrived home, the worst of it was over – the women, with the efficiency their sex brought to the whole business, having tidied all the mess away. Only the smell of disinfectant gave a hospital aura to the house – that, and the prevailing quiet, was the only unusual thing. Dorothy must have taken the children off somewhere, he thought. Well, that showed sense on her part at least. He knew it hadn't been easy for Edith, these past few days, having the house so full, although on reflection, it might be of some benefit to her just now to have another woman around, even if that woman was one with whom she wasn't always on the best of terms. He very much hoped so. In the kitchen sat the midwife, having a cup of tea. 'You can go upstairs, if you like,' she said, in her soft Irish accent. 'Just for a minute, mind. Mother'll be wanting her nap.'

And indeed Edith was too tired to say more than a few words to him. Yes, she was feeling as well as might be expected. A bit uncomfortable, that was all. 'The baby's all right, isn't she?' she whispered. 'Another girl. You don't mind, do you, Fred?'

'I wouldn't have wanted any other kind,' he replied, with perfect truth. 'Now no more talking. You're to get some rest.'

'All right.' She was already half-asleep. He stooped to kiss her, inhaling, in that moment the scent of her warm body, its familiar smells overlaid by the sharp tang of placental blood.

'Time's up,' said the midwife. 'But you can have a hold of your lovely daughter, before you go.'

'Describe her to me, would you, Nurse?' It wasn't the kind of request he'd usually make of anyone but Edith. But his present mood of mingled exhaustion and euphoria overruled his natural reticence.

'She's beautiful – aren't you, my darling? Such a lot of hair, and those lovely big blue eyes . . .'

'Like her mother's.'

'. . . and such a fine pair of lungs! What a yell she let out when she came into the world, God love her . . . Here,' said the nurse, conveying the swaddled form of his sleeping daughter into his arms. It was then that the realness of Joan became apparent to him: her warmth and her weight, and her musky-sweet, unmistakable, baby smell. He breathed it in: blood and ashes. Very lightly, he brushed her forehead with his lips. She stirred, emitting small snuffling sounds, but did not wake. In that moment, he knew that he would die to defend her.

He was helping the midwife on with her coat, having ascertained from her what time she would call next day, when the back door opened and Viktor walked in. 'Is it good news?' he asked immediately. Rowlands told him that it was. '*Herzlichen Glückwunsch!*' he then replied, seizing the other's hand and shaking it vigorously. 'We will drink the little one's health tonight, *ja?*' Preoccupied with seeing the nurse off, Rowlands did not at first reply. Only when she had gone, after many admonitions that he was not to make too late a night of it, but was to 'get a good rest now, because we can't have Daddy looking peaky, now can we?', did the thought that had been hovering at the back of his mind now surface:

'Where's Dottie? Isn't she with you?' Although plainly she was not – his sister's presence not being one that could easily be overlooked. 'Only I thought . . .' He'd thought, or rather hoped, she might be prevailed upon to stay with Edith. They couldn't very well go off to the pub and leave the poor girl on her own.

'Oh, Dottie had to go out. A friend had need of her.' Viktor lowered his voice, although there was no one to overhear. 'A sad case. The man had promised to marry her, and then reneged on his promise, the swine. In her despair, the girl did a very foolish thing. She has made herself very sick.'

'I see.' He would rather he did not. 'So I suppose you've no idea when she'll be back? Dorothy, I mean.'

Viktor sighed. 'It could be very late. You know Dottie. She can never say no to someone who has need of her.'

Except when that someone is a member of her own family, Rowlands thought, and then reproached himself for the thought. Whatever one said about his sister, she had a big heart. 'Then I think our celebratory drink will have to be put off,' he said pleasantly. 'I can't leave Edith, you know.'

'But of course not!' was the reply. 'I will fetch the beers, *ja*? Then we will drink to our good fortune, in having two such women, you and I.'

In the flat grey fields, there was no sign of life. Only the bare stumps of trees, which had once been alive, and the twitch of something at the periphery of vision which might have been living, gave the lie to this. A child was crying. On and on it cried – would no one come to its help? He struggled up, as if out of a black pit, and found himself, gasping for breath, in his own bed at home. 'It's all right,' Edith said. 'Go back to sleep. I'll manage.' Because by then the wailing had stopped, to be replaced by the small contented sounds of a baby being fed. He slept once more, and woke again, perhaps an hour later. This time it wasn't the baby's crying that woke him but another sound, much softer: the click of a latch. This brought him wide awake. Taking care not to disturb Edith, or the baby, he got up and put on his dressing gown.

In the kitchen, he found Dorothy. 'You're very late,' he said. 'Or should I say early?' It was half past five by his watch.

'Yes,' she said. 'I was just going to make some tea. Would you like a cup?'

'Please.' He sat down at the table while she busied herself filling the kettle, and setting out cups and saucers. 'So,' he went on, 'how was your friend, when you left her? Viktor told me about it,' he added.

'He shouldn't have done,' she said. 'It's nobody's business but that of the people concerned.'

He thought she was being rather hard on Viktor. 'I asked where you were. He had to say something.'

'I know.' Then she said nothing more until after the kettle had boiled, silencing it just as it reached its shrieking crescendo. 'If it's all the same to you, I'd rather not talk about it,' she said, in a funny wooden voice that didn't seem quite like her. Suddenly she burst into tears. 'Oh, Fred, it was awful,' she cried.

'There now, you mustn't upset yourself.' He got up, and took her in his arms, stroking her hair as he had done when she was a child and something had gone wrong. After a while, her shuddering sobs quietened. 'That's better,' he said. 'Now, you're to sit down and drink your tea,' he went on, 'and then you're to get off to bed and get some sleep.'

'All right.' She allowed him to pour the tea, although in truth he made rather a mess of this, slopping half of it into the saucer. Then she sat silently while it cooled. Dead tired, she must have been, he thought afterwards, because she didn't even ask about Edith.

By the time he'd shaved and dressed, and got himself some breakfast – a bit of a scratch affair, but it didn't do to be overparticular about the consistency of his porridge or the thickness of his two slices of toast on this day of all days – he went up to see if Edith was awake. He found her feeding the baby. 'I've come to take your order for breakfast, madam,' he said: their old joke.

'Ooh,' she said. 'Breakfast in bed. What a treat!' As if it were champagne and caviar, instead of tea and toast.

'You'll be all right, then, old girl, until the nurse comes?' he said, when he had returned with the tray, and set it down where she could reach it.

'I'll be fine.'

'If you need anything, I'm sure Dorothy can fetch it,' he added, without conviction. He hoped his sister would spare Edith the details of last night's errand, although judging by how upset she'd been earlier, it seemed unlikely she'd refer to what had happened at all. 'I'll be off then,' he said. If he left now he'd be in time for the quarter to eight train. He kissed Edith, taking care not to wake the baby. 'Bye-bye, girls,' he said. Three of them now. It would be quite a household of females. Not that he minded; he'd had enough of the society of men in his Flanders days.

He was in the office by ten minutes past the hour. The telephone was ringing.

'Good morning. Saville and W—'

'Is he there?' said Celia West abruptly.

He felt himself flush. Try as he might – and he *did* try – he was unable to dispel the memory of their last encounter. 'I don't think Mr Willoughby's come in yet.' In the time – now over a week – since he'd been attacked, he'd exchanged no more than a few terse words with her. These brief conversations *'Put me through, would you?' 'At once, Lady Celia . . .'* made no mention of that meeting. It might never have happened at all. But he knew it had happened. That night, and all that had taken place in that brief hour they had been together, was seldom out of his waking thoughts. Nor were his nights exempt. It was if a fever had got into his blood. All he could think of was her voice, her touch. *Her naked body, so tantalisingly close to his . . .* 'I'll just check,' he said.

'Could you hurry?' she said. 'Only it's rather urgent.'

'Of course.' But there was no reply when he buzzed the extension. 'I'm afraid he isn't in his office. Shall I ask him to ring you as soon as he arrives?'

'Yes.' There was a curious flatness to her voice. 'Do that, please.'

There was a click, and the line went dead. For a long moment he sat there, his mind a blank. It was as if she drove all thoughts out of his head except those that were of her.

At a quarter past eight, Willoughby walked in.

Swiftly, Rowlands conveyed Celia West's message. 'It sounded urgent,' he ventured to add.

'Did it, indeed? Then you'd better get her for me straight away.'

She answered on the first ring.

'Gerald? Is that you?' He'd never heard her sound more agitated.

'It's Frederick Rowlands, Lady Celia. I've got Mr Willoughby for you now . . .'

'What's all this about?' he heard Willoughby say, and then she said, in a low voice: 'Oh, Gerald. Thank God. You've got to come at once. Something's happened.'

More than twenty minutes had passed, he noticed, with that part of his mind that kept track of the length of calls. A long time, even by their standards. He ran his fingers over the board to check that the number 13 doll's eye was still down, and inadvertently flicked the switch to open. He heard her say: 'Oh darling, I've been so frightened . . .'

'Shh. Everything's going to be all right. Listen, Celia. This is v-very important. Have you told the police you were at Claremont last night?'

'I . . . I don't think so.'

'Well, d-don't. In fact, say nothing about it to anyone. I'm coming over to Hill Street now; I shouldn't be more than ten minutes, if I can find a cab.'

'Oh darling, you will hurry, won't you? I don't think I can stand it a moment longer without you.'

He just had time to return the switch to its neutral position before Willoughby came dashing out of his office, knocking into one of the desks in his haste. 'Hell and damnation.' His voice sounded curiously hoarse. 'I'll be out of the office for the rest of the day, Rowlands. Something's come up. N-needs my urgent attention.'

'Yes, sir.'

'Anybody wants me, I'll be in as usual tomorrow. Take any messages, won't you?'

'Of course, sir.'

'Good show.'

The door banged shut behind him.

Rowlands was still thinking about what he'd heard when Carrie Gilbert arrived, murmuring about the buses. He cut her short as civilly as possible. But she seemed disposed to chat. 'So how *is* she?' she asked eagerly.

It took him a moment to realise it was Edith she meant. 'She's fine,' he replied. 'Very well indeed.'

'And the baby,' she rattled on. 'I want to hear all about the baby.'

Cursing the propensity of women to find such topics endlessly fascinating, he gave her as brief an account of his wife's travails as possible. Still she wouldn't be satisfied. 'Another girl, is it?' she asked, with a hint of wistfulness. Mrs Gilbert had no children. 'It wouldn't be fair to Wilf,' was all she'd ever said on the subject.

'Yes.'

'How lovely. Have you thought of a name?'

He answered her questions with as good a grace as

he could, although all he could think about was the conversation he'd just heard. *Something's happened* . . . How desperate she'd sounded! And what was it that Mr Willoughby had said about the police? Perhaps there'd been a burglary at Hill Street . . . although it was Claremont that Willoughby had mentioned. And why should it matter if she were there or not? He couldn't make it out.

The rest of the day passed without incident. He felt as if he were going through the motions. *Switch. Flick. Switch.* His hands seeming to act quite separately from his brain. It was with a feeling of immense relief that he heard the big clock outside his window strike half past five. He'd never been more thankful to go home. All the way back on the train to Honor Oak Park, the nightmarish refrain ran through his head: *Claremont . . . Claremont . . . Claremont . . .* Of course, he hadn't had much sleep the night before. Tiredness could make you jumpy. Even so, the clutch of alarm he felt as he walked into the, *surely unnaturally quiet,* house was out of all proportion. Stupid, to be so on edge about nothing. 'Hello?' he called. 'Anybody there?'

But then the children appeared. Serious Margaret, lively Anne, and Billy, his sister's child, who was neither serious nor lively, but only Billy. A funny little chap, he thought. Very much his mother's pet.

'Hello, Daddy.'

He gathered the girls to him, kissed each sweet-smelling

head in turn, and ruffled Billy's hair. 'You're very quiet, all of you.'

'Aunt Dorothy said we're to be quiet. Because of the baby,' said Margaret.

'Quite right. And what do you think of the baby?'

'She's very nice.'

'I helped Margaret make Mummy a cup of tea,' interjected Anne, perhaps feeling that the baby had been the centre of attention long enough. 'Billy helped,' she added grudgingly.

'That was kind of Billy. Now let me go and find Mummy.'

Edith was lying on the sofa, with a rug over her knees. She seemed pleased with the roses he'd brought. 'How sweet. Pink ones, too – that was clever of you.' Although it wasn't, he recalled too late, a colour she'd ever liked. 'Could you put these in water for me, Margaret? That child's been a marvel,' said Edith, when this request had been complied with. 'What with her running around after me – to say nothing of your sister – I haven't had to lift a finger all afternoon.'

'That's as it should be. How's the baby?'

'Asleep. Dorothy's just putting her down.' As she spoke, he heard his sister's step on the stairs. A moment later, she came in. 'Did she settle all right?' asked Edith, yawning.

'Good as gold,' was the reply.

'That's a relief,' said Edith. 'One forgets how little sleep one gets at first.' She yawned again. 'Have you brought a newspaper?' she said to Rowlands.

'Only the *Evening News*.'

She took it from him. 'Thank you, Margaret,' she said, the child having returned with the flowers. Their fragrance filled the air. 'Just put them there, will you?'

'I think Meg deserves a medal, don't you . . .' he started to say, when there was a gasp from Edith.

'Good God!' It was quite out of character for her to blaspheme; he'd learned not to do so in her presence. 'None of your army language,' she'd say, if he forgot himself. So the words were as shocking as if she'd used a much stronger oath.

His first thought was that she must have been taken ill. She was doubtless still weak from loss of blood. 'Edith, are you all right?'

Yes, yes,' she said, impatiently. 'I'm perfectly fine. It's him!' She flapped the paper under his nose, as if it might convey something to him.

'Who are you talking about?'

But she seemed incapable of explaining. 'I can't believe it,' was all she would say. 'It was only a few weeks ago that we were talking to him . . .' Her tone was half-fascinated, half-appalled.

'Who do you mean?' he said sharply, aware of something in the room beyond his control.

But she didn't answer. 'Out you go, girls, into the garden,' was all she said, in the high, bright tone she used when she was upset or angry. 'You too, Billy.'

'But Mummy . . .'

'*Off you go.*'

'What's happened?' he asked, when he judged the children were out of earshot.

'It's Lionel West. He's been murdered,' Edith said flatly.

He stared at her, unable to bring out a word.

'It's true. They found him this morning, at his place in Surrey. Shot dead.'

'But that's impossible,' Rowlands said, finding his tongue at last. 'I mean . . . I was only speaking to Lady Celia this morning,' he added foolishly. He thought of the call he'd intercepted. *Something's happened.* 'My God.' He fumbled for the back of a chair, and lowered himself into it, with the sensation that his legs were about to give way. 'Perhaps that was why she sounded so upset . . .'

'Do the police have any idea who did it?' said Dorothy.

His wife scanned the paper. Turned a page. 'No. They're appealing for witnesses to come forward,' she said. 'Oh, and the driver of a green Lagonda, seen in the vicinity, late last night.' She shuddered. 'I imagine a man like that must have quite a lot of enemies. Although he seemed pleasant enough, that time at Ralph's garden party.'

'Yes.' He hadn't liked the man – knew him for a bully and a brute, in fact. Still there was something chilling about the bare fact of it: *shot dead.*

'I'll tell you one thing, though, his wife won't be too sorry to be rid of him.'

'Edith, *really* . . .'

'Well, it's true, isn't it? Everybody knows they've led separate lives for years. And she won't be left poor, *that's* for certain.'

'Even so, I hardly think this is the moment . . .'

'Why ever not? She can't hear us.'

'No, but . . .' It was a question of delicacy, he wanted to say. Of good taste. To hear Celia West's marriage reduced to such crude banalities struck him as indecent.

'The baby's crying,' he said.

'I'll go,' said Dorothy.

Further discussion of what had happened was necessarily curtailed until after supper, when the children were in bed, although for those few hours, it proved hard to think of anything else. Murder. It had a dreadful sound. They had been joined by this time by Viktor, who had seen the headlines, he said, on the news vendors' stands as he came back from another fruitless trip to the Labour Exchange. His observations, like Dorothy's earlier, were mercifully brief. He was sorry for the man's wife, who had seemed a pleasant enough young woman, he said – if somewhat thoughtless and self-centred, like all her class. Of the man himself he preferred to say nothing, since there was nothing good to be said. He and Dorothy had gone off for a walk, the evening being a fine one. It was then that Edith unfolded the paper once more. 'Would you like me to read you the full report?' she asked.

'If you wouldn't mind,' Rowlands replied. He was

still angry with her for what she'd said about Celia West. Making her out to be some kind of gold-digger. If you only knew the truth of it, he thought.

'Very well.' She cleared her throat. '"*Police were called this morning to Claremont Court, the Surrey mansion of financier Mr Lionel West (47). On entering the handsome Georgian property, they found a grisly scene: the body of a man in his forties, later identified as Mr West, was found in the library, dead from a single gunshot wound to the heart. Entrance to the house is thought to have been effected through a downstairs window, in which a broken pane was found. Signs of a struggle suggested that Mr West may have attempted to overpower the intruder, before meeting his untimely end. The body was discovered at six o'clock this morning by Miss Elsie Binns (18), a housemaid, and was later identified by Mr West's wife, Lady Celia West (25), who had spent the night at the couple's house in Hill Street, Mayfair, after returning from a party . . .*"' Edith paused for a moment, as if to let the implications of this sink in. '"*Police have appealed for witnesses, and in particular for the driver of a dark green Lagonda, seen in the vicinity at around midnight, to come forward. Mr West is survived by his wife. There are no children.*" Perhaps it's just as well,' she concluded, putting down the paper. 'About the children, I mean.'

'Perhaps.'

'I expect she'll marry again. She's still young, after all. And with all that money . . .'

'Yes. Edith, do you mind if we don't talk about this just now?'

'Not a bit. I was forgetting,' Edith said coolly, 'that she's a particular friend of yours.'

The office was quiet as the tomb that Saturday morning, with only a couple of the lawyers in, and so Rowlands spent the morning putting his files in order. It was a system he'd devised himself, using a sequence of holes punched into the upper right-hand corner of each file, for ease of recognition. A rudimentary Braille. He'd got the idea from his time at the Lodge. 'You should always be able to identify a document with the merest touch of the fingertips,' the Major had said. The original system on which Louis Braille had based his language of dots and spaces was called 'night-writing', he'd added. It had been intended for the use of soldiers in the field. 'For passing messages in the dark, d'you see? Just what we're doing ourselves, every day . . .' It was the sort of job that could be done with the minimum of effort, leaving one's thoughts free. Time and time again he contemplated the knowledge that had come into his possession: Claremont, and the fact of her presence there last night, which had to be concealed . . . 'Say nothing about it to anyone,' Willoughby had said. But why, Rowlands asked himself. *Why?*

At midday, the telephone rang. It was the Inspector, his tone drier than ever. 'Is himself there?' he enquired.

'Mr Willoughby hasn't been in today, Inspector.'

'Pity,' was the reply. 'I wanted to let him know that we've arrested Caparelli.'

'Oh!' In all the excitement of the past twenty-four hours, he realised that he hadn't given a single thought to the fire conspiracy case. 'That *is* good news. Would you like me to try his home number?'

'Arrested him for murder, that is,' continued Douglas. *Murr-da*. 'Picked him up two hours ago in the Great North Road. Driving a green Lagonda.'

In spite of the heat of the day, Rowlands felt himself grow cold all over. 'I don't understand. You can't mean he's the one suspected of killing Lionel West?'

'That's exactly what I do mean. He and West were partners, you know. But *that's* usually no impediment to murder.'

'Has he confessed?' asked Rowlands, still trying to make sense of this news.

The Inspector laughed. 'Not he. Swears blind he had nothing to do with it, of course. But we'll wear him down eventually. The funny thing is,' Douglas went on, 'he admits he was at the house last night. Says he went to see West – even owns up to having quarrelled with him. But draws the line at having killed him.'

'Did he say what the quarrel was about?'

'Och, aye. He had a great deal to say on that score. It seems he wasn't best pleased at West's having decided to bear witness against him in the fire case. No, he wasn't too pleased about that.'

Of course, thought Rowlands. A man with Lionel West's ambitions would never have allowed himself to be compromised by association with anything his erstwhile business partner might have done. There had been too much at stake for that. He recalled Willoughby's gleeful remark of a few days before: *It means our case is as good as won* . . . Meaning the case against Caparelli. With West willing to testify against him there'd be no need to wait until the bogus claim for the warehouse fire came in. They could proceed straight away. No wonder Caparelli had been so angry that day. Thinking how close Willoughby had come to a bullet in the heart made him shiver.

Chapter Eight

Lionel West's murder was not, as it happened, the only violent crime to have taken place that summer. Perhaps the hot weather had something to do with it, Rowlands thought, exacerbating passions that might otherwise have remained in check. Whatever the reason, hardly a day seemed to pass without the papers reporting some horror. *On the 1st August, the bodies of Percy Williams (46) and May Kelly (22) – rumoured to have been lovers – were found by a passing labourer, in a copse outside Lymington. Both had been shot dead by the gun found in Williams' hand. On the 3rd of the month, Harry Trotman (40), of Queen Mary Road, Sheffield, was brought before local magistrates on a charge of wilfully murdering his son, Ernest, aged seven, by striking him on the head with a poker. On the 7th, Alfred Thornton (39), of no fixed abode, was charged at Southwark Police Court with cutting a woman's throat in a railway carriage. At Tower Bridge Police Court, on the following day, Arthur Merchant (26), of Long Lane, Bermondsey, was charged with the murder of his wife Mary (24), and his sons Edward, aged four, and Robert, aged seven months, by striking them each several blows with an iron firedog.*

But these events merited no more than a paragraph in the newspapers. They were commonplace crimes, committed by ordinary people. Cut-throat razors, pokers, firedogs, and hatchets were, for the most part, their chosen weapons of dispatch (the Lymington lovers' suicide pact being the exception, but Percy Williams had been on active service in France, and retained his service revolver). In short, they were crimes of poverty, fuelled by drunkenness and despair. For the readers of *The Times* and the *Morning Post*, they were crimes over which one could shake one's head, and wonder what the lower orders were coming to. Whereas *this* crime – the cold-blooded shooting of a wealthy man by a professional villain (and a foreigner, at that) – had about it something else. Call it glamour, if you will. The glimpses afforded by newspaper coverage of the trial into the life led by

Lionel West and his circle were thrilling enough, for was this not a man who had been presented to the King, and vacationed at Biarritz and Monte Carlo?

And what of the woman in the case – the beautiful Lady Celia? She was surely worth a whole column, with her chic black dresses – the latest Paris models – her hats, her gloves, her shoes, her furs, her pearls? As a married woman, you could not say she belonged to a fast set, and yet what kind of married woman went about so much without her husband? Such speculations gave a delicious flavour to an otherwise humdrum reality, revealing a world of hitherto unsuspected irregularity behind the bland formalities of the court circular.

If Rowlands felt any misgivings at the deception he was practising, these were alleviated by his conviction that he was acting for the best. All he wanted was to find out the truth. That couldn't be wrong, surely? As for what he did with the knowledge, once he'd found it, he couldn't afford to worry about that yet. He'd know the right thing to do, he thought, the way he always had. What mattered was to be in possession of all the facts. Because sitting here, at his switchboard, was the only time he felt in control. With its cords and switches allowing him access to any one of a hundred conversations in any given day, it might become for him an instrument of detection, making him privy to information not readily available to others. How could he not take advantage of the fact?

He'd have been a fool not to. For once, he needn't be at a disadvantage to everyone else, but ahead of the game. Even so, he could feel his heart beating unnaturally fast as he made the call. Front key back. Cord inserted into jack. The connection made, and the Mayfair operator answering. *Number, please.* He gave the number. *One moment, please.* And then the ringing tone.

'Mayfair four-two-nine-oh . . .'

'Is that Lady Celia West's residence?'

'Her ladyship is not receiving calls at present. Who is that, please?'

'Inspector Douglas of Scotland Yard,' he said, making as good a fist as he could of the policeman's Scots accent. 'We're investigating the murder of Mr Lionel West.'

'Oh!' The girl sounded frightened, now. 'I'm not sure I ought . . .'

'Nothing to worry about, Miss . . . What did you say your name was?'

'Meadows, sir.'

'Christian name?'

'Agnes, sir. But I'm not sure I . . .'

'Just routine questions, you know. Can you tell me what time your mistress came home, the night before last?'

'One o'clock, sir. I was sitting up for her.'

'Been out for the evening, had she?'

'Yes, sir. Mrs Fisk's party, sir.'

'Of course. We'll be speaking to Mrs Fisk. And what happened then?'

'What happened when, sir?'

'I mean after Lady Celia came home. You turned in, I suppose?'

Yes, sir. Her ladyship said I needn't wait up.'

'But there was no need, surely, if she'd gone to bed?'

'No, sir. But she was going out again, you see . . .'

'Was she, indeed?' His heart was hammering. He did his best to make his voice calm and steady. 'And where might that have been?'

'Her ladyship didn't say, sir.' She hesitated a moment. 'For a drive, I suppose. She says it helps her sleep.'

'For. A. Drive . . .' he repeated, with the heavy deliberation of the born policeman. 'Very good. We're almost done now. All I need to know is what time your mistress came back.'

'I couldn't say, sir. I was asleep, you see.'

'Of course you were. Well, thank you, Agnes. You've been a great help.'

'Thank you, sir.'

'One other thing . . .' He tried to make his voice sound as gruffly professional as possible. A voice you could trust. 'No need to worry your mistress about all this, just now. We'll have questions enough for her later.'

'I understand, sir.' The girl's voice wavered slightly. 'Oh, sir, you will catch him, won't you? The man that's done this dreadful thing . . .'

'Don't you worry yourself about that,' said Rowlands, his mind still reeling with the implications of what she'd told him.

'"*Dramatic scenes took place in Court Number 1 at the Old Bailey yesterday . . .*"' Edith read aloud, '"*. . . on the third day of the* Crown *v* Caparelli, *where the defendant stands accused of the murder by gunshot of Mr Lionel West, the entrepreneur. Calling Lady Celia West to give evidence, Sir William Davenant, KC, acting for the Crown, first conveyed his deepest sympathies for Lady Celia's loss, then asked her to say in her own words what her late husband's relations had been with the accused. Speaking in a low voice, at times barely audible to those in the gallery, Lady Celia, who was wearing a plain black dress and coat, ornamented with a diamond brooch, replied: 'I believe Mr Caparelli may have been a business acquaintance of my husband's . . .'*"' Did you say something?' his wife said.

'Just clearing my throat.'

'Then I'll go on, shall I?' She gave the paper a cross little shake. '"*Sir William thanked Lady Celia for her clear and succinct answer, and said that he was fully sensible of the ordeal it must have been for her, to appear before the court that day, under such trying circumstances. Cross-examining, Mr Bernard Stansfield asked Lady Celia if she was aware that her late husband and the defendant, Mr Caparelli, had been in partnership together? The following exchange then took place:*

Lady Celia: 'My husband was not in the habit of discussing his business affairs with me.'

Mr Stansfield: 'Be that as it may, Lady Celia, I should like you to answer the question . . .'" Where are you off to?' Edith said, as Rowlands got to his feet.

'Just going outside for a smoke. You carry on with your paper.'

'Oh, *I'm* not particularly interested in the affair,' she said. 'I thought you were.'

'Not really. If you want to know, I'm a bit fed up with it all.'

'I know exactly what you mean,' said his wife, casting the paper aside with an exaggerated yawn. 'I suppose they have to fill the newspapers with something.'

Of course, as he was well aware, he wasn't being quite straight with her, nor she with him, if it came to that. Although the greater fault – call it lack of candour, or downright dishonesty – was certainly his, he thought grimly. In the past few weeks, he'd become quite a practised liar. But there were limits. Because sitting there, listening to an account of a trial whose every detail was already known to him, through the simple fact of his having been there in person, was too much, even for one with his new-found taste for dissimulation. Oh, he'd meant to tell Edith that he'd attended the trial that day, but somehow the opportunity to do so hadn't arisen. Then it was too late – a lie having been persisted in becoming that

219

much more of a lie. Adding to his feelings of guilt was the sense of having been, somehow, in collusion with Dorothy about the matter.

It was all because he'd borrowed one of Viktor's hats. He himself no longer possessed such an article, never having worn a hat since he'd lost his sight. Hats shaded one's eyes – it was what they were designed to do. As a rule, he wanted all the light he could get. And so, as he was on the point of leaving, he took what he judged to be the least disreputable of his brother-in-law's various items of headgear from the stand in the hall. It wasn't until Dottie spoke that he realised she must have been standing there all the while. 'I should try the fedora,' she said. 'The homburg doesn't really go with that coat.'

He couldn't restrain a nervous start. 'Thanks. I meant to ask, only . . .'

'Oh, Vic won't mind a bit,' she said. 'Here, let me . . .' She adjusted the angle of the brim for him. 'There! That's better. You look quite presentable, dressed like that. Going somewhere special?'

'Not really. That is, I thought of going along to the Old Bailey.'

'Ah.' She seemed to consider this. 'To watch that murder case being tried, I suppose,' she said.

'Yes. I . . .'

'Of course you know her, don't you?' said Dorothy. 'Celia West. We met her that day at your brother-in-law's, as I recall.'

220

'Yes.' He was conscious of lowering his voice, although to the best of his knowledge there was no one else in the house but themselves. 'Listen, Dottie, I wonder if you'd keep it to yourself for the present – that I'll be attending the trial, I mean. Only I haven't yet had a chance to mention it to Edith.'

'Oh, don't worry,' his sister said. 'I won't breathe a word.'

By the time he reached the court, a crowd had gathered in the street outside – he could hear its excited murmur, like that of a swarm of flies about to descend on a piece of carrion. He elbowed his way through, provoking indignant mutterings from some, 'Hi! Watch where you're going, can't you?', and climbing the broad flight of stone steps that led to the doors of that austere edifice, over which, he dimly recalled, the figure of Blind Justice brandished her sword. A set of scales, too, if he wasn't mistaken. That was to symbolise that everyone was equal under the law. Unless it was to point out how easily the balance of a life might be upset – by misfortune or through wrong doing, it mattered not. There was a queue for the public gallery; he joined this, shuffling one step at a time up the stairs by which it was reached. All the seats were already full, he discovered, but then a woman at the end of a row moved up for him. She was youngish, he guessed from her voice, no more than thirty, and she smelt of Parma Violets. He was uncomfortably reminded of the girl in St Mary Woolnoth, the one who'd watched him as he listened to the music. His new acquaintance, too, seemed disposed to make friends. 'Come far?' she enquired. He said that he had not. 'I'm up from Dagenham, visiting my sister. Thought I'd make a proper day of it.' She spoke as if attending a murder trial were merely a superior form of theatrical entertainment, which in a way it was, thought Rowlands. 'I must say, I *do* like him,' she went on, referring, he gathered, to Caparelli. 'Quite a card, *he* is! I think he's like Ronald Colman, with those dark looks, but my sister says Valentino . . .'

She prattled on. He was glad when the usher called for silence, and the play, as it were, could begin. From the excited stirring of people in the seats around him, he deduced that the leading actor in this particular performance had been brought up from the cells, and now took his place in the dock. 'Poor soul,' whispered Rowlands' companion. 'He's looking ever so pale.' Caparelli's was not to be a speaking part that day, however. Instead, it was members of what one might have designated as the supporting cast, who held the stage. The housemaid who had found the body. The murdered man's French valet. Lady Celia's personal maid. Her chauffeur. All were questioned and cross-questioned, with a thoroughness which might have seemed tedious, had the events alluded to not been so sensational.

A great deal of time was devoted to what seemed,

on the face of it, to be inconsequential details. What was the *exact* time, the defending counsel, Mr Stansfield, wanted to know, that M. Gaspard (the valet) had heard a car draw up outside? Oh, so he hadn't heard it *draw up*. He thought it was driving away. He – Mr Stansfield – hoped that the members of the jury would appreciate the distinction. So what time did he – M. Gaspard – hear this vehicle *drive away*? Was it one a.m.? Two a.m.? Later than that? And how could he be sure it was the *same* car he'd heard arrive earlier? Oh, so he *hadn't*, in fact, heard Mr Caparelli's car arrive? Then the other car might very well have been an entirely different one, mightn't it? This exchange was typical of the defence lawyer's strategy, Rowlands began to see, sowing doubt in the minds of the jury without explicitly contradicting the witness' statement.

It did seem to Rowlands that the said witness, Pierre Gaspard, was uneasy about something, although that might have been merely the result of being cross-questioned by so adept an inquisitor as Bernard Stansfield, whose refusal to let even the most apparently trivial fact go unchecked bordered on the relentless. Whatever the reason, Gaspard grew increasingly monosyllabic in his answers to Mr Stansfield's questions, his French accent making some of his replies unintelligible to all but the keenest ear, so that the judge was obliged on more than one occasion to ask him to repeat himself.

When it came to the turn of the unfortunate housemaid, Sir William, acting for the Crown, was all fatherly solicitude. She was Elsie Violet Binns, of 11, Peabody Buildings, Islington. She had been in the employ of Mr West and Lady Celia for the past twelve months, had she not? She confirmed in a faltering voice that this was so. Would Miss Binns oblige the court, Sir William continued, by recounting in her own words the events of the morning of July 29th? 'Yes, My Lord,' replied Elsie Binns, evidently overawed by the magnificence of her interlocutor's manner, as much as by her surroundings.

'You need not address me in that way, you know,' said Sir William, to general amusement. 'That is only when you are speaking to His Lordship. "Sir" will do quite well enough for me.'

'Yes, My . . . sir,' said the girl.

'Now, Miss Binns. Will you tell us what happened that morning?'

'Well,' was the halting reply. 'I got up, see?'

'Indeed you did. And what time was this?'

'Half past five. And then I had my wash and . . .'

'I think we might dispense with your ablutions. At what time did you descend?' The girl must have stared at this, for Sir William amended smoothly, 'I mean, what time did you go downstairs?'

'Six o'clock sir. Same as usual.'

'And so it was at six a.m. that you entered the library, I take it?'

'No, sir. Not till five past. Because I always shake out the doormats first of all, sir. I like to get a breath of air,' she added in a small voice, as if conscious this might be seen as reprehensible.

'Very well,' went on the prosecuting counsel, with the air of one displaying infinite patience, 'five minutes past six, then. And was it your habit to start with the library?'

'No, sir. Usually I'd begin with the morning room, to get the fire drawing nicely before they'd come down for their breakfasts, and then do the drawing room and after that, the library and the smoking room, but that day I went straight to the library, after I'd shaken out the doormats, see, because I could see that the lights had been left on. And so I knew the fireplace would want sweeping out, and the room airing, which it always did when he'd been sitting up late smoking . . .'

'By "he", I take it you mean your employer, the late Mr West?'

'Yes, sir.'

'And what did you find when you went into the library at five minutes past six?'

There was a pause. Rowlands, leaning forward in his seat, heard what sounded like an intake of breath. 'Oh, sir,' said the girl, sounding close to tears. 'It was awful.'

'Now then,' said Sir William. 'No need to upset yourself. Just tell us calmly what you saw.'

'Him, sir.'

'Mr West, you mean?'

'Yes, sir. He was just *sitting* there, in his dressing gown . . .' Tears threatened to overwhelm her once more. 'Dead as a doornail, bolt upright in his chair.'

'And you could be absolutely sure of this from where you were standing – that he was dead, I mean?'

'Oh yes, sir,' said Elsie Binns. She blew her nose sharply, adding in a firmer voice: 'Blood all over, there was. On his dressing gown. Soaked through, it was, all down the front. On the chair. On the carpet. I noticed that particular,' she added. 'Blood's a difficult stain to get out of carpets.'

Lurid details such as these aside, there was not much more to be learned from Miss Binns' testimony. Having made her frightful discovery, she had at once called for help, she said. Help had arrived in the form of 'Monsieur', Mr West's 'Man'. It was he who had telephoned for the police. Rowlands thought he detected a glimmer of animosity towards the Frenchman, in her account of this. 'Monsieur said as I was to leave the room exactly as it was,' she said. '"Touch nothing", he said. As if I would've!' she added, with some resentment. What had been the condition of the room, Sir William wanted to know. Could she describe it for the court? She need not, he added, say anything further about Mr West. Invited to expand on a topic about which she was something of an expert, the clearing-up of other people's mess, Elsie Binns gave a succinct account of what it was she had found. The overturned chair and the cooling ashes in the grate. The broken glass on the floor, and the smell of whisky, not quite masking another, more dreadful smell . . .

After Mr Stansfield, the defending counsel, had declined the opportunity to question the witness further, the court rose for lunch. Going outside for a smoke, Rowlands found that the crowd had thickened, its ranks evidently now augmented *Gangway there! Press!* by photographers and newspaper reporters. Because of course the day's main attraction had yet to arrive. It occurred to him in that moment that the last thing he wanted was for anyone – and that person in particular – to see that he was there. And indeed a few minutes later, as a car drew up, to a chorus of whistles and shouts from the gentlemen of the press, he drew the borrowed hat down over his eyes. There came the slamming of a car door, followed by an excited murmur from the crowd, as Celia West, accompanied by her lawyers, Rowlands supposed, swept up the steps and into the building; a progress marked, for him, by the surging forward of those around him, and by an increase in the volume of their voices. When he was satisfied that the danger was past, he slipped back inside the building.

Back in his seat, saved for him by the thoughtful Parma Violets, Rowlands settled himself down to listen. From around him rose the minute sounds – creaks, sighs, intestinal rumblings – that denoted the presence of others: participants in the stately ritual of the trial, or, like himself, spectators of it. Although strictly speaking, you'd have to call him an auditor, he thought. It was something he'd become good at, over the years: paying attention. Others might rely on the evidence of their eyes; he, with so much less to go on, was obliged to make the most of what there was. When she came in, he knew it before anyone had spoken, by the whispering, like that of the wind passing over a cornfield, that moved around the courtroom. 'Lovely she looks, in that black costume,' sighed his neighbour, close to his ear. 'Like Gloria Swanson, only fair . . .'

Certainly there was something of the film star about Celia West, although he could not have said which one. Going to the pictures wasn't something he got much out of any more; the theatre was more to his taste. And there was a smoothness about Lady Celia's performance in the witness box that day that suggested a well-rehearsed West End production. Something starring Miss Lawrence, perhaps (they'd seen her last year in *Oh, Kay!*) or the one with the pretty laugh who'd played opposite Mr Coward in *The Constant Nymph*.

The witness took the oath, and, in a low voice – which might have been inaudible to anyone less attuned to its cadences than Rowlands – confirmed her name and address.

'Lady Celia,' said the counsel for the prosecution,

in his mellifluous baritone. 'Allow me to offer my condolences – and, I feel sure, those of the rest of the court – for your sad . . . your *very* sad loss. I very much hope that we will not have to detain you long.'

'Thank you.' The words, though spoken in an undertone, reached Rowlands as if they had been meant for him alone. Conjuring up a memory of the last time they'd been together. Not that you could compare that . . . *intimacy* . . . with this public show.

'Now, Lady Celia, I have one question I should like you to consider, if you would be so kind. I should like you to tell me in your own words what your late husband's relations were with the accused.'

'I believe Mr Caparelli may have been a business acquaintance of my husband's.'

'Thank you for your admirably clear and succinct answer, Lady Celia,' said Sir William. 'I should add that I am fully sensible of the ordeal it must have been for you, to appear before the court today, under such trying circumstances. I have no further questions, My Lord.'

'Do you have any questions for the witness, Mr Stansfield?' enquired Mr Justice Trevelyn, with an air of weary patience.

'I do, My Lord.'

'Then you may proceed.'

'Thank you, My Lord,' replied Mr Stansfield. 'Lady Celia,' he said, in a sharper tone, 'I wonder if you are aware that your late husband and the defendant, Mr

Caparelli, were in partnership together? That is rather more than a mere "business acquaintance", do you not agree?'

'My husband was not in the habit of discussing his business affairs with me,' said Celia West coolly.

'Be that as it may, Lady Celia, I should like you to answer the question.'

Rowlands found he was holding his breath. But then came an intervention.

'I believe Lady Celia has already answered the question,' said the judge. 'When a lady says she and her spouse do not discuss business together, I think we can infer that she was unaware of the relationship alluded to.'

'Yes, My Lord,' said Mr Stansfield, not sounding altogether convinced.

His Lordship was not quite finished, however. 'In my opinion,' he went on, to general laughter, 'it is a very good thing that wives do not interest themselves overmuch in their husbands' affairs. For my part, the last thing I feel like, on returning to my own hearth after a day spent quibbling over the finer points of English Law, is to have my rulings rehashed over the tea table.'

'I take your point, My Lord,' said Mr Stansfield. 'Lady Celia . . .' Again, his voice had a colder sound. 'I should like you to return your thoughts to the night of July 28th. Could you describe the events of that evening, for the benefit of the court?'

Sir William must have risen at this point. 'My Lord,'

he said, his tone one of profound disappointment. 'The court is well aware of the events to which Mr Stansfield refers. It seems to me that there is little to be gained from asking Lady Celia to describe them – a task which is bound to be distressing for her.'

'Nonetheless . . .' Stansfield again, it was better than a radio play, Rowlands thought, 'I should like to hear Lady Celia's account.'

'Proceed, Mr Stansfield. But try not to be too long about it. One can only hope,' added his Lordship, in a ruminative tone, 'that it is not beyond the bounds of possibility that we might conclude these investigations before tea.'

'I will do my best, My Lord.' The Counsel for the Defence turned once more to the witness. 'Lady Celia, you were, I understand, absent from Claremont Court on the night of your husband's murder?'

'Yes.'

'You were attending a party, I believe?'

'A private dinner. With friends.'

'But not your husband . . .'

'I fail to see what bearing this has on the matter in hand, My Lord,' objected Sir William.

'Do get to the point, Mr Stansfield.'

'Yes, My Lord. Lady Celia, at what time did you return home after this private dinner?'

'I believe it was around one.'

'One in the morning. Rather late for a quiet dinner with friends, was it not?'

'I don't know,' she said, in a bored tone. 'I suppose so.'

'Did you go straight to bed on your arrival at your house in Hill Street?'

'I don't remember. I might have done.'

'Because a witness has said she saw you going out again in your car. A midnight-blue Hispano-Suiza, is it not?'

'Yes, that's right – I remember now. I went for a drive. To clear my head. I often do, after a late evening . . .'

'Do you, indeed? And where did you go, at just after one o'clock, on the morning of July 29th?'

'I don't recall exactly. Around and about.'

'Is it conceivable, Lady Celia, that your drive might have taken you in the direction of Claremont Court?'

Sir William was on his feet again. 'My Lord, this is outrageous.'

'It does seem an unusual line of questioning, Mr Stansfield,' remarked the judge. 'I hope there is some point to it?'

'I believe so, My Lord. Lady Celia, did you, in fact, visit Claremont Court in the small hours of 29th July?'

'No.'

'Even though a witness says he heard a car drive away at around two o'clock that morning?'

'That car was a green Lagonda,' interposed Sir William. 'There is not the smallest shred of evidence which implicates Lady Celia in this.'

'No. Indeed. I think, Mr Stansfield, that you might do

well to remember who is on trial here.'

'I will bear it in mind, My Lord,' replied the other. 'Lady Celia,' he then went on, 'we have heard Miss Meadows' statement', this was her maid, 'to the effect that she was asleep in bed and therefore could not say what time you returned from your drive. Can *you* tell us what time it was?'

She hesitated a moment. 'I'm not sure exactly. Around three. Or perhaps half past . . .'

'Half past three. Rather a long drive, wasn't it?'

'I suppose so.' The bored note was back. 'I hadn't thought about it.'

'So that – correct me if I've got this wrong – you have no proof of your whereabouts during this, let us say, *crucial* period between one and three-thirty . . .'

'Mr Stansfield, I think we have heard quite enough of this,' interjected the judge. 'Lady Celia has shown exemplary patience, in my view, in answering your questions thus far. After all,' went on His Lordship, 'who amongst us in this courtroom could provide a better alibi as to his whereabouts at the time? I myself have only my wife's say-so to prove that I was asleep in bed.'

The laughter which greeted this sally had not quite died down, when it happened:

'She's lying! She was there that night, like he said . . .'

It was the prisoner who had spoken. A moment of electrified silence followed. Then, like a wave rising, and curling, and breaking with muted thunder on a shore, a shocked murmuring of voices began. The repeated exhortations of the ushers to silence were powerless to quell the commotion. 'I shall have the court cleared if this does not stop at once,' said the judge, to greater effect. When the court was quiet once more, he addressed the prisoner: 'You would do well to remember, Mr Caparelli,' he said, 'that this is an English court of law. We do things by the rules here and not by making wild and unfounded accusations against innocent people. If there are any further such interruptions from you, I will have you taken down to the cells. Do you understand?'

'Oh, yes, Your Lordship,' said Caparelli. 'I understand very well.'

In the street, trams were clanging their bells, newspaper vendors were shouting 'Evening *Speshul*!', but Rowlands was oblivious to it all. He'd walked and walked, hardly aware of what direction he was going, and ended up back at the office, like some blessed homing pigeon. He wasn't sure why he'd come back here. The office would be closing soon. But somehow he felt himself reluctant to go home just yet. And so he pushed open the heavy doors, and took the lift to the fifth floor, quite as if it were the beginning of a working day and not the end. A few people passed him, coming out of the office, as he went in. He returned their greetings mechanically. 'Forgotten something, have you, Rowlands old man?' enquired Jackson cheerily, and he agreed that he had. What he really wanted was to be alone, to think things out in peace and quiet for an hour. He sat down at his desk, his limbs suddenly as tired as if he had been marching all day over rough country, rather than sitting in a stuffy courtroom, listening to the elaborate circumlocutions of lawyers.

Quieting his conscience about the dubious nature of what he was doing proved easier the second time. His fingers moved rapidly, confidently, over the switchboard, connecting the cords to their jacks. He pushed back the front key. 'Get me Esher five-three-two, will you?' he said to the operator. 'Yes, that's all right. I'll wait,' when the other replied that it might take a few minutes. He was surprised at how calm he sounded, although his heart was pounding like a trip-hammer, and it was an effort to keep the pace of his breathing slow. There was the familiar series of clicks and crackles, followed by the hollow sound that was to him like the soughing of wind through pine trees. More clicks, and bleeps followed, until at last a connection was made.

'Esher for you, caller.'

'Thank you.'

There was a moment's charged silence before the telephone started ringing. A mental image of the instrument, as it vibrated into life, filled his mind. He pictured it now – either a candlestick model or a more substantial, wall-mounted instrument, trilling with peal after peal of urgent sound, from the marble-topped hall table or purpose-built cupboard where it had been placed, awaiting just such an eventuality. Although for the life of him, he didn't know what he was going to say when somebody answered. A few moments passed – long enough for him to contemplate abandoning the attempt, but not so long that he had time to do so. Perhaps they hadn't got back yet, although it had been a good four hours since the court had risen for the day. But then all of a sudden there was a voice: nervous-sounding, hesitant – as if the young woman to whom it belonged were not quite sure how to deal with this unlooked-for event.

'Yes?'

'Is that Esher five-three-two? The West residence?'

'Yes. Who wants to know?'

'The police,' he said.

There was a sound between a gasp and a wail. Then the girl said in an agitated tone, 'I've *said* all I'm going to say! I said it to the judge. I *said* what I'd seen . . .'

The housemaid, he guessed. What was her name, again? Elsie something. Briggs? No, Binns.

'Yes, yes,' he replied in a soothing tone. 'It's just for our records, Miss Binns. It *is* Miss Binns, isn't it?'

'Yes. I've *said* . . .'

'You were the one that found the body, weren't you?'

In a small voice: 'Yes. But I've *said* . . .'

'It must have been a great shock for you.'

'Only I told the judge, I said. I've never been in any kind of trouble with the police.'

'Of course you haven't. This is just a formality, you know.'

'I'm sure I don't know how I'm ever going to get another place,' said Elsie Binns, her voice trembling on the edge of tears. 'Not with this hanging over me.' Her voice dropped to a terrified whisper. 'I mean, *murder*. It's not very nice, is it?'

'No, it isn't nice at all. Miss Binns, I promise I won't keep you long. It was just one thing you said in your evidence today that I . . . that the police . . . want to get clear. You said there was broken glass all over the floor in the library. That was from the broken window, I take it?'

She seemed taken aback for a moment. 'Window? I don't know about no window. It was from the glass that he'd had in his hand . . . *He* said I wasn't to clear it up – not till after the police had been. Nor the other glass, that was on the table, still half-full of drink, neither . . .'

'So . . . let me get this quite clear. There were two glasses. One broken into pieces on the floor and the other . . .'

'On the table. Yes.'

'Only you didn't mention this – the second glass – when you gave your evidence.'

'Nobody asked me, did they?' she said, with a certain truculence.

'That's very true, Miss Binns. But I'm asking you now: was it your impression that there might have been two people in the library that night?'

But this proved beyond her to envisage. 'I couldn't say, really,' she said. 'Maybe you should ask *him* . . .'

'I take it you're referring to M'sieur Gaspard?'

'That's right.' Her voice, subdued until that moment, assumed a scornful accent. '*He* was there that night, you know. The night it happened. If you want to ask somebody questions, you could ask *him*. Knows everythink there is to know, does Monsieur.'

Perhaps it was the slightly louder tone in which she had spoken, or merely the fact that he himself had been mentioned, that attracted the valet's attention. A moment later, there came another voice on the line. 'Allo? Who is this?' and then, in an undertone to the mortified Elsie Binns: 'Be quiet, you stupid girl!'

When Rowlands replied, it was with a Scottish burr that, he hoped, would be convincing enough to deceive the Frenchman, as it had Lady Celia's maid: 'Guid evening, would that be M'sieur Gaspard I'm speaking to?'

'*Oui*. Gaspard 'ere. And who is this?'

'Inspector Douglas, of Scotland Yard,' Rowlands replied.

There was a pause, as Gaspard considered this. 'Ah, *oui*. *L'Inspecteur*,' said Gaspard, apparently satisfied. 'You were at the court today, yes?'

For a moment, panic seized him. *Had* Douglas been

in court today? He'd no way of knowing. If this were a trap, to catch him out, Gaspard couldn't have come up with a better one – had he but known it. Well, there was nothing for it . . . 'I was in court, as you say. Although,' he added, 'not called upon to give evidence.'

'I am not likely to forget a man like you,' said Gaspard, with what might have been a veiled irony. 'Such a great tall man, with such red hair! And so what may I do for you, *Inspecteur*?'

'I was explaining to Miss Binns just now that I need to ask you both a few questions for our records,' said Rowlands. 'Just routine, ye ken.'

'But I tell you everything already, *Inspecteur* – is it not so? The judge, too.'

Rowlands took a breath. 'Not *quite* everything, M'sieur, now was it?'

'I don't know what you're talking about,' said Gaspard, all traces of good humour gone from his voice.

'Let me refresh your memory,' said Rowlands. 'When you were being cross-examined by Mr Stansfield you said something very interesting. You said . . .' He made it sound as if he were reading from his notes, '"He tells me I can go to bed . . ."' – meaning Mr West, I take it – "and so I leave them and go upstairs . . ." Who was it you meant, M'sieur Gaspard?'

'I don't understand,' said the Frenchman sullenly.

'Och, I think you do. You said you left "them" –

239

Mr West and someone else. It couldn't have been Mr Caparelli, because he'd already gone. So who *did* you mean?'

'I meant nobody. My English is not so good.'

'You're too modest, M'sieur Gaspard. I should remind you,' said Rowlands evenly, 'that perjury – which is what we call lying under oath – is a very serious crime. You could get seven years.'

There was a faint gasp at the other end of the line. 'Who are you?' said Gaspard. 'You are not a policeman. Or at least, not the one you have said. *Monsieur L'Inspecteur* is not so tall – nor does he have red hair.'

'Never mind who I am. Let's just say I've a pretty good idea of what really happened that night . . . but I want to hear it from you.'

'Why should I talk to you? It might be better for me if I were to tell *Monsieur L'Inspecteur* what you have done.'

'I don't think you'll do that. And if you don't want to find yourself in more trouble than you are already, you'd better tell me the truth. From the beginning.'

Alone in the deserted office, with nothing but the creaks and groans of the cooling radiators to disturb the silence of the vast building, Rowlands heard once again about Caparelli's arrival at around midnight, in a green Lagonda motor car, which he'd left parked at an arrogant angle in front of the house, 'instead of taking it round to the stable yard, like a gentleman', said Gaspard. He heard about the quarrel between Caparelli and M'sieur West, which had degenerated into fisticuffs, and which might have ended in worse if, he, Pierre Gaspard, had not intervened. 'He had a gun, *vous savez* – but me, I am not frighten' of guns. I was at Verdun, me. After *that*, I am frighten' of nothing . . .' He heard about Caparelli's threats, 'He said he will kill him. M'sieur, he laughs in his face . . .' And about West's insistence that he, Pierre, should go on up to bed. 'If he had only permitted me to wait up for him,' Gaspard had interjected, with the first sign of real emotion Rowlands had heard in his voice, 'He might still be alive and well . . .'

All of this he already knew. He interrupted Gaspard: 'There's something else you have to tell me, isn't there? Something you didn't say in court . . .' Then, when the other said nothing, 'Whose *was* it? The second glass? It couldn't have been Caparelli's. You don't offer a drink to a man who's just threatened to kill you. So – whose was it?'

'I didn't hear nothing,' said Gaspard sullenly.

'No, indeed. You *saw* something, though, didn't you?'

There was a long pause. When the Frenchman spoke at last, it was in a subdued tone that contrasted sharply with his earlier pugnaciousness. 'I don't want to get nobody into trouble,' he said.

It was an effort to preserve his studied evenness of tone. 'What did you see, M'sieur Gaspard?'

'It wasn't much . . . No more than a *glimpse* . . . is that the word?'

'Go on.'

'A . . . a *flash,* out of the corner of the eye. Nothing else, *vous savez.*'

'Who was it that you saw?'

'I couldn't see her face, you understand. Just her *robe.* The red one, with the golden dragons on it. Milady's *robe de chambre.*'

Chapter Nine

He'd been surprised to find, on coming in on Monday morning, that someone else had evidently been using the switchboard. Two of the cords had been replaced in the wrong jacks, so that they were all tangled up, and one of the front keys had been left open – not a thing he would ever have done. He couldn't believe that Carrie Gilbert, absent-minded as she could be at times, would ever have been so careless. Bert, when questioned, indignantly denied having touched the switchboard without permission. Old Mr Cheeseman, the caretaker, said he hadn't been near it either. Which just left him. Because of course, he was the last person in the office on Friday night. It had been then that he'd put through that call to Claremont. He supposed, in the agitation of the moment, he must have been the one to leave things in a mess. And yet he knew it wasn't so. So who was it, then, who'd come along after him, and tangled up the wires? Who'd made a call and then left the evidence for him to find?

He puzzled and puzzled over it, until he thought he must be going mad. The uncanny idea that *someone* had been there after him, that hands other than his had moved amongst those cords and switches, made the hairs on the back of his neck stand up on end. *Had* there been someone in the office after him? Surely he'd have heard him, as he came in? Unless he – the invisible man – had waited until Rowlands was gone . . . but then, how would anyone have entered the building without a key? With the feeling that he was missing something which ought to have been plain as daylight, he went over and over the events of that day, trying to recall anything untoward. The truth was, he'd been so preoccupied with all he'd heard at the trial – Celia West's evidence, and then Caparelli's extraordinary intervention – that he hadn't been paying attention to much else. Although there *had* been something, hadn't there? Those footsteps he'd heard, descending the steps behind him, as he'd left the courtroom. There'd been something odd about them. Yes, that was it: the fellow'd had a limp. Not that that was such an uncommon thing, these days.

Now he came to think about it, he was convinced

he'd heard that step again. It had been as he'd waited to cross at the lights at Ludgate Circus when someone – a little chap, wearing a mackintosh – had taken his arm to guide him across the street. He'd called out his thanks, as they'd reached the other side, but the Good Samaritan, whoever he was, had disappeared into the crowd, dragging his lame leg after him. At the time, Rowlands had dismissed the impression from his mind. Now he wondered if he should have paid more attention to it. Had that unseen someone been beside him, all along? Dogging his footsteps along the street and following him into the building? Standing over him as he sat at the switchboard, and listening in to his conversation? He couldn't rule it out. And yet, he told himself, going over each minute detail of that day in his mind, surely he would have noticed something? A footfall on a creaking board. The sound of someone breathing. He, usually so attuned to all that was going on around him, could not have missed these telltale signs – or could he? The smell of another's hair and clothes, or that of an unfamiliar brand of tobacco . . . Over and over, he examined each separate moment of that fatal hour, for traces of a secret sharer.

The day 'Count' Caparelli was called into the witness box, the court was full to overflowing, with spectators crowding into the public gallery and queuing all down the stairs and out into the street. That the victim had come from what some of the members of this audience would have called the 'smart set' added to the frisson surrounding the case, as did the character and notoriety of the accused. For if the murdered man and his wife might have been said to belong to the upper echelons of society, Giovanni Caparelli could certainly be regarded as belonging to the better class of criminal. It was evident in his dark good looks, and his well-cut suits (a different one for every day of the trial). The haughtiness of his bearing – aristocratic, as befitted his soubriquet – was in no way disgraced by the finer points of his sartorial style: his highly polished shoes and immaculate spats, his elegant gloves, his faultlessly barbered hair. Call him murderer, arsonist, embezzler – what you will. You could never call him badly dressed.

'To see him sitting there, with a silk handkerchief in his pocket, and a diamond as big as your fist in his tiepin, you'd have thought he was cock-of-the-walk,' said Jackson, who had attended the trial the previous day. 'Which, considering how things are likely to turn out for him, shows pluck, you'll admit.' Rowlands made a sound indicative neither of agreement nor of disagreement. Jackson took it as encouragement to go on. 'Yes, you'd have laughed to see him, looking as pleased as Punch, while Counsel put his questions. And the way he answered! Cool as you please, the scoundrel. "Mr Caparelli,"' said Jackson, mimicking Sir William's pompous tones, '"Here is a photograph of a Lagonda motor car, registration PX 23L48. Colour – green. I wonder if you can tell the court when you last saw such a vehicle . . ." To which our boy replies, "I don't-a rightly remember. Seems to me I might-a once have taken her for a spin . . ." What a card!' chuckled Jackson. 'I'm telling you, the Old Bailey hasn't seen anything like it since Thompson and Bywaters.'

Difficult as it was to have to listen to such stuff from Jackson, or from the ever-communicative Bert, who had been following the progress of the trial in the *Evening News*, it was nothing compared to what Rowlands had to face at home. Ever since the news of Lionel West's untimely death had burst upon their household, Edith had made it her business to keep him informed of developments, supplementing what she could glean from the newspapers with the titbits provided by her brother. For in this – somewhat dubious – interest, she and Ralph were once more united, Ralph having the benefit, as it were, of a ringside seat. After a slow start – for he had only become aware, he said, of what had taken place so thrillingly on his doorstep by reading about it in the papers – Ralph had since made up for lost time. 'When he happened to walk past last week, there was a policeman outside the gates. To deter "trippers", Ralph thinks,' said Edith. 'Extraordinary, how ghoulish people can be.'

To which Rowlands, thinking of the telephone call he'd received at the office a few days before from Ralph, could only give a non-committal grunt. He wondered what Edith would make of her adored brother's having been mixed up in the affair, if only because of his dubious financial activities. 'You won't say anything to Edie, will you, old boy?' Ralph had said. 'I mean about our little chat the other day. Water under the bridge, what?' When Rowlands had reassured him, he'd become expansive. Relief at having so narrowly escaped retribution mingled with an unlovely gloating: 'Yes, I'd say it's a pretty ghastly business, all told. Although if you ask me, a man like that had it coming. *Nil nisi bonum*, and all that, but he was a poisonous type, was Mr Lionel West. Shame he never got that title he was so keen on,' he added nastily. '*Some* justice in the world, I s'pose you might say . . .'

The heat which had been building up all day was at its most oppressive when he got off the train; by the time he'd reached home, he was running in sweat, beneath the unwarranted layers of flannel and wool. Why *did* one wear so many clothes? he wondered, thankful to be able to discard his jacket and tie at last. Remembering bygone summers when, dressed for rowing, he'd enjoyed the freedom of singlet and shorts, he marvelled at the human animal's propensity for making itself uncomfortable. In the kitchen, he turned the cold tap on full and, bending down, took great gulps of the lukewarm, metallic-tasting water, splashing handfuls over his face and neck until the front of his shirt was drenched. It wasn't until he straightened up that he noticed how quiet the house was. They must all be out. But in the garden he found Dorothy. 'You're back early,' she said.

'There's not much doing at work.' He sat down, with a grateful sigh, on one of the wicker chairs his sister had dragged out onto the lawn. 'Are we on our own?'

Dorothy yawned. 'Edith's taken the children to the park. Vic's gone to buy beer.'

'I wouldn't mind a beer myself.'

'I dare say you'll get one,' said his sister. 'If you play your cards right.' She seemed in better spirits today, he thought. Of late, her moods had been volatile, a consequence, he supposed, of her weeks in prison. An experience like that changed you. And for a sensitive creature like Dottie, it must have been particularly shocking. 'They're going to hang Caparelli for that murder,' she said, as if there had been no change of subject.

In spite of the heat of the day, Rowlands felt a shiver run through him. 'Have they reached a verdict, then?'

'Yes.' She flapped the newspaper at him. 'Want me to read it to you?'

'No, thanks.'

'It *is* a disgusting business, isn't it?' she said. 'The trial, and then the ritual bloodletting . . .' She shuddered. 'Quite primitive, really.'

'It's the process of law.'

'Yes, and how very sure we all are that our laws are the right ones!' There was a histrionic note to her remark that told him she was working herself up.

'They're all we have,' he said wearily. It was too hot for this.

'We can change them, can't we? I mean,' she added, in a curious, tight voice, that sounded as if she could not get enough air. 'There must be instances when we get it wrong. By hanging the wrong man . . .'

So close was this to his own thoughts on the matter that it struck him as uncanny. '*Do* you think they've got the wrong man, in this instance?'

She hesitated. 'I don't know.'

'Well, I do. It seems to me . . .' He broke off again. 'Well, that there's room for doubt, at the very least.' When she said nothing, he went on: 'I've found out – don't ask me how – that Caparelli might not have been the only one to visit Claremont Court that night.'

'Have you?'

'Yes. Dottie, you mustn't breathe a word of this to anyone.'

'I won't. Who was it, then?'

'I'd rather not say. If I'm wrong, it might do untold damage to this . . . person's reputation.'

'But if he's the murderer . . .'

'I've no evidence to suppose anything of the sort. It's all circumstantial – the fact that this . . . individual . . . happened to be there at the time the murder was committed. It could mean nothing at all.'

'That's not very likely, is it?' she said. 'I mean, if this man were innocent, surely he would have come forward?'

He was silent a moment. 'I've thought and thought what I ought to do,' he replied at last, 'but there seems no easy solution. If I say nothing, an innocent man may hang. But if I speak out, another, who may be no less innocent of the crime, will pay the price in his stead.'

'Quite a conundrum,' murmured Dorothy. 'But surely you've other reasons for supposing this *person* to be a murderer than just the fact of his being at the scene of the crime?'

'Yes.'

'Motive being the most important one, I'd say. I mean, what *are* the usual motives for committing murder?' his sister asked, in a speculative tone. 'There's money, of course, and revenge. That seems to have been Caparelli's motive. Then there's love – or rather, jealousy . . .'

The garden gate creaked open, and then banged shut. 'Hello,' called Viktor. He joined them on the lawn. 'Who's ready for a Bass?'

'That'd be nice,' said Rowlands.

'Coming up.' Viktor busied himself removing the tops from three bottles of beer. 'You're looking very serious, Fred,' he remarked, when this operation was complete. 'I hope Dottie has not been talking politics again. It is much too hot for such things.'

'We were talking about murder, if you want to know,' said his wife.

Viktor made a sound indicative of disgust. '*Ach*! Murder, nothing but murder. I am sick of this, you know? Always the newspapers are full of these ugly stories. The trial. And then the hanging. It is not civilised. In my view,' he went on, putting one of the bottles he'd just opened into Rowlands' hand, 'those who commit murder should not be put to death at all, but should be sent to hospital until they are well in their minds.'

'Rather hard luck on their victims,' said Rowlands, taking a swig of his beer. 'And don't you think your hospitals might become rather full, with all these murderers you want to save?'

'Oh, Viktor wants to save everybody, don't you, dear?' Her mood had changed again; now she seemed girlish, lighthearted. 'If he had his way, we'd all be living in a perfect paradise, with no need for money, or wars, or any of the other horrid things to which we're so addicted.'

'You laugh, Dottie, but you believe in this too, I think,' Viktor calmly replied. 'Have you told Friedrich of our news yet?'

'What news is that?' he asked.

'I was waiting for you to get back. It isn't just *my* news, you know. The fact is, I'm expecting again.'

'That's splendid.' That must be why her moods were so up and down.

'A little brother for Wilhelm,' said Viktor happily.

Since the collapse of the fire conspiracy case – for with the chief suspect sentenced to hang in three weeks' time, and the rest of the conspirators small fry, who could be dealt with by a magistrate's court – Willoughby seemed to have lost his *raison d'être*. In place of the cheerful young officer of Rowlands' recollection, there had come a shambling stranger. Unreliable as to timekeeping, and unkempt as to personal habits, Willoughby – once so fastidious in his dress, in whose wake a scent of Bay Rum

252

always pleasantly wafted – now smelled of infrequently changed linen, and, increasingly, of whisky. 'Have a drink with me, won't you, Rowlands?' he'd said one day, when he'd stopped by the office to collect his messages. It was late in the afternoon, but not as late as all that.

Rowlands had declined. 'Thanks, sir. Not for me,' he'd replied, as gently as he could. 'A bit early in the day.'

'Is it? I suppose it is,' said Willoughby.

Afterwards, when he'd gone, taking the reek of spirits with him, Bert, who had been lurking nearby, doing precious little as usual, had delivered himself of a remark: 'Letting hisself go a bit, ain't he?'

'You mind your manners,' Rowlands said sharply.

'I was only saying as he hadn't *shaved*. Not like Mr Willoughby not to shave.'

'That's quite enough of that sort of talk.' If there was one thing Rowlands couldn't stand, it was people making personal remarks. Mingled with his anger was sadness that it should have come to this: that the man he revered above all others should have lost his self-respect to such a degree. Even without being able to see it for himself, he could discern enough about Gerald Willoughby's physical deterioration to fear for his mental state.

'Nervous strain,' was Mr Saville's explanation when, a few days after this incident, he'd called Rowlands into his office to say that the junior partner was taking a few days' holiday. 'The bother of this wretched trial, you know. He knew the man, it seems . . .'

'Yes, sir.'

'Lionel West, I mean. Seems to have hit him hard, all this.'

Rowlands had murmured his agreement. For himself, he was glad he wouldn't have to face Willoughby for a while. It was hard enough dealing with his own sense of the wrongness of what had happened, without having to deal with Willoughby's guilt as well.

There was a feral stink to the place: an atmosphere of unwashed male bodies, mingled with something else – fear, perhaps? – that no amount of Lysol could disguise. It was a sharper reek than that of the women's gaol, one that got you in the back of the throat if you breathed too deeply. The sounds were louder, too. Doors were slammed, here, with just that much more force; tin trays banged down on tables with less regard for the noise they made. The effect was of a constant reverberation of sound throughout the great labyrinthine building, whose tiled walls only magnified the echo. When he was shown into the visitors' room, Caparelli was already seated at the table. He realised this only when, the guard having conducted him to a chair, he heard the other man's voice: 'So you've come to 'ave a look, 'ave you, at the condemned man? Well, let me tell you, *cieco*, there isn't anything to see – even if you *could* see.' A burst of jeering laughter followed.

'I've brought you these.' He pushed the pack of

Player's across the table. 'I didn't know what brand you preferred.'

'Anything I can get,' was the humorous reply. 'And anything's better than the filth you get in here, I can tell you.' There was the sound of the packet being ripped open. 'Got a match?'

'Here.' He handed the box over. 'Keep them, if you like.'

'They don't allow that in here. I might burn the place down,' said Caparelli dryly.

'I see that.'

'Do you, *cieco*? It seems to me that you *see* rather more than is good for you. How *is* that black eye of yours? Tell me, does it hurt just as much when you can't see out of it?'

'Since you ask, it hurts just the same.'

'Of course it does. You must forgive my little joke. You must see – ha! – that I'm a little bit angry with you. You wanted to put me in prison for making fires – you and that boss of yours. That Willoughby.' The Italian gave a scornful laugh. 'I suppose he thinks he's got the better of me. But he'll find out how wrong he is very soon, you may be sure. And when he does, *I'll* be the one laughing at him. Oh yes, I'll make him pay. The beautiful Lady Celia, too . . .'

'You've got no business dragging her into this.'

'Haven't I?'

There was a calculated insolence to Caparelli's tone that made Rowlands long to hit him. He restrained himself, however. 'It's a pretty low trick, trying to hide behind a woman,' he said coldly.

There was a hissing sound, as if the Italian had drawn in his breath sharply, then silence. 'If you had said that to me outside these walls, it would have been the last thing you said,' Caparelli murmured. Then he laughed. 'But I like your spirit, *cieco*. You are – how do you say? – a *gentleman*. You think all women must be protected, from men like me. Because I am *not* a gentleman. Maybe,' he added, his good humour evidently restored, 'that is why women like me . . .'

There seemed no answer to this piece of braggadocio, and so Rowlands said nothing.

After a moment, Caparelli said: 'You didn't come just to bring me cigarettes.'

'No. I wanted to ask you something.'

'Ask away. I'm not going anywhere.'

Rowlands drew a breath. 'Did you go to Claremont with the intention of shooting West?'

Caparelli considered the question. 'You're not so stupid, are you, *cieco*?' he said at last. 'If you want the truth, my intention was only to frighten him. He'd done me a bad turn, by going to the police. I was angry. I let him know it. But as for *killing* him . . .' Again he laughed: a softly unpleasant sound. 'If I'd been going to kill him, I'd have chosen another way.'

'So you didn't in fact return to the house that night?'

Again came a burst of laughter. 'What are you, *cieco* – some kind of lawyer? You heard what the judge said. I returned later that night, in order to carry out a "ruthless and cold-blooded murder". . . '

'I'm asking you what really happened.'

'And what good will it do, *cieco*, if I tell you?' Caparelli sighed. 'What I *will* tell you is what I *would* have done if I'd wanted to kill Lionel West. I wouldn't have wasted time going to his house, in a car anybody would have been able to identify, and where the *servitori* could overhear everything that went on between us. No. That would have been stupid. And I,' said the Italian with a certain fierce pride, 'am not so stupid. What I *would* have done is to wait for him one night outside his office. I would have taken him to a little bar I know – quite quiet, very discreet – and filled him full of good Italian brandy. Then I'd have walked him back to his delightful house in Mayfair, where the so-charming Lady Celia – ah, *la bella*! – would have been waiting for him. Except that he wouldn't have reached his house. The so-beautiful wife would have looked for him in vain, not that she would have shed many tears, that one! . . . A week later, his body would have been fished out of the Thames. No marks, no bullet wounds – nothing on it to tell the story. You want me to say what happened? That's what *would* have happened,' concluded Caparelli. 'That's how I'd have killed Lionel West. Not waving guns around at two in the morning.'

'Let me get this straight,' said Willoughby, after a silence so long that Rowlands wondered if he'd heard him the first time. 'You're asking me to accept a month's notice?'

'Yes, sir.' Conscious that he was under scrutiny, Rowlands squared his shoulders and looked straight ahead, as if he'd been called to attention.

There was another pause. 'May I ask the r-reason for this decision of yours?' Willoughby said at last. He didn't sound angry, only faintly perplexed.

'My sister's husband has asked me to go shares in a . . . a chicken farm,' replied Rowlands. His face felt oddly stiff and expressionless; he'd never been more conscious of his blindness.

'I asked you what your reason was for leaving – n-not what you intend to do afterwards,' said Willoughby, with the first flash of temper he'd shown. 'You can't s-seriously expect me to believe that you'd prefer that kind of work to this? That a man w-with your ability and training would be content to give it all up in order to m-muck out poultry. I mean, damn it all, Rowlands, you must take me for a fool if you think I'd swallow *that*.'

Since there was nothing to be said to any of this, Rowlands said nothing. A few seconds passed. His employer gave an exasperated sigh.

'I'm sorry. That was unforgivable.' There was a pause, while Willoughby lit a cigarette. 'Oh, I'm sorry – do you want one?'

Rowlands shook his head. The truth was, it would have choked him. The very smell of the things brought back uncomfortable memories. Hadn't it been that which had given the game away, that night at her house in Hill

Street? When she'd played him for a fool, taunting him with her touch, her naked flesh, while he lay there at her mercy? Whispering her honeyed words into his ear, while Willoughby stood by watching?

'Suit yourself. So,' Willoughby asked, 'are you going to tell me what this is all about? I mean, you have to admit that, if nothing else, your decision seems a s-somewhat eccentric one. Given that you've been with us, six – or is it seven, years . . .'

'Seven years.'

'. . . seven years, and have therefore attained a certain, shall we say, s-seniority in the firm – a seniority, moreover, commanding a good deal of respect . . .'

'Yes, sir.' If he'd felt wretched before, it was nothing to the way Rowlands felt now, at this reminder of all he stood to lose. It was an effort to keep back the treacherous tears. Respect wasn't the half of it.

'. . . to say nothing of a fairly decent salary. Not as much as it should be, of course, but . . .' Willoughby stopped short, as if the thought had just occurred to him. 'Is *that* what this is about?' he said sharply. 'Is it more money you're looking for? Because if it is . . .'

'It isn't the money.' He couldn't suppress a pained grimace. That Willoughby should think *that* of him . . . In rehearsing this conversation, over all the sleepless nights and distracted days which had led up to it, Rowlands had never anticipated this particular moment: having to put into words the one thing that couldn't be said. Now he stammered, as if he were the one afflicted with that habit of speech. 'I . . . I . . .'

'Sit down, man, won't you, for heaven's sake,' said Willoughby. 'You're not on parade now, you know.'

'No, sir.' Rowlands found the back of the chair that stood in front of Willoughby's desk and sat himself down upon it. In that brief moment, he pulled himself together. Came to a decision. 'The fact is, sir, my wife needs a change of scene. She hasn't been quite herself lately . . . not since the baby came. I . . . we both feel the country air would do her good. The children, too. My girls,' he finished lamely, feeling the blood rise to his face at the brazenness of the lie.

'I see.' There was a brief pause, as Willoughby considered this. When he spoke again, it was with none of his earlier vehemence. 'Well, I'm sorry to hear your wife hasn't been well. I suppose that puts a different complexion on things.'

'Yes.' It was the first and only time he'd ever been glad that he couldn't look Willoughby in the eye.

'Is it her nerves, do you know, or something more, ah, physical?' went on this cool, dispassionate voice. 'Only w-women do get nervy about all sorts of things.'

'I . . .' Again, the hateful stammer appeared to have taken hold of Rowlands' tongue. As if he were engaged in some cruel mockery of the other man. 'I believe it's more of a physical ailment.'

'Ah. Pity. Because I was going to r-recommend a good "nerve man". Harley Street, you know. Helped a f-friend of mine no end . . .'

Rowlands inclined his head to show his appreciation of this suggestion, when all the time he wanted to cry out, 'For God's sake, don't you see the whole thing's impossible? Knowing what I know makes me an accessory after the fact – isn't that the term? An accomplice to murder. You know that as well as I do'.

'So it seems we're going to lose you, after all,' Willoughby said. 'Since you clearly don't have much choice in the matter. Under other circumstances,' he added, 'I'd have suggested sending your good lady and the children to the seaside for a month. Never fails, you know, as a cure for every kind of illness. But I can see you're set on going.' There was an odd tremor in Willoughby's voice. 'And nothing *I* can say will persuade you to stop.'

'Captain Willoughby. Sir, I—'

'It may perhaps strike you as foolish, but I shall miss you, you know,' his former O.C. went on, as if Rowlands had not spoken. 'We've been through a good deal together, you and I. A good deal. Some of it pretty bloody, of course – you'd be the first to agree with me about *that*! – but all of it the kind of experience that binds men together . . . for life, one might have thought. You'd think it would count for s-something, at any rate. But perhaps, after all, it doesn't.'

The bleakness with which he said these last words was enough, when he recalled it afterwards, to make Rowlands weep.

* * *

All the way home, on the rattling train from London Bridge to Honor Oak Park, he'd been dreading what Edith would say – rehearsing arguments in his head, none of which seemed convincing, even to him. He knew she wasn't going to like it. What woman would? Being asked to give up everything – because that's what it would amount to. Even though she'd never been happy in Gabriel Street – still, it was the only home they had. Now even that was in jeopardy. Walking back along the quiet street, his footsteps seemed to him to have the ring of an assassin's; the turning of his key in the lock had a no less ominous sound. With the knowledge of what he had to say – and of Edith's likely reaction to it – weighing on his mind, it was an effort to eat his supper. He'd had enough experience of his wife's darker moods to expect the worst, when he faced her with this crisis. But, for once, she was reduced to speechlessness by his announcement. There was a gasp, then, after a silence: 'You're not serious?'

'I'm perfectly serious.'

'But . . .' She sounded utterly at a loss. 'What's happened? What have you *done*?' The last word emerged as a wail.

'Edith . . .'

'Have you been given the sack, is that it?'

'No, of course not . . .' Even though he was prepared to go through with this – the sacrifice of everything he'd worked for – his pride wouldn't allow him to let her think the worst.

'Then *why?*' She was still struggling to comprehend the enormity of what he'd done: the wanton throwing away of a good job, with prospects (albeit limited) and wages that, though they could never be described as princely, were at least adequate for their needs. 'Was it about the money?' she said, jumping to a conclusion. 'Your asking for that payrise, I mean? Because if it was . . .'

'It wasn't about that.'

'Are you sure, Fred? Perhaps they thought it was too much . . . Although two pounds a week extra *isn't* a lot of money,' Edith said. 'Not when you've got three children to support, to say nothing of . . . Oh, Fred!' she cried suddenly. 'How *could* you have given up that job? You'll never get another one as good, not the way things are nowadays . . .'

The truth of it overwhelmed her all at once, and she burst into tears.

'Edie. Dearest. Don't take on so.'

But when he moved towards her, to comfort her, she pushed him away. 'Don't touch me.' She was trembling now, with rage and grief. 'I don't know how you can bring yourself,' she went on, between sobs, 'to do this to your children. Even if you don't care what happens to me . . .'

'Edith, please . . .'

'. . . you might at least think twice about letting them starve.'

'They're not going to starve. I've already told you. I'm going in with Vic, in this chicken farm of his. He thinks it's a good thing . . .'

'Oh yes.' Her tone was scathing. 'The chicken farm. And what, may I ask, do you – or Viktor, for that matter – know about that, or any kind of farming?'

'We can learn.'

There was a brief, incredulous silence. When his wife spoke again, it was with the cold politeness she employed when she was really angry. 'Indeed. It's always good to learn something new, isn't it? After all, it only took you two years' hard work after you came back from the war to learn typing and telephony. Another two years should do it. You're thirty-seven now, so you'll still be under forty when you start your new career . . .'

'Edith, if you'd just listen to me for a moment . . .'

'. . . that is, if you and Viktor and the rest of us haven't ended up in Queer Street by then. I'm sorry,' his wife concluded, sounding anything but, 'that I can't share your enthusiasm for this new life of yours. In fact, I've a good mind to write to Mr Willoughby and tell him so.'

'You'll do no such thing.'

'Won't I?' She was almost breathless with anger now. 'Just you watch me. If *you* won't see reason, I'm sure Mr Willoughby will. Maybe he'll agree to give you another chance.'

He'd never raised a hand to her in all their married life, and yet he came close to it now, rage blinding him to all but that maddeningly superior voice of hers. 'Edith, I absolutely forbid you to write to Mr Willoughby.'

'Do you? Why? Are you afraid I might get at the truth about all this?'

It felt for an instant as if his heart had stopped beating. 'What exactly do you mean by that?'

'I mean that Gerald Willoughby is doubtless as mystified as to why you've decided to quit your job as I am. Unless there's something you haven't told me . . .'

He was silent a moment, making an effort to get his temper under control.

'Mr Willoughby has accepted my resignation,' he said, conscious that his voice was not perfectly steady. 'If you go against my decision by writing to him, you'll only make me look a fool.'

'It seems to me,' said Edith, 'that there's nothing *I* could do in that respect that you haven't done already.'

Chapter Ten

Strange that in dreams the landscape was utterly silent, when at the time it had been a place of hellish noise; the sound of the shells whizzing overhead was the loudest, like an express train going full tilt, some of the men said, with the impact of a giant door slamming. He himself thought the sound resembled that of an iron-shod wheel going round the corner of a gritty road. A sound to set one's teeth on edge, followed by the juddering *whoomp* of the explosion, that shook one to the very core. Then there was the rattle of machine gun fire. *Atta-atta-atta* . . . The *crump* of the big five-nines. The whinnying of the horses that pulled the gun carriages, a sound whose comforting evocation of domestic scenes (milk cart or brewer's dray) could turn, all too soon, to horror. How the poor beasts could scream! It was worse, somehow, than the screaming of men – although that, too, was hard to bear.

Yet when he found himself back there again, it was not the sounds his unconscious mind recalled, nor the smells, although these had their own power to awaken the past. Even now, ten years after his own particular war had ended, he had only to pass a saddler's shop for the smell of burnished leather and polished brass to catch him by the throat. Cordite – that was another smell you couldn't forget. The way it clung to your hair and clothes, after the shell had been fired. The acrid smoke that hung in the air for minutes afterwards. Nor were these the foulest smells; what *those* were didn't bear too much thinking about. It was something you couldn't guess, unless you'd experienced it – how rapidly the living body could be reduced to a stinking mess of blood, and brain matter, and shit. Yes, it was surprising, considering that his dreams were odourless. As if the brain, overloaded with sensory information, had retained only the barest details: a strip of earth, a patch of sky, a tangle of wire. A flicker of movement at the edge of vision.

It had been agreed that he'd work out his notice. Because, after seven years, there wasn't much about the firm's way of doing things he didn't know, to say nothing of the intricacies of running a switchboard. As Edith had pointed out, it had taken him long enough to get the hang of the thing. Now it was a sequence of actions and responses so much a part of his life that he suspected he'd be lost without them. That he'd miss not only this routine of call and answer, of connections made and unmade, but also his relationships with other people – his colleagues, the clients – was never in doubt. To leave all this for what looked certain to be a more solitary existence, tending chickens in a field, would be hard; he could hardly bear to think about it. If there were times when reflections such as these were enough to give him pause – to bring him to the brink of reconsidering his resignation – the thought of what had driven him to it was an instant corrective to such backsliding. Simply, he knew he wouldn't be able to live with himself. He was giving up a job he loved, friends, colleagues, his professional standing, for what? A matter of principle. He supposed he might dignify his scruples enough to describe them as that. The irony was that no one but himself had the faintest idea about any of this. Even Willoughby . . . well, perhaps Willoughby had an inkling of the truth. But then Willoughby's conscience must be in much the same state as his own.

Reactions amongst his colleagues to the news of his imminent departure were varied, although most expressed unequivocal regret. 'Sorry to hear about your wife,' said Jackson, startling him at first, until he recalled the lie he'd told to Willoughby. 'I must say I was very surprised to hear of your leaving us,' was Mr Saville's response, delivered with an air of icy disapproval. 'Very surprised indeed.' 'You could've knocked me down with a feather,' was Bert's more unbridled comment. 'I'd never have thought it. I said to Mr Cheeseman, I said, "Can you believe our Mr Rowlands is leaving us for good?"' Only Carrie Gibson expressed a positive pleasure at the news. 'Oh, I do envy you!' she exclaimed, when her colleague's plans were made known to her. 'It's what I've always wanted – a little place in the country, with a few chickens. If Wilf were only well enough, that's what we'd do . . .' At the prospect of having to work with someone else, she seemed resigned. 'I suppose I know enough to show them what's what,' she said. 'It's not so very difficult, when you get used to it.'

It occurred to Rowlands that maybe the prospect of becoming the senior telephonist in his stead was not without its appeal. Perhaps they'd raise her wages, he thought, bitterly aware of exactly how much the loss of those same wages would mean to him. Because Edith was right; by giving up his job, he was risking everything. Not only his own future, but that of his children. It was sheer lunacy, whichever way you looked at it. And yet, turning it over in his mind, as he'd done every night since he made his fatal announcement to Willoughby, he couldn't see what else he could have done. To have carried on as if nothing had happened, knowing the truth about who killed Lionel West, would have been tantamount to colluding in his murder.

He realised, of course, that he was taking the coward's way out. Running away from the dilemma, instead of confronting it head-on. If he had any guts, he'd take the whole matter to the police, and hang the consequences. As it was, it would be an innocent man who would pay the price. It was this, more than his own situation, uncertain as it was, that came between him and sleep. When he'd left Wormwood Scrubs that day, after visiting Caparelli, he'd almost been physically sick at the thought of the horror that was to come. Somehow, the brutality of the punishment was lessened when one knew the condemned party to be guilty of the crime. That Caparelli – reprobate though he undoubtedly was – would suffer that hideous fate undeservedly, made its savagery all the more starkly apparent.

Now, in place of the grey strip of mud, the white strip of sky, the barbed wire with its fluttering scrap of uniform, had come another dream. It was as silent as the first, and as muted as to colour. There was the grey light that came filtering through the barred window. A grey room, in which three men, dressed in grey, were standing. The man in the middle wore a grey hood over his face. His hands were bound. The man on the right tapped him on the shoulder to make him step forward. The man on the left stooped to release the lever . . . Then he was choking, fighting for breath. He clawed at his throat, to tear the dreadful ligature away . . .

'Wake up,' said a voice in his ear. 'Fred. Wake up. You're dreaming.'

'I'm sorry.' His heart was pounding. 'Didn't mean to wake you.'

'I'm surprised you haven't woken the whole house,' said his wife. 'Do you want me to make you some cocoa?'

'No, that's all right. Go back to sleep,' he said.

'You, too.' Within seconds, her breathing told him she'd drifted off again. One thing about Edith, she'd always been a sound sleeper. A good thing, too, given that his own nights were so often disturbed. In the weeks since he'd given in his notice, they'd achieved a rapprochement of sorts. Having evidently come to the conclusion that nothing she could say would make him change his mind, Edith had taken up a different line. Now she was forever reading out bits from the newspaper about the beneficial effects of country air on children, and of how much might be saved per annum by the simple expediency of growing one's own vegetables. It occurred to him that his wife was one of those who liked a challenge. She'd certainly proved that much, when she married him.

It was the first Sunday in September. They'd been to church, and had their lunch, and then Edith had taken the children for a walk. Dottie and Viktor were off somewhere, too. He was alone, for the first time in weeks. Had things been as usual, he'd have enjoyed this brief respite from domestic life; as it was, he found it impossible to keep his thoughts from the subject which had now become his obsession: that a man was dead, and that, in a few weeks' time, another man would die, unjustly, on account of this. There was no getting away from these hard facts, and so, since he could not forget them, he tried to distract himself as best he could. Reading was, as ever, his preferred distraction. It was his one consolation: the ability to immerse himself, when reality seemed intolerable, in an invented world. He had been thus engaged for half an hour or so, when there was the sound of a motor car pulling up in the street outside. This was a rare enough occurrence in their quiet neighbourhood, to take his attention, momentarily, from the book he was reading – his fingers arrested at the moment of Rodolphe's seduction of Emma Bovary:

Oui, je pense à vous continuellement! . . . *Votre souvenir me désespère! Ah! pardon! . . . Je vous quitte . . . Adieu!*

He felt sorry for Emma. That Rodolphe was an artful beast. What chance did she have, poor silly little woman, and with a husband like that Charles, who couldn't even see what was going on under his nose. 'Who's there?' he called, hearing the click of the garden gate. 'Edith – is that you?' Although even as he spoke, he knew it wasn't his wife's step.

'I hope I'm not disturbing you,' said the intruder. 'Oh, don't get up . . .'

Although it wasn't politeness which had brought him to his feet, but the knowledge that, seated, he was at a disadvantage. As if she were some deadly adversary, about to inflict a blow. Absurd. He felt his face grow hot with shame – as much at the nervous start he'd given when he heard her voice, as at the memory of the last time they'd been this close to one another, when he'd been all the more at her mercy, being unaware of what she was. Well, he wouldn't make that mistake again.

'Lady Celia. I . . . I'm afraid my wife isn't at home just at present.'

'It isn't your wife I came to see,' said Celia West. 'May I sit down?'

He hesitated only a moment. What, after all, did he have to fear from her? 'Please do.' He gestured towards the wicker chair he'd just quitted.

'Oh, the grass will do for me. It's quite dry. I say, what a pretty garden! Lovely roses . . .'

'Thank you.'

'Aren't you going to sit down?' she said.

He knew he must look foolish, standing there like a wax dummy, and yet he was reluctant to surrender what little advantage his height afforded him. To sit down beside her on the grass – for if she refused to take the chair, he couldn't very well do so – felt like conceding too much. As ever, he felt subtly wrong-footed by her.

He sat down.

'But I see that I *have* disturbed you,' went on his unexpected guest. 'You were reading. What is it? May I look?'

'Of course. But . . .'

There was the faint creak of the stiff pages being turned.

'How very clever you must be,' she said, 'to be able to decipher all these strings of dots as words.'

'It isn't so hard, once you get the hang of it.' In spite of himself, he was being drawn into conversation. As if they were merely two civilised people, passing the time of day, in an English garden. Not that he and she, in the normal run of things, would ever have found themselves together in this, or any other kind of garden. Their worlds were too far apart. It was a brutal aberration – murder – which had brought them together.

'Getting the hang of it must take an awful lot of will power,' she said.

'Not really.' His face felt stiff. His lips were those of an automaton, moving in jerky simulation of real life.

'But then you strike me as just that sort of person. I shouldn't think you'd easily let yourself be beaten by circumstance, would you?'

'If by that you mean what happened in the war, there are a lot of people like me.' He shrugged. 'One had to get on with it, that's all.'

'That's what Gerald says, too.'

The sound of that name had a peculiar resonance, invoking all that had so far been left unsaid. She seemed aware of this, because when she spoke again, it was with a deliberateness that showed she had come to the heart of the matter: 'Gerald tells me that you've given in your notice at Saville and Willoughby's.'

'Yes.'

'Rather rash, wasn't it? I mean – forgive me for saying so – but you're hardly in the best of situations, are you?'

'That's my business,' he said.

'Now I've offended you. I'm sorry. Only . . . what do you intend to do for a living, Mr Rowlands?' He started to speak, but she went on. 'I know, I know. You'll tell me to mind my own business again, but don't you *see*? You've sort of *become* my business, in a way . . .'

'I'm not sure I understand.'

'Gerald's dreadfully cut up about your leaving,' said Celia West. 'He blames himself.'

'Mr Willoughby has nothing to blame himself for.'

'But he *does*, you see. He thinks that something he's said or done must be behind it.'

'It's nothing he's said or done.' He hesitated, choosing his words. 'You shouldn't have come,' he said.

'I can see you've already formed an opinion about all this.' She didn't sound angry, only perplexed.

Disappointed, he thought, as if she'd expected something better from him.

'It's not my business to have opinions.'

'And yet you've expressed what you think as clearly as if you'd shouted it from the housetops.' The brief pause that followed was loud with the sound of bees. Soft scents of rose and lavender surrounded them. They might have been a thousand miles from here, on a deserted hillside, overlooking a blue bay, instead of in the heart of the great dirty city. It wasn't an illusion which could last very long, Rowlands knew. Sooner or later, something – the rumble of a passing dray, or the shout of a rag-and-bone man in the street – would call them back to what was real. Although it wasn't, he thought confusedly, a reality of bricks and mortar alone, but a whirling vortex of lies, half-truths and subterfuges, and all the other miseries from which people's lives were made. That was it: that was the city. Nor could either of them escape it, except temporarily.

'I wonder,' Celia West said at last, 'what exactly you think of me? Oh, don't worry, I'm not asking you to tell me. That would be too shaming – for both of us, I imagine! It's just that it does seem a little harsh,' she went on, in a voice whose lightness of tone belied the seriousness of what she was saying, 'to be judged and sentenced, as it were, without being given the chance to appeal.'

'Are we talking about Giovanni Caparelli?'

She laughed. 'Perhaps. But then again, perhaps not . . .

At least,' she added, 'Mr Caparelli has had the benefit of a trial, before being condemned.'

'Yes,' said Rowlands evenly. 'He's certainly had that.'

'And yet you evidently believe him innocent,' she said brightly.

'I never said that.'

'No. But it's written all over your face. You've a very expressive face, Mr Rowlands.'

'Have I?'

'Oh yes. So if you don't think Mr Caparelli killed my husband,' she went on, in the same airy tone, 'then who do you think *did*?'

He opened his mouth to reply but no sound emerged.

'Oh, come, Mr Rowlands,' said his guest, with a tremor of laughter in her voice. 'Surely you can do better than that?'

'I don't think you should be here,' he said, finding his voice at last.

'Why ever not?' she replied, deliberately misunderstanding him. 'It's the twentieth century. I'm hardly likely to be compromised . . .'

'Mr Willoughby wouldn't like it.'

'I don't suppose he would. He'd think I was putting you in an unfair position, which I am, of course. But I wanted to give my side of it. I suppose it must strike you as odd,' she went on, before he could say anything, 'that I'm not more upset by my husband's death?'

'I haven't thought about it.'

'Oh, I imagine you have. Be that as it may,' she said,

'I have to confess that I'm not sorry about it at all. Our marriage wasn't a success, you see . . .'

'Lady Celia . . .'

'No, let me speak. It was, I suppose you'd say, a marriage of convenience. Suiting both parties, you see, for different reasons. Lionel wanted a wife – of the right sort, you know – and I . . .' Her voice tailed off. 'Well, let's just say that I was looking for a comfortable life.' He said nothing, and after a moment, she continued: 'It wasn't all bad, at first – I wouldn't want you to think *that*. For the first year, you know, we managed to be more or less happy. It was only after I found out about the first of Lionel's little peccadilloes, that things started to fall apart.'

'I know he treated you badly,' Rowlands said in a low voice.

'Do you, indeed? I hadn't realised it was as obvious as all that. He said I was making a fuss about nothing, of course. Perhaps I was.' She gave a little unamused laugh. 'Then, you know, I met Gerald again, after all those years, and realised what a sham my life had become.'

Against his better judgement, he felt himself overcome with pity for her. 'Couldn't you have left him – your husband, I mean?' he said.

'You didn't know Lionel,' she replied. 'He wasn't the sort of man who'd put up with that.'

Into the silence, came the sound of a child's voice: 'No, Billy, you mustn't . . .' and then the squeak of the garden gate, followed by the creaking of the heavy pram on its sprung wheels.

'I've told you and told you not to scuff your shoes like that,' said Edith. 'It ruins the leather . . . Oh!' she exclaimed, evidently catching sight of their visitor. 'Lady Celia. I'd no idea . . .'

'Do forgive my dropping in like this,' said Celia West. 'Only it was such a lovely afternoon. In fact I was just saying to your husband that I hoped he . . . that is, all of you . . . might be able to join me for a drive. I thought of running down to Brighton. Do say you'll come.'

There was an excited murmur from the girls at this – Anne's voice, as usual, rising above the rest. 'Oh *do* let's, Mummy!'

'Be quiet, Anne. It sounds like a lovely idea,' said Edith to their visitor, 'but I really don't think we can accept.' She gave a forced little laugh. 'There are rather a lot of us . . .'

'Heaps of room in the car,' said Lady Celia.

'Then there's the baby,' Edith persisted.

'Yes, I see,' replied the other woman, with a considering air. 'Not much fun for a baby, really, the seaside, is it?'

'Well . . .'

'Babies can't eat ices, or play on the sand, can they?' Celia West went on. 'They can't run and jump and splash about in the waves . . .'

'Oh, Mummy, *please* . . .'

'That's enough, Anne.'

'Of course, one way around the difficulty might be if you were to let me borrow your husband for a

279

few hours,' said their guest. 'Then the girls can have their afternoon by the sea, and you and the baby – such a *sweet* baby, by the way! – can have a nice quiet time together. Ah, *do* say yes. It would give me such pleasure to give the kiddies a treat, having none of my own, you know.'

'Well,' said Edith. 'It's very kind of you I'm sure . . .'

'That's settled, then,' said Celia West sweetly.

At the garden gate, they met Viktor and Dorothy returning from their walk. Rowlands effected a hurried introduction. 'This is my sister and her husband.'

'I believe we've met before,' said his guest.

'Yes,' said Dorothy.

'At my brother-in-law's garden party,' supplied Rowlands, irritated by his sister's refusal to make more of an effort. However much she disapproved of the Celia Wests of this world – and they were of course, the very sort who had once provided her with a living – she might at least try to be civil.

'Ah yes – the house opposite Claremont,' said the object of his solicitude. 'That was it. I knew I'd seen you somewhere.'

'Lady Celia has kindly offered to take the children to Brighton for the afternoon,' put in Edith.

'I hope that's all right?' murmured Celia West, already opening the car door.

'Well . . .'

'Aunt Edith said I might,' said Billy to his mother. 'Because I'll be company for Anne and Margaret.'

'In that case, of course you may go,' said Dorothy, with what seemed to her brother to be an artificial politeness.

Being here with her was, he decided, a kind of vivid dream; it could not be taking place in his real life, and yet, evidently, it was. A moment out of time – did she feel it too? Perhaps they were both dreaming. Caught up in a space that was neither here nor there; an illusion, built out of things that could never be. He knew it was nothing but that. Those few hours, walking with her by the sea, were among the best of his life, it seemed to him afterwards. It was as if all his ugly thoughts had been magicked away, leaving only what was good and pure between them. By mutual consent, they had avoided the topic which was uppermost in both their minds – or at least, in his. He thought, 'It doesn't matter what she's done, or hasn't done', and for that brief time, he believed it.

They were walking along the esplanade. The girls and Billy had run on ahead; he could hear their voices drifting back faintly, above the sound of the waves, and the crying of seagulls. A warm, salt-smelling breeze blew in their faces, and he could feel the glow of the September sun through his closed eyelids. He heard her let out a sigh, as if her heart were full. 'How awfully nice it is, being out of London,' she said. They walked a few paces further, her hand resting lightly in the crook of his arm, as if he were the one leading her, instead of the other way about. *To have her beside me, like this . . .* he thought, and then could think nothing more. The feel of her hand, the soft swish of her skirts – discernible to him even over the deep sighing sound the waves made, as they tumbled onto the shore – above all, the delicious *scent* of her, prevented thought. 'Such a pretty view,' she was saying.

'Describe it to me.'

'All right.' She took a moment to consider her subject. 'It's a little after three in the afternoon,' she said. 'The sun won't be setting for a couple of hours yet, but the shadows are already lengthening. Everything – that is, the white, stucco-fronted houses along the esplanade, the buildings on the pier . . .'

'Are we looking towards the pier?'

'We are. Everything, as I've said, is bathed in the most beautiful golden light, so that it's all as sharply defined as it can be . . . and yet, somehow, soft. Almost Mediterranean, if you can picture that . . .'

'We never got as far as the Mediterranean. But there were some beautiful days on the French coast, before they sent us north.'

'Well then, imagine that golden light, and you'll know just how the shingle looks at this moment – such a glorious warm colour, speckled with grey and white. The strip of sand along the water's edge is the same pale gold as the pebbles higher up the beach. It's darker where the waves have reached it. There's a ragged sort of edge, which is the exact shape of the

282

drier ripples of sand left by previous waves . . .'

'Yes, I remember.'

'. . . and all the newer ripples are frilled with sea foam, as well as bits of seaweed, and tiny shells, and all the other things the sea casts up . . .'

'Tell me about the sea.'

'I was coming to that. Near to the shore, at the place where the sea meets the land, the water's quite clear – you can see the pebbles underneath it . . . and bits of coloured glass, worn smooth by the waves. We used to collect them as children, Rollo and Johnny and I . . . Further out, the sea turns to a deep green, which grows deeper and greener the further out you go. Like the best kind of emerald, which can be almost black, you know, at its centre . . . By the time you get quite far out, almost to the horizon, it's purple. Like crushed blackberries, or wine . . .'

'"The wine-dark sea". . .'

'I remember one of my brothers quoting that – Homer, isn't it? At the horizon itself, it's dark – a great smudge of violet. There's a boat out there, a little white one, looking just like a bird in flight. Above it the sky is immense. The palest blue. Like . . . oh, I don't know . . . A thrush's egg. It's criss-crossed with cloud. Fine-weather clouds. I don't know what you call them . . .'

'Cumulus, I think. When I was a child, we called it a mackerel sky.'

'Then there's the pier, marching away towards the horizon in that way piers have of seeming not quite to have made up its mind whether to become a bridge or not. It's gleaming white, the pier – they must have given it a coat of paint – and there are strings of coloured flags going from end to end . . .'

'What colour are they?'

'Red and yellow. Awfully jolly, like a gypsy caravan. There's a man with a bunch of balloons. Another selling ices. A fortune teller. "See Your Future in the Crystal Ball." I'm not sure,' she said with a little gasp, between laughter and horror, 'that I want to see mine . . .'

'Will this do, do you think?' she said, as they took their seats, at a table that seemed not quite steady, next to a plate-glass window slippery with steam, and in an atmosphere redolent of over-boiled milk and burnt toast. 'It looks all right.'

'If you'd prefer somewhere else . . .' he started to say, but she stopped him by the simple expedient of putting her gloved hand upon his.

'No, no, it's perfectly fine. Quite amusing, in a rather rustic way, with those gingham curtains – I suppose that stuff *is* gingham – and such lovely thick cups.' She gave a little shudder of laughter. 'I'm sure they must do tea. *Do* you do tea, and all the rest?' she said, addressing their waitress, whom he could not see, but of whom, nevertheless, it was possible to form an opinion.

'Two teas,' said the girl sternly. 'Anythink else?'

'Oh, I think so. We'd like cakes, wouldn't we children?'

'That would be very nice,' said Margaret, appointed their spokesman.

'And . . . bread and butter, I suppose, and all of that . . .'

'Cakes,' said the girl. 'Plain or fancy?'

'Which do you recommend?'

'Well . . .' said the waitress uneasily.

'A selection of both, please,' said Rowlands, taking charge. 'And three glasses of milk.'

'Milk.' She had a habit, this young woman, of breathing through her mouth; adenoids, he thought, wishing all at once that they'd chosen another, more elegant, establishment in which to have tea. But this, he guessed, rather poky little place had been the first they'd come to, although the Grand Hotel was only a hundred yards further along the seafront. Only Celia West had dismissed his suggestion. The Grand was fearfully stuffy, she said. This was much jollier. And what luck to have found an unoccupied table.

'Oh, Daddy, couldn't we have lemonade, as it's a treat?' This was Anne.

'You must certainly have lemonade,' said Lady Celia. 'And make sure it's China tea,' she added, to the waitress. 'Isn't this fun?' she said, when the latter had been dispatched. 'I adore the seaside. It makes me feel ridiculously young. As if I ought to be turning cartwheels, or . . . building sandcastles.'

'You're hardly old now.'

'Oh, but I *feel* a hundred. It must be nice,' she said,

apropos of nothing, 'to have a family to bring up. I've never had children. I rather regret it, sometimes.'

You still might, he would have said, if it had not seemed an impertinence.

'Here's our tea,' she said. 'And such splendid cakes. I don't know that I've ever seen such a variety, with such wonderfully *lurid* icing. Now, they're all to be eaten,' she said to the girls and Billy. 'Because one thing I do know is that, in life, you mustn't waste your chances. So tell me,' she went on, addressing Margaret, he surmised, 'what do you like doing best?'

Margaret thought about it. 'I like reading,' she said.

'Then I suppose you must be clever. That's a good thing, for a girl. I was never very clever,' said Celia West. 'It wasn't encouraged, you know . . .'

After they'd had their tea, and skirmished over who was paying the bill – an argument Rowlands won – they walked back along the front towards the pier. The children had raced ahead, as was their wont, for which he was grateful. This brief hour would be all that he and Celia West would have together. A few moments out of time. He didn't want to waste it in idle chit-chat, when there was so much to be said. And yet he half-dreaded what she might say . . . But in the end it was nothing very startling. A confidence, not a confession: 'You know, Gerald and I have been friends almost the whole of our lives.' They had been walking for a while, with only the sound of the waves

– hypnotic in its rise and fall and rise again – to fill the silence. 'He and Johnny, my elder brother, were at school together. He used to stay at Claremont during the holidays. That was when . . .' Her voice seemed to catch in her throat. 'Well, let's just say he and I became quite fond of one another. My brothers used to joke that he – Gerald – was only waiting until I grew up to marry me. Brothers can be awful beasts. Do you have any brothers, Mr Rowlands?'

'One. Killed at Mons.'

'I'm sorry.'

The silence that followed was filled with the crying of gulls. Such a mournful sound, he thought; its eerie wailing like that of souls in torment. Yet he knew it signified nothing at all. Just a lot of rapacious creatures, fighting over scraps.

'I suppose you could say we were meant for one another, Gerald and I,' she went on, in the same reflective tone. 'Except that it didn't work out like that. Things so seldom do, in my experience. Because then the war came along . . . of course you know all about *that*! And after Johnny was killed . . . and then Rollo, my younger brother, six months after . . . nothing was ever quite the same again.'

They had reached the shore's edge, where he felt, beneath his feet, the pebbles give way to firm damp sand. Here, the sound of the waves was louder, almost drowning out her words. 'Yes, it's a sad story – if you like sad stories, which I don't. Because then there was just Mummy and me, rattling around in that great big house, and trying to sort out the mess – all those unpaid bills, you know – which had accumulated after Daddy died. Death duties. All of that. It got so bad we thought we'd have to sell the house. Which of course would have broken Mummy's heart. And mine. It's all we had left, you see . . . I mean of the life *before*. I don't know if that makes sense to you?'

'Perfect sense,' he said.

'Yes, well it was a wretched time, I can tell you . . . It was then that Lionel came along. Handsome, rich, and in search of a wife.' She was silent a while. There was nothing but the remorseless hissing of the waves. 'Oh how tired I am!' she cried suddenly. 'I sometimes wish . . .'

But what she wished he was never to hear, for just then Billy and the girls ran up, shouting about a Punch and Judy man, and the moment was lost.

Chapter Eleven

On his last day at work he'd arrived a few minutes early, and fell flat on his face. A chair had been moved from its customary position and now stood in his way – a fact he'd only become aware of when he'd fallen over it. He'd been lucky not to break his neck. The caretaker, who'd heard his shout, was full of apologies. He'd been told to give the front office a good going-over, he said. It was on account of the new receptionist starting. He'd meant to put the chairs back the way they were when the floor was dry. He hoped Mr Rowlands wasn't hurt. Nursing a bruised shin, Rowlands told him that it was all right. 'No harm done,' he said, feeling his way gingerly towards his desk. Only when he was seated at it, still trembling a little from the shock, did it occur to him that something wasn't right – hadn't been right, in fact, for a long time. He'd had a feeling of foreboding hanging over him for days; he couldn't quite put his finger on why it was, only that it made him feel very much as he did now. As if someone had been moving the furniture around, and he'd fallen over it. As if someone had been watching his every move, and staying one step ahead of him, all the time. It occurred to him then that everything Celia West had said to him had been a lie. Either that, or he was going mad. Of the two possibilities, he almost wished it could be the latter.

It was hard to believe a month could have gone by so quickly. He'd cleared his desk of all the things that were his to take: the pen tray, the little jar covered with seashells Anne had made him, and which held paperclips; the pen wiper and matchbox cover that were Margaret's handiwork. He'd made sure his files were in order for his successor, Miss Stanley, although *she*, Carrie Gilbert said, would doubtless have her own ways of doing things: 'You mark my words, she'll have all *this* out and a new system put in, before you can say Jack Robinson.' What the formidable Miss Stanley would or wouldn't do once she was in charge was of no interest to him. Once he was out the door, it would be as if all that had happened in those seven years had never been. Even so, he couldn't resist running his hands over the switchboard one last time. The feel of the keys under his fingers; the smooth fit of the jacks into the sockets; the *tick-tick-tick* as the dolls' eyes fell down – these had been part of the fabric of his being. He wondered, as he checked, from force of habit, the lie of the cords – making sure that they ran straight, and had not been left in a tangle – how long such sensations would continue to appear in his dreams, so much had they been a part of his waking experience.

'Said your goodbyes?' asked Mrs Gilbert, perhaps picking up something of her colleague's melancholy mood.

'I have.' There'd been an awkward little gathering at lunchtime in the George. Mr Jackson had stood him a pint, and a couple of the others – young Mullins and Mr Fairclough – had shaken his hand and wished his luck. Because he was leaving of his own accord, there was no presentation clock, or anything of that sort, for which he was glad. He couldn't have borne any kind of fuss. Let him vanish, like the shadow he was. Even so, he couldn't help but regret that Mr Willoughby hadn't been into the office that day. In spite of all that had happened, he'd have liked to say goodbye.

'I'll be off, then,' said Carrie Gilbert. 'Wilf'll be waiting.'

'Yes, you go,' he said mechanically. 'I've a few things to finish off yet . . .'

'All the best,' she said. 'You'll let us know how you get on?' His incomprehension must have been obvious, for she added, in a mildly reproving tone, 'The chicken farm, I mean.'

'Oh. Yes, of course.'

'Well, cheery-bye.' She rested her hand for a moment on his arm. Even though they'd worked in close proximity for a number of years, they'd rarely touched, except by accident, he realised.

It was strange, being at a loose end again, after seven years of being in work. Days seemed longer and yet emptier. The loss of everything that had filled them had had a curiously enervating effect on him, Rowlands found. It was an effort to get up in the morning. If it hadn't meant losing face with Edith, he'd have been tempted to stay in bed all day, although of course he did no such thing. Just because he'd lost his job, didn't mean he should lose all self-respect. And so he found himself things to do. Household tasks he'd been putting off for months: painting the skirting boards, mending the garden fence. He set himself a programme of self-improvement – learning ten new words a day to increase his vocabulary, brushing up his French – to keep at bay a creeping feeling of uselessness. Because what, after all, had his grand gesture achieved? The loss of a good income, that was all. It wouldn't stop a man being hanged, for something he didn't do. Which meant that man's death would be on his conscience, as surely as if he were the one to pull the lever that would send the poor devil to perdition. This half-hearted protest was the worst of both worlds. He'd have been better off stifling his scruples and keeping his job.

Hard thoughts such as these were going round in his head one day a week later, as he stood digging over the ground in his vegetable plot, in preparation for next spring. Of course the likelihood was that they wouldn't be living here then, but the work needed to be done, and, in any case, the hard physical labour involved suited his present frame of mind. Work like this stopped you from brooding, or, at least, that was the general idea. More importantly, it got you out of the house, where your wife was crashing about in one of her moods. 'Doing out the rooms', was what she called it, but he knew the signs well enough. And so he went at it, turning over spadeful after spadeful of the clayey London soil, until the sweat ran down his back. His people had been farmers once, up in Norfolk. Even though it had been two generations since they came to the city, along with the thousands like them who'd lost their livelihoods due to the bad harvests of those years, some things remained in your blood and bone. Yes, maybe on reflection it would do him good – do them all good – to get out of London. Go somewhere where life was cleaner.

There was the sound of footsteps on the path. A tread he recognised, but couldn't, at first, put a name to. 'Your good lady said I'd find you out here,' said a voice.

He almost dropped the spade in surprise, but controlled himself in time. 'Good afternoon, Inspector.'

'Far be it from me to come between a man and his

work,' said the policeman, 'but I was hoping for a quiet word.' When Rowlands said nothing, he continued: 'Little bird told me you'd cleared out of Saville and Willoughby's. Sudden decision, was it?'

'Not really, no.'

'Oh? Because I talked to that charming colleague of yours, pretty little woman, what was her name again? Gilbert. That's the one. Mrs Gilbert. She seemed as surprised as anything. "I'd never have set him down as the type to go in for farming," she said. You know how women like to chatter.'

Rowlands said nothing to this. There was a queer taste in his mouth, like blood, or iron. Only later did he realise that he must have bitten the inside of his cheek.

'For a man like yourself – meaning no offence, o' course – it can't have been easy, finding a job in the first place, and so I wonder what was in your head when you gave in your notice a month ago? Two days, wasn't it, after sentence was passed upon Caparelli . . .'

He didn't answer straight away, knowing that too hasty or vehement a response might look as if he had something to hide. He picked up the spade he'd set down and resumed digging. After the rain they'd had all summer, the ground was soft and easy to work. 'It sounds as if you think there's some connection,' he said evenly.

'Isn't there?'

'Not the slightest.' He said this without a tremor, but his heart was hammering as if this were a court of law and he himself were a prisoner in the dock.

'Mr Willoughby said you'd left on account of your wife's health,' remarked the policeman, with a speculative air. 'Would that have been your wife I met just now? Dark-haired young lady . . .'

'That's my sister. Mrs Lehmann.'

'Ah.' The Inspector considered this. 'Lehmann,' he repeated, after a moment. 'Now, where have I heard that name before?'

Rowlands stopped his digging. Of course, he thought bleakly, he'll have known all along . . .

'Oh yes, I remember. Dorothy Anne Lehmann. Twenty-eight years old. Married, one child. Husband a German national. Resident – until June 3rd this year – at 12a, Greatorex Street, Whitechapel. Served six weeks of a three month sentence for resisting arrest . . .'

'I'd like you to leave now,' said Rowlands.

'. . . released on compassionate grounds, conditional on good behaviour, to relatives in South London.'

'She's done nothing wrong.'

'No, but as a convicted law-breaker, it wouldn't do for her to get into any more trouble . . . or to be associated with anyone else who's been in trouble with the law.'

'I don't know what you're talking about.'

'Och, I think you do. But I didn't come here to chat about your domestic arrangements. I was hoping,' said the inspector, 'that you'd give me your opinion of this. It's a letter. Anonymous, of course. It was delivered to my office yesterday. I'll read it, with your permission . . .'

Rowlands gestured his assent.

Douglas cleared his throat, then read aloud: '"If you want to know who killed Lionel West then ask his wife where she was that night . . ." Printed, of course, so you can't tell much from the hand—'

'I suppose it's someone with a grudge against Lady Celia.'

'Ah! You think so, do you?'

Rowlands shrugged. 'What else can it be? Anyone who attended the trial might have got the idea she was involved in some way from the allegations made by Caparelli's counsel. Which is nonsense, in my opinion,' he added.

'I take it that you yourself attended the trial, Mr Rowlands?'

To his annoyance, Rowlands felt himself flush. 'Only one day of it.'

'Indeed? And which day might that have been?'

'I don't remember.'

'I'd venture to suggest that it was on the Friday – the day Lady Celia gave her evidence.'

'Perhaps it was. Does it matter?'

Inspector Douglas laughed. 'Only in that it might help to cast some light on this mysterious wee note of mine. I don't suppose you noticed anything at all unusual, while you were there?'

Rowlands smiled. 'I hardly think I'm the best person to ask, Inspector.'

'Why ever not? It seems to me you're rather good at

noticing things, Mr Rowlands. Rather better, in fact, than some of us with all our faculties, I'd say. So, *did* you notice anything? Anything unusual said or done by anybody that might help identify the author of this billy-doo . . .'

He hesitated a moment, wondering whether it was worth mentioning the man with the halting step who'd followed him from the courtroom, but then decided against it. He'd probably been imagining it. 'I'm afraid not,' he said.

'That's a pity. But never mind. We've other ways of finding out what we want to know . . . Why, this must be your lady wife now,' said Douglas, suddenly all affability.

'This is Inspector Douglas,' said Rowlands, as Edith joined them.

'Oh!'

'I've just popped by to see your husband about a little matter concerning the Caparelli case. You'll let me know,' he said to Rowlands, with a sharper emphasis, 'if anything further occurs to you?'

'Of course.'

'Good man. Well, I must be getting along. Pleasure to meet you, Mrs Rowlands. Glad to see you looking so blooming.'

Both waited until the sound of his heavy tread had receded along the path, and the gate had clicked shut behind him. 'So,' said Edith, reaching to brush a bit of mud from the sleeve of Rowlands' jersey. 'Are you going to tell me what all that was about, or do I have to guess?'

'It wasn't anything important,' he said, resuming his digging. He heard her sigh with exasperation. 'But to come all this way,' she said. 'It *must* have been important . . .'

'The fact is . . .' He hesitated. It struck him in that moment that he hadn't been playing fair with Edith. All these weeks, he'd kept her in the dark as to his real reasons for leaving Saville & Willoughby, when any decent man would have taken her into his confidence. She was his wife, wasn't she? At the very least, he owed her the truth. Except that to tell her the truth was to involve her in the appalling moral dilemma in which he himself was enmeshed. It wouldn't be fair. 'I haven't the least idea why he came,' he said, deciding, in that moment, to shoulder the whole of it. He was saved, in any case, from further equivocation by the arrival of his daughters, one in hot pursuit of the other, it transpired.

'Daddy! Tell her she can't have it!' demanded Margaret, breathless with indignation. 'Tell her it's stealing, Daddy!'

As a counterpoint to this stern denunciation, came Anne's passionate rebuttal of the charge: 'It's not stealing! I found it! That means it's mine.'

'Girls, your father and I are talking. You know you mustn't interrupt when grown-ups are talking,' said Edith, with a weariness borne of familiarity with such disputes. 'Stop that noise at once, Anne, do you hear?'

Because Anne's sobs had grown louder. Incoherent

with distress, she clutched her father's arm. 'Daddy. It's mine. Daddy . . .'

He crouched down, so that he was on her level, gathered her to him. 'Now, what's all this about?' It was then that she unfolded her small hot hand to disclose what she'd been clutching: a brooch, made of some sort of metal, set with small faceted stones. Its shape a curious double twist, like a bow or a lovers' knot. 'Where did you find this, Anne?'

'In the garden.' She'd stopped crying, but her whole body still quivered with the resentment of one wrongfully accused. 'On the grass – jus' there! Saw it shinin'. Like di'mons. It *is* di'mons, isn't it, Daddy?'

'May I hold it for a minute?' he asked, taking it from her. 'I want to show it to Mummy.'

'I don't suppose those can be real diamonds,' said his wife. 'Although they're awfully good for paste . . . Oh! There's an inscription: *To darling C from your own G: Ti amo. June 29th, 1927.* What does "Ti amo" mean, I wonder?'

'It's Latin for "I love you". *Only she must have mispronounced 'te' as 'tee'* he thought. I suppose she dropped it that afternoon she was here. Lady Celia, I mean . . .'

'Ah, of course,' said Edith with some asperity. 'Then the diamonds must certainly be real. I can't imagine *she'd* settle for anything less.'

* * *

'Dottie said the police were here earlier,' said Viktor, in the Chandos Arms that evening. It was the first time they'd been for a drink in weeks, Vic not having been in a position to afford it, and refusing to let Rowlands treat him on a regular basis. Well, all that kind of thing was over for him, too. He'd have refused Vic's offer of a celebratory pint (earlier that day they'd signed the paperwork transferring the ownership of the Staplehurst farm) if he hadn't been in such a state. Even Edith hadn't objected when he'd said where they were going. 'It'll do you good to get out of the house,' was all she said. And it was a relief, to be surrounded by a comforting fug of tobacco smoke and beer, and the low rumble of men's voices, even though the place wasn't a patch on their former haunt, being a bit of a spit-and-sawdust, with a clientele whose conversation seemed limited to the merits or otherwise of racing dogs. Still it seemed to Rowlands, standing there at the bar, to be almost like old times. A pang of regret for their Friday evenings in the Lamb, after work, assailed him. How much he'd have liked that old, carefree life back again. But that could never be – he knew well enough that you couldn't turn the clock back. It surprised him, nonetheless, to think that he'd been happy. That was how life went: you didn't realise how happy you were, until it was over.

'That's right.' He raised his hand to summon the barmaid. 'Same again,' he said. Only when the drinks had arrived and the girl had removed herself to the far end of the bar, did he allow himself to expand on this. 'It's not what you're thinking,' he said.

'I don't mind telling you, I got a fright when she told me. Thought they must be after her again. Turned out it was you they wanted to see.'

'Yes. Listen, Vic . . .'

'I don't have to tell you, old man, what it would do to me if anything happened to her,' said his brother-in-law in a low voice. 'I don't think I could stand it, and that's a fact. To tell the truth, it's the only reason we're leaving London – to get her away from all that. Policemen knocking on the door at all hours. I thought,' he added dryly, 'I had left all that kind of thing behind me, when I left Berlin. But it appears not . . .'

'This has nothing to do with her.'

'So she said. I suppose you're not going to tell me what it's all about?'

'Rather not, old chap, if you don't mind.'

'Thought you'd say that. It seems to me,' said Viktor, taking a meditative sip of his pint, 'that Dottie and I aren't the only ones with a reason to make ourselves scarce.'

Another restless night, followed by a day of no less agitated thoughts, decided him. He must have it out with Willoughby. Or warn him, at the very least. Because it was plain that the police suspected something – Douglas' visit had told him that much.

Whether they had any evidence to back up their suspicions was another matter, and one he had no way of knowing for certain. His instinct was that they had nothing, or very little, in the way of hard facts – otherwise why the fishing expedition? All that business about the anonymous letter. It wouldn't have fooled a child. No, the more he thought about it, the more convinced he became that Douglas has been trying to trap him into an admission that something had been going on, which of course it had. The brooch, with its amorous inscription, was the proof of that, if he'd ever doubted it before. And so, after he'd finished his chores for the day, and bathed, and shaved, he'd dressed himself with more than his usual care, in a clean shirt, with a starched collar, and put on his best suit. 'I'm going up to town for an hour or so,' he said to Edith.

'Be careful.' She reached up to straighten his tie, but made no other comment on the way he was dressed. He had his good raincoat on, and his shoes were polished to a glossy shine.

'I will.'

'Do I look all right?' he ventured, suddenly unsure.

'You look very nice.'

'Do I need a hat?'

She thought for a moment. 'A hat would certainly add the finishing touch. Just a minute . . .'

She went away for a moment, then reappeared. 'Here you are,' she said, putting the article into his hand. 'It

302

was Father's. It came from Lock's. I'm afraid it's not the latest fashion, but . . .'

He took it from her. 'Thanks.' He felt an impulse to say something more – to tell her he loved her. But in the end, he confined himself to a brief kiss. 'I've got my latchkey. Don't wait up,' he said.

When he reached Piccadilly Circus, the ticket inspector insisted on taking his arm to guide him onto the moving stair, even though he'd have been better holding the handrail, like everybody else. *Mind how you go now, sir.* People meant to be kind. It was one of the reasons he refused to carry a white stick: their relentless kindness. Even at this time of day, the Circus was busy, or seemed so to him, offering more than its fair share of hazards to the unwary. Around him, as he stood getting his bearings, came the shouts of people hailing taxis. There was the roar of heavy traffic, buses, delivery vans, as it rounded the island with its famous statue of the blind god. From somewhere in the distance came the clanging of an ambulance's bell. As he stood trying to get his bearings, a taxi pulled up in front of him, disgorging a gaggle of shop girls. To judge from their excited chatter, they were on their way – and not for the first time – to see *The White Slave* at the Capitol, Haymarket. Titled beauties abducted by lustful sheikhs. It didn't sound at all his sort of thing. Interrupting their good-natured squabbles as to who owed sixpence to whom, he leant across to speak to the driver: 'Which way to Berkeley Square?'

'Straight ahead, guv'nor. Third turning to your right. You can't miss it.'

Rowlands thanked him, then set off, as the clock on St James', Piccadilly struck seven. It occurred to him that Willoughby might be out. Then he'd have come all this way only to have to surrender the wretched brooch to a housemaid. He decided that if this proved to be the case, he'd ask if he could wait. No sense in coming here if he couldn't see Willoughby. Because the more he thought about it, the more he became convinced that Douglas didn't really have a case. What suspicions he had were founded entirely on conjecture. A few details, in an otherwise straightforward investigation, that didn't add up. The only evidence of any weight was the little token he carried in his jacket pocket, with its tender inscription and its lovers' knot. A lovers' knot that might easily end up fashioning a hangman's noose, if it fell into the wrong hands . . .

He turned down Dover Street. Not far now. A snatch of an old marching song, perhaps suggested by the rhythm of his steps, came into his mind. It was of a vaguely obscene flavour, with an irritating refrain that he couldn't, once he'd recalled it, suppress. Funny how the songs you liked had vanished with all the rest of it, while the ones you couldn't stand stayed with you until your dying day. He was still humming it under his breath, *Inky pinky parlez vous*, when he reached the house.

He climbed the steps, and found the bell, uncomfortably reminded, as he stood there waiting, of the last time he'd made this journey. Then he'd come with a warning; now his intentions were more ambiguous. Because since Celia West's visit, he'd had a clearer view of things. What was done was done. You couldn't bring the dead back to life. Although it was a travesty of justice that a man should hang for a murder he hadn't committed, there could be no justice, surely, in bringing the perpetrator of this particular crime to book? And they'd never get him to say what he knew – that was what he had to tell Willoughby. A man would die, and he wouldn't lift a finger to save him, if it meant he could save *her*.

The room was a large one, he guessed, from the feeling of airy spaciousness above his head. It was walled with books, if the smell was anything to go by: leather and paper, intermingled with the clean scent of applewood from the fire that was burning in the grate; he could feel its comforting warmth even from where he was standing. He cleared his throat, to draw the other's attention to himself, even though the maid had announced him when he came in. It occurred to him, as he stood there, in a silence which began to strike him as ominous, that his former employer and erstwhile commanding officer might still be angry with him. And indeed this seemed confirmed when Willoughby spoke at last, with an abruptness that verged on rudeness:

305

'Well, don't just s-stand there.'

'No, sir.' Rowlands took a tentative step forward, trusting that there wouldn't be any items of furniture or slippery rugs in the way. He supposed Willoughby would sing out if there were. Unless his feelings of displeasure towards Rowlands were such that he'd relish the sight of his old comrade falling flat on his face. He managed to cross the room without incident, however, coming up against the tall back of a leather-upholstered wing chair after three paces. He was glad he hadn't tripped over it. He didn't want to look a fool.

'Sit down, man, for God's sake.'

'Yes, sir.'

'And don't "sir" me! You're not in the b-bloody army now.'

'No, s . . . No, I'm not.'

'Join me in a drink?' Although this wasn't the first drink he'd had, to judge from his speech, which was ever so slightly more hesitant than usual, as if forming his words were an effort.

'All right,' said Rowlands. Because what could it matter now?

There was the sound of a decanter being unstoppered, and then a clinking as it was set down on a table. 'Glasses,' muttered the younger man. 'Now, w-where did I put the glasses? Ah . . .' There was the sound of liquid being poured into tumblers. 'Afraid there's no water.'

'This'll do fine.'

'Well,' said Willoughby. 'Here's luck.'

'Here's luck.' A little gingerly, Rowlands took a sip. The fiery taste wasn't one he'd ever had the chance to get used to. The whisky they'd had in the army, when they could get it, had been pretty poisonous stuff. Rotgut. This was of an altogether superior quality. He wondered, as the fieriness turned to smoothness, whether he'd ever grow to like it, given time.

'So,' said Willoughby. 'Was there something particular you wanted to see me about?'

'Yes.' Carefully setting down his glass on the floor beside him, Rowlands fumbled in his pocket, withdrew the brooch, which he'd wrapped in a scrap of brown paper, and held it out towards Willoughby.

After a pause, Willoughby took it from him. 'What's this?' He started to unwrap it.

Rowlands was suddenly glad of the Dutch courage the whisky had given him. 'I thought it must belong to you, sir. Or rather, to Lady Celia. I . . . I found it on the floor of the office a week or so ago.' It was the best lie he could come up with. He'd already decided to say nothing of her visit.

'Where did you say you found this?'

'On the floor of your office, sir. I thought it must be Lady Celia's, because of the inscription.'

There was a long pause. Rowlands supposed that Willoughby must have been studying the inscription, because when at last he did say something, it was about that: 'It was a birthday present.'

'Sir?' He was finding the habit hard to break.

Fortunately, his former O.C. seemed not to have noticed.

'It's inscribed, you see. With the date.'

'Yes, my wife noticed that.'

'The date of her birthday, as it happens.' Willoughby laughed. 'Quite an expensive little trinket, I'd say. But then she's always liked pretty things. Known how to get them, too . . .'

There seemed no answer to be made to this remark, which struck Rowlands as in rather poor taste. No less surprising was the resentment it conveyed. It seemed all wrong, somehow.

'Because a woman like her does have admirers, you may be sure,' said Willoughby, with the same disconcerting note of bitterness in his voice. 'Oh, yes. Always has done, ever s-since she was a girl. Beautiful women do, you know. You can't blame 'em. It w-would be like blaming the stars for shining.'

It occurred to Rowlands that this might be Willoughby's way of excusing his relationship with Lady Celia. If so, there was no need, as far as he was concerned. 'I hope I did right, in coming to you, sir?' he said, when the silence which had followed Willoughby's observation seemed to be prolonging itself unduly. 'Only it's a valuable brooch, and I thought . . .'

'Oh yes. Quite right,' was the reply. 'You can leave it with me now.'

But when he'd got to his feet, taking this as his dismissal, Willoughby had insisted he sit back down again. He must have another one for the road, said his former O.C. That was only right. Since he'd come all this way, on so 'chivalrous' a mission – that was the word he used, which remained with Rowlands afterwards – he ought at the very least, to take another glass . . . And so Rowlands, conscious that the time was slipping away, with nothing of any significance having been said, sat down again, and waited while Willoughby poured him a second glass. What he *wanted* to say was simply this: that he would say nothing to the police or anyone else of what had passed between Willoughby and the woman who had been, was still, perhaps, his mistress. There seemed no way of conveying this that did not sound impertinent.

In the end, it was Willoughby who spoke first: 'Did I ever tell you,' he asked, 'about what happened at Polygon Wood, my first – no, s-second – month out?'

'I don't think so, sir, no.'

'I'd just been given my first platoon. A good bunch of lads, they were. No end of pluck. I was jolly lucky like that, if it c-comes to that,' Willoughby mused, topping up his glass and Rowlands', although Rowlands' was still three-quarters full. 'Never had to deal with the windy sort . . . What was I saying? Oh, yes. That day at Polly Wood, we'd been cleaning out a nest of snipers. They'd given us a lot of trouble all the p-previous day, and I was determined to beat 'em. As a rule, you know, it would have been a job for the Infantry, but I was a bit full of myself, in those days, and thought I knew how it should be done. All it needed was for me and a couple of the lads to get close enough. Chuck in a couple of Mills Bombs and clear the lot of 'em out.'

Rowlands nodded to show that he was paying attention. The whisky slipped down more easily now. It wasn't so bad, once you got used to it. And Willoughby, in spite of the care he was taking to enunciate each syllable clearly, was obviously very drunk – had been drunk for a long time, Rowlands realised. Although it was only since that matter of the brooch, that it had become obvious. Gentlemen being, by tradition at least, better able to hold their liquor than the lower classes.

'Well, as I said, we had to get ourselves over there, to the far side of the wood, where the firing was coming from. They'd d-done for a couple of our chaps already and wounded four more. One later died of his wounds. So I couldn't afford to let it go . . . I asked for volunteers, and got Tyrwhitt and Arkwright. Both Deptford lads – they were Pals, y'know. Did everything together . . . Odd, really, considering what opposites they were – Tyrwhitt such a queer little runt, with his red hair, and Arkwright such a great big brute of a fellow. They'd worked in the dockyards, both of 'em, before they got called up. Tyrwhitt was a master joiner. Funny, how things s-stick in your mind . . . Anyway. We took our bombs and our rifles, and made our way to where the enemy lay. We had to wriggle most of the way on our bellies, because it was almost daylight. Another hour and the sun would've been up. No chance of not being seen . . .'

'No chance,' echoed Rowlands. The whisky had induced a pleasant feeling of muzziness. It was a long time since he'd felt like this – as if he were suspended a little way outside his body. You got the same effect with morphine but that wasn't an experience he cared to try again . . . I must be tight, he thought, making an effort to focus his attention on what was being said.

'We'd got almost the whole way without being seen,' Willoughby was saying, his voice sounding strangely devoid of expression. 'But we must've been s-seen, because that's when they opened fire, the Germans. Arkwright was killed on the spot. Tyrwhitt and I made it through. We tossed one of our bombs in then, which put a stop to their nonsense. After that, it went very quiet for a bit. "Shall we take a look?" I said to Tyrwhitt. Except that he didn't answer me. Couldn't, you see,' said Willoughby, with a strange kind of laugh, 'because just at that very moment a bullet whistled clean past my ear, and took off the top of his head. He fell down like a stone. Never uttered a sound.'

There was silence for a moment. Then Willoughby went on: 'Well, I saw red, you may be sure, after *that*. Took my gun and ran like a madman through the wire. Didn't stop till I reached the spot where the firing had come from – one of their concrete pillboxes – *you* remember . . .'

'Yes.'

'So I charged up to it, madder than a wet hen, not caring for anything except getting the bastard who'd done it. Didn't cross my mind to wonder why he hadn't shot *me* while he was about it. You don't think of those things until later . . .'

'No.'

'Another splash?' Willoughby suited the action to the words. 'Good stuff, this. Chap I know sends me down a crate every month or so from his estate in Scotland. God knows they need it, with that b-bloody awful climate of theirs . . . Where was I?'

'You'd got to the pillbox.'

'So I had. It'd gone quiet again. No sign of life at all you'd have said, if you hadn't known better . . . And we'd certainly accounted for a few, Tyrwhitt and I. Dead Boche strewn all around. That bomb had done its work pretty well, I'd say. 'Cept that it'd missed one. One skinny little bloke – no more than a boy, really – with a machine gun. He'd run out of ammo, of course, which is why I'd escaped having my head blown off. Nice looking lad, he was, with his big blue eyes, and that flaxen hair they had – you remember? Put up his hands, then, saying "*Kamerad* . . ." If it hadn't been for what he'd done to Tyrwhitt, I might have spared him.'

There was a silence. Rowlands took another sip of his drink. It occurred to him that he'd never given a thought to the man who'd blinded him. He was probably a boy, too, perhaps barely out of his teens. One was always surprised, counting the dead, to see how young they were.

'It haunted me for a long time after that,' said

Willoughby. 'The look in his eyes, when he realised that I was going to shoot him. He didn't cry, or say anything after that, but his chin gave a sort of quiver, as if he was trying his best to be a man. War's a beastly thing,' he added, 'but it does teach you to know right from wrong. Even though you don't always act upon that knowledge.'

It wasn't until Rowlands was descending the moving staircase to the Underground at Piccadilly Circus, that he realised that he'd left his hat behind. He'd handed it to the maid on his arrival, of course, but, having got out of the habit of wearing the beastly things, had forgotten to ask for it back on his departure. The truth was, he'd been so puzzled by what had passed between himself and Willoughby – not to mention being fuddled by all that whisky – that he'd had no thought for anything else. For a minute he hesitated, because it was already later than he'd intended, but then he made up his mind to turn back. It was only a ten minute walk back to Berkeley Square. And Edith would be upset if he lost the thing. Her father's old homburg. Fancy her keeping it all this while. Poor old Harold had been dead a good five years. Smiling, and shaking his head at the sentimentality of women, he retraced his steps along the broad, traffic-loud street. As he did so, keeping close to the wall on his right so as not to collide with oncoming passers-by, he thought about that queer thing Gerald Willoughby had said. *It would be like blaming the stars for shining* . . . As if, in spite of his words, he *did* blame her – Celia West – for the spell she'd cast upon him. Others, too, thought Rowlands. The more he thought about what Willoughby had said, the more uncomfortable he felt.

Afterwards, he wondered at the randomness of the thing – that if it hadn't been for that small act of forgetfulness on his part, he might never have known what had happened until days, perhaps weeks, later. Instead of which, he'd found himself flung from the edge of things to the dead centre. No longer a passive observer – if that word could have been said to apply to him – but a participant. Oh, he'd been that, all right. Not that it was a role he would, given the choice, have chosen. Because after he'd rung the bell, and been re-admitted by the maid, and stated his reason for returning, he'd had a few moments to himself – ones he'd never forget as long as he lived. Waiting there, alone in the echoing hall, for the maid to return with the hat, he'd become aware of a faint but unmistakable sound. It was one he'd heard many times before, albeit in very different surroundings: the sound of a gun being loaded and cocked, in readiness for firing. It was then, in that moment of appalled realisation, that something – call it instinct – took over. There'd been no time for reflection. He'd launched himself towards the sound. There was, of course, a door in the way. Locked. He'd hurled himself against it. 'No!' he'd shouted. 'For the love of God . . .'

But by then it was too late: all the shouting and the hammering on doors in the world couldn't drown out another, more terrible sound – that of a gun going off, and the ringing silence that followed the sound.

One effect of his being always in the dark was that there was no obvious difference between nighttime and any other time of day for him. Midnight and midday were distinguished one from another only by their place in a sequence of habitual activities. When the sequence was broken, as it was now, there seemed no reason to go to sleep at all. All that had happened in the past few hours had had the quality of a nightmare, with events seeming at the same time to be unfolding at breakneck speed and interminably slowly. He wasn't sure how long he'd been here, at the hospital. Three hours? Four? As to where he was, he had only the vaguest notion – a corridor between wards, he supposed, from the intermittent traffic of nurses, and porters wheeling trolleys. He'd asked if he might wait, and this was where they had left him. He didn't mind; he'd wait all night, if he had to, just to hear that Willoughby was out of danger. It occurred to him that the longer he sat there, the better the news was likely to be. Surely if it had been hopeless, he would have heard within minutes?

He was brought out of the waking trance into which he had fallen by the sound of voices. There were two of them: a man's voice, low and placatory in tone, and a woman's. It was this that brought him to his feet.

'What do you mean – he's in the general ward? He should never have been *taken* to the general ward, do you understand?' Sharpened as it was by indignation, mingled with fear, he still would have known it from all other voices . . .

'Madam, I assure you . . .' replied the hapless male, hospital manager or trustee, dragged from his bed in the middle of the night to deal with this emergency.

'I want him moved. At once, do you hear?'

'Of course, Lady Celia. At once,' echoed the other, as the two of them drew near to where Rowlands stood waiting.

Celia West did not seem surprised to see him. 'You've heard, then?' was all she said. Her voice sounded curiously harsh: the tone of one who had yet to give way to weeping.

'Yes.'

'Lady Celia . . .' began the manager.

'Just see to it, will you?' she said.

When they were alone, Celia West addressed Rowlands once more. 'Do you know what happened?'

He hesitated. 'All I know is that . . . there was an accident.'

'Is that what it was?' A small sound, between a laugh and a sob, escaped her. 'Oh, what was he *thinking*?'

The manager appeared again, sounding out of breath. 'Lady Celia . . .'

'What?' Her voice was cold with fury.

'I've given orders that Mr Willoughby is to be

316

transferred into Room 1B. Our *best* room,' he added with some obsequiousness. 'And I shall personally telephone Mr Willoughby's parents.'

'Thank you.' Her voice was scarcely warmer than before. She turned again to Rowlands. 'Walk with me a little, will you?' She took his arm and they set off along the corridor. 'They said I'm to be called if . . . if there's a change. They've got him doped up, with morphine, so at least he won't be feeling anything . . . Oh, *why* did he do it – *why*?' she cried, in the same breathless wail he had heard a few moments before. 'Do you think it was on my account?'

'Of course not,' he said – too quickly, but she didn't appear to notice.

Up and down the tiled corridor they walked, Celia West clinging all the while to Rowlands' arm, as if afraid she might fall. Her heels clicked on the linoleum. Her voice echoed softly: 'Oh *why* did he do it? *Why*?'

The hospital manager interrupted their colloquy with a discreet cough. 'Lady Celia. I'm happy to inform you that your instructions have been carried out.' When she said nothing, the man continued: 'I trust you'll find the arrangements that have been made for the gentleman satisfactory.'

At this, she let go of Rowlands' arm. 'Where is he?' she asked, sounding suddenly much younger than he knew her to be. *A child, afraid of the dark*. 'I want to see him.'

'If you'll come this way . . .' replied the manager, with

something of his former self-important air, accustomed, no doubt, to the vagaries of people's behaviour under such circumstances. Left alone in the middle of the deserted corridor, Rowlands gazed in the direction that they had gone. A door, some distance away, was opened, then shut again. After that, there was nothing but an echoing silence.

In the age between the gun's going off and the door's being broken down, his mind had been filled with a question: 'Why?' And, since there could be no answer to this it was followed by a string of others, no less futile. 'Surely you must have *known*,' he'd wanted to cry, 'that I never would have betrayed you – or her? That my whole intention in coming to see you was to save her – to save both of you?' But by then it was too late for such questions. All he could do when at last the door burst open on the foul reek of cordite was to shout for help, as loud as he could. Then, when the weeping maid ran to telephone, he'd stumbled his way to where Willoughby, his blood already forming a pool on the floor beneath his head, lay spreadeagled. Cradling the poor hurt body in his arms, Rowlands had murmured, over and over, 'This won't do, sir, you know. This won't do at all . . .'

The feeling of that limp weight in his arms was with him still. The sound of the wounded man's groans. Muffled, as if bubbling through a mouthful of blood. At the sound, he'd gently lifted the other man's head, feeling the coarse, springy texture of the hair, the terrible angle of the shattered jaw, thinking that there might be something he wanted to say

– some word that would supply an answer to the question now tormenting him: that 'why' to which it seemed there was no answer. But if there had been anything Willoughby had to say, he did not succeed in saying it. All that emerged from the poor, broken mouth were formless cries, recalling a time when such sounds of pain and distress had been all too common a feature of both their lives.

Now, as Rowlands sat there in the deserted corridor, suspended between one day and another, and breathing in that familiar hospital smell, compounded of disinfectant, surgical spirit, and the smells of blood and sickness they imperfectly concealed, he felt himself transported back to that earlier time. When it was he who lay wounded, in a darkness he did not yet know was to be a permanent condition, while Willoughby sat beside him, smoking cigarette after cigarette, and talking of inconsequential things. The football results. Rowlands had supported Charlton in those days. How much he was looking forward to going home . . . 'Why did you do it, sir?' he murmured, echoing Celia West's bewildered words. 'You know I never meant it to come to this.' Because there was no escaping the feeling that Willoughby's violent act of self-abnegation was – in part, at least – connected to Rowlands' visit. Or rather, to the reason for that visit, which was the diamond brooch. That cursed brooch, which he'd found clutched in Willoughby's hand, and sticky with his blood. The brooch which was now concealed in the pocket of his jacket, a small but terrible reminder of what had passed.

It was after two when he woke from the shallow doze into which he had fallen, his heart pounding, as if at a violent shock. It was the sound of his own name being pronounced, close to his ear, that had woken him. 'Did I disturb you? My apologies,' said Inspector Douglas.

'I wasn't asleep.'

'Yes, it's hard to get more than a few minutes' shut-eye in these places,' said the policeman, pleasantly, as he sat down beside Rowlands. 'Cigarette?'

'No, thanks.' His hand went automatically to his pocket – but the brooch was still there. Proof, if any were needed, that what had happened that night was real, and not just part of some ghastly dream.

'So here we are again,' remarked Douglas. 'I won't ask you what brings you here, because I've a fair idea. What I *am* curious about, is how you came to hear about it.'

Rowlands was conscious of choosing his words carefully. 'I happened to call by . . . at Mr Willoughby's house, I mean. It seems there was an accident . . .'

'Accident be damned. Suicide's a crime, you know.'

His heart gave a jump. 'What makes you think it was suicide?'

Douglas emitted a dry little laugh. 'Oh, we've plenty of evidence, believe me. When you've seen as much of this kind of thing as I have – even the botched attempts – you get to recognise the signs.' For an instant, Rowlands allowed himself to hope. There was no real evidence, then. 'But, even if I

320

hadn't had my suspicions in the first place, finding the note would have convinced me,' the policeman said. 'Och aye . . .' Rowlands having been unable to repress a start. 'We've a splendid note. A confession, too, you'll be interested to know.'

'I don't follow . . .'

'Don't you, by God? Then let me spell it out for you. All the while that we – the Metropolitan police force – were busy pursuing our line of enquiry into what the newspapers like to describe as "the Claremont Court murder", it seems we were barking up the wrong tree.' The Inspector's Edinburgh accent grew more pronounced, the angrier he got. 'Yes, it would seem our Mr Caparelli didn't kill Lionel West, after all. Your Mr Willoughby did.'

'*What*?'

'He says so, as plain as day, in the note he left before he tried to take his own life. Here, let me read it to you . . .' Douglas drew a sheet of paper from his pocket and unfolded it. '"I, Gerald Winstanley Willoughby, being of sound mind . . ."'

'This is hardly the time and place . . .'

'Why ever not? No time like the present. ". . . being of sound mind, have decided to put an end to my life and to what has become an intolerable situation . . ."'

'For God's sake, man, have you no pity?' For Rowlands' sharper hearing had detected the sound of a door opening. Footsteps approaching.

'Go on,' said Celia West. There was a flatness to her

voice which was more shocking than outright hysterics would have been. As if nothing and no one could matter to her any more. 'You were saying something about Gerald . . .'

'Ah, Lady Celia.' For a moment, Douglas seemed almost taken aback by her appearance. 'I'm very sorry about all this. Very sorry indeed.'

'What was it you were saying just now? About Gerald . . .' She gave a gasp. 'That's his writing, isn't it? Give it to me.'

'I'm afraid that's not possible, Lady Celia,' said the policeman. 'You see, it's evidence . . .'

'Evidence of what? What are you talking about?' Her voice cracked suddenly. 'I *insist* you give me that letter.'

There was the sound of a brief struggle, followed by that of a slap.

'You scoundrel,' said Celia West.

'It's as well,' said Douglas, in an even tone, 'that I'm not on duty. Assaulting a police officer's an offence, even if it *is* by a member of the aristocracy. Because it may surprise you to know, Lady Celia, that we're all equal under the law. Equally innocent, until proven guilty, and equally capable of being found guilty.'

'What does it matter now, any of it?' she said tonelessly. 'You've got what you wanted, haven't you?'

'Lady Celia,' said Rowlands. 'Don't. Please . . .'

But she paid no attention. 'Hounding him, until he

was almost driven mad. Driven into a corner. Oh yes, you've got what you wanted, all right . . .' Suddenly, all the fight seemed to go out of her. She collapsed into Rowlands' arms, her body racked with sobs. 'My God. My God,' she cried. 'What will become of me? Oh, what will become of me?'

It was left to Rowlands to say what had been obvious to him since her reappearance. Which was that the worst had happened. 'Don't you see, you fool?' he said to Douglas. 'He's dead. It's all over, now.'

Chapter Twelve

As he emerged from the Underground at Regent's Park, the first flakes were beginning to fall; he felt each one like a spectral kiss upon his upturned face. Snow. He'd always loved the smell of it – the crackle of ice in the air that said they were in for a heavy fall. Although the fact of it was somewhat less appealing. Memories of childhood pleasures, *sliding on iced-over puddles at Camberwell Green*, couldn't obscure the very real dangers the stuff presented. Bad enough, he thought, gingerly ascending steps already slick with moisture, as flakes turned at once to water on contact with the warmer surface, and froze again – bad enough, when you could see where you were going. Potentially fatal, when you were feeling your way blind along pavements transformed to skating rinks, and trying to keep your balance on stairs turned into frozen waterfalls. For the moment, however, it was safe enough. Thanks to Edith, he was wearing his stout shoes. 'I don't like the look of that sky,' she'd said, as he'd been about to set out. 'It's that strange shade of yellow it goes before a storm, or a snowfall. I don't suppose you remember . . .'

'Oh yes,' he'd said. 'I remember.'

Entering the park by the York Gate, he followed the familiar path towards the Inner Circle. There was a fresh, cold smell of moist earth and evergreens – a pleasant change from the noxious fumes of traffic in Marylebone Road – and a definite crispness to the grass underfoot, as he cut across Queen Mary's Gardens. He'd walked here often enough with Edith; it must be ten years ago, when they were courting. It had been summer then, of course, and the roses were in full bloom. She'd told him the name of each one – Ena Harkness, Ophelia, *Gloire de Dijon* – and described their colours. The crimson ones had the strongest scent, he seemed to recall. It was a smell which never failed to conjure up, in his mind, that heady state called being in love. An intoxicating, overwhelming aroma. No wonder women so often wore it as a perfume.

Arriving in front of the house, he found his memory of the place to be as indelibly inscribed, its smallest details as present to him as the rose garden's had been. The way the gate swung inward with a slight metallic groan. The way the gravel crunched under one's feet. The smell of leaf mould arising from the shrubbery. Laurels, if his memory served him correctly. It was twenty paces to the door. Three steps up to the porch, with its tiled floor. His hand remembered the feel of the bell pull, and his ear the muted jangling the bell made. As he stood waiting, he heard the gate open, and a man come whistling up the path. He was evidently not a visitor, for instead of mounting the steps, he followed the path as it curved round to the back of the house. On his way to the workshops, Rowlands surmised. Some slight sound on his part must have attracted the newcomer's attention.

'Hullo!' he said, halting for a moment. 'Were you wanting anyone in particular?'

'I've come to see Major Fraser,' replied Rowlands guardedly. One thing he *had* forgotten was the intense interest everybody at the Lodge took in everybody else's business.

'Oh. Thought you might be the new trick cyclist,' was the reply. 'The old one left last week. Had his fill of the place, I shouldn't wonder. Not that I set much store by that kind of thing. Telling your dreams,' he said, with an accent of deepest scorn, 'to a complete stranger . . .'

'I've never fancied it, either.'

'Don't I know you from somewhere?' said his interlocutor suddenly. 'You sound awful familiar.'

Rowlands introduced himself.

'Well, I'll be blowed!' exclaimed the other. 'Freddie

Rowlands, as I live and breathe! Don't you remember me?' he went on. 'It's Sid Ridley. We played a bit of football together, in the old days. Centre forward you were – and not so bad neither. Till you gave it up for messing about in boats.'

'Of course I remember you.' The two men shook hands. 'But . . . didn't you have a job to go back to, in Sunderland?'

'I did that,' replied the north-eastener. 'Lasted a year, and then they laid me off. Not *suitable* for the work, they said.' He gave a sarcastic laugh. 'All my eye and Betty Martin. They didna want to take the risk of having me fall into the machinery, they said. I told 'em, "It's me that's taking the risk, man . . ."'

The door opened and someone – the Major – looked out. 'Rowlands, is that you? Thought I heard the bell. Where Ellen's got to I can't imagine . . . Who's that with you? Oh, it's you, Sid. Well, don't stand there freezing yourselves to death – come in.'

The first thing Rowlands noticed was that the place still smelt the same: a mixture of floor wax, wood smoke from the sitting room fire, and boiled cabbage; even in his day, the food had been of the institutional variety. As he divested himself of coat and muffler – the coat stand, he noted with satisfaction, was still behind the door, next to the rack for the men's sticks – the Major kept up a stream of humorous remarks, of which Ridley was the principle object. 'Sid's our football coach, you know. We're trying to keep him, even though he could get a lot more money coaching West Ham, or Tottenham, or one of the other big teams. But we don't tell him that,' he concluded in a stage whisper.

'Haddaway, man,' said Ridley. 'You know I could never work for one of them fancy London clubs. Well, best be going. I've a team to get into shape before the final. Good to see you again,' he added to Rowlands.

'And you,' said Rowlands, thinking how some habits of speech never die.

When he'd finished saying what he had to say, a silence fell. Nor did the Major seem in any hurry to break it. Instead, he got up from his chair and went over to the window. There was the sound of the sash being thrown up. A gust of cold air. 'It's snowing quite a bit harder,' he said, closing it again after a moment. 'I think it'll lie. Though it's early in the year. What are we – mid-December? Could mean we're in for a long winter . . .' Rowlands murmured his concurrence with these remarks. After this, there was a longish pause, filled with the minute sounds of the Major filling his pipe. 'Do smoke, if you'd like,' he said, when this task was accomplished to his satisfaction and the instrument was drawing nicely. 'There are cigarettes in the box on the table. Turkish and Virginia. Matches to the right, I think you'll find.'

'Thank you, sir,' said Rowlands, helping himself.

There was a brief, companionable silence, while both had their smoke, each taking the time, it seemed to Rowlands, to consider what it was he had to say. It struck

Rowlands then that he knew hardly anything about Ian Fraser at all, beyond the bare facts of his biography: Marlborough and Sandhurst, followed by a commission in the King's Shropshire Light Infantry; then the Battle of the Somme, which had put paid to his military career, but had led eventually to his stewardship of the Lodge. It wasn't much to know about a man. Yet he would have trusted him above anyone.

'If it's advice your friend's after, I'm not sure I'm the right man to advise him,' said the Major, at last. 'It all sounds a bit out of my league, frankly.'

Rowlands said nothing, sensing more was to follow.

'You say that the man in question – your friend's O.C. – is dead . . .'

'Yes.'

'. . . having taken the burden of guilt for the, ah . . . *crime* upon himself.'

'That's right. The fact is, Major . . .'

'The actual . . . ah, *perpetrator* of the act is still at liberty, I take it?'

'Yes. You see . . .'

'And this friend is the only one who knows the truth of the matter . . .'

'The police suspect something,' admitted Rowlands, with some reluctance.

'Do they indeed? Then I should let them get on with following up their suspicions. It's what the police are for.'

'Thank you, sir.' The feeling of relief was enormous.

'Unless, of course,' the Major went on, with the diffident air that was so characteristic of him, 'it turns out that your friend is in possession of information not available to the police. That, I imagine, would make a difference to what you . . . that is, your friend . . . decides to do. Because that would be withholding evidence.'

'Yes, of course.' Brief as it had been, that moment of respite from the burden of responsibility he had been carrying around these past few months now redoubled the weight of it. Not that he was surprised at what the Major had said. It was what he thought himself. Whether he could bring himself to act upon it was another matter.

There was the sound of a door being pushed open and the tintinnabulation of teacups. 'Ah, here's Mrs Walsh with our tea! Thank you, Mrs Walsh . . . if you'd just put it on the table in front of the fire, we'll help ourselves.' When the door had closed behind the housekeeper, the Major said quietly, 'I'm not advocating any particular course of action, you understand. All I'm doing is setting out the various alternatives. Undoubtedly, your friend will have thought these out for himself but . . .'

'It helps to have someone else say it. Puts it in a clearer light,' said Rowlands.

'If that's so, then I'm glad. The fact is,' said Major Fraser, starting to pour out the tea, 'I've experienced too many what you might call *ambiguous* circumstances, to want to lay down the law to the other chap, if you take my meaning. There were things that happened during the war – I daresay you can think of a few, too – that cured me of any tendency towards judging my fellows. Good men gone to the bad, through sheer brute force of events. Bad men . . . well, let's just say that bad men seldom come off worst, in this world.'

'That's true.'

'Our Lord had it right, I feel. "Let he who is without sin cast the first stone." Drink up,' said the Major, touching Rowlands lightly upon the wrist to direct his hand towards his cup and saucer. 'The sugar bowl's at two o'clock.'

Afterwards, they took a turn around the park. The snow had stopped falling, and the ground was now covered by a thick soft crust that crunched beneath their feet. 'We'll be in for some more of this, before nightfall,' opined the Major, sniffing the air appreciatively.

'My girls'll be pleased.'

'Ah, yes. You've children, of course,' said the Major, who had none. 'How many is it now?'

'Three.'

'Splendid. Y'know, when I took on this job in '16,' the older man went on, 'I thought it'd be for a few months, until I got back on my feet, y'know? Funny, how something can take over one's life. Not that I regret it for a moment, but I've sometimes asked myself, "Did I choose it, or did it choose me?"'

'I believe I know what you mean,' said Rowlands.

* * *

He'd been the only one from the office to attend the funeral. It had taken place in Hampshire, which was where Willoughby's people were from. He'd gone down on the train, and a taxi had dropped him off at the church, just after the service had started. It had been a sparsely attended affair – no more than a dozen mourners, if the raggedness of the singing was anything to go by. Which was strange, when you thought what a likeable sort Willoughby had been . . . although, on reflection, it wasn't as strange as all that. People didn't want to be associated with a suspicious death, that was all. Even though the circumstances of this one had been hushed up, there were still some for whom the rumour of suicide was enough. Afterwards, he'd been on the point of leaving, when a man – elderly, to judge from his voice – accosted him in the church porch, and asked him his name. When he'd supplied it, and given a brief account of himself, the old gentleman had seemed moved. 'Good of you to come all this way. I'm Gerald's father.'

Rowlands held out his hand. 'How do you do, sir?'

'He was a good boy,' said the old man, with a sudden burst of feeling. 'A good boy. Never the least bit of trouble to his mother and me. A good sportsman, when he was at school. Won all the cups, you know . . .' His voice faltered.

'Yes,' said Rowlands, groping for something he could say that would be of consolation. 'He was my O.C., during the war. A fine officer. Very well liked by all the men,' he added, with an unhappy sense of offering false coin for gold.

Willoughby senior had seemed delighted by this, however. 'Was he, indeed?' he'd exclaimed. 'Eunice, my dear . . .' he called to his wife, 'this young feller knew our Gerry during the war.'

Summoned, with a reluctance she was unable entirely to conceal, Mrs Willoughby had bestowed on Rowlands her small, gloved hand. 'There are several men from my son's regiment here, I believe,' she said. 'If you like, I can introduce you, Mr . . . er . . .'

When he'd said his name, there was a brief, but perceptible, pause. 'You were at the hospital that night,' she said.

'Yes. I . . .'

But Mrs Willoughby was addressing her husband: 'I think, don't you, that we ought to be getting back to the house,' she said with a determined cheerfulness that was more terrible than a display of grief. 'I've asked Mrs Driver to set out a cold collation in the dining room. Roberts will see about the sherry . . .'

'Of course, my dear,' was the reply. 'Do join us, if you'd like to,' the old man said to Rowlands. But Rowlands, sensing that his presence could only be an uncomfortable reminder to Eunice Willoughby of certain hours she would rather forget, pleaded a train to catch.

It was only in books that being in possession of a shameful secret proved unbearable to the possessor, so that life became impossible until the dreadful knowledge was revealed. He had read several novels in which this had been the fulcrum of the story – *Thérèse Raquin* being one that had troubled him extremely. But, despite the uncomfortable feelings aroused by this, and other tales of a similar ilk, Rowlands had managed to live with his secret quite successfully. It had got so that, after a lapse of several months, he no longer thought about it very much at all. One reason for this was that he was now living a different kind of life, far from the places where the events in which he had been so caught up had taken place, and from the people who had been involved in those events. If he thought about them at all, it was as if they had happened to someone else, a long time ago, in another country. And despite the obvious disadvantages of his present situation compared to the one he had enjoyed before, where he was now was undoubtedly a kind of a refuge.

It was quiet – that was one thing you could say for the place. The noise and bustle of the city seemed a thousand miles away. The house – two farm labourers' cottages knocked into one – wasn't so bad either, once they'd fixed it up a little. As Edith had pointed out only the other day, they could never have afforded the rent for so a large place on their own. Best of all was the amount of land that went with the house, which was almost four acres, if you counted the orchard. There was a good bit of kitchen garden, and then the field behind the house, where a good many hours of Rowlands' day were spent. It wasn't how he'd envisaged ending up, but it wasn't the worst kind of life. And it was healthier for the children, that much you couldn't deny.

After the cold spring they'd had, followed by a spell of weather so wet it had seemed as if they must have skipped the more clement season altogether and gone directly to autumn, today, the first of August, was warm and dry. The grass, until a few days ago a sodden mass which clung to his trouser legs, soaking as it clung, now parted with a swishing sound, to let him pass, releasing a pleasant smell of meadow flowers. A warm breeze ruffled his hair. It was good to feel the sun on his bare throat and arms – exposed as these were by the rolled-up sleeves of his oldest shirt. 'One for the Old Clothes man,' Edith had muttered that morning, as she'd watched him dress. 'Can't have you going about looking like a tramp.' Himself, he thought it a pity that clothes only became really comfortable when they had lost all vestiges of respectability. At least his present employment didn't require him to look more than presentable. It was months since he'd worn a stiff collar.

Ahead of him, across the field, went his daughters, Margaret leading the way, with the egg-basket, Anne following, pushing the pram with the baby. He brought up the rear of the little procession, carrying the feed and water buckets. Their combined weight, and his reluctance to spill any more of his burden on the ground than was necessitated by the unevenness of the path, meant his progress was the slowest of the three. More than once, he was obliged to set down the brimming pails, in order to rest his arms. 'Come on, Daddy, you slowcoach!' he heard Anne call, by way of encouragement. The coops were in the middle of the field. There were twenty of them, arranged in rows of four around the hut where the tools were kept, and the supplies of worming powder and disinfectant. There was a shotgun there, too, suspended high upon the wall, out of reach of the girls. Edith wouldn't have it in the house, although of course with foxes and other vermin about, they couldn't do without it, Viktor had pointed out. Nor could they; he was just glad he wasn't the one who had to wield the thing. His days of messing around with guns were long over, thank heaven.

Reaching the coops at last, he set down the pails and went to open up. As he slid back the catch on the first cage, there was a feathery hubbub on the other side of the wire, as the incumbents jostled each other aside in their efforts to be first to the feeding tray. Further along the row, he could hear Margaret and Anne talking to their favourites: 'Come along, Henrietta . . .' 'Here you are, Prudence, some lovely scraps for you . . .' Even though he knew it was just one of their games, he disapproved of making pets of creatures destined to end up in the pot. Edith had said he needn't worry. 'Children are much more hard-hearted than you'd imagine.' He wasn't entirely convinced of this. Margaret, it was true, seemed sensible enough, but Anne had developed an anxious streak since she turned six. Refusing to go to sleep without the light on, and complaining that there was 'a man hanging' from the door of the bedroom she shared with her sister. Even when the dressing gown that had prompted this nervous fancy had been taken away, she still persisted in her delusion. A pile of dead leaves at the end of the garden had a similarly malevolent look to her. He'd run the rake into it, to show her there was nothing there. But the goblin she'd conjured up from some childish realm of nightmare was not so easily magicked away.

'Daddy, will my eyes drop out one day, like Mary-Jane's?' she'd startled him by asking, Mary-Jane being her china doll. When he'd reassured her, she'd said stubbornly, 'But *yours* did . . .' Yes, she was going through what Edith called 'an imaginative stage'. So that when, bending to scoop up handfuls of the dry, faintly musty smelling grain, to throw for his newly released flock, he heard Anne shout, 'Daddy! There's a man . . .' he didn't at first pay much attention.

'Margaret, bring the water bucket, will you? Can you lift it all right?'

'Yes, Daddy.'

'A man!' screamed Anne. 'A man!'

'Pipe down, Anne. You'll frighten the hens,' he told her. 'Now, what's all this fuss about?'

But before his daughter could reply, there came another voice: one he hadn't thought to hear again. 'Sorry to butt in on you like this. Your wife said I'd find you here . . .'

337

Rowlands straightened up, brushing the powdery feed from his hands. He didn't smile. 'What brings you here, Inspector?'

'I was hoping for a wee chat.'

It was with an effort of will that he kept his voice level. 'I believe we've said everything we had to say to one another.'

'Ah, but that's where you're wrong,' replied Douglas softly. 'My, what great big lasses you're getting to be,' he added, addressing the girls. 'How old are you now?'

'I'll be nine next birthday,' said Margaret.

'That's a fine great age, to be sure. And what about you, young lady?'

But Anne, having announced the arrival of this interloper in their midst, now steadfastly refused to bring out another word.

'Girls,' said Rowlands. 'I want you to run back to the house and ask Mummy for some lemonade.'

'I'm not thirsty,' said Margaret.

'Run along.'

When he and Douglas were alone together, with the baby still asleep in her pram between them, he allowed his anger full rein. 'You had no right to come,' he said. 'Raking up the past. I said all I had to say at the time. I've nothing more to add.'

'Haven't you, though?' said Douglas. 'You know, you surprise me. Given that you were *there*, all the time it was going on. You must have heard *something*. A sharp chap like you. Wasn't that why you left – because you'd heard something that didn't square with what you thought was right?'

'I didn't hear anything,' said Rowlands. 'Now, if you'll excuse me, I've got work to do.'

'They were lovers all along, you know. How do you think she got him to do her dirty work?'

'I told you. I've nothing to say.'

'Oh, she had him on a string, you may be sure . . . The wonder of it is that string was nearly enough to hang him.'

'I've no idea what you're talking about.'

There was a moment's silence, as if Douglas were trying to judge the truth or otherwise of Rowlands' words from his expression. 'What's surprising,' the policeman went on, 'is that he seems to be willing to let bygones be bygones. Which is odd, you'll admit. But then, he's not the first man to have been willing to throw his life away for the sake of a smile or two from the beautiful Lady Celia. Or rather more than that, in Caparelli's case . . .'

'If you're referring to what Caparelli said in court, you must know he was lying,' said Rowlands coldly. 'Trying to save his neck by dragging her name into it . . .'

'I'm afraid there's rather more to it than that. They're living together, you know.'

It was as if someone had emptied the bucket of water intended for the chickens all over him. 'What?'

'Why man, you've gone as white as a sheet. Has it really come as such a shock, then? Och aye, they left England together a week after he came out of gaol. Now they're living in France in some villa near Monte Carlo. He's calling himself by another name, of course – some Eye-talian sounding thing. Count this or that. But we made sure it was the same man.' Douglas permitted himself a chuckle. 'There aren't too many men with Caparelli's sartorial sense, let's be frank. Although it doesn't seem to bother the lady. Funny how women are attracted to that dago look . . .'

'I don't want to listen to any more of this . . . this *filth*,' said Rowlands. He was almost breathless with rage, so that it was an effort to speak. 'You come here, without so much as a by-your-leave, and tell me a pack of lies . . .'

'I assure you, it's perfectly true. I had it from Caparelli's own lips, in gaol. He says it was her idea – Lady Celia's – for him to go to the house that night. They'd arranged to meet, once the . . . *business* was done. Only . . . she didn't turn up, he says. Or not until later . . .'

'He's lying.'

'. . . by which time he'd gone, leaving his gun behind. He'd dropped it in the scuffle. Oh, yes, he admitted to all of that, did Caparelli. Just not to the actual killing.'

Rowlands thought about what Caparelli had said to him, that time he'd visited him in prison. *If I'd been going to kill him, I'd have chosen another way.* 'You've no proof of any of this,' he said.

'That's true enough,' said Douglas. 'Which is where I thought you might be able to help. You *do* know something, don't you? I can see it in your face. You were uncertain from the first – that's why you went to see Caparelli in gaol . . . Oh yes, he told me. You wanted to convince yourself that he was guilty. Instead, you realised that he was probably telling the truth. Which meant somebody else was probably telling lies . . .'

'I want you to leave now.'

'I did wonder, you know, if it might have been you who wrote me that letter, as a way of tipping me the wink without seeming to, if you get me . . .'

'I didn't write it. Now, if you'll excuse me, Inspector, I've got work to do.'

'Gerald Willoughby's dead, you know. Nothing you can say or do can bring him back . . .'

'I've told you. I've nothing to add.'

'. . . but don't you think you owe it to his memory to clear him of the disgrace of being thought a murderer? You can do *that* for him, at least . . .'

In the silence that followed, Rowlands could hear the soft clucking of the hens, as they clustered around the feed tray. Rising above that comforting murmur came another, not dissimilar, sound – the cooing of his baby daughter, waking up from her nap. Even though he knew she'd lie there contently for a while, before making her presence felt, he went to her at once, and gathered her up. Holding her close to him, as if his physical presence alone might guard her from the evil that had come near, and which threatened to engulf them all.

'Nothing's going to happen to you, you know,' said the policeman, drawing closer, so that they were separated only by the length of the pram. 'You'll be asked to sign a statement, that's all. I doubt whether you'd even have to appear in court, if the thing came to trial.'

In Rowlands' arms, Joan gave a joyful wriggle, exclaiming softly with amusement and pleasure at everything she saw: the sky with its clouds, the field with its chickens, her father in his old blue shirt . . . He felt the warm weight of her, a surprising weight for a child not yet two, and smelled her sweet baby smell. At twenty months, she hadn't yet mastered walking, preferring to shuffle along on her bottom, a fact that worried Edith, used as she was to Margaret's precocity in all respects; Anne's dogged determination to follow suit. But he'd told her there was plenty of time. Hadn't Joanie learned everything she needed to know – to focus her eyes on a familiar face, to smile, to hold her head steady – as soon as she needed to know it? Now, as he held her in the crook of his arm, with one hand resting lightly against her back, he knew she had no need of any further support. Yet, out of habit, he brought up his other hand to cradle the back of her neck. Such a slender little neck, to carry so heavy a head. Joan's head was all the more beautiful, to his mind, for its sparsity of hair. Until lately, when – to her mother's relief – a few feathery curls had manifested themselves, there'd been nothing but a covering of soft down upon that smooth warm dome. If you rested your hand there, you could feel the pulse beating beneath the as yet unclosed-up plates of the skull . . .

He became aware that Douglas was still talking.

Douglas, it seemed, was always talking, or trying to get others to talk. '. . . all you have to do is tell me what you know,' that insistent voice went on, like a hammer in the brain. *Tell me what you know. Tell me what you know,* it murmured, on and on. Offering what kind of absolution? And it would be so easy to tell. To divest himself, at a stroke, of that unbearable burden. The guilt of that knowledge. *Oh, darling I'm so frightened . . .* It would be payment in kind for that double betrayal. Retribution. He could feel the words on his tongue. *She was at Claremont that night. I heard her say so to Willoughby . . .* A death sentence, if ever there was one. Of the two that had heard it – her confession – one was dead, by his own hand; the other now stood in the middle of a Kentish field, with his child in his arms, his mind burning with all that he had heard. He had only to open his mouth, and tell the inspector what he knew. Perhaps then he could be at peace. 'There was one thing,' he said.

'Yes?' Even though he was unable to see the other's expression, he could tell that there was a different quality to his attention, a sharpening, that was not there before. 'And what was that?' said Douglas. In his eagerness, he leant forward, the better to catch whatever revelations might fall from the other's lips. Hungry for the moment of truth. Rowlands gathered this, although he couldn't see it, because at that moment the pram gave a jolt, as if too much weight had been placed upon it. The sudden movement startled Joan. There was a split second of outraged silence, as she drew breath, then she started to cry. As with everything his placid daughter did, it was slow to begin, but wholeheartedly carried out. 'Och, the puir weé thing,' said Douglas, attempting joviality. 'Did the bad man frighten ye? I didna mean it . . .'

'Shh, shh,' murmured Rowlands, stroking the soft curls at the nape of his daughter's neck. Such a fragile neck, not much thicker than his own wrist. So strong, when one thought of the burden it had to carry, and so easy to break. 'The last time I saw Mr Willoughby, he reminded me of something we learned in the army, which was the difference between right and wrong. It was on account of something he did that . . . that resulted in another's death, that he came to this understanding. I think the gist of it was that one should always follow one's conscience in such matters. One's instinct for what is right,' said Rowlands. 'At the time, I didn't understand what he meant, but I do now.' Soothed by the sound of her father's voice, Joan stopped crying as suddenly as she had started. 'If you'd like to walk back with me to the house,' Rowlands went on, 'I'll ask my wife to give you a cup of tea.'

There was another silence, this time of a different nature. When the inspector spoke at last, it was with a calmness that barely concealed his anger. 'You realise of course that she was using him – your precious Willoughby – to get what she wanted? Lionel West's money, and that . . . that *creature* she was in love with . . . If you can call that kind of thing love,' said Douglas, as if the word left a foul taste in his mouth.

'If that's so, then she's paid a high price for it,' replied Rowlands. 'One can't imagine any kind of love that would stand such a test.'

'That's true. It may be that one fine day I'll open the paper and see that Lady Celia's fancy man has snapped her pretty neck for her. A pity, though. I'd hoped to have been the cause of it myself.'

Something else occurred to Rowlands: 'Why wasn't he re-arrested, when he left prison?'

'Caparelli, you mean? Och, we'd have liked to. Only, you see, there wasn't enough evidence for that . . .'

Rowlands frowned. 'But surely, Jarvis' statement . . .'

'Isn't worth the paper it's written on, with the witness himself dead . . .' The Inspector's laugh had a grim sound. 'Fished out o' the Thames by Hungerford Bridge not two days after he'd been to see the police. Not a mark on him, o' course. But quite a lot of cheap brandy in his stomach.'

They'd reached the house by now, and conversation ceased, although Rowlands' mind was a whirl of questions he'd have liked to put – not least about Harry Jarvis' untimely end. A memory of the day it all started, when the man had come into the office, bringing a whiff of the inferno with him, now returned to trouble him. Other questions crowded into his mind. How was it that the police had failed to pump Caparelli for what he knew of Celia West's involvement in the affair? If indeed, he knew anything at all, and wasn't lying, to save his own neck . . . Yes, there was no real evidence against her, he thought, except the knowledge that he himself had chosen to withhold. He guessed that the Inspector, judging by his affronted silence, would cheerfully have throttled him.

Edith came to the door to meet them. She and Dorothy had been baking all morning, and the air was filled with the smell of new bread and scones. 'No, I won't have tea, thanks all the same,' said Douglas. 'I ought to be getting along. I'm expected back at the Yard by six.'

'A long day for you,' said Edith.

'Och, it'll be longer still before it's over,' replied the policeman. He and Rowlands did not shake hands. 'Well,' he said, 'if you change your mind, you know where to find me.' His footsteps receded along the gravel path towards the gate.

'I've never liked that man,' said Edith as, together, they went back inside the house.

'He's only doing his job.'

'Yes, but he does it with such awful *relish*. One imagines he takes a positive pleasure in sending people to the gallows . . .'

'I doubt it's pleasure that drives him,' said Rowlands. 'Merely a desire to see justice done.'

'It's my belief,' said his wife, 'that all such things should be left to a higher power. We're not gods.'

'No,' he agreed. 'We're certainly not that.'

'So what *did* he want to see you about?' She poured him a cup of tea, then one for herself. 'Surely not something more to do with that case? The poor man's dead, isn't he? Such a *strange* affair,' she continued, when he did not reply. 'I never did see what it was he saw in her. Celia West. Not that she wasn't very lovely, of course. But there was something not quite right about her, in my opinion. Something fundamentally unsound. Unhappy, Dorothy thought her, didn't you Dorothy?' she said, as her sister-in-law came in, with the baby, little Victor, in her arms. 'Celia West, I mean.'

'Yes,' said Dorothy, off-handedly. 'I know who you mean.'

'There's a cup of tea in the pot, if you want one.'

'No, thanks,' said Dorothy.

'Please yourself. As a matter of fact,' Edith went on, 'there was a mention of her – Lady Celia – in the paper, the other day . . .' Having decided to suspend her reticence on the topic, it now seemed she couldn't say enough about it. 'I didn't bring it to your attention at the time, Fred, because . . . well, I didn't think it would interest you, that's all. Apparently, she's living in France these days. The Côte d'Azur.'

'Is she?'

'Oh yes. She's in with a fast crowd. Lord Knowles, and Mrs Wyse – that American divorcee – and some Italian count whose name I can't recall. I must say,' said Edith, 'she does seem to have got over what happened remarkably quickly.'

He took a sip of his tea. It was too hot, and he set down the cup again.

'It's strange to think that you and she were such friends, for a while . . .' There was a speculative note in Edith's voice. He knew better than to rise to the bait, however. She could fish all she liked; he'd never admit to anything. 'Ringing you up, out of the blue,' his wife went on, 'and that day she came to the house – do you remember?'

'Yes,' he said. 'I remember. What do you mean, ringing me up?'

'Oh, didn't I tell you?' said Edith. 'It must have slipped my mind. It was one day when you were out. I didn't speak to her myself. She left a message at the pub. Bill Perks brought it round, the cheeky so-and-so.'

'What did it say?'

'Don't look at me like that. It can't have been terribly important, or she'd have written . . .'

'What did it say?'

'Fred, I will not have you *glare* at me like that . . . It said, as far as I can remember, "Thank you for all you've done", or words to that effect. I suppose she meant being with her at the hospital, the night poor Mr Willoughby died. I'm sorry. If I'd thought it was that important . . .'

'It doesn't matter,' he said, getting up.

'Where are you going?'

'To shut the hens up.' He managed to restrain himself from slamming the door.

In the middle of the empty field, he gave in to his feelings at last. *To think that she* . . . His mind recoiled from the pain of that knowledge. He wanted to lie on the ground and howl. To beat his fists against its hard dry surface. He felt the hot tears roll down his cheeks. He didn't even know why he was weeping. Was it for the man he loved, whose death he – albeit inadvertently – had helped to bring about? Or for the woman who'd betrayed them both? *Thank you for all you've done*, she'd said. But what, after all, *had* he done? Because of him, a man had died for a crime he did not commit, while the perpetrator . . . He flinched away from the thought. Blind fool that he was. With his sights trained on what he'd thought to be the target, he'd failed to see the real enemy, just outside his range of vision. Thinking himself superior in understanding to the rest of them, he'd proved no better at finding his way in the dark. How close he'd come, that day, to delivering her up to justice! Only the thought of the penalty she'd have to pay had prevented him. A fresh bout of shuddering sobs overwhelmed him. No, he could not, as it seemed, play God. That much was a consolation.

It was past eleven when he let himself into the building; as it turned out, he'd never got around to handing back his set of keys. He'd chosen his time carefully, making sure no sound of footsteps or passing traffic disturbed the street, although at this time of night, the City would have been deserted for hours. Even so, he stood for a long moment in the entrance hall of the great stone edifice, until he was as sure as it was possible to be that there was no one else about. Minute creaking and groaning sounds, as of hot-water pipes cooling, were all that he could hear, however. He drew a breath, alert for anything unfamiliar – a scent, a motion of the air – but there was nothing. Slowly, cautiously, he crossed the wide mosaic floor towards the stairs. He had already decided not to take the lift. It made too much noise, and there was also the possibility that it might get stuck between floors. He had always had a particular horror of being trapped in such a way, and with all the more reason now. He climbed the stairs. There were five flights of these, and by the time he reached the top, he was breathing heavily. Time was when he'd have run up just such a number without thinking; now he was all too aware of the irregular beating of his heart and of the tightness in his chest. That would be the cigarettes, he thought. No matter what they said about their being healthier than smoking a pipe, he couldn't imagine they did you much good in the long run.

He unlocked the office door, recalling with a pang how many times he'd done so in the past. On the threshold, he stopped and listened again, but there was nothing. He allowed himself to breathe again. At least, he thought, with the grim humour that came to his aid at such times, there'd be no lights to give away his presence to any passing copper in the street below. He'd come and go like the ghost he was, leaving no trace. Moving with the confidence of long habit, he crossed the broad expanse of parquet towards his desk – his no longer, of course – and sat himself down at the switchboard. There he remained for a long moment without moving. Remembering all that had been. Then, his hands knowing what to do, as if they had never left off doing it, he flicked the switch which would give him an outside line, and connected the cords to the right jack for the exchange required. After a moment or two, the operator answered. He requested the number he had in mind (which had never left his mind). 'One moment, please,' she said. A few more seconds passed before he heard the telephone ring, and go on ringing. It was almost with a feeling of relief that he thought, 'There's no one there.' Then came a voice at the other end of the line:

'Mayfair four-two-nine-oh. Who is this?'

Not her, of course, but the maid. And not the one he'd spoken to before, on that earlier occasion, when he'd still believed her faithful. This was an older woman, more guarded in her manner. A housekeeper, perhaps. The lie he'd prepared, which was to say he was some long-lost cousin returned from India, wanting to get in touch with her ladyship after many years, wouldn't wash with this one – even though he prided himself that his accent was educated enough to pass muster with most. So he risked a version of the truth: 'My name isn't important. But I've a message for Lady Celia from Gerald Willoughby.'

There was a moment's shocked silence. 'Mr Willoughby's dead,' said the housekeeper.

'Yes. It was a message he gave me before he died.'

'What is the message?' she said, her voice icy.

'I was to give it to nobody but Lady Celia herself.'

A pause followed, while she thought over the

351

implications of this. Then: 'I'm afraid that's impossible. Her Ladyship is away at present.'

'When do you expect her back?'

'I couldn't say.' Another pause. 'It's very late,' she said. 'I must say, you've a nerve, ringing up in the middle of the night like this. I wonder what the police would have to say about it . . .'

'I shouldn't mention anything about it to the police if I were you,' said Rowlands, keeping his voice steady. 'Not if you've Lady Celia's interests at heart.'

'You're a cool one.' There was a grudging admiration in the woman's voice now. 'Is it money you're after? Because I can tell you, you're wasting your time. She's got nothing but the clothes she stands up in. Besides which, if *he* got to hear about it . . .' She broke off, as if aware she'd said too much.

It was true, then. He wondered why he didn't feel more surprised. 'Nevertheless,' he said, 'I'd like you to give me her telephone number in France, if you will.'

She drew in her breath with a little hiss. 'I'll do no such thing. Even if she were in France, which she's not,' she added, too late.

'Please,' he said softly. 'It isn't what you think. All I want is to talk to her – to say what Mr Willoughby asked me to say. I promise there won't be any repercussions . . .'

'As if I cared about that!' she said scornfully. But she seemed to waver a little.

* * *

Sitting there at his desk in the dark office, he listened to the telephone ring. Peal after peal resounding through a silent house, in a foreign land known only to him as a battlefield. The region where she was now – asleep, or perhaps listening, like himself, to the ringing of the telephone – was far away from there, almost, one might have said, in a different country altogether. The south had not been scarred by the war, in the way the north had been. There, from what he'd gathered, you'd have been forgiven for doubting that there'd ever been a war at all. Not that he'd ever seen it for himself, that world of ease and elegance, with its shuttered white villas surrounded by cypresses and and oleanders, overlooking an azure sea. Where the air smelled of lavender and rosemary, and a warm breeze rustled the dry fronds of the leaning palms. A world in which it seemed nothing bad could ever happen. The telephone rang and rang. After a few minutes, the operator came back on the line:

'*On ne répond pas.*'

'*J'attends.*'

'*Comme vous voulez.*'

But it wasn't until he was on the point of hanging up that the receiver was lifted at last.

'Hello,' she said. 'Who's that?'

'Lady Celia . . .' he said; but before he could go on, she cut across him.

'I'm afraid you've made a mistake. There's no one of that name here.' Then someone who was in the room with her must have said something, because she laughed. An uneasy laugh, it seemed to him, listening in the deserted office. 'Oh, it's nothing,' she said, addressing this other. 'A wrong number. Go back to bed.'

'I must speak to you,' he said urgently.

A silence followed. For a moment he was afraid she'd hung up. But then he heard her voice, speaking so low it was almost a whisper. 'I can't speak now. Ring tomorrow. One o'clock. I'll be alone then.'

Chapter Thirteen

On what he sometimes thought of as the last day of his life, it had rained without ceasing. The air was smoky with it. 'Cats and dogs' you'd have said, although he'd never seen the sense of that. Eels, perhaps. Certainly the air had a rotten, fishy stink to it. Men's feet went bad underneath their wrappings; wounds got infected. It was more like a swamp than any battlefield, they groaned to one another, shivering in their filthy holes in the grey dawn. On that day – it was the 31st July they'd risen before it was light and harnessed the horses to the limber. They hated it too, poor beasts, the rain running in sheets off their flanks, and making the ground a quagmire, so that even before they were halfway up to their position, they were all – animals, men, and guns – as thickly splashed with mud as if they'd been plastered with the stuff. At the top of the incline, he'd looked back over the landscape below – a grey morass of churned-up earth, shell holes filled with green-grey water, black carcasses of trees, and tangled wire. It seemed hard to believe there was anything living in that landscape, and yet he knew for a fact it harboured twenty thousand men. There, too, lay the corpses of many more, a fact made all too horribly apparent by the incessant rain, which washed away lumps of the clayey soil, revealing portions of those hastily and inadequately buried: a hand, an eyeless face.

We go to gain a little patch of ground
That hath in it no profit but the name . . .

He shook his head, dispelling with the gesture the bleak cynicism of the lines. It didn't do to look too hard at things – not here, not now. Later, there'd be a time for such thoughts. Off to his right lay what had once been a farmhouse; beyond it was the village whose name would thereafter conjure up everything that happened there. Just then, it was nothing more than another village. He remembered the rain running down his face and inside the turned-up collar of his oilskin cape. He'd had to discard the cape a moment after, because that was when the firing began in earnest. He and Wilson took the first shift. They were targeting an enemy emplacement, half a mile away across the fields, or what had once been fields before three years of constant shellfire had destroyed them. He'd adjusted the sight – a number 7 Dial Sight with a rocking bar, telescope on the right and range scale on the left. A German model, of course. Theirs were still the best precision instruments. As ever, there was nothing to see at first. Just the flat grey fields, and the dark line of trees in the distance. Only the sudden flashes, followed by puffs of white smoke – growing more frequent now – betrayed the presence of their adversaries. Would the rain never stop? He was looking forward to a cup of hot coffee and a smoke, when this was over.

It was a big place – twelve thousand lay here, although many more had fallen in the fields around. The names of thirty thousand or so, whose bodies had never been found, were recorded on the great curved wall at the far end. He had traced with his fingers the outline of some of the names incised in the stone. Recalling the men they were – a few known to him, most not – their flesh, blood and bone now reduced to just this strip of calcified calligraphy. In spite of everything, he was glad that he'd come. It was better than he'd thought it would be. The geometric symmetry with which the place had been laid out made it easier than might have been expected to find one's way around. He was reminded of his first days at the Lodge, with its grid-like corridors – although those had rung with men's talk and laughter. These corridors were silent. But because it was all straight lines and right angles here, he hadn't had to rely on the sighted members of his party as much as he'd feared.

Now, as he walked between the ranks of graves at a slow pace dictated more by his reflective mood than by any need for caution, he could hear their voices in the distance. Rowntree's, and Thompson's, and Colefax's, and above them the hoarse cockney tones of that other fellow, Horrocks, whom they'd met yesterday morning on the platform at Victoria Station as they'd waited to board the boat train. It was he who – presumptuously, in Rowland's view – had appointed himself their guide. He'd been in the RFA at the same time as Rowlands and the others, it transpired, although they hadn't known each other then. Now, he – Horrocks – was recalling what it had been like before: 'No, no, no. You've got that wrong, old chap. Number six battery was to the east of the redoubt, I know that for a fact . . .'

They'd arrived at Ypres the previous night in time for the Last Post, their little group subsumed into a larger crowd which stood, heads bared, in front of the great memorial to those – almost fifty-five thousand of them – with no known grave. Afterwards, they'd strolled around the town, talking of the way it had been. Several of them, Rowlands included, remembered the place before the shelling had reduced it to a ruin. It had certainly been that by July 1917. Streets and houses obliterated, and rough paths cut through the debris towards the *Grand Place*, which had been one of the jewels of mediaeval Europe. The once magnificent Cloth Hall had been, in those last months, no more than a shattered stump, resembling a broken tooth. They were rebuilding it now, along with the rest of the city. Scaffolding shored up the great tower, and a smell of lime and plaster was everywhere, effacing the smells of burning and decay that had once hung over the place. 'Yes, you'd hardly recognise it now,' said Horrocks, with cheerful tactlessness. In Rowlands' view, it should have been left as it was – a blackened shell, with nothing but the crows to mourn around the fallen tower. That, and not some great triumphal arch, would have been a more fitting memorial to the men who had died. But he kept his opinion to himself.

That morning, they'd hired a car to take them out along the Menin Road, with Horrocks offering his usual commentary: 'Hellfire Corner – remember that? And didn't it just get hot there?' They'd gone through Hooge, bearing north at Clapham Junction, and skirting Polygon Wood. He thought of Willoughby, then. *I'd just been given my first platoon. A good bunch of lads, they were* . . . Nor was he the only one having such thoughts, he guessed. Apart from the irrepressible Horrocks (and even he shut up after a while) his companions remained largely silent throughout this journey. Perhaps they were seeing the landscape as he was in his mind's eye, not as it was now – a placid rural scene, whose scars, though still discernible to those who knew what to look for, had long been covered by a film of green – but as it had been then. Colefax, he knew, had lost a brother here, Rowntree a son. Thompson, like himself, had been blinded by shrapnel. *I was walking through a wood at the time. I remember looking at the little red buds unfurling on the trees – it was a beech wood, you know – and thinking it would soon be spring* . . . Each had his own memories of this defiled country. For him, it was like visiting a graveyard in which the corpse of his own youth was buried. He saw now that everything that had followed, in what he'd come to see as his posthumous life, had come from this.

Now, having reached the spot where his life, in one sense at least, had ended, he was trying to get his bearings. Walking between the rows of gravestones, he tried, and failed, to connect the place as it was now with the way it had been. Even if one could forget, for a moment, that one were in the middle of a cemetery, and suppose oneself back on the field of battle, the smell was all wrong. Instead of the stench of mud and the reek of gunpowder, there was nothing but a clean, dry scent of mown grass, and meadow flowers. Smooth green lawns had long ago covered up all the filth: the mounds of decaying bodies, the tangles of wire, on which scraps of clothing fluttered. What had been a terrain as devoid of life as the moon, pocked with shell holes, and echoing to the noise of battle, had given way to a terraced garden, planted with the dead. The only thing that was even vaguely familiar was the lie of the land – *that* was as it had been. As he made his way up the slope that led to the salient, he felt his body adjust itself to the familiar gradient. A sort of natural earthworks, hadn't Captain Willoughby said? 'It doesn't give us much of an advantage, but by God, what little advantage it *does* give us, we'd be fools not to take.'

It struck him in that moment that it was the first time since Willoughby died that he'd been able to think of him without pain. Strange that his former O.C.'s spirit should, after all, be found here, even though his body lay far away. And yet, in a sense, a part of him – the best part, Rowlands thought – would always be associated with this place. The day they'd captured Abraham Heights – that had been a great day. How exhilarated they'd been, whooping like schoolboys, as the shells hit home. Willoughby shouting louder than all the rest of them. 'A bottle of whisky for the man that knocks out their last machine gun!' he'd cried, a bright colour in his face, as if this were the Glorious Twelfth, and their enterprise merely a superior form of shooting party.

Yes, he was glad, after all, that he'd come, even though he'd resisted the idea at first. But of course it was the only way he could have made the journey here, without exciting comment from his wife . . . Thinking of Edith, he felt a flicker of guilt. Once again, he hadn't been entirely truthful with her. In fact, to put it bluntly, his coming here had been a monstrous lie. What made it worse, was that Edith had been so pleased about his deciding to return to Flanders. 'It's time you made your peace with that place,' she'd said. 'I only wish I could come with you.' What she'd have said if she'd known the real reason for his visit, he hated to imagine. Not only because he'd lied about what had brought him here, but because it was on account of a woman she detested . . . He felt for his watch: it was just after two. That was the time they'd arranged, wasn't it? Then why wasn't she here? It occurred to him that she might, after all, have decided not to come. It would be just like her: to make a promise she'd no intention of keeping . . .

But then he heard her voice. 'Mr Rowlands. I hope I'm not late?' Even though he'd prepared himself for this moment, he still couldn't repress a start, at the sound – still, after all that had happened, retaining its power to charm – and at the surprise of her nearness, her footsteps on the soft turf having made no sound.

'It was good of you to come,' he said stiffly.

'Oh, but the thanks is all mine – that you've come all this way, on my account.'

'It wasn't just for that.'

'No. Of course not. I'm sure you had your own

reasons,' she said. 'But I think even if you hadn't suggested this meeting, I'd have wanted to come. To see this place, as he must have seen it . . .'

'It wasn't like this then.'

'No,' she said. 'I suppose not . . .'

'Nor did he die here – although it might have been better if he had.'

She was silent a moment. 'Then you *do* hate me,' she said. 'I was afraid of that. Was it because of *that* you asked me to come? To tell me how bad you think me?' She laughed. 'Because I can promise you, nothing you can say to me could be worse than the things I've said to myself.'

'It wasn't for that.' Although of course that was a large part of why he'd come. He put his hand in his pocket and withdrew the brooch, wrapped in its scrap of paper. 'I've got something that's yours,' he said.

She hesitated before taking it from him. 'What is it?' she asked. He said nothing, because she had, in that instant, unwrapped it. 'My God,' she said. 'Where did you get this?'

'It was in Gerald Willoughby's hand when he shot himself.'

He'd wanted to hurt her, of course, but he was unprepared for the low cry of horror that came from her. 'No! I won't believe it.'

'It's the truth.' He drew a breath. 'What's worse is that I gave it to him.'

'You?' she cried. 'But how . . .'

Standing there amongst the ranks of graves, he explained how it was he had come to be in possession of the brooch, and why he had visited Gerald Willoughby on that fatal day. He'd thought he was doing the right thing, by handing over the object to his former O.C., but his doing so had precipitated the final catastrophe. 'So you see,' he ended by saying, 'if anyone's guilty of having brought about his death, it's me.'

'But I still don't understand,' she said. 'Even if you thought the brooch was a gift from Gerald, instead of . . . someone else . . . why were you so anxious to return it?'

'I thought, because of the inscription, it might be construed in a certain way, if it were to fall into the wrong hands. That anyone reading what it said would assume it was a gift from a lover. As it turned out, I was right,' he added unhappily. 'Except that I'd thought the man in question was Gerald Willoughby.'

'But . . .' A long pause ensued, during which she seemed all of a sudden to grasp what he was driving at. 'Oh,' she said flatly. 'I believe I begin to see. You think I killed him, don't you?'

'Lady Celia . . .'

She ignored this interruption. 'My husband, I mean, not Gerald. Although you rather blame me for *that*, too, I imagine . . .'

He shook his head, but she paid this no more attention than she had his previous intervention.

'. . . and because you believe me a murderess, you

thought to protect me from being found out. So you returned what you assumed was *evidence . . .*' the word was pronounced with an accent of scorn, 'to the person least able to bear the implications of that evidence.'

It felt as if he had been struck a blow in the face.

'Well?' she said. 'Have you nothing to say in your own defence?'

'No.'

A pause ensued. 'I don't know why I should be getting angry with you,' she said at last, 'when it's myself I should be angry with. Let's walk, shall, we? May I take your arm?' She did so, and he felt once more the light pressure of her gloved hand, her arm in its fur sleeve, pressed against his; the warmth of her body beside him. Both remained silent for a while, as they began walking slowly up the slope together, between the orderly rows of gravestones. Stretching out his hand in passing, his fingers traced the outline of a maple leaf, inscribed on one of the stones. A Canadian battalion, he surmised. A great number of them had died here too, far from home, and from those that loved them. From nearby came the scent of roses, which had yet to succumb to the frost, from the rose bushes that were planted between the graves. Their perfume and hers combined, to heady effect. It had always been like this, he thought – his ridiculous pretensions to objectivity overwhelmed in a trice by the fact of her physical presence. 'I've never been quite certain how it was you knew,' she said, after they had been walking for some time in silence. 'About what happened that night, I mean.' Her tone was light; conversational. But that it was a serious question was not in doubt.

'It was a telephone conversation,' he said.

'Yes, of course. Go on.'

'I . . . I overheard something you said to Mr Willoughby.' He drew a breath. 'About your being at Claremont that night . . .'

'So because you knew I'd been at Claremont, you came to the conclusion that I must be guilty of murder – have I got that that right?'

He made a deprecatory gesture. 'When you put it like that it sounds ridiculous.'

'But you're wondering, nevertheless, why I didn't just admit that I was there to the police?' She gave a sad little laugh. 'As it turned out, it might have been a lot better if I had. Only Gerald told me I mustn't. He said it would look bad for me.' She emitted a small gasp of laughter. 'I seem to have been rather the victim of other people's anxieties on my behalf.' They continued their slow pacing, up and down the garden of remembrance. Her hand rested lightly on his arm, with that knack she always had, of making him feel he was the one leading, whereas in fact it had always been the other way about. 'You've no idea how dreadful it was,' she went on, in a strange, light voice that belied the horror of what she was saying. 'To find him there. Lionel, I mean. I suppose you know well enough what the dead look like . . .'

'Yes.'

'Well, I *didn't,* you see.' Her voice faltered. 'I won't deny that it was a shock. He didn't look peaceful, as dead people are supposed to look, just horribly . . . absent. A body. No, worse than that. A *thing . . .*' She was silent again, perhaps contemplating the image her words had conjured up. When she spoke again, it was in an altered tone, as if she were making an effort to compose herself: 'What's really absurd is that I'd never have gone to Claremont at all that night if it hadn't been for Gerald. Because we'd quarrelled, you see, he and I. He'd been in a black mood all evening – I was really afraid Poppy Frinton or one of the others who were at dinner with us would notice. When I got him alone for a minute I asked him what on earth he thought he was playing at. Did he *want* to get us talked about? Because if he did, he was going the right way about it. Sulking like a silly schoolboy. Oh, I let him have it, you may be sure!'

She broke off. Along the path towards them, people could be heard approaching. Another of the small groups they'd been encountering all day of former soldiers paying their respects to fallen comrades, or mourners searching for the last resting place of their beloved dead. He was relieved that it wasn't his own group. When they'd gone past – both parties murmuring a polite greeting – she picked up the thread of her story: 'Where was I? Oh, yes. Gerald. Well, after I said all *that*, he lost his temper. Told me I'd never really loved him. Said if I cared so much about what other people thought it might be better if we didn't meet again. He finished up by saying that if I wasn't such an awful little coward, I'd have left Lionel a long time ago. "The trouble with you is, you can't bear the thought of giving up the nice life you've had with him, to be with me", was his parting shot. So you see, I had no choice but to go and have it out with Lionel.'

'I'm sure he – Mr Willoughby – can't have meant you to . . . to expose yourself to any . . . well, unpleasantness.' Even as he said it, he knew it was a ridiculous way of describing what had happened.

'I don't suppose he did. But that was the result. Because as soon as I could get away, I jumped in the car and drove straight to Claremont. There wasn't much traffic on the road; I was there before two. The house was very quiet. Which struck me as odd, you know – because the lights were still on . . .' Her voice, so matter-of-fact up till now, seemed, for the first time, to falter.

'Lady Celia . . .' Suddenly he couldn't bear it. That she should say it aloud meant it could never be unsaid. Until then, there was still a chance he might have been wrong, all along. 'There's really no need . . .'

But she wouldn't let him off so easily.

'I let myself in, thinking Lionel must already have gone up to bed. Although as a general rule, you know, he liked to sit up late.' She gave a little sob of laughter. 'Lionel didn't believe in wasting time in sleep – it was one of his maxims. "Plenty of time to sleep when you're dead", he used to say.' Beside him, the woman Rowlands had come to love drew a long shuddering breath, as if nerving herself to continue. 'I was about to go up myself when I saw there was a light still burning, in the library. I opened the door. He was sitting there, in his chair by the fire. I thought for a moment he must have fallen asleep . . .'

'There's no need to go on . . .'

'Oh, but there is. He was dead, you see. I saw it as soon as I drew closer. There was quite a lot of blood.' She gave a little shiver of disgust. I expect you're wondering,' she went on, in a high, strained voice, 'why I didn't call a doctor . . . or the police.'

He hesitated a moment. This, then, was not to be a confession. He wasn't sure if he was disappointed or relieved. 'People don't always think of the right thing to do in such circumstances,' he said.

'Now you're making excuses for me.' There was an eerie calmness to her voice. 'The truth is, I was afraid they'd think I'd done it, the police. It's always the wife they suspect first, isn't it? And I had every reason to want him dead.'

His mouth was suddenly dry. 'You mustn't say such things.'

'Why not? It's true enough. So then I got in the car and drove back to London. I don't remember much about the journey,' she added, with a laugh. 'All I know is I got back, and went upstairs, and fell asleep almost as soon as my head touched the pillow. The next thing I knew was, my maid had come in to tell me the police had arrived, and wanted to speak to me.' She was silent for a long moment, as if telling her story had exhausted her. 'So many graves,' she murmured at last. 'I hadn't realised there would be so many. Acres and acres of them . . .'

'This is only one of many such places.'

'I suppose it must be. Hard to take it in, really. So what will you do?' she asked, as if struck by a fresh thought.

'Do?' His surprise must have been obvious, for she let go his arm, and turned towards him, to study his face, he supposed. She'd remarked on its expressiveness once, which had taken him aback at the time. Until that moment, he'd thought himself impenetrable to others, on account of his blindness. She'd shown him he was as transparent, where she was concerned, as any other man. 'What should I do? There's nothing *to* do.'

She considered this. 'Well, for a start, you might mention what I've told you to the police.'

'I've already told the police I've nothing to add to my original statement.'

She drew a sharp breath. 'They've been to see you, then?'

'Yes. About a month ago.'

'I *knew*, at the hospital, the way that man – Douglas, isn't it? – kept poking and prying . . . I knew then that the police suspected something.'

'I doubt they've any hard proof,' he said.

'No, for which I am eternally in your debt. Speaking of proof,' she added, 'I really ought to dispose of this . . .' He realised it was the brooch she meant. 'I don't suppose you've got a knife?'

He took out his pocketknife and handed it to her.

'Don't worry,' she said. 'I promise not to break the blade.' She must have bent down, then, because there followed a scraping sound, as of a small quantity of dry earth being excavated. 'There!' she said, standing up again. 'That won't be found again very soon. I've entrusted it to the care of Sergeant J. Dalziel, Artists' Rifles, died October 1917. It'll be quite safe with him. Give me your handkerchief, will you?' He did so, and, having wiped the blade, she handed knife and handkerchief back to him. They resumed their stroll. 'I can't tell you,' she said, when they had been walking for some minutes, 'how good it is to see you again.' The note of intimacy was unmistakeable. He'd heard it in her voice from the first. It was the way she had of drawing one in, he thought unhappily. Of making one feel like the only other person in the world. The queer thing was, that even after all that had happened, he still couldn't help but respond to that private signal. 'Oh, I know you must feel quite differently,' she said, with a dry little laugh. 'I can't imagine my presence here can be anything but unpleasant to you . . .'

'That isn't so.'

She ignored what must have seemed a half-hearted protest, although it was no more than the truth.

Whatever she'd done, or hadn't done – and he was by now no longer sure what he believed – her presence would never be anything less than delightful to him. A delight all the more intense, because he knew it was all wrong. Her next words only served to confirm him in this guilty awareness: 'I suppose you've heard,' she said, her tone falsely bright, 'about my present domestic arrangements?'

'I . . .' He felt a painful flush steal across his face and neck, remembering his abortive midnight call. Her voice, addressing that hated other: *It must be a wrong number. Go back to bed.* 'I had heard something.'

'Inspector Douglas again, I don't doubt. Quite why that man detests me so much, I can't imagine.' She laughed. 'Perhaps I offend his Calvinist soul.'

The sound of voices drifted towards them: Rowntree's and Horrocks', arguing about something. 'I tell you, it was over there, the pillbox . . .'

'Your friends are coming this way.'

'I ought to be getting back to them. Tell me one thing,' Rowlands said, with sudden violence. 'Was it going on before he . . . Willoughby . . . died?'

She didn't reply for a moment. When she did, only the coolness of her tone showed how much he'd offended her: 'What must you think of me, if you believe that?'

'Then it isn't true?'

'What? That I was his mistress all along? Is that what *he* told you?' she demanded, in a fierce undertone. 'Your precious inspector?'

Momentarily thrown off balance by her vehemence, Rowlands reached out to steady himself, and encountered sun-warmed stone. It must be the monument which stood at the centre of the place – Horrocks had pointed it out on their arrival. A flight of stone steps led up to a stone bench, set against a curved wall, on which were inscribed the names of the various regiments whose members were interred here. Here they could sit out of sight, until she'd had time to collect herself. 'Let's sit down for a minute,' he said.

'I don't want to sit down.' But she allowed him to guide her up the steps to the seat, which was, thankfully, unoccupied. They sat down. She was still trembling with anger, he could hear it in her voice: 'I must have a cigarette.' There was a brief pause while she unclasped her bag, took out her cigarette case, and fumbled with the lighter. It took several attempts before the thing was lit. 'Oh, I'm sorry. How frightfully rude of me. Would you like one?'

'Please.'

'I'll light it for you, shall I?' There was a further sequence of minute sounds before she slipped the lighted cigarette between his lips, the taste of her lipstick upon it. He drew in a lungful of the exotically perfumed smoke. Turkish, he thought. A few seconds passed. They smoked their cigarettes in what, under other circumstances, would have been a companionable silence. 'If I omitted certain things . . .' She gave a little laugh, without any mirth in it. 'It was because they seemed unimportant. What had happened between me and the man I now have the honour of calling my fiancé had ended – at least so I thought . . .'

'So you didn't plan it with him?' For some reason he was reluctant to mention Caparelli's name. 'The . . . the crime,' he added, in case she should have missed his meaning.

'Your policeman said that, did he?' Her voice was full of scorn. 'No, I didn't plan it. Although it suits *him* to say so.' She, too, seemed unable to name the man who had been – was still – her lover. 'What happened between us was an appalling mistake. I knew that, almost at once . . .'

'But the brooch . . .' said Rowlands, remembering its tender inscription and, more damning still, the significance of its date. A birthday gift, from a lover to his beloved. Small wonder that he'd mistaken the giver's identity.

'Ah, yes. The brooch. How I wish I'd thrown it in the river, the first chance I got! Yes, I suppose the brooch does put me in a rather bad light . . . the fact that I kept it, I mean. Gerald always said I was too fond of pretty things for my own good.' She was silent a moment. 'I don't suppose you'll believe me,' she said, 'but when . . . he . . . gave me the thing, the affair, such as it was, was already over. *He* wouldn't accept it, of course. Threatened to go to to my husband and tell him the truth. That was what he had come for, that night – the night you turned up at Hill Street . . .'

'So it *was* him? I thought there was someone . . .' He remembered the uncanny feeling he'd had of being watched. The shape half-seen against the light. The smell of a Special Mixture cigarette. Purloined, he supposed, from a pack left behind by another man. In such small ways, did one's senses betray one.

'Yes. He came to confront Lionel, but Lionel wasn't there. And then you arrived, like a champion, to defend me.'

'Rather a battered-looking champion,' he said with the ghost of a smile.

'I tell you, I was never more glad to see anyone in my life.'

Then for a while neither of them said anything. Rowlands smoked his cigarette down to the smallest stub, a habit he'd contracted in the army. How long ago it seemed since those hectic, unsettling days, when – doubtless because of the proximity of death – he'd never been more aware of being alive! Extraordinary days, that seemed, to his memory, to be charged with colour and excitement. An hour then was filled with more incident than a week of his life now. One lived more intensely, he supposed, knowing that might be all there was to be of life . . . He thought about what Celia West had said. She'd been lying, of course, when she said the affair had been over. He knew only too well what he'd unwittingly been a party to, the night he'd turned up at her house. Not a cold severing of intimacy, but a passionate renewal of it. If he'd been wrong about the smell of a stolen cigarette, he hadn't been wrong about that other smell – the salty reek of love. He thought about confronting her now with what he knew, and instantly rejected the notion. He'd rather cut his throat. Besides which, what did it matter, whether she was telling the truth or lying? Still, he'd find it in his heart to forgive her.

'Gerald suspected there was someone else, of course,' she said, with a bleakness that wrung his heart. 'I think that's what made him so angry with me that night. But I suppose it wasn't until he saw the brooch, with its damnable inscription—' She broke off.

'I had no idea,' he said tonelessly. 'I thought I was doing the right thing, handing it over.' It was to save you, he wanted to say, but did not. Just as he – the man we both loved – wanted to save you.

'Oh, what does it matter now? He's dead. I suppose we both had a part to play in that . . . but mine was the worse part. Rest assured, though,' she added, with terrible gaiety, 'I'm paying the price for it now. Gerald Willoughby was the love of my life. Now he's gone, my life's a kind of hell. Do you know what it's like, being in hell, Mr Rowlands?'

'I've a pretty good idea.'

'You're referring to the war, of course. I imagine that must have been as close to hell as most people come. By comparison, mine's a very *civilised* sort of hell. But it *is* hell – nor am I out of it,' she murmured, as if to herself.

'Can't you leave him?' he said, with a mounting sense of the horror of what she had been saying. 'Go back to England . . .'

She laughed at that. 'What? And put a rope around my neck? I'm afraid I'm too much of a coward to risk it. Besides which,' she added, exhaling a mouthful of smoke, 'with Claremont sold, there's nothing left in England for me now.'

'Is it sold, then?' he asked, surprised. He'd thought from all she'd said that the place meant a lot to her. Hadn't she as good as said she'd married Lionel West so as not to have to let it go?

'Oh yes. I couldn't have afforded to keep it on. I've only a life interest in Lionel's money, you know – and nothing at all if I re-marry. He made sure of *that*.'

'I see. Then who . . . ?'

'Well, that's the strangest part. He's left most of his fortune – apart from a few legacies to servants – to some child I'd never even heard of, until the will was read. What was the name, again? It's some German name. Lieberman or Liebnitz or some such . . .' She gave an unamused laugh. 'Typical of Lionel, really. To leave his money to some brat conceived the wrong side of the blanket, instead of to his lawful wife. Not that I was much of a wife to him,' she added, as if to herself. Then, with the triumphant air of one performing a difficult feat of recollection: 'Lehmann. That's it. I told you it was German.'

'Lehmann,' he echoed stupidly.

'Why, yes. One of Lionel's little factory girls, no doubt. He always did have a predilection for that type. The child's name, as I recall, is William. He always wanted a son, you know, Lionel. Men do, I believe. It's he who'll inherit everything, in the end. Well, there you have it,' Celia West said brightly. 'My sad story. I told you it was a sad story once before, but perhaps you thought I didn't mean it. Time I was getting back.' She shivered slightly, as if at a sudden chill. 'I'll be missed. Goodbye. I don't suppose we'll meet again.'

'Goodbye, Lady Celia.' He got up, and held out his hand. She didn't take it. There was the fraction of a second's pause, then she kissed him, full on the mouth. His surprise gave way, almost at once, to something more instinctive. It was as if, for that brief instant, he were possessed by another's spirit. That of the brave young soldier who'd gone to his grave, rather than betray her. His arms came up to hold her. Just for a moment, he returned the kiss.

She broke away. 'Forgive me,' she said softly. 'I never meant . . .' But before he could tell her there was nothing to forgive, she'd gone. Melted, like a will o' the wisp, into the air, leaving only the ghost of her scent – roses, ashes – behind. How long he remained there, staring blindly after her, he had no way of knowing. All he could taste was her mouth on his; all he could feel was the warmth of her body in his arms. In that moment, he knew he would go through it all again, if that kiss were to be the end of it . . .

'I say, Rowlands! Where are you, old man?'

'Think he's wandered off somewhere, and got himself lost?'

With an overwhelming feeling of reluctance, he declared himself.

'Oh! There you are. Been having forty winks, have you?'

Horrocks' jocular tones grated on Rowlands' nerves as never before. 'I lost track of time,' he replied, with as much civility as he could muster.

'*I'll* say! We've been looking for you for over half an hour.' Then, in a stage whisper: 'Saw you was with a woman. Not still about, is she?' It was as well for Horrocks that Rowlands' sense of where he was standing was necessarily approximate. Otherwise he'd be nursing a bloody nose.

'No '

'Shut up, Horrocks,' said good-natured Thompson. 'Did nobody ever tell you to mind your own business?'

'It's nothing to me if Rowlands has his fancy woman on the side,' retorted Horrocks. 'Handsome bit o' skirt she was, too, I can tell you! What you'd call a classy piece.'

'She knew my O.C.,' said Rowlands, paying no attention to this. 'Before the war. I believe they intended to marry. Only it didn't work out in the end.'

'Ah. Like that, was it? Didn't I tell you?' said Thompson to Horrocks, with an air of satisfaction. 'She wasn't one of your fancy women at all, but a poor girl who'd lost her man, same as the rest of 'em. That the story, Rowlands old chap?'

'Yes,' he said. 'That's the story.'

Chapter Fourteen

He took the gun from its hiding place on top of the wardrobe and withdrew it from its holster. He knew at once from the weight of it that something was wrong. It was a standard issue Weblcy Mk VI; he'd had it since the model had been introduced, in the second year of the war. Without bullets, it weighed exactly two pounds, six and a half ounces. With, it was heavier. He knew beyond a shadow of a doubt that it had been unloaded when he last held it. Not only was it standard practice to empty the chamber when the gun was not in use, but with children in the house, he'd never have been so careless as to leave it like that.

He broke the gun open, depressing the catch, as he had done so many times years ago, so that the barrel and cylinder swung down. As the barrel dropped, the automatic extractor threw out all six cartridge cases in the cylinder, releasing the six rounds. Holding the revolver in his right hand, he shook them into his left palm and weighed them for a second, deadly pellets. The Dragon's Teeth, he thought; their harvest was only Death.

Holding the thing brought back memories of the last time he'd done so, in the summer of '17. Although in point of fact, he hadn't used the weapon much – it had been principally an officer's weapon, issued to the gun crews for self-defensive purposes only. Its sights were basic, he recalled: a V backsight was fitted above the rear of the cylinder, and there was a large foresight, to compensate for the upward movement of the pistol when it recoiled on being fired. A double-action revolver, it could be fired from a cocked or uncocked position. The former gave a lighter trigger pull, but the hammer had first to be drawn back by the firer's thumb. He did this now, hearing again the familiar oiled soft click. It puzzled him that the gun had evidently not been fired very recently; a sniff of the barrel confirmed this. If what he now knew to be the case were in fact the case, then how could this be, he wondered.

He found Dorothy in the orchard at the bottom of the garden. The children were picking up windfalls, to be made into pies and apple sauce. They ran hither and thither between the gnarled trunks, whose upper branches were still heavy with fruit. He'd have to bring the ladder down to get the best of it. Not that he could think about that now, or any other ordinary task. It felt as if he were proceeding to execution – his own, or another's, it hardly seemed to matter. He felt sick to his stomach. If only it could all turn out to be a mistake – if he could be wrong about this, as he had been wrong about so much in the past. He knew, as he sat down beside her on the fallen trunk he hadn't yet got around to sawing into logs for the winter, that he wasn't wrong, however. He let a moment or two elapse, until he was sure they wouldn't be overheard. The girls' voices, high and fluting as birds, were more distant now, as they wheeled the wheelbarrow laden with their spoils up to the house. There, supervised by Edith, they'd sort the apples, setting aside the bruised and bird-pecked ones for immediate use, and arranging the rest in rows on shelves in the pantry, for the coming winter. He calculated that he had a little time at his disposal – perhaps twenty minutes – before they returned.

But before he could speak, his sister said: 'What's the matter, Fred?' She'd always been able to read him like a book.

He'd intended to lead up to it, although how did one lead up to such a subject? Now he plunged right in: 'It was you, wasn't it, who was at Claremont that night?' he said.

She was silent a moment. Then: 'Why do you ask, since you already know?'

'I wanted to hear it from you. It *was* you, then?'

'Yes.'

Hearing her admit what he had known since his conversation with Celia West ought to have been some relief to his feelings, but was not. 'You killed him.'

'He wanted to take Billy.' Her voice was as calm as if she were discussing the weather. 'It was the price for getting me out of prison. He'd seen my name in the papers, of course.'

He thought of the day he'd been to visit her – of the car that had nearly run him down, and the shilling offered in compensation.

'You haven't the least idea,' she went on, 'how determined he could be.' She gave a little shuddering laugh. 'He said if I refused to take the sensible course – that's how he put it, "the sensible course" – he'd see to it that Viktor was deported. The British government, he said, didn't look kindly on foreign agitators . . .'

'He's his child, then?'

'Yes.'

'Does Viktor know?'

'He knows Billy isn't his child.' Beside him, she made a restless movement. He remembered this about her – her inability to keep still when she was agitated. 'Why do you suppose that he married me? He doesn't believe in marriage, you must know that. He only did it to save my reputation.'

'Viktor's a good man,' he said sharply.

'Do you think I don't know it?' Both were silent for a brief spell. In the branches above their heads, a flock of starlings quarrelled over the spoilt fruit still hanging on the tree.

'Does he know . . .'

'. . . what I've done? No. He hasn't the least idea.' Her voice softened when she talked of Viktor. 'You know Vic. He's never been one for asking awkward questions.'

'Tell me,' he said, 'exactly what happened.'

She drew a breath. 'How did you find out?'

'I'll come to that. First I want to hear your side of it.'

'All right.' She laughed – an oddly mirthless sound. 'I don't suppose I have much choice, do I? After that day – the day he came to see me in prison – he wrote to me,' she said. 'Saying he was going to get his lawyers to draw up a new will, leaving all his money to Billy. The only condition was that I'd have to give up my rights to "his" son, as he called him, and that Billy would live with him from now on – him and that pretty blonde doll of a wife of his. He'd got it all planned, you see. That was Lionel all over.' Saying the name aloud seemed to release something in her. The desire to confess, Rowlands supposed. Because what followed emerged without hesitation on her part, or the need for further questions on his. 'He was as good as his word, too,' she went on. 'The day after I got the letter, I was told I was being released from prison, on medical grounds. My poor health being the reason given. Of course, I knew that wasn't the real reason. Lionel had pulled some strings, I don't doubt. He was very thick with all sorts of people.' She was silent a moment. The chatter of the starlings grew louder. 'How *did* you find out?' she said at last. 'I thought I'd been so careful.'

'You were. Just not careful enough,' he replied. 'You forgot to unload the gun, when you put it back, that's all.'

'The gun,' she echoed. 'Of course. I wasn't thinking straight at all that night. But it hadn't been used, in the end, and so I must've thought . . .' her voice tailed off. 'I don't know what I thought.'

'So you did take it?' He was careful to keep his tone neutral, but she seized on the implication at once:

'I had to have something. You don't know what sort of a man Lionel was . . .'

'I've a pretty good idea.'

'I wanted to even things up. Being a man, you wouldn't understand.'

'Don't be too sure,' he said mildly. 'So you took the gun . . .'

'I've said so, haven't I?' It was the first sign of temper she'd shown. 'It was the day your Joan was born. I took Billy and the girls next door, to get them out of the way of all that business – the baby's coming, I mean. It was then that I made up my mind to go and see Lionel. To reason with him, or so I thought.' Again, came the bitter little laugh. 'That was my first mistake . . .'

'And yet you took the gun?'

'How you do keep harping on about the gun! Yes, I took it. I knew where you kept it, because I'd seen you replacing it on top of the cupboard in the spare bedroom once, when you'd been cleaning it. I got it down and put the bullets in – I'd seen how you opened it, too. Then I put on my hat and went out, just as the midwife was arriving.' Her voice, which had been animated, now assumed a leaden tone, as if the speaker were unwilling to recall the events described. 'I knew the way, of course. We'd done that same journey, the day of your brother-in-law's party.' She gave a laugh that seemed as much a shudder. 'That cursed party! How I wish I'd never agreed to go. Because it was there that Lionel first set eyes on Billy . . .'

'Yes,' said Rowlands. 'Go on.'

She drew another long breath. 'I got off at the station – just a little place it was, if you recall? There was nobody about. I walked across the fields – I suppose it must have been a couple of miles. Then I came to the house. Claremont. I don't suppose you've been there?'

'No.'

'Not that it would have meant much to you if you *had*, poor old Fred,' she said, with a slight softening of her tone. 'I suppose all places must seem pretty much alike to you . . . Anyway, take it from me that it was a very grand place indeed. A great long drive – half a mile long, I'd say – and when you got to the end of it, it was like something out of a picture book. Steps up to the front, and pillars, and one of those – what d'you call 'em? – *porticos*. Like a Greek temple, you might say. Oh yes,' she said, in a jeering tone. 'People of their class do themselves proud when it comes to houses! Not that *he* was of that class – Lionel, I mean – but he was rich enough to make up for it. He'd bought himself a nice wife with his money, and got a nice house into the bargain. Having acquired these things, he'd thought he'd buy himself a child, too.'

'I thought you said he was Billy's father.'

'Oh, he was. Not that he'd ever laid eyes on him before that day at the garden party – I made sure of that. Because by the time Billy was on the way, our little affair was well and truly over. I'd had to leave my job at the factory when I found I was in the family way. Lionel was only too happy to see the back of me, I imagine. The next I heard, he was married to his blonde doll, and I got married to Viktor not long after . . . No, it wasn't, as I've said, until he met me again, at the party, that he remembered that he had a child at all. And what with Billy being such a beautiful boy . . . He *is*, you know, Fred, although you'll have to take my word for it.'

He smiled, although it wasn't a time for smiling. 'I'll take your word for it. Go on.'

The fleeting warmth occasioned by this mention of her son was gone from her voice when she spoke again: 'Well, of course, he wanted him for his own, didn't he? From that very second on. I could tell from the way he was looking at Billy – and me. Then when he read about my arrest in the newspapers, he saw his chance.' She fell silent once more. Nothing was to be heard but the wind among the leaves, and the petty squabbling of birds.

'Anyway,' she resumed at last. 'When I got to the house, it was about six o'clock. The place looked deserted, with half the blinds drawn down. It occurred to me then that Lionel might not be there, after all. Even though the address on the letter he'd sent had said Claremont Court. But then I saw the car, parked round at the back, where I suppose the stables used to be. One of those great big shiny things – a Rolls, I fancy. Lionel always did like expensive things. "Dolly," he once said to me – that was his name for me then – "I was born poor. But I'll die rich." He was right about that, as it happens,' she added, as if to herself.

'What did you do then?' He didn't want to hurry her, but he was afraid the children would return before they were done. And she was still far from reaching the crucial point of the story.

'Do? There was nothing *to* do. My idea was to wait until it got dark, and then try and get inside the house somehow. So I found a hiding place – a little summer house it was – within sight of the house, and settled down to wait. I hadn't been there much more than an hour, when I saw Lionel. He'd just come out onto the terrace, and was smoking a cigar. So then I saw my way in. I waited until he'd had his smoke, and gone back inside the house, and then I slipped in through the French windows, after him.'

'So you didn't break a window to get inside?' he interrupted her, remembering a detail about the case which had puzzled him.

She hesitated a moment. 'That was afterwards. I had to make it look as if someone had broken in.'

He nodded. 'I see.' Her coolness then and now was astounding, he thought. But he kept the thought to himself. 'What did you do then?'

'I went upstairs,' she said. 'I only had a moment to decide what to do, because the longer I waited, the more likely it was that I'd be seen by one of the servants. What I didn't know then was that the house was shut up for the season, with only Lionel's valet there to look after him, and a housemaid and cook. So in fact it was perfectly safe. But I wasn't taking any chances. As quickly as I could, I ran upstairs, and found another hiding place – a linen closet, this time. I waited there until I was sure it was quiet, then I tried a few doors. Lionel's was the third or fourth I came to. I knew it was his, because it was much larger and grander than the others I'd seen. A great high room with a great big bed in the middle of the floor, and naked goddesses painted on the ceiling. There was a set of evening clothes laid out on the bed. So I knew Lionel would be up soon to change for dinner. My idea was to *talk* to him, and make him see reason. I *couldn't* give up my son. Only when he came in . . .' She paused a moment. 'It didn't work out quite like that.'

'What happened?'

'Well, as soon as Lionel walked in – he was surprised enough to see me, I can tell you! – I said my piece about Billy, and how I couldn't give him up. I knew I'd only have a minute or two before he shouted for the servant, to have me thrown out, and so I just came out with it. He laughed, of course.' She allowed a brief pause to elapse. 'It was then I thought to show him the gun.' She laughed. 'Funny what a difference having a weapon makes! He had to listen to me then.'

'What did he say?'

'Oh, that he understood my feelings, but that surely I wanted the best for my child, and all that rot. Lionel could be very plausible. "You can put the gun down now, Dolly," he told me. "You've made your point loud and clear."'

'And did you put down the gun?' said Rowlands.

'Oh yes. It was clear to me by then that Lionel wasn't going to cut up rough. He'd lit a cigarette by this time, and rung down to the servants' hall to get dinner sent up on a tray. "Perhaps, after all, I might let you see the boy, from time to time," he said then. "On condition that I can still *see* his mother . . ."'

Rowlands put his hand on her arm. 'The girls,' he said. Because they could now be heard approaching: Anne's protesting tone, 'But Mummy *said* . . .' counterpointed by Margaret's calm insistence: 'Mummy said we were to take turns. You know she did.'

'What's all the fuss about?' he said, as they came up, trundling the wheelbarrow.

'Mummy said . . .' they both began.

'I'm sure whatever Mummy said she didn't mean you to quarrel about it. Now then, Margaret, let's hear your side of the story.'

'We're to take turns pushing the wheelbarrow, Mummy *said*. Only Anne thinks *she* should do it.'

'That'll do. Anne?'

'Margaret's had her turn. It's mine now.'

'All right. Here's what you're going to do. Margaret, I'm making you Captain of this patrol. Anne's your driver. You're to go over to the far side of the orchard – there, by the big plum tree – and you're to keep a sharp look out for the enemy while you pick up supplies – apples, that is. Then you're to report back to your C.O., that's Mummy, in double-quick time. Understood?'

'Yes, Daddy.'

When their voices had receded to what he judged to be a safe distance, Rowlands said: 'So he offered to let you see Billy?'

'Oh, he didn't mean it for a second. That was just Lionel's way. He liked playing games with people. He'd be all smiles one moment, saying you were the most beautiful thing he'd ever seen, and that he'd give the eyes out of his head to have you all to himself . . .

then he'd be cold as ice. Just then, he was at his most charming. Very pleased with himself indeed. Wanting to show me all over the house, you know, so that I could see what "my son" – as he kept calling him – would be getting. "All this," he said, waving his hand at the ceiling with the goddesses, "will be his when I die, and a great deal more. Now don't you think, Dolly dear, that it will be a better life for our William than anything you or that Bolshevik Jew of yours can give him?"' She was silent a moment. 'Oh, don't think I didn't consider it – the offer he was making. It would've meant Billy could have had all of those things – the house, and the money, and the fine times. He'd have grown up a rich man's son. But it was just *that* I couldn't stand, Fred – not just the thought of losing him forever, but the thought of what he might become . . .' Her voice tailed off.

'You still haven't told me what happened,' he said.

'No.' She sounded infinitely weary. 'What happened was this. We had our dinner, brought up by the servant. "Just leave it outside," Lionel said, to spare my blushes, I suppose, or his. Then, well, things went on from there, as they say. I couldn't have stopped it, even if I'd wanted to. "Yes, I'd like nothing better than to see more of you, pretty Dolly," said Lionel. We were lying in bed by this time. "But I don't think it'd do either of us much good, do you?" I knew then that he hadn't meant a word he'd said – about letting me see Billy.' She was silent again. 'He always was a liar,' she said softly.

'Go on.'

'I was just about to. Well just as we'd finished, there was the sound of a car outside. "Who the devil can that be at this hour?" Lionel said, because it must have been past midnight. He went down to see, and I waited for a while, thinking he'd come back to bed, after he'd got rid of whoever it was. When he didn't, I put on one of *her* dressing gowns – Chinese silk it was, all scarlet and gold – and crept downstairs to find him. It was easy enough, because I could hear him shouting, and then the other man – the Italian – shouting back at him. Calling him a liar and a cheat, and all sorts of other bad names. Most of them true, I'd have thought.'

She laughed. He thought he'd never heard so bleak a sound.

'Well,' she went on, 'as I was standing there, halfway down that great sweeping staircase, there was a tremendous noise – the sound of a gun going off. Quite a shock, it was. Then all of a sudden that manservant of his, Pierre, came running. I heard Lionel shouting, "Take care! He's got a gun . . ." so I knew he – Lionel – wasn't dead. I was outside the library by this time, standing out of sight behind one of the great marble pillars on either side of the double doors. It was lucky I was, too, because just then the doors burst open and the Italian, Caparelli, came out. He was shouting and swearing that he'd get back at Lionel for what he'd done. Lionel was nothing but a traitor, he said. After him came Pierre – a great big brute of a man *he* was. In his hand was the gun he must have taken off Caparelli. Lionel came out, after. "I'll take that," he said to the servant. Then he pointed the gun at Caparelli. "You ought to be more careful," he said, in that pleased-as-Punch way he had. "Waving guns around. Somebody could get hurt . . ."

'Well, of course this set Caparelli off again, and he was all for having another go at him – gun or no gun – until the servant put a stop to it. Put him out, too, still breathing fire and brimstone. He must have decided it was a no go, though, because the next thing was the sound of the car driving off. Then Lionel and Pierre went back into the library and talked some more. I heard the man ask if Lionel wanted him to stay, in case the Italian came back, and Lionel saying no, he could go to bed. I was getting chilly by this time, in nothing but that flimsy silk wrap, and so as soon as the coast was clear, I went to join Lionel. He was sitting by the fire, drinking a glass of whisky he'd just poured for himself.'

'He poured you another.'

'You seem to know all about it! But of course you heard it from Pierre, the day you telephoned Claremont.'

'It was you, then, that day in the office? I thought there was somebody . . .'

'I had to find out what you knew,' she said.

'Of course. I suppose it was you who followed me from the court. Pretending to limp . . .'

'You'd have recognised my footsteps in a flash if I

395

hadn't done that. I put a stone in my shoe,' she added, with what seemed a pardonable pride in her own ingenuity. 'It hurt like the devil. But it did the trick. I borrowed Vic's old raincoat, too, because I thought otherwise you might guess it was me from my clothes.'

'And then you slipped past me into the office.'

'You've no idea,' she cried, 'how much I hated spying on you! My own brother. But I had to know . . .'

He shrugged, as if one more betrayal, amongst so many, were of little consequence. 'Go on,' he said.

But the spell in which she had been caught up all this while seemed now to have been broken. His sister was silent a moment. 'You know the rest,' she said at last.

'Not all.' He would not be done out of this – knowing all there was to know.

'I killed him. There! Is that what you wanted to hear?' She seemed suddenly defiant almost, he thought with horror, as if she were proud of what she'd done.

He ignored the question. 'Did you mean to do so from the first?'

If she understood that he was offering her a way out, she disdained to take it. 'I didn't go there with the intention of killing him, if that's what you mean, but when the opportunity presented itself, I didn't hesitate,' she said.

Her words hung in the air between them, like a cloud of poisonous gas. Perhaps goaded into saying more than she'd meant to by his silence, Dorothy went on in the same dull tone, as if reciting a lesson: 'The way it happened was like this. I'd gone there to persuade him – to *beg* him, if you must know – to give up his claim to my son. It hadn't worked, as I've said. But I suppose I thought, fool that I was, that I might still persuade him. I'd no objection to his seeing Billy, I said. He could visit him whenever he liked. Only I wanted him to go on living with me and Vic, because we were the only parents he knew. Lionel wouldn't wear it, of course. "What's in it for me?" he said. "If this were business, I wouldn't call that much of a proposition." He told me I was a silly girl; I was sitting on his lap, at the time. If I didn't stop saying such foolish things, he'd have to get angry with me . . . He wanted it again, by this time. I suppose the gun going off, and then the whisky, had excited him.' The flatness in her voice was more chilling to Rowlands than the words themselves. 'I made him give me the gun. It was in the pocket of his dressing gown, you see. I said that one weapon was enough for me. That made him laugh, all right. He was still laughing when . . .' She broke off. 'I'd never realised how easy it is to kill someone. I suppose *you* know all about that.'

He said nothing.

'It was lucky that I'd taken off her dressing gown by then,' she added, as if the thought had just occurred to her. 'Or it would have been covered in blood.'

'I wonder you didn't make sure of it,' he said coldly.

'I didn't think of it,' she replied. 'I just wanted to get away from that house . . .' Her voice cracked slightly. 'From that room.'

'You must have wiped off the fingerprints from the glass first,' he said.

'I did.' She laughed. 'I'm not a complete fool. And then I went back upstairs, and got dressed, and . . . and made the bed, if you want to know.'

'What did you do with the dressing gown?'

'What? Oh, that. I hung it back in the wardrobe, where I'd found it. Why? Does it matter?'

'Somebody saw you wearing it, that's all.'

'Who? Oh, Pierre, I suppose. I wonder he didn't mention it to the police.'

'He didn't want her dragged into the affair. Unlike you, he has some sense of right and wrong . . .'

She made a move to get up, as if she'd heard enough, but he put out a hand to restrain her. 'Wait. I haven't finished yet. What about the window?'

She seemed not to understand him at first.

He reminded her: 'You broke a window. To make it look as if there'd been an intruder.'

'It was all I could think of to do. I had to cover my tracks.'

'You seem to have made a good job of it,' he said. 'And of implicating Celia West.'

'That wasn't deliberate . . . not at first. It wasn't until later that I learned she'd been there that night. From you, as it happened.'

'You seem to have found out quite a lot from me.'

'I knew you were in love with her. *That* was as plain as the nose on your face. The rest I worked out for myself.'

He was suddenly furious. 'Do you realise,' he said, 'exactly how much harm you've done?'

'I couldn't let him take Billy.'

'You could have fought for him. There are courts of law.'

She laughed. 'You don't suppose for a moment I'd have won?' Her voice had a scornful ring. Her soapbox voice, he thought. 'The courts in this country aren't set up to defend the likes of *us*.'

'And so you took it upon yourself to be judge and jury. Executioner, too . . .'

He couldn't see her shrug, but it was implied in the cool detached tone with which she replied. 'I've told you – it was necessary '

'That word has been used to justify any number of crimes.'

'If it had been one of your children, you'd have done the same.'

To which he could say nothing.

'Listen,' she said in a gentler tone. 'I'm sorry about your friend. But it wasn't my fault that he died.'

'Nothing, it seems, was your fault,' he said. 'I suppose you know about the money?'

'If you mean the money that will come to Billy – yes,' she replied calmly. 'He *is* his son, after all. It's only right.'

'You and I,' he said, ' have different notions of what is right.'

'Yes,' she said. 'If you recall, *I* was against the war. All that killing – and for what? At least,' she added, under her breath, 'I had good reason.'

'You can't compare the two.'

'Perhaps not.' She fell silent a moment. 'Are you going to turn me in to the police?' she said, all trace of defiance gone. Now she sounded like a frightened child.

'You know I won't do that. Unlike you,' he couldn't resist adding, 'I'd prefer not to be the cause of unnecessary deaths. Not that I accept any death to be necessary, as you call it.'

She said nothing to this, but he heard her let out a breath. Had she really thought he meant to deliver her up to the hangman? 'One thing I do want to know,' he said. 'Was it you who wrote that letter, implicating Celia West in her husband's murder?'

'I . . .' She was silent. He took the silence as an admission.

'Douglas – the Inspector – showed me a letter. It was that which made him sure,' he said.

'Sure of what?' Her voice was almost a whisper.

'Of her guilt. The woman whose life you've ruined.'

She drew a breath, as if about to answer the charge. 'You must know I never intended . . .'

But his sharper hearing had caught the sound of children's voices. He held up a hand to silence her.

'Daddy!' It was Anne, of course, out of breath from running. 'Mummy says . . .'

'It's teatime,' said Margaret, arriving at a more sedate pace.

'Thank you, girls.' He bestowed a glancing kiss on

each tousled head. 'Tell Mummy we're just coming.'

'And the baby's crying,' added Margaret, with her customary punctiliousness.

'I'm coming.' Dorothy got to her feet. 'We'll talk about this later,' she said to Rowlands, as if what they had been discussing was a domestic matter of no more significance than slaughtering a pig, or shooting a fox that had come too close to the henhouse.

The late afternoon sun was warm on his back, although he felt cold all over, and shivery, as if he were going down with flu. His head still rang with her words. Even though he had known it from the first, hearing her guilt confirmed out of her own mouth seemed an unbearable horror. As bad was the feeling, which had been growing upon him all the while they'd been speaking, that he'd never really known her. To have done what she'd done and yet show so little awareness of its enormity struck him as monstrous, inhuman. And yet she was his sister – his own flesh and blood. How could two such apparently incompatible facts coexist? He had the feeling of unreality he'd had during the war, on his first leave home, when the whole of London had seemed to be getting on with business as usual, while just a few miles away, across the English Channel, tens of thousands of men were dying, horribly, each day. One had to hold both thoughts in mind simultaneously – that of the comfortable, everyday life, and the unnamable horror – without letting the one infect the other. So it would be for him from now on, with Dorothy. What had been a relationship founded upon trust had been fatally undermined. Simply, he'd never again be able to believe a word she said.

But it seemed to him as he sat there, with what had seemed such a safe, well-ordered life in ruins, that there was nothing to be done. He must live with the consequences of his mistake. A 'fatal mistake', people said, didn't they? Well, it had certainly been that. He'd got just about everything he could have got wrong, wrong. As for Dorothy . . . but this train of thought was arrested, suddenly, by a faint sound from overhead. It was so small a sound that it would have been easy to miss it, overlaid as it was by the clatter of the starlings, and the sound of the wind in the leaves. But he didn't miss it.

'Who's there?' he called softly, afraid he already knew the answer.

At this, the small indefinite sound became more decidedly itself: a child crying. In the same moment, a fragment of bark or twig fell onto Rowlands' upturned face, as the culprit attempted to squirm out of sight, forgetting, or perhaps unaware, that such measures were unnecessary.

'You'd better come down.' He got up, then, and held out his hand. 'Don't cry,' he said, to soften the apparent severity of the injunction. 'Nobody's cross with you, I promise.' Although it occurred to Rowlands as he said it that, after what the child had just heard, he might be forgiven for doubting the veracity of adult promises. His gentleness of tone must have been convincing, however, for there came a scuffling noise, as the eavesdropper descended from his arboreal perch.

Rowlands took the folded handkerchief from the breast pocket of his jacket and held it out to him. 'Here,' he said. 'Dry your eyes. Now tell me,' he went on, while this operation was being performed, 'how long have you been sitting there?'

At once he regretted having asked the question, because Billy started crying again. 'Don't tell Mummy!' he begged, with an anguish that wrung the other's heart. 'Promise me you won't . . .'

'Shh.' He reached out to stroke Billy's hair, but the child flinched away like a frightened animal. 'It's all right,' he said, wondering, as he made this dubious assertion, what exactly Billy had heard – and how much he had understood – of Rowlands' conversation with his mother.

'Are they going to take her back to prison?' he sobbed, confirming Rowlands' worst fears.

'No. Of course not. Put that thought right out of your head. Nothing's going to happen to your mother.' Which was true enough, Rowlands thought grimly; whatever his sister had done, she had made sure that others, and not she herself, would pay the price for it. 'Come on,' he said, affecting a cheerfulness he did not feel, 'we'd better hurry up, or we'll be late for tea.' He held out his hand, and this time the little boy did not refuse to take it. He felt the small, hot palm slip into his.

'But she said about the police. I heard her say it,' the child insisted, his voice still trembling on the edge of tears.

'Then you must have heard what I said, too,' he replied, as they started to walk back towards the house. 'Nothing's going to happen,' he said again, as if the repetition of this phrase alone could make what he'd said come true.

'And you won't tell Mummy?' He seemed, if anything, more troubled by this thought than by anything he had heard . . . *if* he heard very much at all, Rowlands thought. He hesitated a moment before replying.

'All right. I won't say anything. But you know, don't you, Billy, that it's very wrong to listen to other people's conversations?'

The child said nothing to this. Either he hadn't taken in what had been said in reply or, more likely, he'd merely nodded his head. Unlike Rowlands' daughters, he hadn't been brought up to make his responses unambiguous. But his next remark showed that he'd understood the principle. 'I won't do it again,' he said placidly. It was as if the events of the past hour had never happened, as if he'd never sat, looking down on them from his hiding place in the apple tree, while his mother poured out her poisonous secrets.

'Billy! There you are! I've been looking for you

everywhere.' As if conjured by these thoughts, the subject of them now appeared. 'Wherever have you been?'

'Oh, Billy and I have been having a nice talk, haven't we, Billy?' he said quickly, knowing how hard it was for children to lie.

'Well, you'd better go and wash your hands at once,' said Dorothy to her son. 'Aren't you coming in?' she added, addressing Rowlands in the same falsely bright tone.

'In a minute,' he replied.

'Don't leave it too long. Your tea'll be getting cold,' said his sister.

She, too, behaved as if nothing whatsoever had happened. Which was how he would also have to behave, he supposed. It was a habit of mind they'd learned, after the cataclysm. One had to 'get on with it' – hadn't he said those very words to Celia West? It was what you did when the world was in ruins. You pretended that things were as they had always been. Averting your gaze – metaphorically, in his case – from the horrors that surrounded you. 'We'll talk about this later,' his sister had said; but he wondered now if they ever would. It certainly wouldn't be a conversation he'd initiate. Instead, like scar tissue growing over a wound, their mutual silence on the matter would conceal the truth of it. How she'd explain her son's newly acquired wealth when the time came was another thing. Knowing Dorothy, she'd find a way to do it. Turning his back on the house, he lit a cigarette. Yes, there was nothing to be said. He'd get on with things, the way he always had. He'd had to do it once before; it wouldn't be so very hard to manage the trick again. Whether he'd ever again have peace of mind was a different matter . . . He took a deep drag on his cigarette. The taste, mingling with the smell of the bonfire he'd lit earlier that day, was the taste of his regret. All the things he'd said and done and now wished unsaid and undone. The chances he'd had. All wasted, now. His life seemed to him like a stretch of ground, churned up by the brute machinery of war, and so polluted with that usage that nothing would ever grow there again. Or – worse, perhaps – it was a graveyard, now greened-over and planted with flowers, useful for nothing but hiding the bones of the dead. Yes, that was his life all right.

He thought of the man he had loved, whose body he had held in his arms that terrible day. Of other men he'd known, who'd died before him. All of them good men, and yet so very little good had come of that sacrifice. The same people who had always run the world still ran it, for their own advantage. Dorothy would say . . . But he averted his mind from whatever his sister might have said on this, or any other subject. His thoughts turned instead towards Celia West. *My melancholy baby* . . . He remembered all the times they'd been together. There was the night she'd come to the office. He heard again her voice, as she'd described the view he had never seen from his window, which he 'saw' from that moment on. How enchanting she'd seemed to him then! He hadn't minded that she was another man's prize, as long as that man was Willoughby. He thought of the night he'd turned up at her house in Mayfair. 'Like a champion to defend me,' she'd said. He'd have made a better job of it, he thought, if he hadn't been fighting in the dark . . . He shivered again; the wind was turning chill. It was only now that the encounter – which had cost him so many sleepless nights – made sense to him. The peculiar quality he'd detected in the atmosphere hadn't been fervid excitement, but fear; her nakedness indicative not of any perverse desire to humiliate him, but of her lover's coercion. He pictured the scene again. Himself, dragging the bell pull with him when he fell. The jangling within the house, interrupting the lover's tryst. If it had been that, and not something altogether more brutal. Caparelli bringing the unconscious man inside. Celia West snatching up her wrap, with its pattern of Chinese dragons. And Caparelli: 'No. Stay as you are. He's blind, isn't he? I want to see you like this . . .' Yes, that was how it had been, he thought.

Other times and other conversations went through his head. The time she'd sat in his garden. *I wonder what exactly you think of me?* And then the walk they'd had on the beach, with the salt-smelling breeze blowing in their faces, and the sound of the waves softly echoing all that was said. *I sometimes wish* . . . But he'd never heard what it was she wished. He thought of their last meeting – was it already a week ago? Walking arm-in-arm, like the old married couple they would never be, between the interminable ranks of graves. It struck him that if his life had become a wasteland, hers was another. 'Hell,' she had called it. Condemned to live with a man she hated, because she feared for her life if she did not. It was all wrong, he thought.

And then, suddenly, he saw what had to be done.

Chapter Fifteen

Because of the fog, the boat train was eleven minutes late leaving Waterloo. Even though it had made up the time well before they reached Southampton, he could not stop himself feeling a certain anxiety, on his sister's, as well as his own, behalf. It would not do to miss the boat; he was struck, at the moment of having the thought, by the metaphorical, as well as its literal, appositeness of the phrase. Simply, too much depended on the carrying-out of this venture, for it to be thwarted now, by something as trivial but apparently unavoidable as a delayed train. Dorothy, however, gave no sign that she felt any unease about what lay ahead, merely remarking in a calm voice, as the train pulled out of the station, that she was glad they were on their way at last. It was Viktor who seemed the more worried of the two, fretfully remarking that he hoped they would not find themselves at the back of a long queue when they did eventually reach the quayside, and obsessively counting and recounting the various items of baggage they had brought with them, the larger trunks having been sent on ahead. When it was established that none of these bags and boxes had been overlooked on the platform, or left behind in the train on the journey up from Kent, he seemed satisfied. It was his books he was most concerned about, although Dorothy assured him that there would be bookshops enough where they were going. Would there be toy shops, too? Billy wanted to know; he, too, was reassured on that point, and the journey continued without further set back. Even so, Rowlands could not escape a sense of the ambiguity of his role which was simultaneously that of a loving brother, concerned to see his sister and her family safely embarked on their journey to the New World, and that of a gaoler, resolved to make sure that nothing happened to prevent that journey.

This feeling of – call it guilt, or remorse – was most apparent in his exchanges with Dorothy, of course, in whose manner a certain ironic note was manifest. Their conversation was desultory, both having exhausted, in previous talks, the subject that was still uppermost in both their minds, Rowlands supposed. Even if there were still things to say, they couldn't have said them, in front of Viktor and Billy (the baby had of course been present at several of these earlier interviews). And so their remarks were confined to trivialities: did she want the window left open or closed? She would prefer it left open, she said. Wasn't she hungry? These sandwiches Edith had made were really awfully good. She didn't have much of an appetite, she said. But for much of the journey, his sister spoke little, evidently lost in her thoughts. This was unlike her, so much so, that Viktor remarked on it: 'I say, old girl, you seem a bit down in the mouth. Not worried about being seasick, are you?' To which she must have shaken her head. 'Why, it won't be so bad,' her husband went on, with what sounded like forced joviality. 'You'll get your sea legs in no time, I am sure.' Which prompted the inevitable question from Billy as to what were sea legs and would he get some, too, for which Rowlands was grateful, if only because it drew attention away from Dorothy's morose silence. Ever since that terrible conversation four months before, when she'd railed at him for his heartlessness, and accused him of betraying her for the basest reasons, their contact – in public at least – had been of the briefest. When he'd ventured a remark, on however unimportant a subject, she let it pass in silence, or replied – when it was unavoidable – with a sarcastic emphasis that conveyed plainer than words her resentment towards him.

Even Edith noticed. 'What's got into Dorothy?' she'd asked, only the week before, when his sister had bitten his head off about something. 'You and she used to be such pals. Now all she does is snap. Have you two fallen out?' To which he could only reply that he supposed Dottie must be feeling a bit anxious about the journey. That was understandable enough. Buenos Aires was a long way off. When he'd said to her, in that first confrontation after he'd learned the truth about his sister's past, that it was no good, she'd have to go away, he hadn't reckoned on quite how far it was going to be. Somewhere away from England, was all he'd thought at the time. Somewhere that she and Viktor and the children could make a fresh start. 'Because you must see,' he'd said, 'that you can't stay here. Not now.' It was then, as the implications of what he'd said went home, that she'd screamed at him, calling him a traitor and a coward. He'd never cared about her, she said; all he cared for was fawning over some woman for whom he was less than dirt. He'd let her have her say, fortunately, it was a day that Edith had taken the children into Tonbridge to buy shoes, then he'd said it again: 'You know it's the only thing to do. How can we go on living like this, with what you've done hanging over us?'

Of course she'd refused to listen to him at first. Weeping and wailing so much that she upset the baby, who'd started screaming too, so that the air rang with both their cries. Later, when she was calmer, she'd tried another tack: 'Don't think I wouldn't do it again,' she'd said. It was a moment before he understood her.

When he did, he'd laughed, at the sheer absurdity of it. 'Oh, Dottie! Are you trying to frighten me? Because I might as well tell you that it'll take a lot more than that.' Which had made her angrier still. Yes, it had taken quite a few such conversations before she'd at last seen sense. She'd go, she said, on the condition that he waited until she'd got clean away before he said any of this to the police. Then it was just a question of where she was going to go. When the idea had first come to him, it hadn't occurred to him that it had to be somewhere that the law couldn't reach. There were parts of Europe where that was the case, of course, although he wasn't sure which parts. Albania, perhaps, or Hungary? Everything had changed since the war. But if not Europe, then where? Australia was sufficiently far, but it maintained strong links – and an extradition treaty – with the 'Mother Country'. America was no go for the same reason. Time and again, in successive discussions of this subject, he and Dorothy came up against the same blank wall. 'You see,' she'd said, with the bitter humour which had become habitual, in those last few weeks, 'it isn't as easy to be rid of me as you'd thought . . .'

In the end, it was Viktor who, unwittingly, had come up with the solution to the dilemma. A cousin he hadn't seen since before the war had written from Argentina. He owned a farm there, out in the Pampas, with fifteen hundred head of cattle. After ten years, he'd become a wealthy man. Would Viktor and his family care to join him? It was a great life out here. The only thing he missed was the chance to talk German, now and again. If Viktor was surprised at the alacrity with which his wife had agreed to this proposal, he did not say so to Rowlands. Perhaps he, too, had become aware of an atmosphere in the house. 'I feel bad about leaving you and Edith in the lurch, old man,' was all he said. 'But you know, this is a great chance for us.' Cousin Dietrich, it emerged, was a childless widower, with no surviving relatives apart from Viktor. 'When he dies, I will come in for all his money,' he said, half-apologetically, to Rowlands. 'I don't care for myself, but it will mean Dottie and the boys are secure.' Quite *how* secure, he could not have been aware, it occurred to Rowlands, who gathered Dorothy had as yet said nothing of her elder son's expectations from his late father's will.

These and other reflections had occupied his thoughts on the journey down. Now they were driven out of his head by the painful reality of the immediate circumstances. Because here they were at last, on the quayside at Southampton Docks, having disembarked from the train, into a cacophony of shrieking whistles, and bursts of steam from the engine, and hailed a porter to help with the luggage, and taken their places in the queue (not, after all, so very long a queue) that would bring them in due course to the foot of the gangway. Above them, Rowlands imagined, loomed the great ship itself, the *Araguaya,* which was to take his sister and her family, by way of Tenerife and Rio de Janeiro, to Buenos Aires. From around them, came the shouts of sailors supervising the loading of trunks and boxes from quayside to deck, as well as the more subdued murmur of other passengers' voices, saying their farewells to those who had come to see them off. There was the strong smell that dockyards have, composed of tar and rubber and grain with, beneath it all, the tang of salt water mixed with that of engine oil. Under other circumstances, Rowlands would have relished this whiff of the exotic – have enjoyed, too, the feel of the wind in his face; the sense that this was a threshold, leading to foreign lands. As it was, he felt only desolation. It was because of him that Dorothy was leaving; he didn't think for a moment that she would otherwise have fallen in with Viktor's suggestion. He was losing her, as he had lost so many others he had loved.

Now, forgetting in that moment what had brought them to this point – her ruthless disregard of all but her own desires – he could think only that she was his beloved little sister, and that, in a few moments, they would be saying goodbye for the last time. Because there could be no doubt in either of their minds that this was a final parting. Once gone, she could never come back; nor would it be safe for him to visit her. 'Shall I come on board with you?' he'd asked, to delay, even by a few minutes, this inevitable rift. Dorothy had said no, however. 'It would only prolong things,' she said. There was a sadness in her voice that suggested she, too, understood the irrevocable nature of their leave-taking. 'I want to get the children settled,' she added, as if to explain this.

'Of course. Well, I'll be pushing along then. Goodbye, Viktor old man. Hope it all turns out as planned.' He held out his hand, only to find himself clasped in a bear hug by the other man.

'Dear Friedrich. Dear old friend. You will write, *ja?*' said Viktor, in a voice thick with emotion.

'Yes, of course I'll write.' Although he wondered if he would. 'Bye, Billy.' He bent down to lift up the child. 'Be a good boy for Mummy, won't you?'

'Yes,' replied the little boy, as if this went without saying.

Now it was Dorothy's turn. 'Hold the baby for me, Vic, would you?' she said. Then Rowlands felt her arms go around his neck. 'Oh, Fred,' she said softly, close to his ear. 'I'm sorry it has to be like this.'

'I'm sorry, too.' For a long moment he held her. She was crying, now. He kissed her wet face. 'Goodbye, Dottie.'

'Oh, Fred. Oh, Fred,' was all she could say, as Viktor, perhaps sensing that the moment ought not to be unduly prolonged for both their sakes, gently disengaged his wife from her brother's arms.

They weren't due to sail for another hour and a half, but Viktor said not to wait; it would only upset Dottie, he said. 'The best thing you can do, old man, is to

go and have a drink somewhere. For old times' sake,'
he'd added ruefully, perhaps thinking that it would
be a long time before he saw the inside of an English
pub again. How much Dorothy had told him of her
reasons for wanting to leave the country, Rowlands
had no way of knowing; he supposed she had not told
him very much. It was fortunate, he thought, that there
had been episodes in Viktor's own past life which did
not stand up to close scrutiny. How it was that he had
managed to get out of Germany in '21, for example,
when all the other members of the Communist cell to
which he belonged had paid the ultimate penalty for
their activities, remained unclear. As Dorothy had said,
that day in the orchard, Viktor wasn't the sort to ask
questions. But in that, Rowlands thought, he wasn't
alone, of course . . . He found a quiet pub in one of the
streets near the dockyards, and ordered himself a beer.
Yes, he'd drink to old times – some of them, at least.
Others he preferred to forget. He thought of the day
Dottie had first brought her intended home to their
mother's house in Dagmar Road. Mother had refused
to leave her bedroom that day. 'If you think I'm going
to welcome a German into my house, after what those
people did to my sons, you'd better think again,' she'd
said. He'd felt rather the same, if the truth were told.
But then Viktor had behaved with such open-hearted
friendliness that it had been hard not to warm to him.
'I know you have no reason not to hate me,' he'd said.
'But I would consider it an honour if you would shake

my hand.' Which he'd done. After that, they'd got along like a house on fire.

''Scuse me, my darling, is this seat taken?' came a voice, interrupting these reminiscences. A woman; young, or young-ish, with a soft West Country accent.

'Not as far as I can tell.' He gestured at her to sit down.

'Thanks ever so. You're not from round here, are you?' she said.

'No.'

'Thought not.' A husky, intimate note entered her voice. 'I said to myself, I haven't seen *his* sort around these parts before.' She gave a throaty chuckle. 'Makes a nice change,' she said.

He smiled, because the remark seemed to call for some such response, but really he wished she'd keep her thoughts to herself. He checked his watch. It was ten past two. Twenty minutes to go before they set sail . . . if you could say that of a steamship.

'Got to be somewhere, have you?' said the girl.

'No. The thing is, miss—'

'That's good,' she interjected, before he could finish. 'Because then you'll be able to spend some time with me.'

'I'm sorry, I . . .'

'The shy sort, are you?' she said, not taking 'no' for an answer. 'Don't worry, I'm used to that. I'll have a gin and lime, if you're asking . . .'

'Listen,' he said. 'There's been a mistake. I'm not looking for company.'

'Aren't you, dear? That's a pity,' she said, seeming not the least bit abashed. 'And I thought it was my lucky day.'

He finished his drink, and drew a ten shilling note from his pocket. It was one of the new ones; it felt clean and crisp in his fingers. 'Here,' he said, pushing back his chair. 'Get yourself a drink with that.'

He had agreed to wait until the telegram came before he did anything further, to give her the chance to get away. And so he did nothing; it was a strange time, which seemed to him a kind of limbo. It was lucky, he thought, that he had so much to keep him occupied. With Viktor gone, he was having to manage most of the work on the farm himself, although he'd got a local lad coming in to help with mucking out the cages. Edith would have done more, if he'd let her, but he didn't like her getting her hands dirty. She had quite enough to do with all the work of running the house, without taking on what amounted to manual labour. During those two and a half weeks, he was out in all weathers, reinforcing a fence where a fox had been digging, and nailing tar paper over the roofs of all the coops to keep out the wet. All the time, his mind was elsewhere – on a boat to Buenos Aires or, in the past few days, exploring the city itself. The 'Paris of South America' it was called. Full of bookshops and theatres, he'd read. Not that Dorothy would have time for theatre-going. She'd be on her way to wherever it was they were bound for, she and Viktor. Some remote place in the Pampas; he tried to picture it in his mind's eye, and could only summon up a vast waste of grassland, bare of any other kind of vegetation. Cattle. There'd be cattle, and horses too, he supposed. Those boys – young Billy, and little Victor – would have a fine life. He wished he could be sure that the same would be true for their mother.

The telegram had come at last – it was tersely worded, but then words were expensive – and he had made the necessary telephone call. Now he sat, on a hard wooden bench in a corridor that echoed to the brisk tapping of typewriters from the offices on either side of it, waiting for the summons that would determine everything that was to follow. He didn't have to wait long. A door opened, and someone came out. 'Well, well,' said a voice he knew. 'Mr Rowlands. This is a surprise.'

'Good afternoon, Inspector.'

'Although maybe it's not such a surprise as all that,' went on the policeman. 'Have you something to say to me?'

'I have.'

'I take it that it's to do with the West case?'

'Yes.'

'Then you'd better step into my office.' That there was somebody else in the room was immediately apparent from the sound of a pen scratching. 'This is Sergeant Withers,' said Inspector Douglas carelessly. 'You needn't mind him.'

'I'd prefer to speak to you alone, if you don't mind.'

'Have it your own way. Sergeant,' said Douglas, 'take these files along to Records, will you? And don't hurry back. Now then,' he said, when his subordinate had gone out, closing the door behind him, 'what exactly is it you want to tell me?'

Rowlands took a breath, to steady himself. His palms felt cold. 'I'm afraid that before I say anything, I must have your assurance that you won't act on what I'm about to tell you.'

There was a moment's incredulous silence. Then the Inspector laughed. 'You must know I can't promise anything of the kind.'

'Then I'm afraid I've nothing to say.'

A longer silence ensued. Then Douglas sighed. 'You can't protect her forever, you know,' he said.

'If it's Lady Celia you mean, I won't have to,' said Rowlands.

By the time he left Scotland Yard, the traffic was already building up in Whitehall. Along the broad street roared what seemed an unbroken stream of vehicles – delivery vans, buses, motor cars. You wouldn't have thought the city could hold so many. As he stood hesitating on the pavement, trying to get his bearings, he heard the clock of St Martin-in-the-Fields strike the half hour. He realised he was trembling all over, as if after a violent shock. And yet he had never been calmer than when he gave his sister up to the mercies of the law. Because despite the fact that he'd forced an agreement of sorts from the Inspector that no action would be taken – *to be frank, we've not the resources, even if we wanted to look for her* – he knew such a condition could never be enforced. If they decided to hunt her down, then they would; it was what the police were pledged to do. Even though she had gone away to a place where nobody, he hoped, would ever find her, and from which no legal mechanism could be used to extract her, still her life would never be free from uncertainty. The shadow of the noose would hang over her for as long as she lived. It was small comfort to know that, by giving her up, he had removed that shadow from another woman's life.

Turning in the direction of Trafalgar Square, he began to make his way through the crowds of people now flooding out of banks and offices, on their way to Charing Cross station, and the suburban trains. His own homeward journey would have to be delayed a while. In the big ABC on the corner, he had a cup of tea and a smoke, to steady his nerves. In the old days, he'd never been the nervy sort; now the least thing turned him to jelly, it seemed. A number 15 bus took him along the Strand to St Paul's. After that it was easy: a route he knew like the back of his hand, having spent the best part of seven years of his life getting to know it. Cannon Street, Mansion House, Cloak Lane, Dowgate, Monument. And now here he was once more, grasping the door's familiar handle: a brazen bundle of sticks with an axe at its centre. It was five-and-twenty past six – he should be in the clear by now. He pushed open the door, and stood for a moment, listening. But there was nothing. Again, he took the stairs. Unlocking the door, he breathed in once more the dear familiar smell: floor polish, pipe tobacco (that was Jackson's doing, of course), and that indefinable aroma that was to do with old documents. He crossed the floor, a little gingerly, in case they'd been moving the furniture around again, and took his seat. He adjusted the chair reminding himself to return it to its former position afterwards, then reached for the switchboard. That was the first shock.

Because it was all different. Instead of the arrangement of switches and sockets he'd grown accustomed to, during his years with the firm, this was something else. A newer, shinier version of the system he'd inherited, with, he guessed, lights that flashed when a call came in, instead of buzzers, which had been, for him, a necessary modification. There was a dial, too, he discovered – he'd never used one, except in a telephone box of course, but they were the coming thing. He took a breath and let it out. Well, he wouldn't let it beat him. He supposed all these things were pretty much alike – buzzers or no buzzers. He reached once more, to find the cord that would give him an outside line, but before he could locate it, the electric light went on, flooding everything with a harsh yellow glow. 'What on earth do you think you're up to?' said a voice.

For an instant he froze, his hand still grasping the

cord. Then he turned towards the woman who had surprised him. 'Miss Stanley, I presume?' he said. 'I'm Frederick Rowlands. We have met, once, I believe . . .'

'Yes,' she said coolly. 'I remember you now. You were there when I came for my interview. The question is, what are you doing here?'

'I doubt you'd believe me if I told you,' he said. 'But you have my word that's it's important. A matter of life and death, you might say.'

'Go on.'

'The fact is, I need to make a call. Long distance. A great deal depends on it.'

She considered a moment. 'Just because you used to work here doesn't give you the right to use the firm's property,' she said.

'I realise that.'

'I suppose technically you're trespassing.'

'I know.'

'If I were doing my job properly I really ought to inform the authorities,' said Miss Stanley, her tone suggesting that she had not yet ruled out this possibility.

'That's true. But I very much hope you won't.'

She was silent – studying him, he supposed. He made his face as calm and innocent looking as possible. After a minute, she sighed. 'I only came back to collect my gloves,' she said. 'I'd left them by mistake.'

'It's easily done.' He felt around on the desk in front of him. 'Here they are,' he said. 'You'll need them. It's a chilly night.'

'Thanks.' She took them from him. 'Did you say you wanted to make a long distance call?'

'Yes. To France.'

'Well, you'd better let me do it. From the look of it, you haven't used this particular model before.'

'You're right,' he said humbly, making room for her at the switchboard.

It took her twelve minutes before the connection was made. '*Bonsoir*,' she said to the operator at last, in her accurate, but schoolgirlish French. '*J'ai un coup de téléphone pour vous . . . De l'Angleterre . . . Oui. Un moment, s'il vous plaît . . .* It's ringing,' she said to Rowlands, passing him the headset. 'Remember to lock the door behind you, won't you?' Then, with a brisk clicking of high heels, she was gone. The telephone rang and rang, as it had done on that other occasion, months before. Then, as now, he was afraid that there would be no answer or, worse, that the wrong person would intercept the call. If *that* were to happen, he'd have no choice but to hang up. His message was for one person, and one person only.

But then there came a voice: the one voice in all the world he most wanted to hear: 'Yes?' it said. 'Who is that?'

And he replied: 'It's me, Lady Celia. Frederick Rowlands. I've something to tell you. It's all right. You can come home again.'

It was going on for ten o'clock when he got home, because he'd missed the quarter past eight train, and then there was the walk over the fields from the station.

Not that he minded the walk – it helped to work off his feelings. He'd only had one beer at the station buffet, while he was waiting for the Staplehurst train, but he felt as lightheaded as if he'd been drinking champagne. It was hearing her voice that had done it, he knew. That, and what she'd said when she'd at last understood what he was trying to tell her. 'You've saved my life,' she'd said. 'How can I ever thank you?' That had been thanks enough, had she but known it. Of Caparelli they hadn't spoken; he assumed the man must still be about, if only because, during the whole of their conversation, she had kept her voice low, as if afraid of being overheard. But she'd manage all that somehow, he was certain. A woman like her was practised at the art of deception. Yes, it wouldn't be long before she'd contrive her escape . . .

When he let himself in, the house was so quiet that he assumed Edith must already be in bed. He slipped off his shoes, and was making his way towards the kitchen, thinking she might have left something for his supper – although in truth he wasn't in the least bit hungry – when he heard her call out to him from the sitting room.

'I thought you'd gone to bed.'

'I was just about to. You were a long time.'

'I missed the early train. I . . . I had some things I had to do, after I'd been to see Hoskins.' The ostensible reason for his visit to London was to sign some documents Viktor had left for him at their solicitor's, transferring the ownership of the farm to him. It had taken all of five minutes.

'I gathered that,' she said. There was a hint of dryness in her tone which seemed to demand some further explanation.

'Edith . . .' he started to say.

'Oh, I don't suppose you'll tell me what you've been up to,' she said. 'Although I imagine it had something to do with that woman. The one you're in love with . . .'

'I'm not in love with her.'

'Then it *was* to do with her?'

'Yes. You'd better sit down.'

'I'm sitting down,' she said. 'It's you that's standing.'

He stopped his restless pacing, and sat down facing her. It seemed to him that this was a moment of no return. All he'd been through, in the months leading up to it – all the lies, and half-truths, and evasions – seemed suddenly of less importance than he had thought it. All that mattered was that the woman sitting opposite him should not judge him as harshly as he perhaps deserved. The fire was not quite out, and he could feel its faint glow on the side of his face that was nearest the hearth. A faint, pleasant smell of applewood filled the room – the last of the logs he'd sawn up in the orchard last autumn. He took a breath. 'All right,' he said. 'You want to know what's been going on, so I'm going to tell you. There's just one thing: you must hear me out, before you start asking questions – is that clear?'

'Perfectly.'

'One other thing. It's you I love. It always has been.'

She said nothing to this, and so he could only guess at what she made of it. After a moment, he got up again, and went over to the sideboard, where there was, he remembered, the remains of a bottle of sherry left over from Christmas. He poured himself a glass, and then another, which he handed to his wife. Then he sat down again and, with the drink to give him courage, began to tell his story.

Acknowledgements

In researching any novel, there are works without which the task of recreating period, place – or that still harder to define quality, 'atmosphere' – would have been difficult, if not impossible. *My Story of St Dunstan's*, by Lord Fraser of Lonsdale, was just such a one: a beautifully written and entirely unselfpitying account of the author's journey from the battlefields of the Western Front to stewardship of the first national organisation for the war-blinded.

CHRISTINA KONING has worked as a journalist, reviewing fiction for *The Times*, and has taught Creative Writing at the University of Oxford and Birkbeck, University of London. From 2013 to 2015, she was Royal Literary Fund Fellow at Newnham College, Cambridge. She won the Encore Prize in 1999 and was long-listed for the Orange Prize in the same year.

christinakoning.com